CAUGHT IN THE MOONLIGHT

Stunned at being caught in her nightclothes by a fully dressed rogue, Erica grabbed at her bodice in a futile attempt to gather it into folds, hoping to further conceal her chest. Unfortunately, there simply wasn't enough fabric there to do her any good at all, and she was about to simply turn and run when her host offered, "Here, put this on."

Before she could object, he'd stripped off his shirt and held it up so that she could slip her arms into it. She did so sheepishly, unwilling to tell him that the gallant gesture had actually worsened her predicament. Now *she* was covered, but *his* magnificent expanse of wiry brawn was visible again, and this time, she could actually feel her nipples straining against her gown, desperate to rub against him. Did all women's do so, and polite society simply pretended otherwise? Or was Erica just the weakest woman who'd ever set foot on a beach?

"Thank you, Captain," she murmured. "But I really should go back to my room."

"Don't run off," McCullum protested, stepping so close she could feel the heat from his chest. Then, to her delicious discomfort, he announced in a deep and utterly seductive voice, "I haven't been able to get you out of my mind."

Dear Romance Reader,

In July, we launched the Ballad line with four new series, and each month we'll present both new and continuing stories set everywhere from medieval England to the American West—the kind of passionate, romantic stories you love best, written by the most gifted authors. At the back of each book, we'll tell you when you can find subsequent books in the series that have captured your heart.

Martha Schroeder's atmospheric *Angels of Mercy* debuts this month, chronicling the dreams and desires of three women stubborn enough to join Florence Nightingale on the battlefields of the Crimean War. In **More Than a Dream,** a young woman of privilege wants nothing more than a life as a healer—until a brooding physician tempts her wish for love. Next, Corinne Everett begins the *Daughters of Liberty* series, in which three young women chart their own passionate courses in the wake of the War for Independence. An ardent Patriot meets her match in a dangerously attractive man who may be Loyalist—and who threatens to steal her heart—in **Loving Lily.**

Next, rising star Tammy Hilz continues her breathtaking *Jewels of the Sea* trilogy with **Once a Rebel.** When a woman who despises the nobility's arrogance encounters a handsome aristocrat, she never imagines the adventure that awaits them on the high sea—or the thrilling fulfillment she finds in his arms. Finally, the second book in Kate Donovan's *Happily Ever After Co.* series presents a Boston society beauty and a widowed sea captain marooned on a tropical island—and the once-in-a-lifetime love that results when they're **Carried Away.**

Kate Duffy
Editorial Director

HAPPILY EVER AFTER CO.

CARRIED AWAY

KATE DONOVAN

ZEBRA BOOKS
KENSINGTON PUBLISHING CORP.

http://www.zebrabooks.com

This book is dedicated to Paul,
for twenty-five years
of love and romantic inspiration.
Happy Anniversary!

PROLOGUE

May 1866

"You look so worried, Father." Noelle Braddock settled onto the arm of her father's leather chair and patted his shoulder. "If this match bothers you so much, don't make it." When the marriage broker didn't respond right away, she took the letter he'd been studying and scanned its contents as intently as he'd been doing. "It's not from the prospective groom? It's from his *mother-in-law?* Isn't that rather odd?"

"His wife died in childbirth four years ago, and this Abigail Lindstrom wants to see him happy again. Touching, isn't it?"

"I suppose." Noelle sighed as she finished reading the short but poignant tribute. "Do you suppose he's as wonderful as she says?"

"Why? Would you like him for yourself?"

"You'd like that, wouldn't you? Anyone but Adam, isn't that so?"

Russell Braddock winced at the sharp edge to his only daughter's tone. Not that she didn't have a right to be upset. For weeks he'd been finding excuses not to deal with the matter of Adam Prestley, a wealthy suitor whose arrogance seemed matched only by his persistence. But in Noelle's eyes, the cocky banker was worldly and irresistible. And given his daughter's impulsive nature, Braddock knew he couldn't just ignore the situation. Noelle might decide to take matters into her own hands and elope!

"One match at a time," he suggested evenly. "Allow me to finish with Captain McCullum, and then we'll discuss your young man."

Noelle had found the second letter—the one from the Boston governess—and its contents seemed to disturb her. "These two couldn't be less suited to one another, Father! They live in completely different worlds. Do you honestly dare to bring them together?"

Braddock smiled at the predictable reaction. "It's the riskiest match I've ever made," he admitted. "But there's something about the young woman's letter. Read between the lines, sweetheart. Can't you hear the yearning? It's as though she is desperate to break free from some imaginary prison. And she doesn't want to stay in Boston—she tells us that straight out."

"She doesn't say anything about cooking and cleaning on some leaky old boat," Noelle protested. "Or living on an island in the middle of nowhere. And what if he rejects her? His mother-in-law admits he has vowed to never remarry. And she says his only fault is that he's stubborn. Or"—she eyed him knowingly—"do you read something between those lines also?"

Braddock nodded. "She wants to portray her son-in-law in the best light, and so she uses the word 'stubborn' to convey a myriad of faults. I would guess he may not be as even-tempered and reasonable as she would have us believe. But one cannot doubt her sincere admiration for the man. After all, if her plan works and he marries the governess, the mother-in-law intends to leave her precious grandchildren behind and move back to New England.''

"What makes you think he'll agree to remarry?''

"He has three children, and he's lonely.''

"He's handsome and daring and big and strong, if half of this is true. And he's a sailor, romancing a different woman in every port. He may not be as lonely as you think, Father. A Boston governess will be too prim and proper for him. Can you imagine her scolding him for coming to table without a proper coat? He'll make her walk the plank!''

Braddock grinned. "I'm more convinced by the minute that you want him for yourself. You should see how your eyes sparkle when you describe him.''

"They don't!'' Noelle smiled at the teasing. "I want a solid, respectable pillar of society. Sometimes I wish I *were* an adventuress,'' she added sincerely. "But I'm not. I wouldn't know what to say to a man like Captain McCullum. And the governess won't know either. She needs a man like my Adam.''

"Fine, then.'' Braddock nodded. "We'll match her with your Mr. Prestley—'' He stopped himself, alarmed that Noelle's gray eyes had darkened again so quickly at the mischievous suggestion. "I was only teasing you, sweetheart.''

"My love life shouldn't be a source of amusement,'' Noelle reprimanded him solemnly. "And you haven't given Adam half the chance you give absolute strangers like Captain McCullum. If you'd just get to know him, you'd see he's witty and sophisticated and perfect in every way."

"Well, then . . ." Braddock slipped his arm around her shoulders and squeezed them gently. "I'll see that he gets an invitation to dinner before the week is out—"

"Oh, Father!" She jumped into his lap and hugged him gratefully. "You'll see! He's as wonderful as you are. And almost as handsome."

"He can come to dinner, on one condition."

"Anything."

Braddock took a deep breath. "You're seventeen years old—"

"And you've matched brides even younger than that," Noelle reminded him quickly.

"That's true. Because their circumstances required that they marry right away. You're fortunate enough to have a loving father who provides well for you. Isn't that so?"

She studied him suspiciously. "What's the condition?"

"He can come to dinner, as often as you'd like. But there'll be no talk of marriage until you've turned eighteen."

Noelle pursed her lips and seemed to consider his proposition. "And once I've turned eighteen?"

"We'll discuss that when the time comes."

"When the time comes, there'll be nothing to discuss." The daughter smiled tightly. "But until that day, Adam can come to dinner as often as I wish, and I won't elope— with him or with anyone else. I accept your condition, Father."

Which means I have only six short months to find the perfect husband for my own daughter, Braddock muttered silently. *What greater challenge could a marriage broker face?*

Then he remembered the stubborn sea captain and the adventuresome governess, and had to smile. In its own way, that particular match was every bit as challenging, and would take place not in six months, but perhaps in six weeks—or even less!

CHAPTER ONE

"I'm so, so bored."

"Hmmm? Did you say something?"

Erica Lane folded her arms across her chest and gave her fiancé a disapproving glare. "I said, I'm bored. By *you*."

"What?" Jack Ryerson looked up from his books and blanched at the expression that confronted him. "Forgive me, darling. I was miles away."

"Well, take me with you next time, because I'm bored to death of this house and of this life."

"And of me?" He flashed his trademark boyish grin. "I'm wounded, Erica."

She relented easily. "Where were you, exactly? When you were miles away."

"In the California mountains, at a lumber mill. I hear it's beautiful there. We should consider spending some time there after we're married."

"So that you can evaluate some horrid old lumber mill

as an investment? How romantic,'' she drawled. Still, to herself she had to admit the scenario had its allure. Rugged, lonely men with saws and axes, taming a wilderness. The scent of pine and danger in the air. Maybe even a bear or two!

''Erica? Are you angry?''

''Me? Never. I was just imagining those mountains, and all the big strong men who work there in the fresh air. Doesn't it make you want to do something a little less cerebral?'' She wriggled between the man and his desk until she was securely ensconced in his lap. ''We could go for a ride, into the woods. I'd let you kiss me—''

''That sounds tempting, darling, but I promised Owen I'd have an answer for him tonight. You remember, don't you, that he and Mary are coming to dinner?''

''This investment is not even for you? It's for Owen?'' Erica shook her head. ''It's as though you'd rather do anything but be alone with me.''

''I'm alone with you now.''

''But you're distracted. I want your attention.''

He brushed her thick auburn hair away from her ear and nibbled gently on the lobe. ''Is that better?''

''Mmm, wonderful.'' Erica closed her eyes and allowed the tingling to radiate through her. ''I wish *you* were a lumberjack.''

''Why?''

''I think you'd enjoy me more,'' she explained. ''Because you'd be lonely, and you'd savor every opportunity for female companionship.''

''Where do you get your ideas?'' He laughed and reached past her for a ledger book. ''Run along and visit with Sarah for a while, darling. I have work to do.''

Erica bristled at the familiar dismissal. Not that she didn't enjoy talking to Sarah, of course. The Ryerson family's governess was a delight. More importantly, she was a godsend of sorts, seeing to it that Jack's little sisters were pampered, civilized, educated and generally satisfied. On the other hand, it seemed these days that Jack expected Sarah to keep Erica occupied and out of his hair more often than the children!

"You haven't even kissed me today, Jack Ryerson. I don't think you really love me at all."

"I've loved you since the night you pretended to faint into my arms at the fireworks display over the bay. That was almost two years ago, wasn't it? And I love you more every day."

Erica smiled at the fond memory. "You should have tried to take advantage of me that night. I believe I would have allowed it, you were so handsome and attentive. I might even allow it now," she suggested precociously, stroking his face with her hand while moistening her lips, readying herself for his kiss.

Jack set the ledger down on the desk, turning his full attention to her at last. As his mouth covered hers, she twined her arms around his neck and sighed aloud in anticipation of the seduction to come. Then to her dismay, he grasped her firmly by the waist and lifted her off his lap. "Run along now and stop teasing me. What would your mother say?"

"She'd say you're a bore. And if Father were still alive, he'd take back my hand and tell you to find another girl to rebuff."

"I doubt it." Jack laughed. "I still remember how relieved he was when I offered to take you off his hands."

"He was not!"

"He said you had a worrisome tendency to get carried away, and he feared you'd run off with some fortune hunter or adventurer."

"Well, no one will ever mistake *you* for an adven-

turer—'' Erica caught her temper, knowing she wouldn't
fare well in a quarrel with a logical man like Jack Ryerson.
She'd do better appealing to his soft heart, and so she
wheedled, ''I just want to spend some time with you,
darling. Because I love you so much. Is that so very
wrong?''

His green eyes warmed visibly. ''Let me finish with
this, and then, if you behave yourself at dinner tonight,
I'll take you riding tomorrow. For the entire afternoon.''

''And will you court me passionately?''

''I'm your fiancé,'' he reminded her with a satisfied
grin. ''I'm finished courting you.''

''Jack Ryerson!'' She shook her head in disgust. ''Perhaps you should marry Owen, since he's the only person
you seem to have any time for these days.''

Jack shrugged. ''I have a small interest in this mill,
and so, if Owen decides to invest heavily, you and I will
profit. I'm doing this as much for you as for anyone.''

''You acquire small interests in so many businesses,''
she mused. ''Why is that?''

He studied her for a moment, as though doubting the
wisdom of such a discussion, then explained, ''Whenever
I see an intriguing business that's faltering, I acquire an
interest in it. That allows me access to its books and
accounts. If it seems to be a wise prospect, I recommend
it to one of my associates, and they make a substantial
investment. The business begins to thrive, and my small
interest becomes a profitable one. Do you see how it
works?''

Erica smiled with pride. ''Do you know what you are?
You're the Russell Braddock of the investment world!''

''I beg your pardon?''

''Russell Braddock is that marriage broker in Chicago—the one Owen was telling us about a few months
ago. You're just like him, except you don't put a bride

together with a groom, you put a failing business together with an investor.''

"I suppose you could say that." Jack chuckled reluctantly. "He fascinates you, doesn't he?"

"If half of what we heard about him is true—"

"I'm sure none of it is, darling. How can a man hope to match two persons from just a letter or two? In my business, I have ledgers and inventories to evaluate. What does this Braddock character have? Nothing. I'm sure he has more failures than successes because of it.''

Erica winced, remembering the letter she and Sarah had so solemnly crafted one rainy day in March. They had been so certain that the Happily Ever After Company was the answer to all of the poor governess's prayers. Was it possible Jack was right?

"You seem disappointed," Jack teased. "Were you thinking about ordering a lumberjack for yourself?"

"Would you be jealous if I did?"

"I don't know." Jack pretended to consider it carefully. "It *would* keep you occupied, so that I could concentrate on these books.''

"You're hateful," Erica grumbled, but her thoughts had turned almost completely to Sarah's dilemma. If Jack was right, and Braddock was some sort of charlatan, the poor nanny's heart would be broken. Which meant Erica had to find her right away—before the response came from Happily Ever After—and convince her that she was better off finding herself a man the traditional way.

She knew it wouldn't be too difficult to change Sarah's mind about Braddock. After all, it was Erica who had convinced her to turn to the marriage broker in the first place. The governess had been aghast at the suggestion, and had resisted so valiantly that Erica had ended up writing almost every word of the letter herself.

"When you decide to start behaving, Jack Ryerson, let

me know. Until then, I'll be in the garden with Sarah and
the children, saying horrible things about you.''

"Have fun. And, Erica?"

She turned to glare. "Yes?"

"I love you."

She bit her lip, pleased by the unexpected tribute. Then,
after a playful curtsey, she turned and rushed off toward
the garden, hoping Jack's sisters would still be napping,
so that Erica and Sarah could converse undisturbed.

She was relieved when she spied her friend alone on
a garden swing under an arbor bursting with pink rose-
buds. *If only some charming, unattached gentleman could
see Sarah now, in so romantic and pleasing a setting,*
she told herself wistfully. *We would have no more need
of Mr. Braddock's services at all.*

At that moment, Sarah glanced up and wailed, "We've
done a terrible, terrible thing! I never should have let you
talk me into this."

"Oh, dear." Erica hurried close enough to see the pile
of pages in the nanny's lap. "Are you saying you heard
from Happily Ever After? And the news is terrible? Don't
worry about that one bit. I've been regretting having ever
suggested it. We'll just send all of this back immediately,
with a short note of apology, and pretend it never happened."

Sarah studied her suspiciously. "I was certain you'd
try to talk me into meeting him, despite the fact that he
and I aren't suited to one another at all. If you're honestly
willing to be reasonable, and to help me explain my
change of heart to poor Mr. Braddock . . ." The girl's
soft brown eyes warmed with relief. "Have you really
been regretting it?"

"I'm afraid so. Jack doesn't quite believe Mr. Braddock
can work miracles, and you know what a wonderful judge
of character he is."

"But Mr. Braddock did his best," Sarah countered loyally. "You should read it, just once, Erica. He took such pains to find the right man for me. But for some reason, he chose someone who lives hundreds of miles away."

"Oh? Where exactly is that?"

"In the Caribbean, of all places. When he's home at all, which I imagine isn't all that often. He's a sea captain—"

"I beg your pardon?" Erica stared in delight. "Are you saying Mr. Braddock found you a tropical paradise and a swashbuckling hero?"

Sarah giggled knowingly. "That's more the reaction I was expecting from you. Even though I didn't say one word about a hero *or* a paradise. And the truth is, Captain McCullum sounds like a very reasonable, practical man— not a swashbuckling anything. If he lived in Boston, or even within one hundred miles—"

"But, Sarah! Why would you want to stay here? How can you start a new life with all of the old ghosts—" She stopped herself and grimaced in apology. "Forgive me, won't you? That was an unfortunate choice of words."

"But an accurate one." Sarah smiled. "My parents and my brother are buried here. Do you suppose I would ever consider leaving? I'm surprised Mr. Braddock would make that assumption, knowing from my letter how docile and unadventuresome I am."

Erica grimaced again. "I may have added a line or two, with the best of intentions, suggesting that you needed to make a fresh start. To have some excitement and to see new places—"

"Erica!"

"You need a change, for dozens of reasons. For one thing, you've always been a servant here. That will change with your new life. And your family has been dead for years and years! Pardon me for seeming heartless, but they would never want you to mourn forever. And as long as you stay in Boston, that's exactly what you'll do." Erica tossed her thick auburn locks impatiently. "I think matching you with a sea captain is inspired! Can you imagine the places you'll go? The breathtaking sights you'll see? Give me the letter. I want to find out every detail."

Accepting the pages eagerly, she began to devour their contents, gasping aloud with delight as she read. A tropical paradise, just as she'd suspected. And the man sounded positively perfect for Sarah. Thirty years old, dark hair, deep-blue eyes, rugged and healthy, and fairly well educated for a sailor. He was a widower, with a seven-year-old daughter and twin four-year-old boys. And a mother-in-law who adored him but was tired of living "in the middle of nowhere," raising the children, all because Daniel McCullum was too stubborn to admit that she should take them back to Salem with her until they were full grown. She in turn didn't want strangers raising her little darlings, and so the poor woman was doomed to live on the island unless Daniel found a new wife.

"Doomed to live on the island." Erica shook her head in amazement. "How can she complain about so delicious a fate? Balmy breezes, fresh fruit, fragrant blossoms all year round—"

"She was raised in Salem, and she misses *this* life. As would I. As would most women. But not you of course," Sarah teased fondly. "You're the only girl I know who would actually trade a life of comfort in Boston for a hut on the beach, or worse, a cramped little cabin on a ship. Mr. Ryerson would be jealous if he could see how your eyes glow at the mere prospect."

"I'd love to see Jack jealous." Erica sighed. "And I'd love to see you married to this sea captain. Don't be stubborn, Sarah. There's nothing for you here."

"My brother is here. I'd rather die than leave him. And even if I wanted to, this letter states quite clearly that Captain McCullum is not aware of all this matchmaking. It's strange and unsettling."

"He's loyal to his first wife's memory, the same way you're loyal to your little brother," Erica soothed. "But he needs to marry again, for the sake of his children and his mother-in-law. And you need to put the tragedy behind you, once and for all. Pining away won't bring your brother back, will it?"

Sarah shrugged. "Not in the way he was here before, but sometimes . . ."

Erica frowned at the faraway gleam in the nanny's eyes. "Sometimes, what?"

Sarah took a deep breath before accusing, "You'll say it's silly. Or superstitious. Or worse. But sometimes, I feel as though he never really left. He simply took a different form. Believe it or not, I feel he knows what I'm thinking. And sometimes, I can sense what he's thinking too."

"He isn't thinking at all, Sarah. He's gone to a place where thinking isn't necessary. He's found peace, and so should you. In the arms of a brawny sailor with a heart of gold. That's what your brother would want for you if he could somehow communicate with you."

"He *can* communicate with me! That's what I'm—oh, dear." She shook her head in self-reproach. "Let's not discuss it ever again. We'll simply write to Mr. Braddock, and thank him kindly for his trouble, and wish him the best of luck in finding a bride for Captain McCullum. And we should apologize for having misled him. I still can't believe you actually told him to find me a husband who lived far away!"

"And I still can't believe you want to stay here, where it's boring, and where you have such sad memories."

Erica smiled encouragingly. "I have the most wonderful idea. You'll sleep on it tonight, and try to dream of the sea captain and his island hideaway. If by morning, you haven't changed your mind, I'll help you write the letter."

"I won't dream of Captain McCullum tonight, I'll dream of my little brother, as I do every night. And there's no sense waiting another day. We need to inform Mr. Braddock right away to cancel the travel arrangements and to find another bride for the captain."

"And another groom for you?"

"No. It was a terrible idea. I should never have listened to you."

Erica bit her lip, uncertain of how to convince the girl not to reject this opportunity so casually. A sea captain and a tropical paradise! Was Sarah mad? Perhaps she was, if she honestly believed she could communicate with her dead brother!

If only Mr. Braddock had arranged for Captain McCullum to come to Boston, rather than for Sarah to travel to the Caribbean. Surely, once they met, they would discover they were just what the other needed.

But of course, Captain McCullum didn't even know the match had been made, and would undoubtedly resist any and all efforts to convince him to come to Boston for such a purpose. Sarah simply had to go to the Caribbean. There was no other way to accomplish what Russell Braddock had so cleverly set into motion. Perhaps Erica could convince Jack that they should act as Sarah's escorts for the voyage. What an utterly romantic prospect!

Then she remembered Jack's inattentive, unappreciative mood and sighed in defeat. She could barely convince the man to go for a walk or a picnic. Did she honestly think he'd take weeks away from his precious investments to facilitate a romantic match for a love-starved servant? Other men would undoubtedly jump at the opportunity to seduce their fiancée at sea, but Jack would act as though it were Erica that was being difficult.

"I'll just take you there myself, then," she announced suddenly.

"Pardon?"

"You and I will go to the Caribbean together. We'll meet Captain McCullum—"

"That's ridiculous, even for you," Sarah scolded. "Do you suppose Mr. Ryerson would let you go, even if I were willing to make such a foolhardy trip?"

"Mr. Ryerson would be glad to see me go," Erica assured her. "He treats me as though I'm a pest. I'm sure he'd help me pack, although I doubt he'd take time from his busy schedule to come down to the dock to wave farewell."

Sarah's brown eyes saddened. "Did you and he quarrel?"

"I never dare quarrel with him," Erica reminded her. "He always wins. But I did ask him if he'd be jealous if I ordered myself a burly lumberjack from Happily Ever After, and do you know what he said? He said it was an appealing idea because it would keep me occupied, so that he could finish his work."

Sarah giggled fondly. "He was teasing you, Erica. You know how much he loves you. If you really did allow another man to pay attention to you, Mr. Ryerson would go mad with jealousy. He'd punch the other man in the nose, and then he'd carry you off and marry you that very day."

"Do you think so?" Erica savored the lusty image. "How I would love to see him that way! Passionate. Obsessed. Aroused beyond any and all ability to think logically. Unfortunately, there aren't many lumberjacks in Boston. We have our share of sailors, of course, but I wouldn't know quite how to go about meeting them—"

"Erica Lane! You mustn't even consider such insanity. Making Mr. Ryerson jealous by flirting with another man might sound appealing, but the truth is, we don't know any men you could trust. We certainly can't trust any sailors!"

"We trust Captain McCullum," Erica teased. "If he's half the man his mother-in-law says he is, we can trust him to make you happy, and to order one of his crew mates to flirt with me and make Jack jealous."

Sarah eyed her sternly. "Don't drag me into your fantasies, Erica. You should try to appreciate Mr. Ryerson, rather than be intrigued by a stranger." Her tone softened slightly. "When you came out here today, you said you had decided this whole plan was ill-advised. Why have you changed your mind?"

"Jack expressed a lack of confidence in Mr. Braddock's ability to make a match, and so I was worried. But now we have proof of the man's genius." She waved the letter from Happily Ever After before the nanny's eyes. "He found you a sea captain and an island paradise. He's as amazing as everyone says, and you should at least meet Captain McCullum before—"

"You aren't listening to me!" Sarah wailed. "If I thought there was a chance Captain McCullum would settle here, with me and his children—or even in Salem at his mother-in-law's home!—I'd gladly consider the match. Although I must confess I'm not as taken with the idea of a sailor as you are."

"A *captain*. And a heroic one, according to this letter. It says his ship was used during the war because it was the fastest ship in the Atlantic! He carried secret documents, and transported important persons—perhaps even President Lincoln himself!"

"It says no such thing." Sarah shook her head in weary reproach. "It simply says it was hired as a revenue cutter

because it was so fast. Which I'll admit is a lovely tribute
to his ship.''

"You really have no imagination at all, do you?'' Erica
teased. ''I don't suppose you've taken even a moment to
picture how bronzed and brawny he must be. With dark
hair and deep-blue eyes—can't you just picture him?
Arriving home after months at sea, and sweeping you
into his arms. . . .'' She paused to take a breath, then
fanned herself with the letter in mock arousal. ''As your
friend, I must insist you marry him before someone else
does.''

"The sooner we write to Mr. Braddock and explain
my decision, the sooner he can find someone else for the
captain. You'll help me, won't you, Erica? I feel so foolish
for having wasted his valuable time.''

"I'll do better than that,'' Erica assured her. ''I'll write
it for you completely, so you don't have to worry about
it one moment longer. It will be my penance, for having
involved you in so silly a scheme in the first place.''

Sarah pursed her lips, as though suspicious of the plan,
but before she could muster a protest, Jack's two little
sisters bounded into the garden and catapulted themselves
into the two women's laps. Erica's affectionate attacker
was little Janie, the six-year-old who looked so much like
Jack, it allowed Erica a glimpse into his childhood, and
how devilishly adorable he must have been at that age.
If their own children proved to be even half so radiant
and precocious, she knew she was destined for a life of
wonder and delight.

"See my new shoes,'' Janie said as she wriggled her
feet. ''They shine as much as your pretty boots do.''

"They're exquisite,'' Erica replied. ''You must take
wonderful care of them, so that they always shine just
so. And as for *you*—'' She pretended to glare at the older
girl, Mary, who had settled easily against Sarah's chest.

"Have you grown again? Since yesterday? Didn't I expressly tell you to stop that?"

Mary giggled helplessly. "I want to be tall, like you."

"If you continue to defy me, you will be taller than I, and I do not tolerate that in a female."

"Jack's tall, tall, tall," Jane taunted. "When you stand with him, you look little, like us."

"What am I going to do with the two of you?" Erica sighed. "You insist on being prettier, and smarter, and taller every day. However will Sarah and I compete?"

"We don't compete with the girls," Sarah corrected carefully, adding to her little charges, "You know, of course, that Erica is teasing you. We want nothing more than for you to surpass us in every way."

"Speak for yourself." Erica smiled, but inwardly, she wondered if perhaps Sarah wasn't too willing to stay in the shadows, raising bright, pretty girls without ever allowing her own comeliness and intelligence to shine. And suddenly, Erica remembered exactly why she had sought the services of Happily Ever After for her modest friend. Only in a letter to a benevolent stranger could Sarah be presented in her best light.

"I should leave you three to your lessons," she said quietly. "What is it this afternoon? Arithmetic?"

"Geography," Sarah answered, ignoring the groans of her pupils.

"The wonders of the seven seas? How fascinating." Erica sighed loudly. "Of course, the lessons would be ever so much more effective if you'd seen or heard of them firsthand—"

"That's enough." Sarah's stern glance warned Erica against further mischief.

It's as though she doesn't feel deserving of more than this, Erica realized suddenly. *Living in the shadow of a tragedy, never allowing another family to take the place of the one she lost in the fire.*

She opened her mouth to argue with the governess, then thought better of it. For one thing, Erica had never been very good at arguing. For another, she had seen more than once how truly stubborn Sarah could be, despite her outward shyness. There had to be a more promising means of finishing what Russell Braddock had started— putting a lonely, love-starved female together with a tough but equally lonely sailor. There had to be some way to salvage this worthwhile venture. . . .

Erica's own words from earlier that afternoon came back to echo in her ears. Wasn't Jack Ryerson a genius when it came to salvaging a failing enterprise? He was just like Russell Braddock, except in a different venue. And in a way, this was an investment, wasn't it? Erica had invested time in it, and Russell Braddock had invested imagination. Sarah herself had invested hope. Now it was up to Jack to figure out how to turn the whole scheme around and make it succeed.

Scooting Janie off her lap, Erica folded the pages of the correspondence from Happily Ever After and slipped them neatly back into the envelope. ''I'll leave you to your geography, then. I need to go see Jack.''

''I thought he didn't want you to bother him,'' Sarah murmured. ''Why don't you work on the response to Mr. Braddock's letter instead?''

''That's precisely what I plan to do.'' Erica gave her friend a reassuring smile. ''Don't give it another thought, Sarah. I'll take care of everything.''

She had to turn away quickly, for fear the governess would see how captivated she had become by the idea of facilitating this match. And it wasn't just the prospect of finding happiness for Sarah that was making her pulse race. It was the thought of working together with Jack.

Perhaps they would travel to the Caribbean together after all! It was so sinfully romantic that Erica could scarcely contain her delight, and as she made her way through the garden and burst through the door to Jack's study, she imagined her eyes must be shining, and wondered how her fiancé would react to the sight.

Then Jack looked up from his ledgers and, to her dismay, he scowled pointedly. "What now, Erica? I thought we agreed you'd stop pestering me, at least until dinnertime."

"Pestering?"

He seemed about to explain, then turned his gaze back to his work instead. Erica waited a full minute before crossing the room to stand next to his desk. "Jack?"

"What is it?"

"You care about Sarah, don't you?"

He sighed, closed his book, and rubbed his eyes as though her question had caused him pain. "Is Sarah ill?"

"She's lonely."

"I can only imagine how that must feel, since I myself am never alone."

Aghast at the unkind implication, Erica spun away, and would have stormed from the room had her fiancé not sprung to his feet and grabbed her by the elbow. "Don't sulk, Erica. It's unbecoming." Turning her to face him, he added gently, "I'm sorry I was cross. As I told you, I need to finish this review before Owen arrives. But since you're determined to interrupt me—"

"I'm the one who should apologize." Erica hoped her expression was as wooden as her tone. "Please allow me to leave, so you can finish your precious work. I won't sulk," she added sharply. "But I also won't be able to join you and the Sawyers for dinner. I have a project of my own that needs *my* full attention over the next few days."

"A project?" Jack chuckled nervously. "The last time you used that word, it cost me a fortune in new furnishings for the girls' bedroom. Don't tell me you're redecorating Sarah's quarters now."

"Sarah needs something quite more than that, and so do I."

"In other words, *you're* lonely too?"

Unwilling to allow him to see how much the sarcastic remark had hurt her, Erica met his gaze directly with her own. "Sarah needs romance in her life, Jack. I've been trying to help her find that. I came in here to ask your advice, but I can see you're busy, so I'll just work it out on my own."

"Romance for Sarah?" He shook his head at the thought. "If that's your new project, my advice is to abandon it now, before you spend time and energy on a hopeless case."

"Jack Ryerson!"

"You think I'm being heartless?" He sighed and shook his head again. "I'm just being sensible, darling. Sarah is a wonderful woman, and I'm delighted to have her raising my sisters for me. But she has never recovered from the fire that took her family away from her. She hides here, Erica. Hides and grieves and nurtures false hopes that she will awaken to find it was just a bad dream."

"But, Jack—"

"If I thought she were capable of having a normal relationship with a man, I would have found someone for her years ago. She's pleasant-looking, and intelligent and well-mannered. But she's also a little off. Haven't you noticed?"

"Off?"

He tapped Erica's temple with his finger. "In her head. You're a little off, too," he added teasingly. "But in your case, it has the opposite effect, and makes you overly romantic. Not that I'm complaining.'' He lowered his mouth to her neck and nuzzled contritely. ''Don't be angry with me, darling. I think it's sweet of you to care so much for poor Sarah. It's the reason you found that mail-order marriage business so intriguing, isn't it?''

''Well, you know how I am. *Overly* romantic and all,'' Erica grumbled.

Jack laughed and patted her shoulder. ''Run along now, and don't waste any more time on this romantic fantasy of yours. It's doomed from the start.''

Resisting an urge to ask him if he was referring to Sarah's romance or their own, Erica backed a few steps away, then watched unhappily as he settled back down at his desk. The words he'd spoken earlier that day haunted her. *I'm your fiancé. I'm finished courting you.* Was it possible he had actually *meant* that? Was this to be her lot for the rest of her life? Being ignored and neglected, and mocked when she tried to inject a touch of romance into their lives? She simply couldn't accept such a fate.

And she couldn't accept it for Sarah either. Jack was wrong, not to mention arrogant, to think the governess couldn't find happiness in the arms of the right man. He was taking Sarah for granted in the same way he did Erica, with no thought to their needs or their desires or their value. It was time someone taught him a lesson, for his own good, and Erica knew just how she intended to do it.

''Say it again! To my face, this time.'' Daniel McCullum tightened his grip on his hapless adversary's neck, pinning him more completely against the ale house wall. ''Be quick about it, too, before I lose my temper.''

"I didn't mean anything by it!" the frightened victim wailed. "I wasn't talking about *you*, McCullum."

"You said *all* Irishmen."

"But you're an American."

"So?" Daniel's eyes narrowed ominously. "You were talking about my cousins, then? My sainted grandparents?"

"No, no—you're choking me—"

"That's the idea," Daniel assured him. "Now say it to my face."

"I take it back!" The sailor tried to squirm and immediately winced in pain. "You busted my shoulder when you threw me across the room."

"This shoulder?" Daniel asked, shoving it briskly as he spoke. "Seems fine to me. Speak up now, man. I'm losing patience. You wish *all* of us had starved to death—"

"No! It was a terrible tragedy."

"Caused by *your* bitch of a queen. Isn't that so?"

"Yes, yes, that's so."

"Say it, then. Tell me about that murdering bitch."

The man nodded as best he could given the iron grip on his throat. "She's a murdering bitch of a queen."

"There now." Daniel released his hold and watched with grim satisfaction as his prey slid to the floor in a heap. "You won't forget it, will you?"

"No, sir."

"Good." Daniel turned to accept a thick, foamy pint of ale from his first mate, taking a long, appreciative gulp before announcing, "You were right, Sean. All I needed was to beat the living tar out of an Englishman. How did you know?"

Sean Lynch chuckled as they wandered back to their table. "I thought for sure it was a woman you've been needing, but you had yourself *two* of them last night and

still had a foul mood on you all afternoon. So I figured
it had to be the other.''

Daniel nodded, impressed by the simplicity of the logic.
Those two girls had done their best to satisfy him, but
had left him wanting more. And even this fight, as rousing
as it had been, hadn't been completely satisfying. It was
enough to make a man wonder if his best days were
already behind him. Even a man who hadn't quite reached
his thirtieth birthday.

''Have you noticed how hard it is to find true inspiration
these days, Sean?''

''Just step onto the wharf and look straight ahead,''
his mate advised him dryly. ''How much more does one
man want?''

Daniel laughed ruefully, knowing that if he did in fact
step outside, he'd be able to see the *Moon Rigger,* his
rakish topsail schooner, waiting patiently in the moonlight
for his return. And hundreds of miles away, his three
children waited also. What more, indeed, did one man
want or need? His crew was solid, Sean in particular, and
Daniel was the master of his own fate to a degree most
men could not even imagine.

He knew it was time to go home, but also knew he'd
find that experience unsatisfying too. There had been a
time when sailing into Crescent Bay and spying his long,
low, white brick hacienda had been enough to soothe
even the most savage restlessness in his heart. Of course,
in those days, Lilli had been there, waiting patiently. Now
it was Lilli's mother who waited, and Abigail Lindstrom
was anything but patient.

That's the truth of it, he growled to himself. *That woman
and her infernal nagging. How is a man expected to enjoy
a fight or a girl when he has a mother-in-law like her?*

''Thinking about Lill, Captain?''

''About her mother.''

Sean shivered with exaggerated dread. "No wonder you're in a foul mood. That woman's as cranky as can be. Of course, she loves those little ones of yours," he added philosophically. "And she takes fine care of them."

"Who asked her to?" Daniel shook his head in disgust. "If she'd just go back to Salem, we'd all be better off."

"Or if you'd let her take the children to Salem with her, like she wants—" Sean broke off in the face of his captain's glare. "Of course, I agree with you, Captain. They belong on the Crescent, at least until they're full grown."

"They're safe there, and so that's where they'll stay," Daniel assured him. "Which means Abigail stays too, since she won't trust me and the servants to raise them. But she complains night and day, about the sand, and the heat, and missing her friends. . . . It's a curse, Sean, pure and simple."

"Aye, Captain, it's a curse for sure." The first mate slapped Daniel's shoulder. "You did a fine job on that Englishman, though. That's something, isn't it?"

Daniel nodded, then revealed quietly, "Abby says she'll go home, and leave Polly and the boys with me, if I take another bride—one *she* approves of—to raise them. She claims it's the only acceptable solution remaining."

"Is that so?"

Daniel found Sean's expressionless face and noncommittal answer annoying. "Have you an opinion on the subject?"

"My opinion is the same as yours, Captain."

"And what is that?"

Sean shrugged. "You're not the marrying sort. Lilli caught you by surprise, that was all. You'll not make the same mistake twice."

"You're calling Lilli a mistake?" Daniel grinned when his first mate blanched. "It's fine, Sean. I've said it myself a thousand times. I'm not the marrying sort, that's true. But Lilli was a bittersweet blessing, and the children are more than any man deserves. I have no regrets, but I'd be a fool to think I could survive it all again. Not with my sanity intact.''

"I thought you'd go mad for sure when we lost Lill.'' Sean's green eyes misted slightly. "I agree with you, Captain. We can't go through that again.''

"I give you fair warning, my friend. Abigail has plans for you as well. She thinks you'd make a fine husband for her niece in New York.''

"What?''

Daniel chuckled, then raised his half-finished drink for a mocking toast. "Here's to staying single, no matter what Abigail Lindstrom wants. You'll watch my back, and I'll watch yours. Agreed?''

"Aye, Captain. We've gotten each other through brawls and squalls, so here's to survival in the face of the greatest challenge yet—female scheming. At least it's a mean old woman who's doing the plotting. If it were a pretty young girl . . .'' Sean grinned self-consciously. "Speaking of which, I'd like to see if Betsy's still awake and agreeable. Care to come along? I'm sure she can find a friend for you.''

"This is the man who's going to save me from women?'' Daniel groaned in feigned defeat. "Go on and have your fun then, but watch yourself. I'll head back to the only female a sailor can ever really trust.'' Taking one last swallow of ale, he shrugged out of his chair and made his way toward the door, secure in the knowledge that the *Moon Rigger,* the sea, and a good night's rest awaited him.

CHAPTER TWO

Erica wasn't quite sure when mischief had turned to foolhardiness, followed by outright defiance, but somewhere in the weeks following the arrival of Russell Braddock's letter, she had clearly lost her mind. What other explanation was there for the fact that she was standing on the deck of a huge clipper ship, heading to the Bahamas, where she would be transferred, bag and baggage, onto something called a "launch" and taken to Captain Daniel McCullum's hideaway on an island called La Creciente?

It had occurred to her, during the days and nights of her voyage, that perhaps the captain had established a "hideaway" for the very purpose of discouraging persons like Erica from invading his life. She had also come to belatedly appreciate the rules of polite society that discouraged proper young maidens from traveling alone. Not that she had been accosted or mistreated by anyone, either in the crew or among her fellow passengers. Still, she found herself suspecting every male glance as being tinged with prurience, and every female stare as a gesture of disapproval. If they only knew how much there was to disapprove!

She had deceived both Sarah and Jack; had appropriated the travel arrangements made by Russell Braddock; and had dared set sail into a stranger's life, intent on meddling to an extent intolerable in civilized society. Of all her miscalculations, her biggest regret was having left Sarah in the awkward position of having to explain it all to Jack. Erica had left him a note, of course, but her fiancé would be likely to demand a more full and dispassionate explanation for his betrothed's disappearance than the enigmatic:

> *Darling Jack,*
> *I'm off to a rendezvous with a brave and lusty sea captain. Remember Father's prediction, that I would be carried away by just such an adventurer? But fear not, my darling. Although it is true that I yearn for excitement and seduction, my only wish for this particular adventure is to find a husband for Sarah. The danger of myself falling victim to the gentleman's advances is slight, and you can rest easily knowing that Captain McCullum would need to be exceedingly bold and persuasive before I would consider jeopardizing the tender, predictable affection you and I inspire in one another. So take care, and we will almost certainly be together again before summer's end.*
>
> >   *Yours as always,*
> >   *Erica*

No, Jack Ryerson would not like that at all. He would be angry and worried and confused. But he would also be jealous, and that would make all this insanity worthwhile.

Because her father had been correct about one thing: Erica wanted to be carried away. And the thought that Jack would come racing after her, enraged and possessive, and would sweep her off her feet and carry her back to Boston for an immediate wedding was the thought that had kept her resolve from weakening—first, when she'd alighted from the carriage and seen the clipper ship moored in the distance, and later, when she'd been shown to her tiny cabin by an eager sailor who couldn't have been more than fifteen years old.

The captain of the clipper ship and his wife had gone to great lengths to make Erica comfortable, insisting that she dine at their table every night. They had been curious as to her situation, but had easily accepted her story that her great aunt Abigail had fallen ill and had sent for Erica. The dutiful niece had made hasty arrangements to come to the Caribbean to care for her three little cousins until the older woman's strength returned.

Auntie Abigail. Erica smiled as she remembered how easily she had taken to the idea of being related to the woman who had written away for a bride for her son-in-law. She liked her already, if only because her transgression made Erica's look somewhat less ghastly. After all, a well-intentioned friend was allowed a bit of matchmaking, but a mother-in-law?

"You look lovely standing there, Miss Lane, with that pretty smile on your face. Were you thinking about one of your many suitors?"

She turned toward her host and captain, John Lawrence. "I was thinking about my aunt, actually. In addition to being one of the boldest women I've known, she's absolutely the most inventive. I can hardly wait to meet—I mean, see her again."

"It's a shame your mother was in Paris when the request for assistance arrived," Captain Lawrence said quietly.

"A pretty girl like yourself should be spending her time being courted and admired, not raising someone else's children, even if they are your own cousins."

"The truth is, I'm pleased with the opportunity to travel. I've never been farther from Boston than New York. Mother wanted to take me to Paris with her, but I didn't want to be so long away from—" Erica broke off, mortified that the truth had almost interfered with her string of convenient lies, not only about Abigail Lindstrom, but also about being relatively unattached, romantically speaking. It had seemed preferable to admitting that she had a fiancé who was so neglectful he hadn't even noticed that she'd run off to the Caribbean!

And as for her mother, that amazing woman actually *was* in Paris, and had indeed begged Erica to come with her. And Erica actually had been foolish enough to believe Jack would miss her, even though he had openly urged her to take the trip. If only she had gone to France, Jack would be miserable and perhaps even jealous by now!

But if she'd gone, she never would have heard of Russell Braddock, and Sarah never would have had the opportunity to marry Captain McCullum. And either way, Jack would be jealous, so this choice, while bizarre, was clearly the better of the two.

"I made some inquiries among my crew about your Captain McCullum," Captain Lawrence told her mischievously. "You say he was married to your cousin?"

Erica gulped. "I've never met him, but yes. It's his children Auntie Abigail is raising. My first cousins once removed, to be precise. I know so little about . . . well, about Daniel. Did you learn anything?"

Lawrence nodded. "He's something of a rogue, I'm told. It's difficult to picture him married at all, much less to a cousin of a sweet girl like yourself. I've met men like him in my day, and they usually marry the sea."

"A rogue?" Erica was struggling not to panic. "Whatever does *that* mean?"

Lawrence grinned. "I didn't mean to shock you. He's a well-respected man, I assure you. Respected for his ability as a seaman, his fighting ability, and his ability to tell a rousing tale. His crew would die for him, I'm told. In the end, that's the only real measure of a sea captain."

"But, a rogue?" She simply couldn't banish the foreboding the word had awakened. "And you're saying he fights? With his fists?"

The captain laughed. "Your cousin must have been quite an adventuress to have married a man like him." Sobering slightly, he confided, "They say McCullum almost went mad with grief when she died. That, too, is a good measure of a man, wouldn't you say? Or at least, proof that his love for her was deep and true. You mustn't allow my poor choice of words to prejudice you against him."

"I've been so looking forward to meeting him." Erica sighed in confusion. "Auntie Abigail didn't share all this with me in her letters."

"I suppose she had her reasons."

"Yes." Erica nodded vigorously, knowing suddenly that "Auntie" Abigail had doctored the truth for fear no decent girl would come to La Creciente otherwise. What nerve!

Of course, Erica had manipulated the truth a bit in her own letter, for Sarah's sake. No wonder Russell Braddock had made such a mess of all this! Matching a proper maiden to a rogue? Wouldn't he be distressed if he knew the truth?

"I didn't mean to upset you, Miss Lane. And I repeat, McCullum's reputation is sterling in its own way. I'm sure he'll be a gentleman with you, in light of the fact that you've unselfishly volunteered to help with his children. He will undoubtedly be greatly appreciative.''

"I wish I could be confident of that," Erica said wryly. "In any case, I've come this far. I might as well meet— I mean, visit with my aunt for a while. But if for some reason I find myself in ... well, in awkward circumstances, how would I go about arranging passage home?''

Captain Lawrence patted her arm. "I've alarmed you for no reason, and I apologize. But if McCullum proves to be a poor host, your aunt can surely assist you in getting word to one of my associates in the area. I'll have Mrs. Lawrence provide you with the names of reliable persons you can trust. But it won't be necessary, I'm sure."

Erica nodded and forced herself to relax. Even if the worst happened, and Abigail was as much a disappointment as Daniel McCullum was proving to be, Jack would arrive before too many miserable days had passed. For all she knew, he was right behind them! He could have chartered a small, fast ship, intent on overtaking his beloved before she even fell into his rival's clutches! Wouldn't that be perfectly romantic?

"There, that's better." Captain Lawrence studied her admiringly. "When you smile like that, you are truly radiant, Miss Lane."

"Thank you, Captain."

He grinned impishly. "My men have been debating the color of your eyes, did you know? They are fascinated by you, and by the fact that you are traveling unescorted, despite their certainty that you have any number of suitors who would have gladly made the trip with you.''

She wondered what he and his crew would say if they knew her fiancé had neither the time nor the inclination to sail with her. It reflected poorly on Jack, but also on Erica, for being unable to inspire devotion in her own true love. "My eyes are hazel," she informed the captain quietly. "They're very like my father's were, although in all other respects I take after my mother."

"You should have gone to Paris with her," he scolded gently. "And I'd say they're more gold than anything else."

"Pardon?"

"Your eyes. They seem golden in color, especially when you smile."

Erica flushed with delight. "Thank you for the lovely compliments, and for taking the time to make my last day aboard your ship so pleasant. Will I see you again before I disembark?"

"I will make a point of it. And Mrs. Lawrence will also. She's grown very fond of you, you know."

"You've both been so gracious."

He bowed slightly. "We'll have that list of reliable contacts for you, although I'm confident it won't come to that. McCullum's a man, after all. I suspect he'll be eager to behave for such a beautiful houseguest."

"I hope you're right," she said, but inside, she knew better. Her view of Captain Daniel McCullum was now as a stubborn, pugnacious rogue who had made himself quite clear on the subject of marriage. He would not be pleased to find an uninvited matchmaker in his home, golden eyes notwithstanding. And he would *not* behave.

So Jack will rescue you from Captain McCullum's bad temper, she decided philosophically. *In some ways, that's even more romantic than a fit of jealousy, isn't it?*

And under the circumstances, a rescue was also more useful, so Erica decided to make the best of the situation until Jack arrived, knowing that whatever happened, she was soon to have the romantic adventure she had been craving all her life.

* * *

She found adventure sooner than anticipated aboard the *Valiant*'s launch. After the comforting stability of the huge clipper ship, the utilitarian sailboat seemed perilously undersized, and as it raced with the wind toward La Creciente, Erica felt a lump in her throat that could only be her heart.

Still, she had never felt so alive, if only because she felt so close to catastrophe, both literally and figuratively. There she was, with the wind whipping her damp hair against her cheeks, as two brawny sailors pleaded with her to sit herself down and stay "abaft the mast." But she wanted to see Daniel McCullum's home as soon as it came into view, in hopes that she could prepare herself more fully for her first encounter with a "rogue."

Then one of the sailors—not the toothless silent one, but the one named Carson who had appointed himself her official escort—thumped her on the shoulder and shouted, "There she is, miss. The Crescent—the most perfect natural harbor in all the world, or so McCullum claims."

"You know him?" She tore her gaze from the choppy sea just long enough to scrutinize her escort. "You've met Captain McCullum?"

"Met him?" The sailor burst into laughter. "Met his fist, more likely. I can't quite picture you in his family tree, miss. You with all your fine ways, and him with his own way of doing things."

"He hit you?" Erica gasped. "Why?"

"He was in a mood." The sailor shrugged. "He didn't mean anything by it. Bought me a whiskey after it was over, and told me about the time he washed overboard rounding the Horn. Ask him to tell you that one! True or false, it's a whale of a story."

Fine, Erica grumbled inwardly. *He hits perfectly sweet men for no reason, then lies about his exploits. What could I have been thinking!*

McCullum was turning into a profound disappointment. The Crescent, on the other hand, was everything Erica had dreamed it would be. Even from this distance, its pink sands beckoned to her. And McCullum's house—she assumed it was his house, since it was the only structure in sight—was like something from a painting, with its low, graceful form and gleaming white brick elegance.

So distracted was Erica by the hacienda's beauty that she didn't even see an approaching swimmer until the soaked figure heaved itself overboard and catapulted itself against her. With a shriek of "Gracious!" Erica backed away, only to be accosted by what appeared to be a little boy in desperate need of a hug.

"Oh, my." Erica returned the child's embrace carefully. "You're drenched, poor dear. How on earth did you get yourself into this dreadful predicament?"

"This isn't a perdicament," the child informed her cheerfully. "It's a launch. Don't you know the difference? I thought schoolteachers were supposed to know everything."

Erica's escort put a firm hand on the child's shoulder. "Where in blazes did you come from, son?"

"I'm not your son. And I'm not your daughter. And if you don't take your hands off me, my father will hang you from the yardarm of the *Moon Rigger.*"

The sailor chuckled and released his prisoner. "You're McCullum's brat? That figures. So? Are you a girl brat or a boy brat?"

Sending the sailor a disapproving glance, Erica pulled the child more securely into her lap. "I know Captain McCullum has two sons and a daughter. And you must be the daughter, because the boys are only four years old. Tell us your name.''

''I'm Polly.'' She smiled shyly. ''Grandma said you might not be pretty, but you'd have a good heart. But you're so pretty, I don't even care about your heart.''

Erica laughed lightly. ''And you're so pretty, I'm quite speechless with confusion. What were you doing in the water? You could have been killed!''

''Killed? By what? There aren't hardly any sharks in these waters, miss.''

''Why does she call you 'miss'?'' the sailor demanded. ''I thought you were her cousin.''

Erica winced. ''Perhaps my aunt doesn't want her to know about the *i-l-l-n-e-s-s*.''

The sailor grimaced. ''Huh?''

''The illness,'' Polly translated. ''Who's sick?''

''You'll be the one who's sick if you continue to behave as you've just done, young lady.'' Erica eyed the child sternly, hoping that she wouldn't notice the change in subject. ''What would your father say if he saw you swimming out to strange boats wearing only these thread-bare breeches?''

''I knew it was you, and I just couldn't wait. Grandma and me could see you through the spyglass, but we couldn't see your face 'cause of all this.'' The girl fingered a lock of Erica's auburn hair and added wistfully, ''It's beautiful.''

Erica smiled and ran her fingers through the child's own hair, which was cropped so short, it was difficult to tell how it might be were it allowed to grow to a decent length. The color was a rich, dark blue-black, though, and it was thick enough, and so she assured the girl, ''You have beautiful hair too; if only you'd let it grow. And your lashes are the most exquisite I've seen.''

''Lashes?''

"Your eyelashes, silly. Hasn't anyone ever remarked on them to you?" She felt a rush of indignation at the clear mistreatment of this child. "Hasn't anyone ever told you how pretty you are? Or how horridly you behave? Swimming half-naked toward strange boats—wait until I tell your father what I think about *that.*"

"You're going to scold McCullum when he gets back?" the sailor said, his voice filled with wonder.

"Back?" Erica frowned. "I was assuming he was here."

"Then where's his schooner?"

"Papa's not here," Polly confirmed. "Grandma says that's best, so we can be ready for him. He won't be happy to see you here, but . . ." She paused, then threw her arms around Erica and murmured, "I'm so happy you've finally come."

The gesture touched Erica's heart, and she cuddled the strange child to her bosom. "I'm pleased to meet you myself, Polly. When exactly do you expect your father to return?"

"Days or weeks. That's how it is with Papa. But when he gets here"—Polly's blue eyes twinkled with mischief—"we'll both swim out to the *Moon Rigger* to welcome him."

Erica grinned and tickled the child's ribs lightly. "My only purpose, in the next days—or weeks—is to ensure you never do such a thing again. You're a pretty young lady, not a rascally boy. It's time you learned to behave. And—oh, dear! What now?"

She'd been so busy lecturing the child, she'd failed to see how near to the shore they'd drawn until the launch actually skirted against the sandy bottom of the bay. With a hopeful glance toward her escort, she asked, "Did we intend to do that? Or have we run aground?"

"Don't worry, miss. We're just going to pull the boat

up onto the beach so you can get out without getting wet.''

Before she could protest, both he and his assistant had heaved themselves over the side and were tugging cheerfully at the ropes.

''I'll go fetch Grandma,'' Polly offered, but Erica grabbed her around the waist before she could follow the sailors overboard.

''You will disembark like a lady, Polly McCullum. Oh, dear, are those your clothes up there on the beach?''

Polly giggled. ''I folded my shirt real careful, just like a lady.''

Erica laughed in return. ''Would you like to know a secret?''

The blue eyes widened dramatically. ''Tell me, please?''

''I have a friend named Sarah who would love to get her hands on you, to teach your how to comport yourself.''

''I thought *you* were Sarah!'' the child wailed. ''Are you here to marry Papa or not?''

''Hush, Polly. We don't want the *s-a-i-l-o-r-s* to hear us,'' Erica teased. ''I can see your grandmother has been keeping you well informed. But there's been a new development, and so it's best that your father is away for a time. It will give us girls a chance to modify our plans a bit.''

''I like the old plan, where *you* marry Papa.''

''Hush now,'' Erica warned again as the brawny sailors dragged the boat right out of the water and onto the sand. ''These men believe I'm your cousin Erica, come to care for you and your brothers while my aunt Abigail recovers from some sickness. Can you pretend with me for just a while?''

Polly's eyes twinkled with delight. ''Can I tell Grandma?''

''Absolutely.'' She turned in time to allow her escort

to assist her from the launch while his companion retrieved her baggage. "You gentlemen must come up to the house with me. I'm certain my aunt would want to offer you some refreshment."

"It's Captain Lawrence we need to please now, miss, and he wants us back right away." The sailor smiled ruefully. "It's been an honor."

"What a lovely thing to say. And after I caused the two of you all this extra work."

"All the men wanted to bring you, but the first mate owed me and Hook here a favor, so we got chosen. Right, Hook?"

Her silent escort grinned in semi-toothless agreement.

"Well, then . . ." Erica hesitated, then offered "Hook" her hand, hoping he would choose to shake, rather than kiss it. Still, when he lowered his odd mouth and grazed her fingertips with reverence, she was pleased, and when her other escort followed suit, she curtseyed and assured them, "I can't remember when I've been treated so gallantly. Give my best to Captain and Mrs. Lawrence, won't you? And take care, both of you."

He flushed, then turned to Polly. "It's been a pleasure, Miss McCullum. Tell your father Carson Beales sends his greetings."

"He'll be grateful that you brought my cousin Erica here," the child said solemnly. "My grandma is ill, you know. That's why she needs someone to help her with us children."

This girl's a born schemer, Erica noted, wondering if Polly got her mischievous nature from her mother's side or her father's. Of course, given Abigail Lindstrom's demonstrated penchant for plotting, she was fairly certain it wasn't the McCullum in Polly that was making her blue eyes sparkle so wildly.

They waved until the launch was sailing freely, then

Erica picked up the child's discarded shirt, frowning as she did so. "This fabric is so rough. How can you abide it against your skin?"

"Grandma says I'm too hard on fancy clothes."

"Just the same . . ." She helped the child slip her arms into the sleeves. "I assume you have a dress or two?"

"Grandma sews them for me, but I hardly wear them. Come and meet her now."

Erica's gaze fixed onto the hacienda as she allowed the child to pull her by the hand. This would be the decisive moment, now that she was actually reconsidering Daniel McCullum as a potential spouse for Sarah. Despite his reputation, he had much to offer Sarah. Little Polly, for one; Sarah would fall madly in love with the child, and more importantly, with the child's potential. And this place! Pink sand, warm breezes, vibrant bougainvillea and hibiscus—some with blossoms as large as saucers and as bright as a rainbow!

And suddenly Erica's heart was pounding, because this was also the ideal place for Jack to come for her. To scoop her into his arms and carry her down the beach, out of sight of the hacienda, where he would make love to her for the very first time. His green eyes would blaze with desire and jealousy and apology, his kisses would sear love right into her skin, and all doubts would disappear forever.

And so, before she shook the sand from her feet and crossed the threshold of the McCullum home, she turned her eyes one last time toward the sea and whispered, "Hurry, my love. I've been waiting my whole life for this—and for you."

Abigail Lindstrom was the soul of propriety and reason, or so she pretended. With the gracious air of a seasoned hostess, she insisted upon taking Erica on a tour of the McCullum home, explaining in minute detail how every feature of the house was designed to keep its occupants comfortable in the tropical climate. Cool, red tile floors; huge windows that allowed for breezes but could be shuttered securely against late summer tempests; airy caned furniture—not a hint of upholstery anywhere save Abigail's rocker!—and beds raised to window height so that cool air would waft right across the sleeping figures, whose faces would be protected if needed by yards of pure white mosquito netting.

The most delightful feature of all to the visitor was the abundance and variety of fragrances that poured through every window, thanks to careful planting of pink allamanda, orange begonias and yellow hibiscus. There was an intoxicating, yet light-as-air quality to the home that made it seem outlandishly romantic—the perfect place to twine one's arms around a man's neck and brush her lips across his in sinful invitation.

"It's all so glorious." Erica sighed aloud. "Did your daughter design it? Surely this can't be Captain McCullum's doing."

"She established the gardens, but it was Daniel and his friend Sean who built and furnished the house. If you are fortunate enough to meet Sean during your visit, you will learn what few persons know—that he's an artist, wasted at sea when he should be creating masterpieces from wood and brick."

"He's Captain McCullum's friend?"

"First mate aboard the *Moon Rigger*," Abigail confirmed. "Daniel recruited him the year he married Lilli. My husband gave them the schooner as a wedding present, primarily because he could not abide having a common sailor for a son-in-law. But a captain!" She sniffed in disapproval. "Both my husband and Lilli found that status to be fraught with respectability and romance."

Erica smiled. "From what I learned during my voyage, your son-in-law was born to the position. And I'm afraid I must agree with the majority—it's a provocative occupation." She lowered her voice so that Polly could not hear. "You didn't approve of the marriage?"

Abigail hesitated, then gestured toward a round mahogany table on which the housekeeper had placed a pitcher of lemonade and a plate of lemon tarts. "Come and have some refreshment, and I'll tell you all about it. Polly? Go and check on your brothers please. They should be finished napping soon. But don't wake them yourself," she added sternly. "They need their rest."

Polly nodded, spun on her heels, and raced down a long, tiled hall.

"She's so darling, Mrs. Lindstrom. I've never been as surprised in my life as when she appeared out of nowhere, drenched by the sea and dressed in boy's clothing."

"And you disapprove? So do I. It's all Daniel's doing, I assure you. I believe he knows enough about men to hope she never attracts one." Abigail smiled fondly. "You asked if I approved of the marriage, and my answer is yes, but only because Daniel McCullum brought a glow to my little girl's face I never believed I'd see. And of course, I thought she would convince him that life at sea was no life for a married man, especially after Polly was born. I was sure they'd give up this isolation and move to Salem to live with Mr. Lindstrom and myself. But Daniel's stubborn. *He* does the convincing, not the other way around."

"You mentioned that in your letter." Erica smiled and accepted a glass of lemonade as she spoke. "But there are a few other details you neglected to mention to Russell Braddock."

Abigail arched an eyebrow. "And was the letter sent by your friend Sarah completely accurate?"

The visitor grinned. "Touché. I believe we've both done a bit of mischief here, but for a wonderful cause. Still, we'd better be brutally truthful with one another now, if we intend to manipulate them into marital bliss."

"The brutal truth?" Abigail shrugged. "I am motivated by selfishness in this, unlike you. I yearn to go home to Salem, and since I know Daniel will never let me take my grandchildren with me, I must find someone wonderful and loving to take my place. Not a servant," she added sharply. "That would be Daniel's solution, but it is an unacceptable one."

"If only you could see how devoted and loving Sarah is to her little charges, you would know that you can trust some servants as much, if not more, than one's own flesh and blood."

"How is it that you came to know her so well?"

Erica hesitated, but what she had told Abigail was correct: They had to be completely honest with one another, and so she explained, "Sarah is governess to my fiancé's little sisters. Jack's parents are dead, and he would have been lost if he hadn't found Sarah to help him."

"So?" Abigail frowned. "You're engaged? I was rather hoping . . ."

"Hoping what?"

"Well, I was hoping *you* were Sarah, pretending to be Erica, for the purpose of evaluating us—and Daniel—without having made any inconvenient commitment."

Erica laughed lightly. "I'm not so adept at scheming as all that, I'm afraid. Although I suspect *you* are."

"Adept? No, but I'm desperate. For the first few years after we lost Lilli, I thought Daniel simply needed time to grieve. He was inconsolable, Miss Lane—almost to the point of true despair. My plan was to stay only for a

while, but now it seems I'm doomed to spend the rest of
my days here unless I find someone to take my place."

"But Captain McCullum doesn't want another wife.
And you say he's stubborn—"

"That's why I made the arrangements myself. I thought
that if I brought a girl here, and gave the children a chance
to grow fond of her, he might relent, if only to rid himself
of me. I haven't been a pleasant person where he is
concerned, believe me. I can only imagine how desperate
he is to see me leave." She took Erica's hand in her own.
"He's a good man, dear. I couldn't have asked for a
better husband for my daughter. Won't you please inform
your friend that she should come immediately?"

"Well . . ." Erica forced herself to swallow her pride.
"You aren't the only one who misled Mr. Braddock.
With the best of intentions, of course. I'm afraid I wasn't
quite accurate when I told him Sarah wanted to start a
new life in a new place. The truth is, she seems determined
to stay in Boston forever."

"What?"

"I'm afraid so. But it's a poor choice on her part. She's
haunted by ghosts there. Here, she would be free of them.
And she would be the lady of a magnificent estate, rather
than a servant. I want this for her," Erica insisted.
"Almost as much as you want to find a stepmother for
your grandchildren. Surely between the two of us we can
find a way to arrange it."

Abigail shook her head. "Daniel doesn't want this, and
neither does Sarah? I don't see how we can succeed under
those conditions."

"He secretly wants it, and so does she. So we *will*
succeed." She studied Abigail with quiet concern.
"You're certain he will be good to her?"

Abigail nodded. "He's a complicated man, although
he'd roar if he heard me describe him so. I believe he

chose a life at sea to escape an unhappy childhood, and at times I think perhaps we should have let him alone there, wrestling his storms and harsh memories. But he is also a loving father, and as I mentioned, he brought something to Lilli's pitiful life that her father and I couldn't supply."

"Her life was pitiful?"

"She was sickly from birth. Never could catch a good, strong breath," Abigail murmured. "It's the reason her father decided to bring her down here, to the estate of an acquaintance in Cuba who swore the sea air and warmth would do her good. That's how she met Daniel, you see. He was a member of the crew on our ship, and was assigned to carry Lilli about."

"She was that weak?"

"At times. She was stronger here, though. Gardening and basking in the sunlight—and in the glow of Daniel's devotion."

Erica could feel her heart weeping in her chest. "It's so unbearably romantic!"

"Yes. Unbearable is the word."

"And he's perfect for Sarah, because in her own way, she is just like Lilli. In need of strength and protection, yet with so much to offer in return. Oh, Abigail!" She reached for the woman and hugged her exuberantly. "Until this moment, I was riddled with doubts. But now I know Sarah is just what the captain needs. She will do wonders for him, and will set *you* free in the process. Oh, my word!" She paused to admire two golden-haired, sleepy-eyed cherubs who had just wandered into view. "Don't tell me these angels are your grandsons!"

Abigail beamed. "Come here, darlings. Meet our new friend, Miss Lane. Erica, may I present Kevin and Little Sean McCullum."

Erica smiled, serenely certain at last. Any man who

could father such adorable children could not be a "rogue," Captain Lawrence's opinion notwithstanding. And if ever there were children who needed the warmth and love of a new mother, it was these. *I thought this match was made by a mortal in Chicago,* she told herself with quiet awe. *But it was actually made in heaven.*

"Are you sure Papa will like my hair in curls?" Polly was worrying three days later as she and Erica played in the pink sand of La Creciente. "He might laugh at me, and then what?"

"He won't laugh," Erica promised, fingering the child's short hair lovingly. "We want him to understand that you're a big girl now, don't we? One day you'll be a fine lady—"

"I don't want to be a lady, I want to be a sailor!" the child blurted. "Sailors don't curl their hair or wear fancy shoes. They must be ready for disaster at any moment."

Erica took a deep breath. "One day you'll change your mind. You'll decide you want men to bring you flowers, and compliment you. And when that day comes, you'd best have long, luxurious hair, and modest lacy attire. If only Sarah were here, she could give you better reasons for behaving, but . . ." She smiled impishly. "I've kissed several boys, and one man, and I can tell you it's all the adventure a girl really needs if it's done correctly."

"Kissing? Ick! I don't want any of that. I want to be a captain, like Papa."

"Don't be ridiculous. Why not be a captain's wife, like your mother was? It's so romantic."

The little girl's jaw jutted out in defiance. "I'll be a captain myself! It's not fair! Just because I'm a girl, no one will believe I can handle a ship of my own!"

"Fine, fine," Erica soothed her. "You'll be a captain,

if that's what your heart wants. You'll be a beautiful lady captain, in a tasteful but practical gown, and every sailor will want to serve under you and do your bidding.''

The girl's blue eyes had widened. "They will?"

"Yes, Polly. You'll be famous.''

"I just want to sail. Like Papa. He needs me to, you know. Kevin and Little Sean can't do it, because they haven't enough air. But I have plenty—'' The child broke off, her eyes dancing as she stared out to sea, and then, before Erica could understand what was happening, Polly was shedding her new dress, revealing the old, tattered knickers she'd hidden beneath them.

"What are you doing?" Erica gasped.

"It's Papa! Don't you see? It's the *Moon Rigger!* Wait here while I help him secure her, then I'll bring him to you!''

Erica lunged for the child, but nimble Polly was three steps ahead, racing for the water's edge, where she turned and waved impishly before plunging headlong into the surf.

Tearing her eyes away from the spot where the child had disappeared, Erica stared at the *Moon Rigger,* a trim, graceful vessel not half the size of the *Valiant,* yet every bit as lovely. Coasting more than sailing, the schooner was still a marvelous sight, and so clearly at home in Crescent Bay that Erica couldn't remember how the horizon had looked without her.

This is insane, she told herself sheepishly as she watched the tiny figure in the water work its way toward the schooner. *How does Captain McCullum allow his daughter to behave in this fashion? And what if she drowned? Or was attacked by mean fish? What would that stubborn rogue do then?*

If Erica had been a strong swimmer, she might have gone after the child, but in truth she hadn't had much

experience in the water, and so she could only hope Polly's
bravado was based in expertise. With eyes that burned
from the noonday sun she watched for what seemed like
hours until the small figure reached the *Moon Rigger,*
where anonymous but clearly strong arms assisted her up
the ropes and onto the deck.

At least she's safe, she told herself grimly as she settled
back down onto the sand to wait for the child's return.
*If I have anything to say about it, that will be the last
time that happens. Abigail has been remiss in controlling
Captain McCullum, but I will not hesitate to explain to
him that he is responsible for ensuring that Polly becomes
a lady, not a sailor!*

Erica's indignation lasted for a time, but after an hour
of waiting for Polly and her father, she reclined completely
into the sand and closed her eyes, hoping for just a
moment's rest. She needed to be at her best, after all,
when she met McCullum. What harm would a judicious
nap do?

Sleep engulfed her, not in visions of children swimming
in a bay, but of a tanned, strapping sailor not unlike those
who had manned the huge sails of the *Valiant,* all the
while casting longing glances in Erica's direction. She
had felt their eyes on her as surely as she'd ever felt Jack
Ryerson's hands, and now, in her dream, one of them
was touching her in places Jack had never dared, and in
ways Jack had surely never contemplated.

There was need in his dexterous fingers, and in her
dream, Erica recognized this man for what he was—a
rogue! An unprincipled scoundrel with a reprehensible
imagination, bent on seducing innocent virgins into lives
of wanton pleasure. Yet even while she wriggled in pro-

test, she craved the moment when he would subdue her and make her his woman. . . .

"Are you deaf, woman? Wake up!" a gruff voice was demanding, and Erica stirred, still dreamy-eyed.

Then she realized this voice was different—more resonant, more impatient, more *real!*—and she shrank from the sound even before she opened her eyes and stammered, "Wh-what do you want?"

"*I'm* asking the questions here," the intruder informed her, his voice an ominous, gravelly growl. "Get up and explain yourself to me."

CHAPTER THREE

He was leaning over her, his bronze chest bristling with wiry black curls, visible because of the billowy white shirt he wore opened almost to the waist and tucked into tight black pants. The sparks in his deep blue eyes and the set to his stern, square jaw warned that he was furious with her, yet he was also greedily memorizing her, from her waist to her quivering lips. She could only pray that he wasn't who he seemed to be, and without thinking, she blurted, "Please tell me you're not Daniel McCullum."

The sailor laughed roughly. "If I thought it would get rid of you, I'd gladly tell you anything you wanted to hear. Unfortunately," he grabbed her by both wrists and tugged her to her feet, "it's my understanding you've come on a mission, misguided as it might be, so let's have a look at you."

"There's no need for that," Erica protested, wishing she knew exactly what Polly had told this irate man. There was the official version—the "governess" story—and then there was the truth. And then of course, there was the *whole* truth, but Polly hadn't even heard *that* one yet, thank goodness. The safest route was to assume the child had done as her grandmother had instructed her, although Erica couldn't imagine how that could have angered McCullum so. Assuming he was McCullum, of course, and not some wicked buccaneer.

In any case, he was waiting, his blue eyes still blazing, and so she tugged with haughty insistence until he released her wrists, then she stepped back and smiled with as much confidence as she could muster. "There's a perfectly innocent explanation for my 'mission,' as you call it, sir. It all started when a mutual friend—"

"A friend of *mine?*"

"No, no. A mutual friend of mine and Abigail's." Erica took a deep breath and smiled again. "This friend heard about the situation on this island, and thought perhaps Polly and her brothers needed a governess. And as luck would have it—"

"My daughter said you were Abigail's niece."

Erica winced and took another step backward. At least now she knew he was McCullum. If only she knew why he was so annoyed over the thought of a visit from a relative! "That's a natural mistake, Captain," she assured him. "You see, on my voyage to your beautiful island here, I didn't want to discuss my personal business with my fellow travelers, so I simply told everyone I was on my way to help my sick aunt. When the sailors brought me here to your island, they confused Polly by referring to me as her cousin, and to Abigail as my aunt, and so . . ." She shrugged and met his gaze directly. "My name is Erica Lane. I'm more than willing to explain myself to you until you're satisfied, but shouldn't you go up to the house first and let your sons know you're home?"

To her relief, a hint of a smile tugged at the corners

of the captain's rugged mouth. "So? Abigail hasn't been trying to play matchmaker between you and my first mate?"

"Pardon?"

"She's been threatening for months to marry him off to her niece in New York. I thought you were the prospective bride, but I should have known from the look of you that you weren't a Lindstrom." His eyes traveled over her with mischievous thoroughness. "You don't look like a governess, either."

"I never said I was a governess." She held up her hand to ward off further misunderstandings. "I assume Polly went up to the house? You and I should join them, Captain. Kevin and Little Sean will be waking from their naps soon, and I imagine Abigail is having a small feast laid out in your honor. They've all missed you," she added sincerely. "You have such a lovely family."

McCullum's eyes had narrowed again. "You're not a governess, and you're not here to marry Sean? So why are you here?"

"Marry Sean? Oh! I'd almost forgotten, but that's your first mate's name, is it not? He must be a wonderful friend for you to have paid him the honor of naming your son for him." Erica bent down to retrieve Polly's discarded dress, shaking it to loosen any sand that may have clung to it. "I want to hear all about him over dinner. And then I'll tell you all about Sarah."

"Sarah?"

"The governess," she explained, adding sympathetically, "I know it seems confusing, but it's really very simple."

"I doubt that," McCullum muttered.

Erica could see he was about to lose his temper again, and was relieved when a chorus of "Papa! Papa!" distracted them both. Turning, she saw that the little McCullum boys were scampering across the sand, their eyes shining despite the fact that each was clearly winded by the effort.

McCullum strode toward the children, scooping them up easily in his muscular arms. "Look at the two of you," he marveled, his voice as gravelly as before, but with a new and touching gentleness. "Catch your breath now— that's my boys. I hear you've done a good job taking care of your grandmother and sister while I was away. And you've had to look after this mysterious redhead too. That must have made it even more interesting."

Erica felt her heart swell with relief despite the jest made at her expense. As flawed as Daniel McCullum might be—and Erica had seen proof that he was indeed an impatient and suspicious rogue of a man—he also had a loving side. And he was a handsome, strapping specimen with a demonstrated ability to produce darling, intelligent children. What more could Sarah ask? Perhaps she could live happily ever after in paradise after all.

Try as he might, Daniel couldn't quite figure out the young woman who had dared invade his hideaway. She clearly wasn't Abigail's niece—not with that tall, willowy shape and those mischievous amber eyes. The Lindstroms were tiny and fair-haired, with wide, pale blue eyes that could look right into a man's soul. Lilli, the twins, and even Abigail had always had a reassuring simplicity of appearance. Erica Lane, on the other hand, exuded complications, from her pouty mouth to that mane of auburn hair to the throaty little laugh that seemed to bubble up unexpectedly at the slightest provocation.

Sean could never have resisted her, Daniel told himself with a rueful smile. *If she'd been Abigail's niece, we'd be having a ceremony on the quarterdeck before the week was out.*

"So?" he demanded finally over a light dessert of fresh fruit in citrus sauce. "I've been patient, but now it's time for an explanation. Polly? Tell me all about Miss Lane here."

"Me?" The little girl squirmed and glanced toward her grandmother. "The sailors called her my cousin, but she's not. One of them didn't have teeth, Papa. And he kissed Erica's hand, and she let him. She's brave."

He pretended to scowl. "Are you keeping secrets from your father, girl?"

She giggled happily. "I don't even *know* the *real* secret yet."

"I see. Abigail? What's it all about?"

The gray-haired woman shrugged. "It's hardly a secret, Daniel. I've been telling you for months that we need to do something about this situation of ours. I'm tired of sand—"

"I agree. That's not a secret," he growled. "Miss Lane? You mentioned that you and Abigail have a mutual friend?"

"That's correct." The visitor moistened her lips, then explained, "When he heard you needed someone to help you with the children, he suggested my friend Sarah. He believes she's someone both you and Abigail can trust."

"And where is this Sarah?"

"In Boston. She's employed by my fiancé as nanny to his young sisters."

"And you're saying that, once you and he marry, she'll be needing to find another position?"

He could see that his guest was weighing her words carefully as she replied, "It's not only that, Captain. Boston holds sad memories for Sarah. I believe she needs to start a new life elsewhere. And I can't imagine anyone being unhappy here, amid all this tropical beauty.''

"Abigail manages to be miserable here," he reminded her. "Hasn't she read you the litany of complaints? No shops, no meat, no parties, no newspapers, no social life, no—what else, Abigail? I know I'm leaving something out."

The older woman frowned. "No doctors, no playmates for the children, and no winter."

"My friend Sarah doesn't need any of those things," Erica interrupted firmly. "She loves children, and you have three adorable charges here for her to raise. She loves to read, and embroider, and write in her journal. She has the most agreeable disposition, and she's really very pretty. Chestnut hair and brown eyes—"

"Why would I care what color eyes she has?" he demanded. "And if this situation is so perfect for her, why didn't she come here herself? Why send you?"

"Isn't it obvious?" Abigail snapped. "Sarah is reluctant to make so long a voyage when it's possible you might reject her. You heard Erica say she is presently employed. She can hardly disappear for weeks on end until she's certain she has another position."

"But Miss Lane can disappear for weeks on end?" Daniel turned his full attention to his guest. "Your fiancé didn't object to your coming here alone? To the home of a complete stranger, hundreds of miles away?"

"I didn't think of Abigail as a complete stranger. I felt an immediate rapport with her, even before we met, just from reading her letter. And in the three days since my arrival, I've learned that my instincts were correct. We get along wonderfully."

"You're two of a kind, that's for sure." He nodded. "Neither one of you is capable of giving me an answer to a simple question."

''Perhaps that's because I'm not accustomed to being interrogated,'' Erica replied evenly. ''Do you always treat your houseguests this way?''

''The ones I invite, or the ones that come uninvited to meddle?''

''Daniel McCullum!'' Abigail gasped. ''Erica came at my invitation, out of concern for your children. I think you should apologize to her immediately.''

''That isn't necessary.'' Erica tossed her auburn hair with clear disdain. ''This is Captain McCullum's home, and if he doesn't wish for me to be here, I'll leave first thing in the morning—''

''No!'' Polly wailed, flying into Erica's lap and hugging her fiercely. ''I don't want you to go. Please, please stay.'' She turned desperate eyes to Daniel. ''Please, Papa? Won't you apologize so Erica will stay?''

Daniel grimaced at the child's sincere distress. ''I didn't mean to be rude, Miss Lane. I'm frustrated by your refusal to answer my questions—''

''That's an apology?'' Abigail eyed him sternly. ''Very well, Daniel, since you must have answers, I'll give them to you—''

''Abby, *don't,*'' Erica warned quickly. ''Don't argue with him. It isn't—'' She hesitated, then gave Daniel a sheepish smile. ''I'm the one who should apologize, Captain. After weeks at sea, you came home to relax with your family, but instead, you have these complications because of me. Why don't you get a good night's rest? In the morning, if you still want me to leave, I'll go cheerfully. And if by then you'd like to discuss this, that would be fine too. It's your house,'' she added reverently. ''We all respect that, despite my bad manners in showing up uninvited.''

He studied her with grudging admiration. Not only had she managed to evade all his questions, she had also kept

Abigail from doing so, on the pretense of making amends. It was an impressive talent for so young a woman, and he had the feeling this was just the tip of the iceberg. Again, Sean was fortunate that this one was already engaged. If she set her cap for a man, Daniel was fairly certain the fellow would be done for.

Still, he wasn't about to be manipulated, and so he turned away from the pretty guest, confronting his mother-in-law instead. "Out with it. *Now!*"

"Don't take that tone with me, Daniel McCullum. If this is the way you're going to behave in front of my grandchildren, I'm not willing to leave them here with you, even if you *do* marry Sarah. I'll take them to Salem with me instead, and—"

"*Marry* Sarah?" Daniel stared in disbelief. "Suddenly you have me married to the governess?"

"She's a governess now, but she wants to be married. And she's one of the few educated, decent women in the world who would consider marrying a stubborn, ill-mannered sailor like yourself." Abigail's pastel eyes had narrowed with frustration. "You should be grateful for this chance, rather than roaring like a wounded lion and offending a sweet girl like Erica. I'm sure she's wondering why she ever considered allowing her friend to marry the likes of you."

Flabbergasted, he turned to his houseguest only to see her edging away from him as she'd done on the beach. Now, of course, he knew why she'd been so wary then. "So? You came here to find a husband for your friend? And you thought it best to lie about it?"

She hesitated, then shrugged. "I thought it best to introduce you to the concept gradually. After all, you've sworn never to remarry—"

"You *knew* that? Yet you still—" He broke off, almost speechless at her audacity.

An eerie silence settled over the room, and for the first time he became aware of the children's eyes—huge as saucers and filled with questions. Some of those questions, he knew, had nothing to do with the current issue, but everything to do with the stormy relationship between the grandmother they loved and the father they adored. Still, they must also be wondering about the sanity of two females who would try to arrange a marriage between two strangers when one of those strangers had not consented to such efforts.

His houseguest had also noticed the children's interest, and he was grateful when she announced cheerfully, "You mustn't worry over this, darlings. Your father is within his rights to be annoyed with me, but once I've explained it all to him, we'll sort it all out and become the best of friends." She kissed Polly's forehead, then stood and crossed to where the twins were sitting. Rumpling their hair affectionately, she suggested, "Run along now and jump into your beds. Your grandmother will tuck you in while your father and I have our chat."

"You needn't bear the brunt of this, Erica," Abigail protested.

"I shan't bear the brunt of anything," the auburn-haired girl assured them all. "The captain and I intend to have a civilized discussion. Isn't that so, Captain?"

Her glance told him he'd better agree, for the children's sake. And for that reason, and that reason alone, he nodded. "I'm looking forward to it."

"There now!" Erica beamed. "Say good night to your father and run along." Her eyes sparkled like sunlight as they watched Abigail and the three little ones shuffle down the hall. But when she turned to face Daniel, he saw that a storm was brewing. "I have something to say to you, Captain McCullum. About your sons. May I speak freely?"

"My sons?" He was confused by the unexpected topic of conversation, but she had effectively piqued his curiosity, and so he muttered, "Will it take long?"

"Only a moment." She settled back down at the table. "Abigail told me the sad story of how you lost your first wife in childbirth. Which means, of course, that those two boys never met their mother, and never saw how you were with her. From all accounts, you adored her and never raised your voice to her, but sadly, your sons never witnessed that. What they have witnessed—and I fear, more than once—is your relationship with Abigail. When they try to imagine how it was with you and Lilli, this will be the only example they have."

Daniel studied her expression carefully before nodding. "I've thought of that. Not in just that way, but in knowing it can't be good for them to see how it is with us. Abby's miserable here. And I'm full up with her complaining."

"And you both know it needs to change, but you have conflicting solutions." Erica smiled sympathetically. "The problem is, you're both correct. I agree with Abigail that the children need more exposure to civilized society. On the other hand, this is the most glorious and protected place I've ever had the pleasure to visit, and in some respects, the perfect place to raise a child. And they should be with their father as much as possible. Abigail's solution, of taking them with her to live in Salem, is a flawed one. I agree with you in that regard, and I've told her so directly."

Grudgingly impressed, Daniel asked, "How did you come to hear about us?"

She cocked her head to one side. "I would gladly tell you if I didn't think you'd lose your temper again."

Daniel grinned. "It's that bad, is it? Give me a minute, then." He strode to the mahogany breakfront that housed his rum and brandy, pouring himself a generous portion of the latter. After a moment's hesitation, he poured a second glass and brought it to set in front of his guest. Then he settled back down at the table, took an appreciative sniff of the heady aroma, and nodded for her to continue.

Erica swirled the liquid in her glass just as Daniel had done, then held it up to her nose and inhaled gingerly. "How lovely. Thank you, Captain."

"Let's hear it now. Straight out. No lies, and no omissions."

"I rarely lie, and only omit details if I feel they'll provoke or bore someone," she replied sweetly. "If you promise to listen patiently until I've finished, I promise to tell you the unembellished truth."

When Daniel had nodded in assent, his guest continued softly. "There is no sweeter girl in the world than Sarah Gibson. Her family was poor and so she educated herself, with amazing results. She undoubtedly would have caught the eye of a gentleman and been married by now, but when she was not quite fifteen, her parents and baby brother died in a fire."

"That's a shame," Daniel murmured sincerely.

"It happened almost eight years ago, and Sarah has been mourning the loss ever since, especially the little boy, with whom she was apparently quite close. I didn't know her then. I became acquainted with her when I began to pay visits to my fiancé's home. And in the last few months I've been spending so much time there, our acquaintanceship has blossomed into a valuable friendship.

"It became clear to me eventually that Sarah wasn't really *living* in the Ryerson home, she was merely existing. I knew she would never make a life for herself if I didn't intercede. And so, I convinced her to contact a gentleman in Chicago who has a reputation as a marriage broker."

"A what?"

She smiled shyly. "It sounds absurd, I know, but I heard such amazing stories about Mr. Braddock and his Happily Ever After Company. I just knew it was the perfect solution. Sarah resisted at first, but I can be almost as effective a bully as yourself when I put my mind to it."

Daniel chuckled. "I don't doubt that. So? This Braddock fellow put you in touch with Abigail? He's a friend of hers?"

"He's a friend to all of us," Erica confirmed.

"But how did he hear—?" Daniel's grip on his brandy snifter tightened. "Are you saying that meddling witch wrote a letter to a matchmaker? About *me*? Behind my back?"

She fixed him with a haughty glare. "If my honesty is upsetting you, I can stop. Even though there's more you need to know."

He resisted the impulse to storm down the hallway and give Abigail a tongue-lashing on the spot, not only because he wanted to hear the rest of this travesty, but also because his houseguest had been correct—he needed to watch himself more carefully when the children were around, no matter how insufferable or annoying his mother-in-law was. "Go on."

Erica sifted her fingers through her lustrous hair as though considering what to say next. Then she reached her hand across the table and patted Daniel's arm. "Abigail said the most endearing things about you in her letter. It was a tribute, Captain. To your fine character and your devotion to your family. She told Mr. Braddock how fortunate her daughter was to have found you, because you made the short time she had left on this earth so magically wonderful."

Tears were sparkling in his guest's golden eyes, and while he suspected she was manipulating him, he had to admit she was correct about one thing. For all of Abby's complaints, the woman had never once said she wished Daniel hadn't married her daughter. She had always admitted, even during the worst of their disagreements, that Daniel's love for Lilli had been a blessing.

Erica sighed and continued. "There will never be another Lilli for you. But your children need someone to care for them and to love them. Someone who is content to live here, despite the lack of shops and doctors and parties. Russell Braddock found that person for you. A sweet, intelligent, generous, loving woman who would never make any demands on you. With Sarah here, Abigail could return to Salem, and this house would be what you meant for it to be—a tranquil paradise."

Daniel took a swallow of brandy. "I'm not looking for a wife. It's as simple as that."

"Were you looking for a wife when you met Lilli?"

"That's none of your business," he growled. "Which brings us to the most important question of all—what are *you* doing here? Why didn't this girl Sarah come herself? And don't tell me it's because she might jeopardize her employment with your fiancé. I'm sure you have *him* wrapped securely around that little finger of yours." He couldn't help but chuckle at the haughty look that remark drew from her. Then he repeated firmly, "Why didn't she come herself?"

"I wish she had. But she had some reservations. About *you*, to be frank. She was more respectful than I of your claim that you don't want to remarry. And she has concerns about your way of life. She's looking for marriage, not adventure."

"She leaves that to you?" Daniel teased.

Erica smiled. "I had heard wonderful tales of Mr. Braddock's talent. It seemed to me we shouldn't just ignore his advice. He read those two letters, and saw a good

match there. I decided to come and see for myself."
Taking a deep breath, she added quietly, "I now believe
Mr. Braddock was correct. Sarah could start a new life
here, away from painful memories; your children would
be happy; and Abigail could resume her own life, knowing
her grandchildren were well-loved. And you could sail
to your heart's content, knowing the children were happy.
No one's asking you to fall madly in love again," she
added gently. "But over time, I believe you would come
to care for Sarah, if only because she's so gentle and
decent. And she's pretty too, although she doesn't seem
to know it."

Daniel wasn't sure if it was the brandy, or the golden
eyes, or the sentimental touches to his guest's story, but
he wasn't angry any longer. Not even with Abigail. His
mother-in-law wanted to go home to Salem, which was
her right. And she wanted to leave her grandchildren in
good hands. Could he blame her? Clearing his throat, he
asked, "Would this Sarah consider coming here as a
governess rather than as a bride? Not that I'm convinced
it's a good idea, but I'd be willing to consider it, as long
as there were no other expectations."

Erica sighed. "I know I gave you that impression
before, but I'm afraid it simply wouldn't work. She won't
lose her position with my fiancé after we're married.
Why would she choose to leave a home in which she is
comfortable, minding children she adores, unless it will
enable her to have a home and children of her own?"

"To escape those tragic memories you mentioned?"

"It's a strange thing about tragic memories," Erica
mused. "One is not always as eager to escape them as
might seem logical. In some ways, Sarah feels closest to
her dead brother there in Boston. It would take more than
a position as a governess to lure her away from that."

"*Lure* her? She doesn't even *want* to leave Boston?"

Daniel could feel his impatience returning in a wave. "Are you saying you came here to match a reluctant bride to a man who wants no part of marriage? All on the advice of a charlatan—"

"He's not a charlatan! You sound just like Jack! Mr. Braddock is a romantic genius—" She caught herself and murmured, "I came here to see if a lonely girl and a needy family could find happiness together, and in the three days I've been here, I've become convinced that it's an inspired match."

He watched in annoyed amusement as she took a delicate sip of brandy. She had almost lost her temper, and he was learning that was something this female never allowed herself to do. She had clearly had words with "Jack" over this, but Daniel suspected she hadn't raised her voice for long that time either. After Lilli's submissive manner, and Abigail's outright nagging, his guest's tactics were something of a mystery to him. Intriguing, but also exasperating. He didn't blame "Jack" for putting up with it all, of course. Occasional frustration in exchange for bedding this girl would be well worth it. But as a meddling guest, she was wearing on his patience.

"Really, Captain, you mustn't be overly stubborn in this matter. Even if Sarah were interested in coming here as a governess, and even if I advised her to do such a thing—which I would not—you're forgetting about Abigail. She won't trust the children to a servant. She wants to know there's a familial bond here before she can tear herself away."

"Then it's settled."

"I beg your pardon?"

His glare was no longer playful. "I don't want to hear another word about it. You're welcome to stay for a few days, although I'm not sure why you'd want to. Do you need me to make arrangements for your return home?"

"No, thank you."

"I assume you thought you'd sail with me when I rushed to Boston to claim my bride," he reminded her sternly. "What will you do now?"

"I have a plan, sir. You needn't concern yourself with it."

He grinned despite his annoyance. "You're angry?"

"Certainly not. I must say, though ..." She took another sip of her brandy, then eyed him with haughty disapproval. "I don't judge you for having a temper, or even for your reputation as a brawler. I doubt you have control over either. But I must say this stubbornness of yours is a profound disappointment. I honestly don't believe you've listened to a word I've said about Sarah. And to dismiss Mr. Braddock as a charlatan without any regard for his well-deserved reputation is incomprehensible to me. You might as well say you *want* to spend the next ten years bickering with Abigail rather than enjoying your beautiful hideaway. It doesn't even make sense."

"My reputation as a brawler?"

"That's correct. I made some inquiries before I came here. I knew Abigail's letter was something of an exaggeration, but until I actually met you—" She pushed back her chair and stood up abruptly. "Thank you for the brandy, Captain. Perhaps when you've had time to think about all I've said, we can talk again."

"Wait!" He stared in disbelief. "Did you not hear me say it was settled?"

"I'm simply saying you might change your mind—"

"Me? I thought I was too stubborn for all that." He stood and moved to within inches of her. "You can stay for a while, as Abby's guest. But I don't want to hear another word about marriage, or governesses, or the sainted Mr. Braddock. Is that clear?"

"It's alarmingly clear," she said with a nod. "Good

night, Captain. I wish you pleasant dreams, if only so you'll be in a better mood in the morning.''

"Wait," he instructed her again, grabbing her arm gently to ensure her obedience. He half-expected her to struggle, but she simply stood rooted to the floor, her eyes cool but not defiant.

"What is it, Captain?"

"I want to hear you say it."

"I beg your pardon?"

"I want to hear you say that the subject of marriage in general, and Sarah in particular, is closed for the remainder of your visit."

He could see she was searching for just the right response, and in that moment he knew she was every bit as stubborn as she had accused him of being. Perhaps she was even worse! But she wasn't going to argue with him—she'd made it clear that that was not in her repertoire. She also wasn't going to give up her quest to marry him to her friend, despite the fact that neither he *nor* this Sarah had shown any interest in such a match. In fact, he was beginning to suspect Sarah was as firmly and openly against it as he himself was!

It was ludicrous, and if Polly hadn't become so attached to their guest, he might have insisted Erica pack her bags and be ready to leave at dawn. Instead, he decided to give her a wide berth for the next few days, then hustle her aboard the schooner and take her to Havana, where they'd find a ship bound for Boston that would take her off his hands.

Releasing his grip on her arm, he gestured toward the guest quarters. "Get yourself to bed then. If you want to plot a marriage, think about Jack, not about me. Is that clear?"

Her eyes flashed, and he was sure she was about to lose her temper for the first time, but after visibly tacking, she shrugged instead. "I won't give *you* another thought. You can be certain of that. Good night, Captain."

He watched in fascination as she sashayed down the hall, wondering what exactly had made her so angry at the end. His mention of her precious Jack? Or more likely, she'd been angry with herself, for having revealed her fiancé's name in her previous flare of temper. Either way, it was nice to know there was a sore subject on the horizon for her as well. With any luck, that, along with Daniel's stern instructions, might be enough to keep her in line for the remainder of the visit.

Dear Sarah,

I've finally met him, and he's everything I hoped he'd be for your sake. I've never quite understood what a ROGUE was until now, and I'm happy to learn it isn't at all distasteful. I almost wish Jack had a touch of that, if only so he wouldn't be so maddeningly practical and calm. Can you believe he still hasn't arrived to sweep me off my feet? I picture him bargaining for a better fare, or looking for a faltering shipping line so that he can evaluate an investment at the same time he dashes to my side. It's maddening!

Captain McCullum has his faults, of course, most notably the stubborn streak Abigail mentioned in her letter to Mr. Braddock. But he is also magnificently handsome, and DON'T YOU DARE say such things don't matter to you. Imagine a man as tall as Jack, but with muscles bulging through both sleeves, and hands so huge and rough they could tame an entire ocean without help. And the sun has tanned him to a golden brown, while his eyes are the same color as the sea he sails.

*And he loves his children. That's the true measure
of a man, is it not?*

*And if that weren't enough, he has a voice that
resonates like the growl of a wild animal. And he
has curly black hair on his chest, which I imagine
feels quite provocative when he embraces a female
and they rub against one another.*

Erica flushed and set down her pen, embarrassed to
have put on paper the silly thought she'd been having
since she first met Captain McCullum on the beach. Somehow, the sight of his bare chest had burned itself into her
memory in some sort of erotic and unacceptable way,
probably because of the provocative dream she'd been
having just before he awakened her.

Picking up the pen again, she scribbled out the last
line, then tucked the half-finished letter in a drawer with
the others she'd written to Sarah since her departure from
Boston. There were at least a dozen of them now, the
latest ones filled with descriptions of La Creciente and
the McCullum children. Flattering descriptions, but also
the grim details—of Polly's unladylike behavior, and the
twins' sobering affliction with the same breathing problems that had taken their mother's young life. Erica was
certain Sarah would know what to do on both counts.
She'd pamper and scold Polly, and perhaps she'd find
games the boys could play that would allow them to romp
without wheezing and gasping for air.

If only you were here, Sarah. Erica sighed inwardly. *I
should have found a way to convince both you and Jack
to come with me. Captain McCullum would never growl
and threaten and manhandle you the way he does me—
the person he sees as a meddler. And Jack and I could
make love on the beach . . .*

It was almost as though the pink sands of the Crescent

had been designed for lovemaking, Erica had noted wistfully. By day, the endless blue sky and sparkling water contributed to the blissful effect, but it was by night that the sensual overtones became completely irresistible. Balmy breezes, glittering stars, and most of all, the privacy provided by the sea and the darkness—such privacy in fact that, for the first time since childhood, Erica had actually dared, evening after evening, to step outdoors in her nightgown. Or rather, the lightweight nightgown she'd borrowed from Abigail, her own having proven much too bulky to allow the island breezes to cool her while she slept.

Moving to the mirror, she wondered how Jack would react if he could see her in this sleeveless, whisper-thin garment. After months of respectful self-control, would he finally grab her, allowing his needy body to find pleasure against hers? If only Jack had a chest like Captain McCullum's, it would be even more delicious! Her nipples would feel the wiry roughness easily through this gauzy muslin fabric.

"Listen to yourself," she scolded her reflection. "Mother was right about you. You have a weakness for men that will lead to your ruin if you don't watch yourself. You love Jack, don't you? So why do you notice the others so easily? It's the same sort of weakness that led Grandmother into an endless string of affairs, and as Mother so aptly observes, the family simply can't continue to weather such scandals."

Despite her sincere appreciation of her mother's position, she couldn't help but smile as she pictured that prim and proper redhead in Paris. Simone Lane had claimed she was going back to visit her childhood home, but Erica knew better. Her mother was lonely, and now that she'd finished more than a proper mourning period for her husband, she wanted to spend some time in the company of gentleman admirers. She would behave herself of course, but still, she would enjoy herself in Paris in ways she would never dream of doing in Boston. It was almost comical, yet touching too.

"At least she was faithful to Father while he was alive, even during all the months of his illness," she informed herself wryly. "You haven't even married Jack yet and your eye is already roving. It was bad enough when you started noticing the delicious variety of men aboard the *Valiant,* but Captain McCullum's *chest?* What next?"

Still gently mocking her romantic lapses, she pushed aside the shutter doors that opened from the guest quarters onto the beach, ready for her midnight adventure. She'd taken this stroll every night since her arrival, impressed with the fact that she could actually cross an entire island on foot in less than half an hour! Sarah would probably say that that made La Creciente something less than an island—an islet, perhaps?—but to Erica, it was just the right size.

The moon was a crescent, like the island it lit, and Erica had to tread carefully as she wandered, for fear of cutting her bare feet on an unseen shell or coral remnant. The pink tone and softness to the sand was due to the fact that it was actually pulverized coral, or so she'd been told by Polly. And every plant on the island had been brought here, either by Daniel or by the buccaneers who had used it as a shelter more than a century earlier. According to Abigail, Daniel had found actual remnants of those days, buried beneath the sand when he'd built the house and dug the gardens for Lilli. As Erica made her way across the dark expanse, she wondered if those early rogues had brought their women here too. If so, it must have been romantic for them, with danger as well as privacy to seduce them.

"Miss Lane?"

"Oh!" She shrank from the soft but clearly male voice, knowing from the gravelly overtones that it was McCullum, but not particularly reassured by that fact. What was *he* doing out here! Why wasn't he exhausted and sleeping soundly, like any decent man would be after weeks at sea?

He was wearing the same clothes he'd worn to dinner— a soft black shirt and tailored black trousers. He'd discarded his boots, however, in favor of bare feet, and had rolled his pant legs up his muscular calves, presumably for wading in the surf.

Stunned at being caught in her nightclothes by a fully dressed man, Erica grabbed at her bodice in a futile attempt to gather it into folds, hoping to further conceal her chest. Unfortunately, there wasn't enough fabric there to do her any good at all, and she was about to simply turn and run when her host offered, "Here, put this on."

Before she could object, he'd stripped off his shirt and held it up so that she could slip her arms into it. She did so sheepishly, unwilling to tell him that the gallant gesture had actually worsened her predicament. Now *she* was covered, but *his* magnificent expanse of wiry brawn was visible again, and this time she could actually feel her nipples straining against her gown, desperate to rub against him. Had her grandmother's breasts misbehaved so flagrantly? Did all women's do so, and polite society simply pretended otherwise? Or was Erica just the weakest woman who'd ever set foot on a beach?

"Thank you, Captain," she murmured. "But I really should go back to my room."

"Don't run off," McCullum protested, stepping so close she could feel the heat from his chest. Then, to her delicious discomfort, he announced in a deep and utterly seductive voice, "I haven't been able to get you out of my mind."

CHAPTER FOUR

Erica wondered what the sailor would say if she admitted she'd been thinking about him too. She even wondered if perhaps he already knew it! Perhaps he'd seen the curiosity in her eyes, from the first moment she'd spied his bronzed body and rugged jaw. And those brilliant blue eyes that seemed to peer right through her clothing—not that her nightdress was presenting much of a challenge in that regard at the moment.

Was he going to suggest something wicked? Until now, she'd teased herself about this moment, and used it as a means of engendering jealousy in Jack, but hadn't really thought there was any possibility McCullum would actually try to seduce her. Not that she'd succumb, of course, but it would be awkward, especially if he sensed that her resistance was less than complete.

It was possible, of course, that the captain had been thinking of something perfectly innocent. Or worse, he might be about to tell her he was sending her packing in the morning. It might have nothing to do with his manly needs and instincts. In any case, she wasn't ready to hear what he was about to say, and so she assured him coolly, "It's late, Captain. Whatever it is, I'd prefer we discuss it in the morning."

"I wasn't thinking about a discussion. I was thinking about the apology I owe you." A rueful smile spread over his features. "I don't have guests here often, and I'm not a gracious fellow by any stretch of the imagination. But I shouldn't have been gruff with you. You came here to help your friend. It's admirable. Annoying, but admirable."

"Does this mean I can talk about Sarah—"

"No. It means I apologize for my manner, pure and simple. The rules still stand."

"I see."

"We can talk about anything else. For example"— his eyes twinkled impishly—"feel free to tell me all about Jack."

"If you must mention my fiancé, could you please call him Mr. Ryerson?"

"Jack Ryerson?" McCullum grinned. "Never heard of him."

"And I'm sure he's never heard of you, either," she said with a sniff.

The sailor's grin faded into a frown. "He's never heard of me? Doesn't he know you're visiting us here?"

Flustered but also annoyed, Erica returned the scowl. "I meant, he never heard of you before Mr. Braddock told us about you."

"You have a bad habit of never answering my question," McCullum observed. "Does he know you're visiting me or not?"

"I'm visiting Abigail, not you. And yes, of course he knows all about it."

The captain studied her intently. "And he had no objection to your taking so long a voyage without him?"

"He suggested an even longer one, actually. All the way to Paris, with my mother. He's making a serious effort to tie up loose ends in his business now, so that he can give his full attention to me when we marry in December."

"December?" It seemed to amuse the sea captain. "He's a patient man."

"He has infinite patience," Erica agreed. "It's one of the reasons I love him."

"And he trusts you to run around the world unescorted, looking as pretty as you do?"

"I'm hardly running around the world," Erica protested, ignoring the compliment. "I sailed on a perfectly respectable vessel, under the watchful eye of Captain John Lawrence and his wife, who are dear friends of mine. And now I'm here, visiting a charming family. There's no reason to make it sound scandalous." She folded her arms across her chest. "This is the oddest apology I've ever received."

"I'm done apologizing," he told her with a laugh. "Now I'm just trying to figure you out."

"Well, good luck with that. And good night."

"Wait!"

She knew before he grabbed her wrist that he'd do so. For some reason, he seemed to feel it was proper behavior. Perhaps it was time someone told him otherwise. "Captain, you must unhand me this instant. When you want my attention, simply ask nicely, and I will almost always cooperate."

"Almost always?" he quoted with an exasperated grin. "You have a way of saying things that doesn't say much at all. Are you this way with everyone? With Jack?" When she simply stared at his hand on her wrist, he laughed again and released her. "Please stay for a moment, Miss Lane."

"That's better. What is it you want?"

"I want you to talk to Abigail for me. About hiring a governess. It's a good idea, and she seems to respect your opinion. And it's like you said at dinner: with the right governess here to take care of the children, Abby can go home to her old life without worrying."

"Did I say that?"

He nodded.

"I believe I also said she would never agree to it unless the governess was a member of the family. Fortunately, I can arrange that—" She winced at the flash of annoyance in his eyes, and without thinking she grasped his arm and pleaded, "Forgive me, Captain. I honestly didn't mean to vex you."

He arched an eyebrow. "If you want my attention, Miss Lane, you need only ask for it. There's no need to assault me."

Erica bit back a smile. "I have a proposition for you."

"Eh?" His grin widened. "This sounds promising."

"It is. I propose that we join forces. After all, we agree on one fundamental truth: the situation here cannot continue as it is. Abigail should go home to Salem as soon as possible."

He seemed both startled and pleased by her pronouncement. "Whether I marry or not?"

"Yes, Captain. Marriage is the preferable course, but either way, it's not good for the children to see her so unhappy. She needs to go home."

His eyes narrowed. "Are you suggesting the children should go with her? Because—"

"No! No, never. Not unless you moved to Salem yourself—"

"Which I'll never do."

She exhaled in sharp exasperation. "In other words, you must have everything your way. Fine. I agree that Abigail should go to Salem and the children should remain here, with their father."

"You're willing to tell her that?"

"I've told her half a dozen times already."

His face relaxed into a grateful smile. "I know it seems like pure selfishness to you that I want the children here, but there's more to it. They're safer here. Especially the twins. The weather in Salem during winter is too hard on them." His tone grew wistful as he added, "The Lindstroms never should have raised Lilli there. She was sick more often than not until I brought her here; did you know that?"

"Abigail is the first to admit it. Not that it was your idea, though. She told me she and her husband were already moving Lilli to the Caribbean, to live with friends, when you met her. She said that's how you and Lilli met—on the ship. Isn't that so?"

"They were bringing her to Havana to see if it made a difference in her breathing," he confirmed. "But her father never would have allowed her to stay there permanently. He wasn't the sort to rearrange his life for anyone, even the daughter he supposedly loved."

"Abigail told me he went to California, after Lilli died." Erica sighed. "It's sad, isn't it?"

"Good riddance." McCullum shrugged. "If you truly want to meet a selfish man, you should meet up with *him* sometime."

I never said you were selfish," Erica soothed. "I think your devotion to the twins' health is touching. A bit overdone, perhaps, but—"

"Overdone?"

She bit her lip, surprised by his sharp reaction. "This is the reason I wish you'd agree to meet Sarah. She could tell you these things without offending you. And you'd listen because you could see how skilled she is at raising children. She did wonders with Jack's sister Janie when she wouldn't eat—''

"Erica?"

"Yes?"

"You were criticizing me about the twins. Could we get back to that?"

She flushed apologetically. "Did it sound critical? I only meant to say, I don't believe they're as sickly as you and Abigail seem to think. They seem like normal boys to me. They simply can't run without wheezing. Otherwise, they're as healthy as horses."

"If they were in Salem, you'd see more signs of the trouble."

"I don't doubt that. But they aren't in Salem, they're here. Four-year-olds treated like toddling infants—''

"What?"

She jutted out her chin defiantly. "There's no need to growl at me. I'm only saying they're healthy, and living in paradise, yet they aren't given the chance to enjoy it. Abigail hovers, and I've heard all *your* rules, which are stifling to them, I'm sure. And according to Polly, you won't allow them to learn to swim. Considering that you're a sailor and they live a stone's throw from the ocean, I feel that's a bit overdone." Grabbing his arm again for fear he'd turn away from her nagging, she added apologetically, "You're such a wonderful father to them. Please don't take this as criticism. If Sarah were here, she could explain it all better."

"You're doing a fine job yourself," he murmured. "You think I should teach them to swim? With those lungs of theirs?"

"Little boys want to be just like their father, and I assume you're a powerful swimmer. They watch their sister with pure envy," she told him firmly. "I'm not saying they'll go for miles as Polly does—and by the way, I don't approve of *that* either—but at least they could explore and play along the water's edge safely if you'd give them a lesson or two."

Realizing that her hand was still latched onto his arm, she released him and smiled sheepishly. "It seems I owe you another apology. Forgive me, Captain. I don't know what I was thinking."

"You can advise me on my children whenever you like," he assured her huskily. "And you can touch me whenever you like, too. I like the feel of you on me." He rested his hands lightly on her hips. "Why do you think I kept grabbing you before?"

His touch was gentle, and she knew he was testing rather than actually insulting her. All she needed to do was back away and fix him with a haughty glare, and the situation would return to normal. McCullum would laugh, and perhaps even apologize, and everything would be fine. But Erica couldn't seem to do what needed to be done. Her feet wouldn't cooperate, and even her breathing and speech were inexplicably beginning to fail her.

"You're a fascinating girl, do you know that?" he murmured seductively. "Coming here out of nowhere, with that pretty mouth of yours."

"My mouth?"

McCullum nodded. "I haven't been able to get it out of my mind, for wondering how it tastes." He dipped his head down and brushed his lips across hers, once and then again, then cocked his head to the side and studied her with his startling blue eyes.

She knew he was fully expecting her to protest. Once again, he would take his cue from her reaction, but there *was* no reaction beyond a paralyzing sort of curiosity over what he'd dare do next. And so, for a long moment charged with confusion and anticipation, they waited, each for the other, until McCullum's patience evaporated and he pulled her completely against himself.

She heard herself gasp, in delight rather than protest, just as his mouth covered hers, and then he was enjoying her with the sort of delicious abandon she had craved for longer than she dared admit. She had wanted Jack to be the one to introduce her to such kissing, but he'd never even come close to it. Because he respected her, he'd always said. But now, in the dizzying haze of pleasure McCullum was skillfully inflicting on her, she wondered if "respect" was the word for it at all. Disinterest seemed closer to the truth.

By contrast, McCullum's attentions were absolutely devastating! His demanding hands seemed to know just how to imprison and stroke and tantalize every inch of her love-starved torso, while occasionally cradling her neck, urging her to respond even more scandalously to his kisses.

How can you allow this? she asked herself groggily. *How can Jack allow it!*

Because by now, Jack Ryerson had surely read the note, and thus knew Erica would be alone with a roguish sea captain, but as yet he hadn't bothered to come for her. He *knew* she was in this man's arms, with this man's tongue in her mouth and his hand groping her breasts. If Jack didn't care, why should Erica?

She slid her hand up McCullum's chest, not in protest, but in tentative exploration of the smooth muscles and wiry mat of black curls. She had longed to feel her own chest against his, but his right hand had laid permanent claim to her breasts, while his left had found the small of her back and was mischievously urging her against himself. Breathless from his onslaught, she looped her arms around his neck and pulled her face away from his in order to gasp for a needed mouthful of air, fully intending to allow him to kiss her again once she'd gotten her second wind.

She didn't know what the sea captain's greedy eyes saw in her own at that moment, but it must have been some outrageous sort of permission, because he grinned victoriously and locked his pelvis to hers, grinding himself against her with a hedonistic sort of abandon that jolted her back to reality in a way no kiss, however wicked, could have done.

And so, with all the force she could muster, she wrenched herself free and wailed, "You mustn't, Captain! You mustn't do *that!*"

There was a blaze of frustration in his eyes, but his hands were gentle as they pulled her back against him. Then he was kissing her again, with a new and seductive sort of tenderness that almost proved to be her undoing. Still, there was no doubt now as to what he wanted, so she set her hands firmly on his chest and pushed him away again despite the yearning of her body to submit.

He took a deep breath, then chuckled as though he'd known from the start that she would thwart him before he'd had his way. "So?" he teased. "Jack hasn't had the honor yet?"

"The honor?" Her hand flew to her mouth as she realized what he'd suggested, then she glared with absolute disgust. "He most certainly has not!"

"What's he waiting for?"

"Be quiet! What makes you think I'd discuss that with you?"

"You'd rather just *do* it with me?" He laughed at her horrified expression. "Like I said, you're a fascinating girl."

"Be quiet! Let me think!"

"I don't want you to think," he protested, reaching for her again.

"Don't! And for the love of heaven, take *this!*" She stripped off his shirt and stuffed it into his hand. "Cover yourself, please?"

She waited for him to don the garment, but his attention had fully shifted to the sight of her in her thin gown, and she could almost hear him cataloging the parts of her that he had touched. Or perhaps he was too busy imagining the ones he'd *almost* touched! Mortified, she blurted, "It was the brandy!" then she spun away and sprinted across the sand toward the comparative safety of her room, covering her ears as she ran to blot out the sound of his raucous laughter.

If he dared come after her, she wasn't sure what she'd do. Scream for Abigail, she supposed. *Like a hypocrite,* she taunted herself. *That rogue knows the truth about you now. He knows you've done things with him you've not yet done with Jack, and he knows how much you enjoyed it.*

But McCullum didn't come, and as she slammed the shutters closed behind her, she told herself grimly that he wasn't a rogue after all. He was a decent widower with three children, who had only done what any man would do when a girl allowed it so easily. Wrapping herself in a comforter despite the warmth of the night, she shuddered in remembered delight at the sensations he had aroused in her.

"That's how it will be with Jack on your wedding night," she promised herself in a hoarse, unfamiliar whisper. "You've had a taste of that night, nothing more. Once Jack takes you into his arms and makes you his wife, this night will pale in comparison.

She took one deep breath, and then another, and was relieved when her body finally stopped its unfamiliar throbbing. She certainly hadn't ever felt this way after one of Jack's kisses, but she wasn't about to feel guilty over it. He could have kissed her that way—excited her that way—any time he'd wanted. He'd chosen not to do so, and this was the unfortunate consequence.

She did feel mildly guilty over having kissed Sarah's intended, but decided to view it as research. Wasn't that why she'd come all this way? To determine if McCullum would make a good husband? Wasn't it convenient to have ascertained so accurately that he would be a sensational lover?

Erica's dual "mission," as Captain McCullum had called it, was to make Jack jealous and to evaluate the sea captain as a romantic prospect. With one outrageous but harmless kiss, she'd managed to accomplish both. And so, with a sheepish smile on her still-swollen lips, Erica dug out her pen and stationery and proceeded to share the good news with her lonely, faraway friend.

All his life, Daniel McCullum had yearned for excitement and had hungered for variety. Most of all, he had craved the unexpected. He could measure the first thirty years of his life by such events: the first time he'd sailed close to the wind; the first time he'd climbed a mast during a hurricane; the nightmare voyage rounding Cape Horn in the *Moon Rigger;* the first time he'd had a woman; the first time a woman had had him! Absolutely perfect experiences, eclipsed in many ways by the amazing moment when he'd realized a pale, sickly, soft-spoken girl named Lilli Lindstrom had stolen his heart right out of his chest.

There were other events that should have been perfect ones, but had not. The night Polly was born—they had almost lost Lilli then. With the twins' births, of course, it had happened. Other men spoke of childbirth as a miracle, but Daniel was not one of those. His children were miracles, but their births had been hell—for Lilli, for himself, for Abigail, and most surely for the motherless offspring themselves.

Since Lilli's death, there had been precious few perfect moments, and damned few surprises. In fact, Daniel had begun to believe he would never have one again. Brawls, trysts, storms, war—nothing seemed to excite him anymore. It had taken an auburn-haired meddler with a pouty mouth and supple body to prove his predictable existence was still worth living, and as he stood on the beach on the morning after their outrageously thorough kiss, he had to admit he had never felt more alive, or more sheepishly pleased with himself.

Sean had been right—he *had* needed a woman to draw him out of his gloom! But not in the way either of them had suspected. Daniel hadn't needed to bed a woman— he did that all the time. And while he never tired of it, there were precious few surprises in that arena these days. But Erica Lane had surprised him, with her combination of innocence and sensuality. Her unavailability, combined with complete accessibility, if only for just the briefest of moments. He'd never quite experienced that before, and in that moment, she had proven to him that life still had new challenges and sensations to offer him.

He grinned as he remembered the look in her golden eyes when he'd introduced her to his manhood. That gleam had been better than gold itself! And the true beauty of the moment had been its ultimate irony—the thought that he could be the man who saw it, but didn't need to be accountable for it. That would be Jack Ryerson's job, and he was welcome to it. The last thing Daniel wanted was that sort of unending responsibility.

And until now, avoiding responsibility had always

meant avoiding virgins, for fear they'd want some sort of commitment. He'd never quite considered the potential of an *engaged* maiden for offering ripeness without commitment—innocence without responsibility.

"And you'll never find it again," he assured himself with a grin. "She's one of a kind, that one. Just be grateful you were the man lucky enough to kiss her when she needed kissing most."

His grin broadened as he contemplated the perfection of the moment. Her wide eyes, her yielding body, her fascination with his chest. And just before she'd bolted back to her room, he'd had the pleasure of seeing her in her nightdress, her breasts aroused to the point where they'd actually seemed to be searing their way through the fabric. It was an image he intended to remember long after his guest left the island.

"Which will be soon enough, after last night's indiscretion," he assured himself without a trace of remorse or longing. Because as much as Erica was a marvel and an inspiration, she was also a meddler and a nag and an all-round pain in the behind, and the sooner she left the island, the better it would be for everyone concerned. She'd served her purpose in Daniel's life. It was time for her to return to "Jack."

And there was no doubt in his mind that she'd be gone by the day's end, without any further involvement or fault on his part. Had he followed his first instincts and sent her away as soon as he heard about the matchmaking, Polly would have been upset with him, Abigail would have been unbearable, and he would never have had the pleasure of kissing her. Instead, thanks to that very kiss, he was certain she was packed and sitting on her bed at that very moment, mortified beyond belief, and hoping only to scamper back to her fiancé at the first opportunity. She would make some improbable excuse in that roundabout way she had of avoiding the truth, and by noon, she'd be nothing but a fond memory.

"Captain?"

He spun, literally speechless at seeing her there in the daylight, rather than cowering in her room. *Full of surprises, right to the end,* he realized with wary admiration. *What will she do next?*

When he didn't respond other than to stare, his guest persisted without a trace of embarrassment. "I was hoping we'd have a chance to talk about last night."

"It was the brandy," he reminded her carefully.

"No, actually, it was entirely my fault."

"Entirely?" he echoed, impressed by her willingness to accept full responsibility, especially given the extent to which Daniel himself had misbehaved. She seemed determined to continue being unpredictable, and so he decided to relax and enjoy it. "You're saying I'm blameless?"

"I'm afraid so. I've always had an unfortunately tendency to be curious, and sometimes it causes me to forget myself. It's not something I'm proud of, but I'm not ashamed of it, either. My grandmother was notorious for it, and—" She flushed and added lamely, "I just didn't want you to think it meant anything. About you, or about Jack. Or about my friendship with Sarah. It reflects on myself alone, and I apologize for it. It won't happen again, I assure you."

"Your grandmother was notorious?"

"Notoriously susceptible to men," Erica explained. "It's a long story, and I don't know much of it. I only know my parents continually warned me against following in her footsteps, and I was doing rather a good job of it until lately."

He grinned sympathetically. "I can have you on a ship,

sailing home to Ryerson, by this time tomorrow. How does that sound?''

She seemed startled by the suggestion. ''Are you asking me to leave? I know this is a bit awkward—''

''I'm not *asking* you to go,'' Daniel corrected her quickly. ''I thought you'd be anxious to put this whole adventure behind yourself.''

Erica shrugged. ''I'm not going to allow *my* indiscretion to ruin Sarah's chances for happiness. There's so much I haven't told you about her yet! Also, you asked me to speak with Abigail about the advisability of hiring a governess. And I want to watch you teach the twins to swim. I simply can't leave yet. It's out of the question.''

''You're still matchmaking? Even after last night?''

''Especially after last night,'' she assured him smoothly. ''You didn't force yourself on me, Captain. You were quite a gentleman, actually, given the extent of my misbehavior. Sarah would be fortunate to marry a man like you. And you clearly want a woman in your life—that was painfully obvious from the intensity of your interest in me. I'm more convinced than ever that you and Sarah are made for one another.''

He had to laugh despite his annoyance. ''Wanting a woman and wanting a wife are two different things, missy. Last night had nothing to do with wanting a wife.''

''Of course it didn't. But to be fair, you knew I wasn't available.''

''You *seemed* available,'' he teased.

''I've apologized for that!'' Erica paused to regain her composure. ''It's a personal failing on my part and I'd rather not discuss it any further.''

Daniel felt a surge of affection for his guest. ''You're judging yourself too harshly. Any girl in your situation would have done the same thing.''

''Well, *you* certainly have a high opinion of yourself.''

Daniel laughed at the haughty reaction. "What I meant was, any girl in your situation, knowing she might be facing her last opportunity to kiss a man other than her future husband, would be curious. There's no crime in that. And you put a quick stop to it, because you love Ryerson. It was a momentary impulse, and an innocent one. Don't make more of it than it was."

"You're very kind." She tore her golden gaze from his and looked out over the bay instead. "Your ship is very pretty, Captain. May I ask why you called it the *Moon Rigger?*"

He watched as she sifted her auburn tresses through her fingers, casually changing the subject, as she did whenever it suited her. One of her many unusual habits— endearing yet annoying, like the refusal to argue or answer questions directly. He was tempted to insist on discussing the kiss at length, but knew he'd feel guilty later, so he decided to let her tactic succeed. It was almost as though she was more upset by his refusal to acknowledge her "misbehavior" than by the misbehavior itself.

And so he explained, "Martin Lindstrom gave that schooner to me and Lilli as a wedding present. Until then, I'd been first mate on a clipper ship. He didn't want his son-in-law in so lowly a position, so he made me a captain." Daniel paused to remember the mixed emotions that had accompanied that change in his life. Like any true sailor, he had dreamed of owning his own ship. But it had been tough to accept one as a gift rather than earn it. And the schooner, as lovely as she was, wasn't exactly the ship for which Daniel McCullum had yearned.

Still, he loved the *Moon Rigger,* and most of the memories he had of her were fine ones. "Sean and I were trying to decide how to outfit her for her maiden voyage. We knew we'd have to rig her differently depending on where we were taking her. So I asked Lilli where she wanted to go first, and she said she wanted to sail straight up to the moon.''

"So that's how you rigged the ship, and that's how you named it too," Erica murmured. "How romantic! Did Lilli sail with you all the time in those days?"

Daniel shook his head. "She wasn't strong, even at her best. I think she wanted to come along, but it seemed like the ceremony was barely over and she was already carrying Polly. That was hard on her. Almost killed her, in fact. She never sailed with me after that."

Erica touched his shoulder. "I'm sorry, Captain."

He shrugged away the unhappy memories and turned his attention to the present. "I've been thinking about those swimming lessons you keep nagging me about. I'm ready to make a deal with you about them."

"Oh?" She smiled uncertainly. "What exactly are you suggesting?"

He eyed her with playful admiration, then admitted, "I want you to promise not to mention Sarah, or marriage, for the rest of the day. Can you do that?"

Her golden eyes sparkled with amusement and relief. "I can try."

"I'll go convince Sean to come ashore, then. That way both boys can learn at one time, and I'll have help if anything goes wrong."

"Nothing will go wrong." Erica looked out at the schooner again. "Are you saying your friend spent the night out there when he could have had a nice warm meal and a soft bed?"

"And an earful of matchmaking," Daniel added. "He's determined to avoid Abby for a while. Wait until I tell him she's brought in reinforcements."

His guest moistened her lips and then asked, "Are you going to tell him what happened last night?"

"Are you asking me not to?"

"I don't suppose it matters." She sighed. "But he'll meet Sarah and Jack one day, and I was hoping to spare *them* the details."

Daniel scowled at the thought that she might actually force him to meet the infamous Jack Ryerson. He'd much rather picture that particular fellow as a pale, boring and inept buffoon to whom Erica would compare Daniel favorably, but he suspected that any man who could win this girl's heart was anything but a buffoon. "I don't plan on meeting either of them, so why would Sean?"

"It will be unavoidable, since we'll all be at the wedding when you marry Sarah." She grinned teasingly. "Forgive me for mentioning all that, but you asked a direct question, so what was I to do?"

Daniel chuckled ruefully. "Do you want to come out to the *Rigger* with me?"

"No, I'll wait here. Will you be long?"

He shook his head. "I know better than to leave you and Abigail alone to plot against me."

Her laugh was light and melodious. "Hurry back then. We'll feed Sean first, then have the lessons. And, Captain?"

"Yeah?"

"You're not nearly as stubborn as everyone says. Your sons are fortunate to have you for a father." She curtseyed gracefully, then turned and began a leisurely climb up the beach to his house.

Daniel enjoyed watching the gentle sway of her hips for a while before heading out to the schooner to fetch Sean. As much as he'd wanted Erica to leave, he had to admit her staying had its advantages, if only in terms of sheer entertainment. It would be fun to watch her handle Sean, especially if she decided to aid Abby in her efforts to match the first mate with the niece in New York.

And it would be interesting to try to kiss her again

tonight. He didn't think she'd allow it, but then again, he hadn't thought she would the night before either—and she'd allowed much more than a kiss. She was "curious," wasn't she? And he would be more than happy to satisfy that curiosity for her.

Other men's fiancées. You should have discovered them years ago, Danny, he told himself with a grin as he tore his gaze from her backside and hurried down to the rowboat that awaited him at the water's edge.

"That went quite well," Erica congratulated herself as she shook the sand from her bare feet outside the tiled entryway of the McCullum home. "I believe you and he have put last night's indiscretions behind you. And with any luck, Jack will come rushing to your side at any instant now, and you will have a more appropriate moonlit rendezvous tonight."

"Who are you talking to?" Polly poked her head through the open window of Daniel's study and giggled mischievously.

"I was talking to myself, but I'd much rather talk to you. Where were you this morning?"

"In the courtyard with Belle. I wanted to go down to the beach with you and Papa, but Grandma said not to. She said you were having private talks with him."

"Your father and I don't have any secrets from you. Feel free to join us any time."

"Grandma said you and Papa look romantic together."

Erica flushed. "Your grandmother needs to learn the rules of matchmaking. I'm already spoken for, as I keep telling her. And your father needs a docile wife."

"Docile?" Polly frowned. "What's that?"

"He needs someone to agree with him and try to please him."

"You don't agree with Papa?"

Erica gave the girl's short hair a tousle. "Your mother agreed with your father. She was very docile, according to your grandmother. That's the sort of woman your father likes. Do you remember those days at all?"

Polly giggled. "Papa says you never answer his questions. And you didn't answer mine neither! It's fun."

"But not very docile of me." Erica grinned. "Do you know where your father is right now? He's gone to fetch his friend Sean. Did you and Belle make enough food for two hungry men?"

The girl nodded, then spun to call out over her shoulder. "Grandma! Uncle Sean's coming to eat! I'll go tell him to hurry!"

"Wait a minute, young lady," Erica protested. "Don't tell me you're going to swim out to the ship again. You know how I feel about that."

Polly's blue eyes danced. "Papa likes it. So does Uncle Sean."

We'll see about that, Erica promised her silently. Aloud she cajoled, "Wouldn't it be more fun if we went and prepared the meal for them? So everything was just right when they arrive?"

Polly answered by disappearing inside the study, only to reappear in the doorway, flash Erica a mischievous grin, then dash past her toward the beach.

Thwarted, Erica watched the child dive into the water, then sighed and walked around the perimeter of the house until she reached the outdoor kitchen, where McCullum's housekeeper, Belle, was already busy preparing an impromptu feast of grilled shrimp and fresh fruit. Belle was a huge reserved woman who, according to Abigail, was devoted to Daniel McCullum because the sailor had once rescued her, her husband Theo, and their three children from a capsized ship during a hurricane.

The children were now grown, and Theo worked the port in Havana, visiting his wife whenever he could. According to Abigail, he sometimes brought his grandchildren to play with Polly and the twins. When he visited, he restocked the larder or brought a string of fresh fish for which—again according to Abigail—Daniel overcompensated him shamelessly.

There was another kitchen, inside the servants' quarters behind the main house, but it was in this outdoor "mud" kitchen, as Belle called it, that the housekeeper plied her culinary talents. She had already tempted Erica with a myriad of exotic dishes, from turtle eggs and yam soufflé to fried bananas and hot, sweet peppers.

Perching on a stool, Erica encouraged the housekeeper to brag about her grandchildren, loving the warm, genuine affection Belle could exude at such moments. "They sound so darling, Belle. Do you suppose they'll visit soon? I'd love to meet them."

"I'm never sure when that husband of mine will bring them. I only know they'll come as soon as they start missing my cooking."

"Then they should be here at any moment." Erica nibbled greedily from the platter of delicacies in front of her. "These peppers are so scrumptious."

"This is Mr. Sean's favorite dish."

"What sort of man is he, Belle?"

"He's a gentleman. Always polite. Always hungry."

Erica grinned, suspecting this to be Belle's description of the perfect male specimen. "Is he handsome?"

The cook nodded.

"As handsome as the captain?"

The cook arched an eyebrow. "Shame on you! You're promised to someone else."

"I can still admire a handsome man, can't I?"

"No."

Erica laughed with delight. "I've seen you admire Captain McCullum when you think no one's looking."

"And I've seen you *kiss* Captain McCullum when you think no one's looking." Belle grinned at the shocked expression her announcement had elicited. "It was a long kiss, too. A *very* long kiss."

"Hush," Erica scolded. "Abby doesn't know about it, does she?"

"Her? She doesn't notice anything. Too busy complaining, that one."

Erica smiled, relieved that the subject had shifted away from the kiss on the beach. The current topic—the rivalry between Belle and Abby over who should rule the McCullum household when the captain was away—was never far from either of the two competitors' thoughts. Belle complained constantly about the mother-in-law's scolding of the captain, while Abby decried what she perceived as her son-in-law's overgenerosity toward Belle and Theo. Fortunately, when it came to the children, they managed to cooperate.

"You're going to be sweet to Sarah when she marries the captain, aren't you, Belle?"

"If she's good to him, I'll be good to her."

"She'll be wonderful," Erica promised.

"She's your friend?"

"Yes."

"But you kissed her man?"

"Hush!" Erica eyed the housekeeper sternly, then stole one last shrimp from the tray before wiping her fingertips on a soft cotton towel. "Excuse me now, but I'd better go freshen up. I want to look my best when I meet the captain's friend."

"Why? Are you going to kiss *him* too?" Before Erica could retort, Belle added casually, "I hear their voices."

"Oh, no! I'm not even wearing shoes. Gracious. . . ."

Smoothing her soft yellow skirt and brushing a speck of sand from her lacy white blouse, Erica turned toward the house just as Captain McCullum and a sandy-haired companion strode into view.

CHAPTER FIVE

Erica wanted to take the opportunity to study the first mate, but couldn't manage to tear her gaze from the rugged sea captain. Now that she knew McCullum a little, she could enjoy the hint of danger—the determined set of his jaw, the glint of command in his eyes, the powerful rippling of his muscles—without being actually alarmed by any of it.

Sean Lynch provided an interesting contrast, with his fair hair, lanky body and warm, crooked smile. There was nothing ominous about him, yet a girl could feel safe with him around, knowing instinctively that he was both a gentleman and a protector. Erica could easily see why Abigail wanted to entrust him with her niece. She was almost tempted to switch allegiance herself and recruit the first mate for Sarah!

''This is the trespasser I was telling you about,'' Daniel boomed. ''What do you think, Sean?''

To Erica's delight, the newcomer simply stared at her

as though he'd never seen a barefoot girl before. There was an innocent sort of admiration in his green eyes that confirmed her first impression: he was a warm and gentle man, through and through.

"Say something to her before she thinks you're dim-witted," Daniel complained mischievously.

Erica held out her hand. "I'm Erica Lane. And you're Sean Lynch? It's a pleasure, sir. I've heard wonderful things about you."

"I've heard about you, too," Sean admitted. "But the captain forgot to mention how beautiful you are. I see now why he has such a twinkle in his eye today."

Annoyed to think that McCullum had bragged about their moonlit encounter, Erica sniffed, "It was just a kiss. Don't let him tell you anything else."

Sean spun toward his captain, incredulous and clearly impressed. "You *kissed* her?"

"A gentleman never tells." Daniel grinned. "I didn't think a lady did either, but my guest is full of surprises." To Erica he added, "Your reputation is safe with me. I only told him enough to prepare him for your ways."

"My ways?"

"Sure." He helped himself to a juicy orange slice from Belle's platter. "I told him you won't argue, no matter how angry you get, and you won't give a direct answer to a man's questions."

Erica relaxed enough to smile toward Sean. "It's true that I don't argue. But I'm perfectly willing to answer any appropriate question, assuming I *know* the answer, of course."

Daniel arched an eyebrow toward the first mate, as though to say, "Do you see how she is?" then he turned to Belle. "You're starving Sean to death, woman."

"The food looks delicious, as always," Sean soothed,

giving the housekeeper a quick hug. "You made my favorite."

"Go on into the dining room, then, and I'll serve the two of you."

"There are three of us," Erica complained mischievously.

"And you already ate half the platter," Belle countered. "But go on with the men, and I'll bring you some tea and cookies."

Erica could see from the captain's expression that he was enjoying the banter. Given the contentious conversations he'd undoubtedly overheard between his mother-in-law and the housekeeper, she could hardly blame him, and she was tempted to observe that, were Sarah to ever come to the island, the mood would be bright and friendly twenty-four hours a day. But he'd probably warned Sean about the matchmaking, too, and so she needed to be a bit less obvious for the time being.

"Miss Erica?"

She blushed as she accepted Sean's arm and allowed him to escort her into the elegantly furnished dining room. Its red glazed tiles were cool on Erica's feet, and as she settled into her chair, she acknowledged that, when it came to island life, shoeless dining made as much sense as cooking out of doors and making soup from turtles. It was all so beautiful and relaxing, especially in this particular room, which was the most fragrant in the house, thanks to the bougainvillea planted in abundance under every window. Not to be outdone, Belle proceeded to cover the table with a myriad of delicacies that assaulted the diners with a heady array of pungent, exotic aromas.

"Abigail tells me you made all the furniture in this house, Sean. It's absolutely wonderful."

"I enjoy working with my hands," he replied simply.

"He did all the cabinetry on the *Rigger* too," Daniel bragged. "He has a real talent for all that."

"Isn't that wasted at sea?" Erica sighed. "Abigail tells me her brother in New York could establish you in business—"

"There!" Daniel roared with laughter. "Didn't I tell you? She'll have you married to the niece before the month is out."

"And *you'll* be married to the governess?" Sean shot back.

"Wouldn't that be wonderful?" Erica beamed. "Two such handsome grooms, each with a charming bride."

"Don't forget yourself and Ryerson," Daniel drawled.

"I never do. He is always in my thoughts."

"Except when you're kissing the captain?" Sean interrupted with a hesitant smile.

Erica eyed him reproachfully. "You mustn't believe everything you hear, Mr. Lynch."

"But I heard it from *you*."

"Still, it's not how it sounds," she assured him. "I'd really prefer you not mention it again."

"And you won't mention the niece or the governess?" Daniel demanded.

"Agreed."

"Do you see how she is?" he asked his first mate cheerfully.

"I see." Sean smiled.

"Go ahead. Ask her a question. See if you get a straight answer."

"I have a question of my own," Erica interrupted. "Where is Abigail?"

Daniel gestured toward the hall. "She went to see if the boys are awake. And be forewarned: She's not too happy with the thought of them learning to swim."

Erica turned to Sean. "What do *you* think about it?"

"I agree with you."

Daniel chuckled. "There's a surprise. Sean agreeing with a beautiful girl."

Erica glanced down at her plate, surprised and pleased to hear her host describe her that way so casually. Not "pretty," but "beautiful." Had he been thinking that the night before, when his hands were roaming over her and his breath was hot on her neck? Sean had said it too, of course, and Jack said such things routinely, and so she was being silly to be so thrilled—

"Erica?"

"Hmm?" She met Daniel's gaze and blushed to see pure annoyance in his eyes. So much for compliments. "Did you ask me something?"

"Why would I bother? You'd just find some way to change the subject. But Sean hasn't learned his lesson yet."

"Oh." She turned to the first mate. "Forgive me, Mr. Lynch. What did you ask?"

"I wanted to know if you can swim. And"—he took a deep breath—"I want you to call me Sean, if it's not asking too much."

"And you must call me Erica." She smiled. "And to answer your question, I'm from Boston, Sean. There's not much need for swimming there, with the water so cold, even in summer."

"Can you swim, yes or no?" Daniel growled.

Erica sighed with exaggerated disapproval. "Yes, Captain, I can swim."

"Good. You can help me and Sean teach the twins."

"Are you serious? What would I wear?" she scolded. "There are two of you, and two of them. What do you need me for?"

"Entertainment," he teased. "And you can wear the skin God gave you, the same as us."

Erica gasped and turned to Sean. "He's teasing, is he not? You'll wear clothes, won't you?"

The first mate nodded reassuringly. "If you want to join us, I can find something for you to wear, too. The water's warm as toast here, Erica. You shouldn't go back to Boston without enjoying it at least once."

Pleased by the invitation, Erica assured him, "Perhaps another time."

"That means never," Daniel translated, then he turned to grin at her, his expression nothing less than a dare.

Erica looked at him and waited, knowing that silence was the one thing these men feared in a woman. She'd seen it with Jack, and had managed to use it once or twice to her advantage. Now she would teach McCullum a lesson. And Sean Lynch too, if he wasn't careful.

It only took seven seconds for the men's grins to vanish, and it was then that she yawned slightly. "This island air makes me so sleepy. I honestly need a nap or I'll never be able to keep my eyes open during dinner. But I'll want to hear every detail of the swimming lesson, so pay close attention, won't you? And until then, please excuse me—"

"Wait!"

Predictably, Daniel's hand had latched onto her wrist. And just as predictably, he released it with a sheepish smile as soon as she gave it a condemning glance.

"I shouldn't have teased you," he apologized. "Come down to the beach with us and watch, at least. The twins will want you there, and it was your idea after all."

"That's true."

"We'll behave," Sean added solemnly.

"Well, then. . . ." She gave them the coolest smile she could muster. "How can I resist? Can I ask one favor first, Captain?"

"Sure. What is it?"

"Will you tell Polly to keep her shirt on while she swims with you and the twins today?"

He cocked his head to the side as though bewildered by the request. "Don't worry about that girl's skin. It's tough, even in hot sun."

"Just the same, I'd consider it a personal favor if you'd ask her to keep her shirt on." Erica pushed her chair away from the table and smiled toward Sean. "It's been a pleasure, Mr. Lynch. I'll see you on the beach. And, Captain? Thank you, as always, for your hospitality."

She could feel their eyes on her as she walked away, and so she forced herself to move slowly and gracefully, despite the urge to run. McCullum was annoyed—she knew that without having to see the expression on his face. But he also wanted her to attend the swimming lesson, for moral support if for no other reason. And so he was holding his temper. And if Erica could teach him to do *that*, Sarah Gibson would owe her a debt of gratitude in the coming years!

"They're still babies! And they can barely breathe *out* of the water, much less in! What were you thinking, Erica?"

Erica watched in helpless frustration as Abigail Lindstrom paced the beach in a panic. "The captain and his friend won't let anything happen to them."

"They were there when Lilli died! What good did they do? They can't stop it. If the twins can't catch their breath—"

"They're not having babies, they're learning to swim. If they can't breathe, Daniel and Sean will stop the lessons. It's nothing like childbirth, Abby."

"How do you know? You've never had a baby. And

you've never watched your daughter suffocate before your eyes.''

''Gracious, Abby, I see now why the captain is so anxious to send you back to Salem. Sit down and relax. They aren't even *wet* yet!''

It was true. Daniel wasn't taking any chances with his sons, and had spent almost fifteen minutes instructing them on the beach before allowing them to step foot into the gentle surf. With Polly as his example, he was carefully illustrating how to move hands and feet, how to breathe, and how to signal discomfort.

''How can he be so impatient with us, and so patient with the children?'' Erica marveled.

''He'll listen to you, Erica. Tell him to wait another year.''

She patted Abigail's arm. ''It's time. Look at their faces. They're glowing.''

It was true. Kevin was grinning from ear to ear, while Little Sean laughed proudly at one of Polly's arm flappings. Then Daniel grabbed one boy, Sean hoisted the other, and they were suddenly waist-deep in the water, holding the twins in position just beyond the gentle waves.

The sun was fiercely bright, dancing off the sea as though it were a mirror, and as the light hit Daniel's arms and chest, they glistened with strength and prowess. Erica could remember the feel of those arms, that chest, those rippling, untamed muscles, and knew how masterful they could be.

And Sean Lynch was impressive too, with his lanky height and reassuring smile. His manner was light and as breezy as the air around him, but one could sense from his every cautious move that he wasn't about to let anything happen to his namesake.

No wonder Grandmother was so weak, with so many wonderful men in the world. Erica sighed to herself. *If only Abby could see them through my eyes, she could relax and enjoy herself.*

"Look at Polly," Erica gushed. "Captain McCullum must have told her to wear her shirt in the water! That's an improvement at least, don't you agree? Soon we'll have her wearing dresses and dancing a waltz!" She glanced with sympathetic impatience at her hostess. "Try to enjoy this, Abby. It's a big day for the boys."

"I keep remembering the day we lost Iris," Abigail murmured.

"Iris?"

"Lilli's twin sister. She was the weaker of the two—"

"Lilli had a twin?" Erica bit her lip. "No one told me that. How did she die?" Aghast at the ominous expression on Abigail's face, she blurted, "She didn't drown, did she?"

"She might as well have," the annoyed hostess complained. "She was weak, just like the twins. In her case, it was consumption that took her, but if she'd been insane enough to swim—"

"Gracious, Abby! It's hardly the same thing," Erica began, intent on reassuring the distraught woman once and for all. But at that moment, before her disbelieving eyes, Little Sean's body began to convulse, right in Sean Lynch's arms. Alarmed, she sprinted to the water's edge, only to realize belatedly that the child was sputtering but fine. Laughing in fact.

"I swallowed water," he gasped toward Erica. "It's salty."

"Well, I should think so," she murmured, taking her own slow, steady breath to calm her racing heart. Then she saw that Daniel was eyeing her with brazen self-satisfaction. Grimacing sweetly, she insisted, "I think that's enough for the first day."

"No!" the boys chorused. "We want to swim more."

"Five more minutes, then." She turned before they could protest, and worked her way up the beach until she was again at Abigail's side. "They're fine. They're almost done."

The older woman had apparently managed to relax at long last. "Look at their faces. I can't remember ever seeing them this excited."

It was true. The glow of pride and accomplishment on the innocent young faces was enough to make Erica want to run back to Jack and tackle him into the nearest bed, just so that she could have a darling little baby of her own. She could only imagine the wonderful years Sarah had ahead of her here, on this island, with this amazing family.

Above all, Captain McCullum was mesmerizing Erica with his every move. Brash one minute, gentle the next. Teasing and coaxing the children, and earning in return not only smiles, but performance as well. Little Sean in particular seemed actually to be swimming unaided, at least for a moment or two at a stretch. And Kevin, with his father's confidence, seemed ready to take on the world.

Then five minutes had passed, and a very obedient Sean was hurrying the group out of the water despite a flurry of protests.

"Come here this instant," Erica urged, pulling Kevin into a warm towel and rubbing him briskly. "You don't want to spend all night coughing, do you?"

"Did you see me swim?"

"You were magnificent. Are you tired?"

"No, I'm good. I want to swim more."

"Perhaps later. You've worn your father and your uncle out for now."

The little boy wrapped his arms around her neck and asked, "Can *you* swim, Erica?"

"Not as well as you," she assured him. Then she

remembered Daniel's claim that she never answered questions directly, and so she added sheepishly, "But to answer your question: Yes, Kevin. I can swim."

"Me too."

She looked up to see Daniel grinning at her. "I see we all learned something today."

"I certainly hope so," she said with a sniff. "Kevin? You and your brother should change into dry clothes now."

"Come on," Daniel instructed, grabbing both twins and hoisting them up into his arms. "Sean? Are you coming?"

"I'll be up in a minute," the first mate said.

"So?" The captain arched an eyebrow suggestively, then turned and strode up the beach with Abby and Polly trailing close behind.

Erica smiled uncertainly. "Did you want to ask me something, Sean? I'll try to give you a straight answer, despite what the captain says."

The first mate stretched out on the sand and studied her carefully. "It's about all the matchmaking."

"Oh, dear." Erica sat on her blanket and sighed. "I know the captain sees me as a meddler, and I suppose you do too. But I assure you, I wouldn't have come here if I weren't convinced it was an inspired match. On the other hand," she said quickly, "I haven't met Abby's niece, and I have no reason to think you and she are right for one another. So you're perfectly justified in asking me not to mention *that* match again."

"That's a relief," the sailor admitted carefully. "But it's the other that has me worried."

"Sarah and the captain? Why?"

"I've known him a long while. Did you know that?"

"You helped him build this house eight years ago. So I knew it was that long, at least."

"We were boys together, until he left Ireland for America. Danny wasn't quite seven years old then. Younger than Polly is now. He came here with his uncle, and I didn't meet up with him again until I came over as a young man, and made my way to New York. I became ship's carpenter on a lovely clipper ship, where Danny was serving as first mate."

"That must have been a wonderful reunion."

"Aye, it was fine. Danny was filled with dreams back then. To be the captain of a clipper ship, and sail the world. He wanted to see every port in the Pacific—"

"The Pacific?"

Sean nodded. "He likes the danger of it. Rounding the Horn. Sailing hundreds, sometime thousands of miles from the nearest dry land. The coastal trade isn't adventure enough for Danny, except in hurricane season."

"But this is his home."

"Aye, the home he made for Lilli and the children. And her being the way she was, he didn't dare leave her alone for too long a stretch. So he settled for coasting. Not that *I'm* complaining. This life suits me fine."

"But it's too tame for Captain McCullum? That's what you're saying?"

"I shouldn't be saying anything," Sean hedged. "But I thought you should know. He sails from Havana to Salem in a schooner, because that's the life that protects his family best. The last thing he needs is someone else to protect."

"You make it sound as though he's unhappy with his life, but how can that be?" Erica protested. "This island is paradise. He calls it his hideaway."

"That's what it is. He found it when he was just a deckhand. Claimed it for his own—as a place to come between adventures. He built himself a hut, like the buccaneers who lived here centuries ago. They didn't need anything but this place and the sea. He wanted to be like them.''

''Then he met Lilli and a hut wasn't enough.''

''And then he lost Lill, and it almost killed him.'' Sean eyed her sadly. ''Like I said, he left Ireland as an orphan. He saw his mother die of a fever before his eyes. Lost three sisters and a brother when they were still infants, and an older brother in a skirmish. All before Danny was old enough to read. And the rest of his family didn't fare any better, from the little he's told me since then.''

Erica bit her lip. ''How awful.''

''As a lad, he saw more sickness and death than most men have to face in a lifetime. So when he came to America, he had his own personal ''declaration of independence''—to be free of all that, for all time. When I met up with him again, his motto was Live Aloft, Die Aloft. If Lilli hadn't come along, he probably would have, as reckless as he was back then.''

Erica stared out over the sea and tried to imagine how Daniel must have felt when he realized he'd lost his freedom from pain when he lost his heart to Lilli. To his credit, he hadn't turned away. Instead, he had loved and protected her, despite all his plans to the contrary. And now he stayed with the children, when every instinct was warning him to run. To enjoy life. To avoid commitment. Love. Loss. To live aloft. And alone.

''I thought he had everything a man could want. Except a wife, of course,'' she mused.

''He has enough to satisfy most men. But Danny McCullum isn't most men. What he needs, a wife and children can't give him.''

''It's confusing,'' she admitted.

Sean touched her cheek. ''You should go home to your fiancé, and stop your matchmaking.''

''I suppose you're right.''

"Some day, the twins will be grown, and Danny'll trade the *Rigger* for a clipper and head off to China."

"That's years from now!" Erica protested.

"True. So don't make it longer by saddling him with a new wife and new babies."

She smiled ruefully. "You make it sound as though I really could."

"You're a persuasive girl," Sean told her quietly. "If anyone could convince Danny to marry again, it would be you."

"I won't try any more." Erica jumped to her feet and squared her shoulders. "I'll convince him to leave the twins in Salem with Abby, and go off on his adventures. He could bring Polly with him, couldn't he? She's an adventurer too."

"Don't waste your breath," Sean advised. "He's not about to shirk his responsibility for those little lads, no matter how much it costs him. We've all tried to talk to him, but when it comes to guilt, the Good Lord gave Danny more than his share."

"You're saying he blames himself for Lilli's death? I keep hearing about that."

"Think about it, before you give him someone else in his life to love and lose. I'm sure the governess is a lovely girl—"

"She really is, Sean. In fact, since she's not going to marry the captain, you ought to think about her for yourself. She's more perfect for you than she is for the captain—"

"What?" Sean sat up straight and tried to glare. "I hope you're joking."

Erica grinned sympathetically. "I'm just asking you to meet her, for your sake as well as hers. Every man should fall in love at least once in his life."

"Love and marriage are two different things," Sean

assured her, standing and brushing sand from his still-damp breeches. "I've fallen in love half a dozen times in my life."

"Oh?"

"It's a fine feeling, I'm the first to admit. I don't need a matchmaker to teach me that."

"Are you in love now?" When Sean winced, Erica clapped her hands in delight. "Who is she? Does Captain McCullum know her?"

"Listen, Erica—"

"Don't worry, I won't tell him. Is she married?"

"No."

"Engaged?"

"No. She's not the marrying kind, which suits me just fine, since I'm not either."

"All girls are the marrying kind," Erica corrected. "Have you thought of asking her?"

"She's had opportunities—"

"But not with *you*. I'll bet she's in love with you too. How could she not be? You're so darling and strong and loyal." Erica hugged him effusively. "This is so wonderful. I came here to play Cupid and now I've succeeded. And I'll find someone else for Sarah—you've convinced me Captain McCullum won't do. And *you're* spoken for. Tell me her name."

Sean looked as though he was feeling sick to his stomach. "I don't want to get married, and neither does Betsy."

"Betsy? Oh, Sean! That's one of my favorite names. It's an omen, don't you see?"

"Listen, Erica." His green eyes pleaded with her to understand. "I don't want you talking to Danny about this."

"You underestimate him, Sean. He wants you to be happy, and if marriage to Betsy is what you want, it's what he wants for you too." She smiled and added gently,

"Don't look so worried. I can keep a secret as well as anyone."

"There *is* no secret."

"Then why can't I tell him?" She laughed at her irrefutable logic. "I'm teasing you, Sean. I won't say a word to the captain."

"Thank you."

"On one condition."

"Huh?"

"You have to promise to ask Betsy to marry you the very next time you see her."

"But—"

"Didn't Captain McCullum tell you I won't argue?" She brushed a film of pink sand from her soft yellow skirt, then linked her arm through the sailor's. "Be a gentleman now and escort me to the house. I have a very difficult letter to write, and the sooner I begin, the better."

It was easier to find words to break the news to Sarah than Erica had suspected. After all, the governess hadn't wanted to leave New England, and hadn't been nearly as taken with the idea of marrying a sea captain as Erica had been. She would probably be relieved, and hopefully, willing to write to Russell Braddock again, only this time, Erica would have Sarah compose the letter completely herself, so that the matchmaker would select a more sedate, but equally attractive, groom.

No, Sarah wouldn't be disappointed. So why was Erica so miserable over the turn of events?

Because Jack should have been here by now, she finally admitted to herself. Even allowing for weather and travel arrangements, he should have been able to set sail within three or four days after her departure, propelled by a combination of jealousy and concern for her well-being.

She had been able to make light of the delay for a few days, blaming Jack's practical nature and love of a good bargain, but without the matchmaking to distract her, she had to ask herself why she was staying on the island. Wouldn't Jack's arrival be somewhat anticlimactic after so long a wait? Would she even allow him to sweep her off her feet and carry her away to a secluded spot to make love, or would she be too angry and resentful? And what if *he* was angry, over the loss of time and the inconvenience?

He has his nerve being angry, after the way he's neglected you, she fumed silently to herself. *You ought to do something truly wicked, to teach him a lesson. You should kiss Captain McCullum again! He's not Sarah's man any longer, after all. And you've kissed him before, so there's no real harm. It's just as he says: you've a right to be curious about such things, and if Jack Ryerson doesn't care enough to come and put a stop to it, why should you?*

She wouldn't do it, of course, but just the thought of so bold a revenge made her feel a little better, and she was actually able to smile and pay attention to the children's antics during dinner that evening. The twins chattered incessantly about the swimming, until one would have thought they'd crossed Crescent Bay end to end! And Polly wore a frilly dress to the table, with matching ribbons in her hair, drawing compliments from her uncle Sean and gentle teasing from her father.

Erica took it all as a comforting sign that her long voyage hadn't been a complete waste of everyone's time. If nothing else, she had made new friends, Sean and Abby in particular. She intended to keep in touch forever with the feisty grandmother. And of course, she would see to it personally that Sean and Betsy were married before the year's end.

And as for the other matter—Captain McCullum's wanderlust—she intended to take care of that too. In the time remaining, before Jack arrived, she would persuade the sailor to follow his dreams without further delay. She would remind him that she'd been right about the swimming, and then she'd convince him that his children would be fine in Salem for months at a time while he sailed to his heart's content. Abby would take good care of them, and Mr. and Mrs. Jack Ryerson would be less than twenty miles away, ready and willing to help in any way possible. And of course, Mr. and Mrs. Sean Lynch would be available to do their part. And the McCullum children would play with the future offspring of both happy couples.

"She's got that matchmaker gleam in her eye again," Daniel observed dryly. "This might be a good time for us to go outside and have those cigars."

Erica laughed lightly. "I'll just say good night to both of you then. Once I've helped Abby tuck the children safely into bed, I'll be retiring myself."

The sea captain arched an eyebrow. "I thought for sure we'd be hearing about Sarah and the niece for hours. Or did you bedevil Sean enough about all that during your private conversation on the beach?"

"You've asked me not to mention Sarah again, Captain," Erica said sweetly. "And so I have no intention of bringing her up."

His eyes narrowed with suspicion, then he shrugged. "I know better than to believe that, but any reprieve is a welcome one. Don't go to bed yet, though," he added casually. "There's something I want to talk to you about."

Erica hoped the others couldn't see how quickly her cheeks had warmed. After the prior evening's indiscretion, there was something a bit too intimate about his suggestion, whether he'd meant it that way or not. "Couldn't it wait until morning, Captain? I can't remember when I've been this fatigued."

McCullum shrugged again. "If you change your mind, you'll know where to find me."

"Enjoy your cigars, gentlemen." She stood and curtseyed gracefully, and was pleased when Sean jumped to his feet. It would have been nice if McCullum had done so also, but in a way, she found his lack of gentility reassuring. He wasn't a suitable mate for Sarah, after all. He belonged at sea, miles from civilization, not married to a proper Boston governess.

Erica could think of half a dozen good reasons to take her moonlit stroll that night. In addition to the fact that it was a healthful experience and a delight to the senses, the romantic ambience would allow her to think amorous thoughts about, and eventually to forgive, Jack.

And if by chance she encountered Captain McCullum, she could find out what it was he'd wanted to discuss with her. And she had two topics of her own that needed to be addressed. Polly's behavior, and McCullum's destiny at sea.

There were really only two reasons *not* to take her walk. The first was the simplest: McCullum might misinterpret it as a sign that she was interested in repeating the prior evening's misbehavior. The second was more complicated: she might actually *be* willing to indulge in further mischief. Which meant, of course, that she shouldn't go, no matter how many good reasons she could invent for venturing out into the moonlight.

But she knew herself well enough to know that arguing with herself was futile, and so she settled for wearing a matronly brown dress, on the theory that most of the confusion had been caused by her scanty nightclothes. If perchance she crossed paths with the captain, he would see immediately that circumstances had changed. And if she did not encounter him, she would embrace the opportunity to think sweet thoughts of her beloved Jack.

Still, as she approached the spot where she and the captain had kissed, her pulse began to race, and when she saw a blanket spread on the ground beside a basket from which a wine bottle protruded, a dizzying wave of anticipation swept over her.

"You're late. *And* overdressed," came a familiar growl from behind her, and she spun in time to catch the twinkle in his deep-blue eyes.

Erica flushed and backed away. "Must you always be so rude? Not to mention, presumptuous? You said there was something we needed to discuss. I should have known better than to take the word of a sailor."

Daniel chuckled. "I was expecting a reward, not more badgering. I made Polly wear the shirt, didn't I? And I taught the twins to swim. Have you no gratitude, woman?"

Erica bit back a smile. "My company is your reward. Shall we sit for a while and talk? That is, if you can behave yourself."

The sea captain watched as she settled onto the blanket, primly arranging her skirt about herself. "Would you like some wine?" he asked.

"Certainly not."

He grinned, then stretched out beside her on the blanket, his head propped up on his hand. "Talk."

She took a deep breath. "You mentioned Polly. She looked so pretty at dinner tonight, but I have some concerns about the way she usually dresses."

"She doesn't have much use for fancy clothes here, Erica. Breeches and a shirt are more practical."

"She won't be here forever. Do you suppose any boy will pay attention to her—"

"I don't want any boys noticing her," he interrupted

cheerfully. "You've just convinced me to let her dress like a boy for ten more years, at least."

"It's not modest."

"She's a child."

"A child who's developing bad habits. You can't change nature, Captain. In no time, her body will begin to curve. I'm sure your men will love *that*."

"Huh?"

"She'll swim out to the schooner, dripping wet and dressed in less than nothing, climbing up the rope—"

"You've made your point," he growled. "I'll take care of it. Anything else?"

Erica smiled at the annoyance in his tone. "My father reacted in this very same way the first time he saw a boy pay attention to me. I remember it so clearly. David Watson brought me flowers, and Father chased him right off the porch."

"Because he knew what the Watson boy wanted," Daniel agreed. "I don't want men having those kinds of thoughts about Polly."

"She's a pretty girl, Captain. I'm afraid it's inevitable."

"True. In certain situations, what happens between a man and a woman *is* inevitable." He raised himself up enough to press her back into the blanket so that he loomed over her, then started to lower his mouth to hers.

"I love Jack," she protested just before their lips touched.

"I know."

Erica wriggled away and sat up again. "Before you kiss me, there's something you should know."

"This should be interesting."

Erica glared. "It's important, so we don't have any misunderstandings. I love Jack with all my heart, but I'm annoyed with him right now. Because he hasn't yet come to rescue me."

"To rescue you? From me?"

"More or less," she admitted sheepishly. "He knew I was coming here to convince you to marry Sarah. But he also knew you were a lonely, attractive man who might attempt to take liberties with me."

"And so he objected to your coming here?"

"I didn't tell him—"

"I knew it!"

"I didn't tell him to his face, but I left a note." She grimaced in acknowledgment of her guilt. "I know I gave you the impression he had consented—"

"The impression?"

"Do you want to kiss me or not?"

Daniel burst into laughter. "More than ever, if that's possible. Are you done with your confession?"

"Not quite." She blushed. "I want you to understand why I'm willing to misbehave."

"To punish Ryerson?" Daniel suggested playfully.

Erica smiled. "I suppose you could say that. Also, I've been thinking about what you said this morning. That any girl in my situation—knowing it was her last chance to kiss a man other than her future husband—would have been tempted."

"And then there's your natural susceptibility to such temptations," he teased.

"It's true, Captain. You said any girl would have a *momentary* impulse, but I've been having such impulses all my life, and they're far from momentary." When he grinned and tried to reach for her, she scooted away quickly. "I may have *had* them, but I never acted upon them until last night. I suppose it's just as you said: I wanted to punish Jack, and I was curious."

"Any reason is fine with me."

"Yes, I know," she said with a sniff.

Daniel chuckled and urged her back down, hovering over her expectantly. "Are we through talking?"

"Almost." Her heart was beginning to pound. "Tell me how you found this island."

"Later."

"Captain!" She blushed happily. "You're exactly like the pirates who used to live here. Lusty and impatient. Do you suppose they brought women to this very spot, and tried to have their way with them, just as you're doing now?"

He nodded, his eyes beginning to blaze, and Erica knew in that moment that he could make love to her in a way no other man could ever do. Because just as she yearned to be carried away by adventure and romance, this man lusted to do just that to her.

"Can you imagine?" she whispered hoarsely. "Perhaps once, long ago, a princess was on her way to marry a prince, and a pirate captain kidnapped her, and brought her here to wait for the ransom. And they were attracted to each other, and he wanted to make love to her. And she wanted it too, but—" Erica took a deep breath and stared straight into his eyes. "It was very important that she still be a virgin when she left this island. Because of the ransom."

Daniel nodded again, clearly inflamed by the message she was giving him. "There are ways it can be done, if that's how the princess wants it."

"It's not that I don't love Jack," she reminded him weakly. "But I want this too."

"To punish him," Daniel agreed, his voice thick with desire. "I don't want anything from you but this, Erica. You'll go back to him a virgin, but you'll remember me and this night."

"Yes, Captain," she gasped. "That's what I want. More than anything."

He loomed over her, his eyes blazing again, and she wondered what she had done. He was going to take her now, and nothing would ever be the same. Already, before he'd even touched her, her loins were throbbing and her breasts were swelling with the need to be stroked and petted. He seemed to know it, and so, when he lowered his mouth, it was not to cover her lips, but to suck gently through the fabric of her bodice, teasing her nipple into a fevered peak and sending jolts of arousal through her in the process.

Then she heard him groan, but with frustration rather than desire, and he lifted his head as though listening to the wind. But it wasn't the wind. It was a child's voice, calling out to them cheerfully, and Erica lurched into a sitting position in time to see Polly bounding toward them.

"Oh, no . . ." Erica murmured, pulling a handful of her thick auburn hair forward to cover the wet, puckered spot on the bodice of her dress.

"Well said," he growled. "What's she doing out here at this hour?"

"Hush, Captain." Erica waved as she scrambled to her feet. "Hello, darling. What a nice surprise."

"Shouldn't you be in bed?" Daniel demanded.

"Erica said I should come join you next time, even if you looked romantic," the girl informed him evenly.

"What?"

"Never mind," Erica scolded. "We were just talking about the pirates who used to live here, Polly."

"The buccaneers," she corrected. "Papa always tells us stories about them."

"You should tell her one now, Captain." Erica gave him a stern glance, hoping her own eyes weren't as glazed with lust as were his. Her insides were still throbbing, and she would have given anything to convince the child to leave quickly, while they were still so heady with need for one another.

But she also knew she'd just been given a valuable reprieve, and she'd be thankful in the morning that she'd taken it, so she announced quietly, "This island life is exhausting. I'd better be off to bed."

Polly seemed amazed. "Don't you want to hear the story?"

"Perhaps another time, darling." She gave the girl a quick kiss on the cheek, then smiled sheepishly toward Daniel. "I'll see you in the morning."

He nodded, his face expressionless. "Sleep well, if you can."

She blushed at his meaning. They would both toss and turn, she imagined. Would it be worse for him? Probably not. After all, he'd had dozens of women before, and would have dozens in the future.

Turning away, she trudged back toward her room, trying without success to convince herself that the interruption, while frustrating, had been for the best. After all, did she *want* to be one of the many dozens this man had had? She would have remembered the night forever, but to him, it would have blurred with the countless others.

And what did he mean by "ways it can be done"? She couldn't help but be curious. Would she honestly have emerged from the encounter with her virginity intact? And if so, would she feel any better than she did now? *He* would have been satisfied, at *her* expense, but wouldn't she still have tossed and turned?

"Ways it can be done," she muttered aloud. "Wouldn't *that* have been a disaster? Betraying Jack so some rogue could enjoy himself? What were you thinking, Erica?"

Locating her stationery and a pen, she settled into bed without changing into her nightclothes. She would write Jack a letter, filled with love and anticipation at the thought of seeing him again soon. She would force herself to remember why she'd fallen in love with him in the first place. The fireworks display over the bay. His lavish courtship. His boyish smile.

Even if he was waiting for a reasonable fare, or for a decision to be made by one of his accursed investors, it surely wouldn't be long now before he arrived and carried her back to the sanity of Boston. It was time she stopped thinking about buccaneers and started remembering who she was.

But the feelings that were coursing through her body and her mind had little to do with love, and nothing to do with Jack Ryerson, and so she crumpled up the blank sheet of paper. Then she rolled over so her face was buried in the pillow and shrieked with frustration, hoping that morning—and Jack!—would arrive quickly.

CHAPTER SIX

Sleep well, if you can. . . .

McCullum's parting wish had been a true omen, and while Erica managed to doze off eventually, it was a restless, unsatisfying sort of sleep, much like the abortive lovemaking of the prior evening. Sometime during the night, she decided that it would have been best to have simply gone through with it. She felt miserably unfaithful to Jack, despite her relatively untouched condition, yet she had none of the blissful memories that might have balanced out the guilty ones had the sea captain been allowed to work his magic on her.

She hoped he would growl and complain the next morning, so that she could be disgusted with him. But instead, he was cordial and distant, which made her feel as though the entire episode hadn't made much of an impression on him at all. Feeling like the useless meddler he apparently saw her to be, she wandered aimlessly while the captain and the first mate divided their time between playing with the twins and moving most of the heavy furniture up the stairs to the loftlike interior balconies that lined the main living areas of the house.

"Daniel says the rains will be here soon," Abigail explained. "In a month, or perhaps even sooner. Sometimes the island floods, and it's best just to move everything upstairs, open the doors and shutters and allow it to happen."

"Oh, dear."

"If it threatens to get deeper than a foot or two, the children and I move to one of the larger islands—usually Cuba—for a few days. I actually look forward to it, since it's one of the few times I have a social life." She smiled fondly as she added, "It's such a treat having you here, Erica. It makes me glad Daniel's so stubborn."

"Pardon?"

"It will take you weeks to convince him to marry Sarah, and during that time, I'll have your company. I'm sure your fiancé didn't intend for you to stay longer than a week or two, but he didn't know how Daniel can be."

"None of us did," Erica mused. "And as for marrying Sarah, I'm not so sure I'll be convincing the captain—"

"Nonsense! He trusts your judgment to an amazing extent. In just two days you convinced him to allow the boys to swim, and to speak with Polly about behaving like a lady rather than an urchin. I wouldn't have believed it if I hadn't heard it with my own ears."

"He spoke with her?"

"Over breakfast. You should have been there. It was quite touching. Almost as though Daniel saw her as a girl, rather than just a child, for the first time."

"And how did Polly react?"

"I believe she was both confused and flattered. In any case, Daniel told her to listen carefully to you over the next few days, and to take your advice to heart, and she agreed.''

"Well, I'm confused and flattered myself,'' Erica admitted sheepishly. "It's been such a strange few days. And last night—'' She twisted a thick lock of auburn hair around one finger. "Last night I wondered if I'd made a huge mistake, coming here. But perhaps it was for the best, after all.''

"We all slept poorly last night, because the air was so still,'' Abigail explained. "It's this way before a storm— that green haze in the air, and no breeze at all.''

"Doesn't it frighten you?''

"No. Daniel says it'll be just a short squall. Practice, for the ones to come later. We've gotten quite accustomed to this way of life, Erica. In some ways, I feel safer here than anywhere. That's part of the problem, I suppose. It's why Daniel wants the children here rather than Salem.''

"But I think they belong in Salem, at least for part of the year.''

Abigail stared. "You do?''

Erica nodded. "I've changed my mind about it, and I intend to speak to the captain. I was going to do that last night, only—''

"Only Polly interrupted you?'' Abigail laughed. "I scolded her for bothering you, but she had a wonderful time telling stories with Daniel for hours. It's really been the nicest visit they've had with him that I can remember. We're all grateful to you, Erica. And now, if you're honestly willing to convince him to move us all to Salem—''

"I'm going to try. And I'm not going to mention Sarah anymore. I no longer believe they're a good match, Abby. I hope you'll respect my opinion on that.''

Abigail studied her mischievously. "You're attracted to Daniel yourself, aren't you?''

"Don't be ridiculous. I simply don't think he needs another wife. Some men are meant for marriage—my fiancé being one of those. Daniel McCullum is not that sort." She hesitated before revealing, "I told the captain last night that my fiancé will be joining me here in a day or so. Did he mention that to you at breakfast?"

"No."

Erica smiled in apology. "I'm sorry I kept it from you. I wanted it to be a romantic reunion—secretive and intimate—and so I didn't share the details with anyone, but now it's necessary. I want you to understand why I continue to visit, even though I no longer want the captain to marry Sarah."

"It's romantic," Abigail agreed quietly. She seemed disappointed, and Erica knew that the woman had seen, and misinterpreted, the magnetism that had developed between Erica and the captain. If only she knew how fortunate they were that it was nothing more than a fleeting attraction, fed by Erica's unfortunate penchant for flirting with temptation, and a sailor's natural inclination to plunder any willing female.

"When you meet Jack, you'll see why I love him. He's handsome and charming and patient and kind. He wants to marry me, and have dozens of children, and live in the house his father built, without ever yearning for another world. He's someone I can count on, Abby. And he was able to count on me too, until I got carried away by the idea of finding a husband for Sarah."

"All this time . . . ?" Abigail caught herself and smiled ruefully. "That's why you always look out to sea? You're expecting Jack?"

"Yes. What did you think?"

The older woman shrugged. "It doesn't matter. The important thing is, you love your Jack, and he'll be here soon. I'm happy for you, Erica. And it's best that Daniel won't be here. That might confuse the matter unnecessarily."

Erica bit her lip. "The captain's leaving?"

"Why do you think he's been moving the furniture? And he's on the beach now, sending Sean ahead to Havana to gather the crew—Erica! Where are you going?"

Erica had almost reached the doorway, but whirled to explain, "He mustn't leave on my account. The children are enjoying the visit so. And a storm is coming—you said so yourself. Excuse me, Abby, but I must speak with him."

"Erica, wait!"

Ignoring the older woman's plea, Erica burst through the doorway and sprinted onto the beach in time to see a trim sailboat in the distance, heading east, away from the *Moon Rigger*. And standing on the berm, watching the sails intently, was Daniel McCullum.

"Captain!"

He turned, his face expressionless. "Is something wrong?"

"Abby tells me you're leaving." Erica gasped for a breath before continuing. "Is it on my account? Because you mustn't allow my—my bad behavior to interfere with your visit. The children are enjoying you so."

"There's been no bad behavior, unfortunately."

Erica winced. "Is that it? You're leaving because I've frustrated you? If so, I'm the one who should leave, not you. Please, Captain. Won't you reconsider?"

"And what about the romantic reunion with Ryerson?"

She winced again. "That needn't take place here. I imagine he'll sail, as I did, to Kingston, or to Cuba first. I can leave word where he can find me. I'll willingly leave today."

"So?" Daniel's blue eyes were still cool. "You've

decided to abandon the matchmaking? Because you've decided I'm not worthy to marry your friend?''

"Of course not! What a thing to say."

"It's because of last night, then?"

"Nothing happened last night," she retorted with a haughty sniff.

For the first time, a hint of a smile touched his lips. "Don't remind me."

She tried not to smile in return. "Polly's timing was unfortunate from your point of view. But for myself, it was a godsend. I've put all that behind me now, Captain McCullum. Jack may not have rushed here as quickly as I would have liked, and I may not have been as faithful to him as one would have hoped, but at least when he does arrive, I'll be relatively untouched, and we can have a romantic reunion. That's all I want now."

"You don't want me to marry Sarah?"

"Correct."

"And you don't want to kiss me anymore?"

"Absolutely not."

"But you're staying indefinitely?"

She laughed sympathetically. "With your permission. I'll try not to be too much of a nuisance."

He was grinning as he shook his head. "Stay, but I'll be going. A man can only take so much torture." Before she could protest, he touched her cheek gently. "It's time for me to go, Erica. My men will be getting restless. Stay as long as you like. You can have your romantic rendezvous with Ryerson, down on the beach in the moonlight. The same memory," he added quietly. "Only a different man playing the role of pirate."

"It's not a role Jack could play." Erica sighed, adding quickly, "Nor would he want to."

"You're a frustrating girl," Daniel complained. "Would you like some advice?"

"I'd like to trade advice with you." She smiled in what she hoped was an encouraging manner. "Let me say first that I've been wrong to try to match you with Sarah. Not because you wouldn't make a fine husband, because you've proven that you would. It's something quite different. Quite wonderful, in fact. Something I've learned to appreciate about you."

"I never understand a word you're saying," he said with a rueful chuckle. "What's on that mind of yours now?"

Erica flushed. "I'm trying to tell you why I decided against matching you with Sarah. Because I can see you were right. You don't need another wife."

"I don't?"

"You need more freedom, not less."

The answer seemed to surprise him. "Freedom from what?"

"Responsibility, of course."

"What are you talking about?" he growled. "When have I ever turned my back on my responsibilities?"

"Never," she assured him hastily. "That's why you don't need any more of them."

"Oh." He nodded. "Go on."

"If I continue, do you promise not to bite my head off?"

Daniel nodded again.

"I think you should compromise with Abigail. She could be here with the children during the winters, and they could be in Salem with her during the summers. It's lovely there then, and they'd be away from the storms, would they not?"

"Erica—"

"Let me finish. You could take longer voyages, and of course they'd miss you, but your visits would be longer too, and they'd love that. And Polly could go with you, as long as she brought her lessons along and dressed modestly. Of course, as she grows older, she should occasionally stay in Salem. I'd visit her, or she could come and see me in Boston, and I could introduce her to boys and girls her age from good families.''

Daniel placed his huge, rough hands on her hips. ''What's this about?''

''It's about you, seeing the world.'' She draped her arms innocently around his neck. ''Don't you see, Captain? I'm about to embark on a wonderful adventure—marriage to Jack. I want that for *you* too. But for you, marriage wouldn't be an adventure, or at least, it wouldn't be a new one. You've already done that. Now you should see the world. Sail the seas. Visit strange and exotic places. That's what I want for you.''

''Why?'' he asked, his voice hoarse with confusion.

''Why not?'' Erica kissed his cheek. ''Will you think about it at least?''

''I'll think about you,'' he grumbled. ''A meddler, right to the end.''

Hurt and confused, she pulled away from him, but he grabbed her back to himself and insisted, ''If you weren't so beautiful, one of us would have throttled you by now.''

''One of us?''

''Ryerson or myself,'' he explained with a grin. ''Now it's my turn to offer some advice.''

Erica felt her cheeks flush. ''What is it?''

''When he gets here, he'll ask if I touched you. Tell him I didn't.''

''You're saying I should deceive the man I love? The man I'm going to spend the rest of my life with?''

''That's exactly what I'm saying.'' Daniel leaned into her and brushed his lips across hers, then teased, ''Don't tell him about that one, either.''

Erica pulled free quickly. ''What will your children

think? Kissing me in broad daylight? Go and say good-bye to them now, and stop all this foolishness.''

"This foolishness has been an honor, Miss Lane.''

Erica bit her lip. "You can be so romantic, Captain. It almost makes me wish you and Sarah could have found happiness together, but . . ." She studied him wistfully. "You're not the marrying sort, isn't that true?''

"True enough.''

"Well, then.'' She stepped backward and gazed out toward the *Moon Rigger*. "When will you leave?''

"Sean went to round up the crew. When he comes back in that small sailing boat you saw, we'll be heading out.''

"Small sailing boat? Are you referring to the launch?''

"Spoken like a true sailor.'' Daniel grinned. "Except that one was a cutter.''

"Oh.''

"Sean asked me to say good-bye to you for him. And he sent along a message.''

"Oh?''

"He'll follow your advice concerning his future. I don't suppose you're going to tell me what that means?''

Erica smiled at the thought of Sean married to his mysterious Betsy. "You'll find out soon enough, Captain. Shall we just say, he won't be in any more danger of marrying Abigail's niece?''

Daniel cocked his head to the side. "That's how Sean explained it, too.''

"Well then, it must be true, mustn't it?''

He hesitated, then asked carefully, "Do you want me to stay? Are you worried that Ryerson might not—''

"Don't be silly!'' She smiled at the thought. "If you knew him at all, you wouldn't doubt him. He'll come, at his own pace. He'll bargain for an excellent fare, and he'll conduct business along the way, but eventually he'll

come to claim me. It's that practical, patient side that
both draws me to him and makes me want to scream
But he's a good man, Captain, and he loves me truly. If
it's time for you to leave, you should go.''

"I want to make one more run to New England before
the storm season starts," Daniel admitted. "It looks to
be a late one this year, but still, if there's no reason to
stay, I should go."

No reason to stay—in other words, no chance of kissing
her again. It was flattering, but it was also for the best
that he be gone before Jack arrived, and so Erica agreed,
"It's settled then. Godspeed, Captain McCullum, and God
bless."

Daniel seemed startled, then he shrugged and bade her
"Good luck with the marriage," turned abruptly, and
strode back toward his house to say good-bye to his
children.

Settling onto the sand, Erica did her best to turn her
thoughts away from the rugged sailor and toward the
fiancé who could arrive at any moment. *Think about the
first time Jack kissed you,* she counseled herself shakily.
*Remember what he said? That you were the most beautiful
girl he'd ever seen? That he'd been waiting his whole
life for you? Doesn't that mean more than a silly pirate
fantasy with a self-proclaimed wanderer?*

And it did indeed, because Erica wanted to be the center
of a man's existence—his greatest reason for being—
and she could be that for Jack. Despite how it seemed—
that he valued his investments more than his engagement—she knew it wasn't true. Jack's desire to succeed
at business was rooted in his determination to provide a
wonderful life for his family—Erica, his sisters, and the
children he'd one day have. What more could any girl
ask?

You can ask for a little romance, and Jack will just have

to learn to give it to you, she decided with characteristic boldness. "Lesson number one" was already in progress—Jack Ryerson was at that very moment steaming, or sailing, toward a lovely, remote island, where he'd either seduce, or be seduced by, the girl of his dreams. After that, she had a feeling "lesson number two" would follow without too much prompting on her part. In fact, she'd probably need to reprimand him, lest he take too many liberties and leave nothing for their wedding night.

Because of the importance of concentrating on Jack, Erica avoided Captain McCullum despite her desire to watch as he visited one last time with his children. As attractive as the touching farewell might seem, it would distract her, and she had no intention of allowing that. When she closed her eyes, she could see Jack's handsome face clearly, and could almost remember how his lips felt when they caressed her cheek or throat. The last thing she needed was to witness a poignant display by the sea captain whose lips had dared do so much more than simply caress her.

Still, when Sean Lynch returned in the graceful little cutter, and Daniel waded out to climb aboard, she was tempted to run to him, one last time, if only to repeat her last minute instructions. *Let Abby take the children to Salem. . . . Sail the world, visit exotic ports. . . .* And of course, to Sean, *Marry Betsy!*

"Leave them alone, Erica," she chided herself in wistful amusement as she watched the two men confer. Then, to her surprise, Daniel was leaving the cutter and returning to the beach, where he stood and stared up in the direction of Erica's room. It was a look she hadn't seen before. Quizzical. Hesitant. Lacking in confidence, in a way she'd thought impossible for the brash seaman.

And suddenly, she wondered if it was possible he'd fallen in love with her. Abby had implied it, Polly had openly craved it, and Erica herself had fantasized that, in some small corner of his heart, he'd been beguiled. Yet now, it terrified her. What would she say? What would she *do?* There was Jack to consider, after all. She loved him, didn't she? And even if she didn't—which of course she did—McCullum wanted to sail the seas unfettered and unwed, so what was *he* thinking? That she'd be his *mistress?* Was he insane?

Just tell him you're flattered, but you're engaged to a wonderful man, she pleaded with herself. *Don't think about the rest of it. Don't think about the way he looks at you, or makes you feel. There's no future there. Not for either of you.*

Then Daniel drew closer, and she could see the unfamiliar furrows in his brow. He was worried about something. About being rejected? It didn't seem likely. He had to know how irresistible he was. He had to know that if he said the right words, and made the right promises—

"Stop it!" she instructed herself aloud. "You're being a goose. Go and see what he wants, and remember you're an engaged woman."

She hurried out, into the courtyard and then onto the crest of the beach, meeting up with him just as he was stomping the last vestiges of wet sand from his feet.

"Captain?"

His gaze swept over her, from her loose, free-flowing hair to her bare feet, then he locked eyes directly with hers. "Sean brought a letter for you."

"A letter? Oh! Are you saying it's from Jack?" She moistened her lips, confused by the unexpected turn of events. Then she accepted the envelope and opened it warily.

"He must have been delayed, and didn't want me to

worry," she explained, half to herself, as she unfolded the single sheet of stationery and began to scan the contents.

My darling Erica,

I have made arrangements for your safe return to Boston. If Captain McCullum or his inestimable mother-in-law could transport you to Jamaica, my associate there will see to the rest. I know you are disappointed that I did not rush to your side despite the demands of my business. You will take it as another sign that I don't love you enough. But it is precisely because I do love you that I resisted the urge to run after you. It's time to stop playing games, darling. I did not for one moment believe your suggestion that you might allow the sea captain to seduce you in Sarah's place. Your note was poetic but foolish. And Sarah has confirmed that you intended to make me jealous. Don't be angry with her. She admitted it only because I guessed at your deceit. While I am mildly annoyed by these constant manipulations, I must admit I miss you. Therefore, I am inclined to move the wedding date. December seems much too far away. Shall we say September instead? Don't sulk, darling. Hurry back to me, and we'll put this foolishness behind us forever.

All my love and devotion,
Jack

She handed the letter to Daniel, then turned away, trying her best to understand the new emotion that was bubbling up in her heart. It wasn't anger. At least, not exactly. Nor was it disappointment. It was much too strong to be that. It was a new kind of hurt, laced with a profound variety of humiliation that made her want to dissolve right into the soft pink sand. Fortunately, there were no tears. At least, not yet.

"He's a horse's ass," Daniel assured her softly. "But it's clear from this that he loves you."

"Is it?" she murmured, her gaze fixed onto the ground.

Turning her to face him again, he put one finger under her chin and urged her to look up into his deep-blue eyes. "Try to understand why he didn't come. He's trying to be strong for both your sakes. He misses you—"

"So he says. I suppose I should be flattered he took the time to write so long a note." She moistened her lips before asking, "Could you take me to Jamaica, Captain? Jack's associate will see to the rest of the arrangements."

"You'll sail with us to Salem," he corrected. "We'll leave at dawn. That will give you time for a final visit with Abby and the boys. We'll let Polly come along, to cheer you up. How's that?"

"It's more than I have a right to ask," she murmured. "It was wrong of me to come here. And Jack's right, I am deceitful."

"That's enough," Daniel soothed. "He didn't mean a word of that. He moved up the wedding date, didn't he? September is only six weeks away. He's missing you more than he lets on, Erica. Be angry with him, but don't be hurt. And when you see him again, holler at him, and slap his face. If he's half a man, he's expecting that. He might even enjoy it."

She smiled wryly. "You're trying to cheer me up? That's sweet, Captain." She glanced out over the sea, toward the *Moon Rigger.* "Your men are ready. Shouldn't we leave right away? I'm anxious to go home. To face him. To look him in the eye. . . ."

Daniel nodded. "If that's how you want it, that's how it'll be. The *Rigger* is at your disposal."

* * *

She was glad to go through the motions. Glad for something to do, rather than to lie on her bed and cry her eyes out. She hugged Abigail, with promises to correspond religiously, then allowed Belle to feed her one last time before embracing her fondly. The twins were darling, right up until the moment when she stepped foot onto the rowboat, with a self-consciously demure Polly, dressed in a sturdy blue frock, at her side.

Through it all, Daniel McCullum was a rock, refusing to allow her to wallow in her disappointment, yet just as firmly reassuring her that it wasn't her fault. That she was perfect. That Jack Ryerson was the luckiest, least appreciative, most lovestruck horse's ass in the world.

Still, she felt numb. Betrayed, although she wasn't sure if it was Jack or her own instincts that had betrayed her. She had been so certain he'd come after her. She had even suspected he'd welcome the opportunity to be bold and impetuous. To make love to her, despite his gentlemanly instincts, which had forced him to wait for the wedding night.

Worst of all was his cold statement in the letter that he wanted her to stop playing games. Was that possible? It had been a game that had brought them together! A silly little "manipulation," on a chilly July evening, when she had pretended to feel faint, and he had gallantly caught her in his arms and eased her onto a picnic blanket. He had whispered her name, his lips mere inches from her ear, and she had stirred against him, loving the feel of his arms around her.

And for the next two years, he had warmly teased her about that night, but had it actually bothered him all that time? Did he see it as a lie or deceit? Those were the words he'd used in his note. "Deceit." It sounded so harsh. So judgmental. So fundamentally unloving.

Was it possible he didn't love her after all? At the very least, he clearly disapproved of her. It was as simple as that. He disapproved of the very qualities that made her the woman she was—playful, impetuous and amorous. Apparently, he had *always* disapproved of her. Had always hoped to change her. To tame her.

And wasn't she just as guilty as he? Hadn't *she* tried to change Jack—to undermine his practical nature and force him to abandon his even-tempered ways? Was it possible *she* didn't love *him?*

Daniel stowed her bags in a tiny stateroom in the aft cabin, then insisted that she come up on deck for fresh air while his crew hoisted the schooner's pure white sails. It was a truly lovely sight, and for a few minutes, Erica almost forgot her misery. Then she remembered how she had expected Jack to arrive in just such a glorious vessel, and her heart ached anew.

Even when they sailed into Havana, to load a shipment of cigars that Daniel would sell to merchants in Salem, Erica could barely force herself to pay attention. Had she honestly fantasized about exotic ports and exciting adventures? She would have traded it all at that moment for some true reassurance that she hadn't wasted two years of her life. Of Jack's life. Of hopes and dreams and aspirations and plans. Yet somehow, as she cried herself to sleep, in the narrow but comfortable bed that the first mate had designed and built for the tiny guest stateroom, she knew that that was exactly what she had done.

* * *

The *Moon Rigger* was already underway when a bleary-eyed Erica climbed out onto the deck the next morning. She had known from the motion of the schooner that the seas were rough, but wasn't prepared for the overcast skies and biting wind that greeted her.

"Good morning, Miss Erica."

She turned to smile toward Sean. "Have we been at sea for long?"

"Since dawn." He gestured toward the crewmen, who were busily working the sails. "You'll see what it's all about now. Nothing like your voyage on the *Valiant,* I'll bet."

"You sound as though you actually prefer bad weather."

"I learned that from Danny," Sean admitted, then his voice softened. "Are you feeling any better?"

"What did the captain tell you?"

"That your fiancé's a horse's ass, but we aren't going to beat the living tar out of him because you claim to love him."

Erica giggled. "Lucky for Jack."

"Aye." The first mate stepped closer. "Only a fool would hurt a sweet girl like you. You ought to think carefully—"

"I already have," Erica interrupted. "I was wrong to think that a man like Jack Ryerson should chase after me whenever I decide to run off to the Caribbean."

"Seems to me chasing after you should be the best part of loving you."

Erica smiled self-consciously. "That's so pretty, Sean. Remember to say such things to Betsy."

The sailor winced, then glanced about furtively, as though worried his captain would overhear. "Are you hungry, Erica?"

"I don't quite have my sea legs yet," she admitted. "But I'd love something to drink. Is there tea?"

"For you? Anything. Go on up and see the captain while I fetch it. He'll be glad to see you aren't wasting away in your stateroom."

Several of the crew members had noticed her, and were smiling with the same mixture of reassurance and admiration that she remembered so fondly from the *Valiant*. Captain Lawrence had explained to her that, in the early days of sailing, a red-haired woman on board a ship had been considered bad luck. "Nowadays," he had assured her gallantly, "any sailor worth his salt appreciates having a beautiful girl on board, red-haired or otherwise."

Polly's voice, calling her name, brought Erica's thoughts back to the present. "Look, Papa. Erica's awake."

Erica looked past the child, transfixed by the sight of the dashing captain. He was dressed just as he'd been the first time she'd seen him—his white shirt open to the waist and billowing in the brisk wind that was blowing across the quarterdeck. He could have been a buccaneer, like the ones that had populated his little island so long ago, had his eyes not been so filled with tenderness and concern.

"I'm fine," she assured him quickly. "You needn't look so worried." A gust of wind whipped her hair across her face and she gathered it back with both hands, exclaiming, "I'd best go below and braid this, Captain. Will you tell Sean—"

"You won't be braiding your hair. I forbid it."

"Pardon?"

His blue eyes twinkled. "You're aboard my ship now, and you'll do as I say. And I say I like your hair loose around your shoulders, so that's how you'll wear it if you know what's good for you."

Polly giggled. "That's how Papa is on the *Rigger*, Erica. Sometimes on the island, Grandma gives the orders—"

"Her? Give the orders on *my* island?" he roared. "That's mutiny, girl."

The child giggled again. "And sometimes, it's Belle who tells us what to do. But here, it's always Papa."

Erica laughed lightly. "I'll try to remember that. Do you have any other orders for me, Captain McCullum?"

"Aye." He nodded. "Watch after this little brat. The sea's in a feisty state today, and I don't want anyone washing overboard. Especially not you, my lady."

Erica smiled, warming to the game. "We'll try to behave ourselves, sir."

"One more thing," he announced, grabbing her by the waist and pulling her so that her ear was next to his mouth. Then he whispered playfully, "Cooperate with me, and your captivity will be pleasant for both of us."

"Pardon?"

He shrugged and released her. "You can enjoy our time until the ransom is paid, or you can resist. Either way, I have plans for you tonight."

"The ransom? Oh!" She flushed nervously. "I didn't realize you were teasing."

"I'm not." His gaze roved over her with exaggerated admiration. "Enjoy the hospitality of the *Moon Rigger*. My crew has a bloodthirsty reputation, but we know how to treat a lady, especially one as pretty as yourself."

"He's pretending to be a pirate. It's a game," Polly explained. "He told me all about it this morning. He's the leader, and I'm an orphan he rescued from a whale, and you're a princess. A king is going to pay a big ransom if we return you safely."

"I see." Erica eyed Daniel coolly. "What a clever idea. Unfortunately, I've decided to stop playing games."

"You'll play this one," he assured her confidently. "Or you'll walk the plank."

She tried to scowl, but a smile tugged at the corner of

her mouth instead. He was obviously trying to cheer her up, so why not play along with him? It would help keep her mind off of Jack, and Polly was clearly enjoying it. And he couldn't possibly be expecting her to welcome any amorous advances, despite his impish reference to "plans for tonight." His pretense at being a rogue aside, she knew he had true sympathy and respect for her precarious situation with Jack. The last thing he'd want to do was cause her further grief where such matters were concerned.

Sean appeared at that moment, with fragrant tea and hard, sweet biscuits, which he served to her in the chart room off the quarterdeck. It was a wonderful place, paneled in lustrous mahogany, with comfortable leather chairs and a huge, multidrawered table bolted to the floor. A tall cabinet against one wall housed a profusion of instruments behind clear glass doors, and a small footlocker, also bolted into place, was filled with pens, brushes, pads, and books, all of which enabled Polly to continue with her lessons when she traveled with her father.

"I can't remember a nicer room, Sean," she said with a sigh. "Abby wasn't exaggerating your talent."

He flushed with pride. "The captain told me what he wanted. All I did was build it. But I agree, it's a fine spot. My favorite on the schooner."

"Mine, too."

"You haven't seen Papa's quarters yet," Polly interrupted. "You'll like that best, Erica. It has a big, *big* bed."

Erica blushed at the incendiary suggestion.

"I can't imagine I'll have occasion to see it." When Sean chuckled, she eyed him sternly. "That's enough."

"I was just thinking about—"

"I know what you were thinking about, and I'd appreciate your not mentioning it again."

"And you won't mention Betsy?"

"You and the captain, always bargaining," she said with a laugh. "Fine, I won't mention her."

"Who's Betsy?" Polly demanded.

"My mother," Sean replied evenly.

The girl seemed unconvinced and turned to Erica for confirmation, but she only smiled and asked, "Would you like to take me on a tour of the ship? I imagine you could identify almost every part and sail."

"Not just almost," the child assured her. "I know every inch of her, good as Papa and Uncle Sean."

"Well, then, I'm in for a treat, aren't I? Shall we return these dishes to the galley first?"

"The galley first," Polly agreed. "And Papa's room last, 'cause you should always save the best for last. Or at least, that's what Papa says."

Ignoring Sean's laughter, Erica gathered up the tea tray and followed the child out onto the deck.

Her only thought at the start of the day had been to salvage a pleasant moment or two despite her troubles with Jack Ryerson, but she soon realized that this day needed no salvaging—it was a pure delight, despite the nasty weather. Polly proved to be an excellent tour guide and teacher; Sean seemed obsessed with keeping Erica well-fed and entertained; the crew flattered her with their unspoken compliments as they moved about their business, taking care to position themselves to have their passenger in view whenever possible; and Captain Daniel McCullum persisted in his role as pirate leader, eyeing her lasciviously from a distance, or whispering suggestively whenever she ventured close.

As much as she enjoyed the attention, she was even more enchanted when she'd catch the men off their guard,

going about the business of taming the sea. They climbed
the ratlines, hoisted and furled the sails, and flexed their
muscles in an endless display of brawny prowess that
teased at Erica's imagination despite her vow to stop
engaging in such dangerous reveries. She had McCullum
to blame for it, she knew. Him and his pirate fantasy.
And his looking so much the part . . .

By the time Polly ushered her into the captain's quarters,
Erica herself was completely absorbed in McCullum's
little game, to the point where she saw the rich, dark
wood and gleaming brass through the eyes of a captured
princess who, despite her valiant efforts, could not resist
the potent sexual allure of the rogue who had kidnapped
her. This was the place, she fantasized playfully, where
he would make an attempt on her virtue, putting her lofty
morals, her royal breeding, and her grandiose future to
the test.

Daniel's stateroom was twice the size of any other
compartment on the schooner, accommodating an over-
sized bed, handsomely carved chests, and a chess table,
along with rows of books behind locked glass doors. The
chests, Erica assured herself, were filled with treasure,
plundered from other vessels by the crew. And the books
were a tribute to the leader's cunning—he studied tactics
and cultures to develop the strategies necessary to outwit
even the most talented opponent. But the ultimate strategy
was the simplest—the crew had a reputation for being
bloodthirsty, did they not? And from the gleam of the
swords fastened to the wall over Daniel's bed, she decided
they had earned it.

"So? I see you're as anxious as I am, wench."

She spun toward his growl, and blushed at the mischievous look in his eye. "Really, Captain McCullum, that's
enough." She inclined her head in Polly's direction as a
further warning. "Behave yourself."

Daniel turned to his daughter. "Your uncle's going to let you have a go at the wheel if you're there by the time he counts to ten."

"Oh!" Without a backward glance or word to Erica, the girl bolted out of the stateroom.

"Well, that was rather crass."

"Don't take that tone with me," Daniel warned, closing the door as he spoke. "You may be a princess where you come from, but here, I reign supreme."

"This game has grown tiresome— Oh!" She tried to wriggle away as he backed her cheerfully against the door. "Daniel McCullum, behave yourself."

"This was your idea," he reminded her. "And it's a fine one. Just what we both need."

"Why do *you* need it?" she demanded, then she flushed and added, "You're suggesting I need it because of Jack's letter, but why—"

"I'm a man, and you've been teasing me for three days straight, and so," he grinned wickedly, "I need it."

"I didn't mean to tease."

"It's your nature, and I'm not complaining about it, believe me. It's your finest quality, and I'm grateful to your grandmother for passing it along to you."

"I'm an engaged woman."

"My favorite kind," he said with a chuckle. "I've decided to dedicate myself to providing every engaged woman I can find with one last chance for variety before she ties the knot."

Erica laughed despite herself. "Polly could come back at any moment."

"Then stop wasting precious time," he suggested in the gravelly voice she had come to adore. "All I'm asking for is a kiss."

"One kiss?" She felt herself weaken easily. "I suppose

that's the least I can do, after teasing you for three days straight.''

Daniel grinned triumphantly and leaned down to nibble at her neck, while his fingers moved to the tiny pearl buttons on her blouse. She wanted to stop him, but a familiar paralysis had come over her. She couldn't protest, and she couldn't move away, yet she could feel him, even in places where he was not yet touching her.

Then his hand slipped inside her blouse, scooping her breast from under her silky camisole. His lips came down to greet the nipple, as they'd done on the beach, only this time, without sturdy brown cotton to impede him, he was able to tease and taste with his rough tongue, then pull gently at the peak with his teeth before burying his face against her bosom and nuzzling her with rapacious thoroughness.

Erica moaned as one sensation after another assaulted her, dragging her into a new and more dangerous fantasy—a world without Jack Ryerson. A world of being petted and aroused and adored. A forbidden world, yet for the moment, the only one in which she could feel valuable. And so she buried her face in his thick black hair and whispered, ''Daniel?''

He raised his head and demanded, ''What do you want?''

''I want you to kiss me. On my mouth.''

His blazing eyes would not accept her answer. ''Tell me the truth.''

''I want you to kiss me. I want—'' She gulped and admitted, ''You said there were ways.''

''Ways to do what?''

''To do what you want, and I'd still be a virgin.''

''And that's what you want?''

''Yes, Captain.'' She sighed, curling her arms around his neck. ''That's what I want.''

"More than anything?"

"Yes."

"Well, it'll have to wait until tonight. Polly won't be gone long." His smile was sympathetic. "For now, all I can do is kiss you. How does that sound?"

"Glorious," she admitted sheepishly, raising herself onto her tiptoes and brushing her lips across his. He caressed her cheek gently, then slipped his hand behind her neck and lowered his mouth down to hers.

Her lips parted eagerly, allowing his tongue to plunder and explore, while her own tongue played with him, alive with curiosity and hungry to please him the way he so easily and completely pleased her.

Then he pulled away and bowed deeply, the perfect pirate rogue. "Until tonight, my lady."

When Erica stepped aside and curtseyed, his gaze lingered for a moment on her still-bared breast, then he threw open the door to the stateroom and strode away without another word.

CHAPTER SEVEN

Despite the lack of a full-length mirror in Erica's tiny stateroom, she knew exactly how she looked as she meticulously dressed for dinner in the captain's quarters—the pirate captain, no less. She had decided to dress the part of the captive princess, wearing a lavish black and gold gown she'd purchased months earlier, but had never worn. She had been waiting for just the right moment in which to dazzle Jack Ryerson with it, and had been certain enough that that moment would come in the Caribbean to have dedicated her largest traveling bag to transporting the gown and its accessories.

It would be wasted on Jack, she now knew. He might say and do all the appropriate things, but would he be mesmerized, or aroused, or reckless? No, of course not. He might even be secretly disdainful of the flight of fancy that had prompted the purchase of so ostentatious a garment.

And so she would wear it for Captain Daniel McCullum,

knowing that he would appreciate it. Knowing that he would remember this evening, despite the many women he'd enjoyed. When he visualized her, in days and weeks to come, Erica wanted to look ravishing and desirable and worthy of a king's ransom.

The black silk bodice of the gown was lightly quilted, and cut so as to define and emphasize her bosom. The skirts, like the sleeves, were black taffeta, with an infinite number of golden threads pulled through the fabric in a sumptuously random pattern. A heavy gold chain dangled provocatively between her breasts, while a band of gold embedded with diamonds—an inheritance from her feisty grandmother—adorned her hand. Two lovely combs of gold and onyx, also gifts from her grandmother, would have completed the effect, but Erica remembered the pirate's command that she wear her hair loose, and so she tucked the combs back into her bag and settled for brushing her auburn locks to a blazing sheen.

Then she slipped her feet into delicate black satin dancing slippers, moistened her lips, and took a deep, calming breath. It was only dinner, after all. With Polly and Sean as chaperons. And for an hour or so at least, the mood would be light, and the chances for error few. And after that, when she erred, it would not be the first time. . . .

"Nor will it be the last," she counseled herself softly. "So go and have this night with him. It should have been Jack, perhaps, but it has fallen to Captain McCullum instead.

"After spending last night in tears, can you question whether this innocent transgression is right or wrong?

"You will return to Boston either way," she added philosophically. "So why not return with one glorious night to hold close to your heart forever? It should have been with Jack, yes. But Jack chose not to come. And so it is the captain, and you would be lying if you said that doesn't have its appeal. So . . ." She squared her shoulders, fluffed her skirts, and smiled with sheepish confidence as she stepped into the passageway.

Daniel leaned against the wall of his quarters and watched as the galley boy put the final touches on the handsomely appointed dinner table. Starched linens of pure white, intricately patterned silverware, delicate blue and white porcelain plates, shimmering crystal goblets—the finest the *Moon Rigger* had to offer. Even the weather had chosen to cooperate, and so, while there was a gentle roll to the schooner, and a soft whistle of wind in the rigging, there was no indication that the captain might be called away at an inopportune moment, and that was important tonight in a way it hadn't been important for years.

"Am I pretty, Papa?" Polly asked.

He turned toward the bed, where his daughter had been playing with a small assortment of toys, and was amazed to see that she'd been brushing her short black curls with a silver hairbrush. And she was staring at her reflection in a silver hand mirror! For the first time, he realized she was wearing a dress rather than the breeches and rough muslin shirt she usually sported, especially aboard the schooner.

And she did look pretty. Like Lilli, only without the fair hair and sky-blue eyes. Or the pale complexion. Polly's hair was black as coal; her cheeks ruddy; her eyes a rich ocean blue—all like her father. But she had Lilli's smile, and that was a splendid asset for any young woman.

"You're a beauty," he assured her, moving to sit on the edge of the bunk. "Where did you get these things?"

"From Erica. She's had them since she was little, but now they're mine. She says my hair will be as long as hers one day if I brush it one hundred strokes every night. But I want it to grow faster, so I'm brushing it two hundred times.''

He liked the glint of pride in her eyes, so like the glow he'd seen on the twins' faces when they'd been allowed to swim for the first time. All of it was Erica's doing. Bringing out the best in each of them. Except in Daniel, of course. In him, she was bringing out the rogue—the man who would take advantage of an innocent virgin's hurt feelings and parlay them into a tryst that might endanger her future with the man she loved.

He heard the door open behind him, and knew from the sound of rustling skirts that she had entered. He also knew that if he turned around, he'd weaken. She was a beautiful girl, after all. But someone else's girl.

''You *are* a princess!'' Polly was clapping her hands in delight. ''Oh, Papa! Look at Erica! She's playing the pirate game again!''

The galley boy was staring, much in the same way Sean had stared two days earlier when he'd first glimpsed the lovely visitor. Daniel could almost see the reflection of his guest's beauty in the poor lad's eyes. But Daniel was not a lad. He was a man—a healthy, experienced man of means who could easily find another pretty girl in the next port. This particular girl was spoken for, and more importantly, she was deserving of his respect, for the sizable contribution she'd already made to his predictable existence.

And so, as he shrugged to his feet and turned toward her, he vowed to behave himself, no matter how tempting she might be.

Then he saw her, and grinned in defeat.

''Good evening, Captain.'' She curtseyed shyly. ''I hope I didn't keep you waiting.''

His gaze traveled over her, taking in the provocative

neckline and treasure-laced skirts of the outrageous gown. And her hair, worn just as he had commanded, in lustrous, seductive waves over her shoulders and down her back. And the look in her eyes! Curiosity and anticipation, laced with desire so palpable he could restrain himself only because of the presence of his daughter.

Striding to within inches of her, he complained gruffly, "You bring out the worst in me, wench."

"I was hoping my appearance might please you, sir," she chided playfully. "Are you going to make me walk the plank? Or are your plans for me even more dangerous?"

Daniel sucked in a deep breath, then turned to Polly and tried for a normal tone. "Go and see what's keeping your uncle."

The child jumped to the floor. "I'll be quick!"

"Not too quick," he murmured. As soon as she'd dashed by them and out into the passageway, Daniel fixed the galley boy with an ominous glare. "Get out."

"Aye, Captain." The lad edged past him cautiously, as though fearing for his life. Still, when he reached the door, he dared to nod at Erica and gasp, "It's been a pleasure, miss," before bolting out of sight.

"Come here," Daniel instructed, reaching for her and kicking the door closed in one smooth, greedy motion.

But she jumped clear of his grasp, protesting, "Really, Captain! You mustn't."

"You shouldn't have worn that dress," he informed her with a grin. "There won't be any dinner now until I've had my fill of *you*."

Erica laughed with delight. "Behave yourself, Daniel McCullum. Do you really like my dress?"

"I'll like it better when it's off you—"

"Off me?" she gasped. "Are you saying you're planning to disrobe me?"

Daniel glared in confounded annoyance at the true distress in her voice. Hadn't she suggested this seduction herself? Yet she seemed completely stunned at the thought he intended to go through with it!

The pattern was growing more familiar by the minute. And as usual, he wasn't sure whom she was disappointing more completely, herself or her would-be lover. In any case, it appeared his own dilemma—whether to behave as a gentleman or as a rogue—had been an academic one all along.

Erica had flushed to a fiery crimson. "Don't be angry, Captain. I didn't know— Oh, dear." She grimaced in apology at the sound of knocking on the door. "It's Sean and Polly. Please behave, won't you? We'll have more than enough chance to discuss this after the meal is over."

"There's nothing to discuss," he assured her between gritted teeth. Then he grasped the door firmly by the handle, flung it open and announced dryly, "Join us. Erica promises to be as entertaining as ever tonight, and the cook made good use of those chickens we bought in Havana. What more can any man ask?"

Erica was miserable during dinner, knowing that somehow she had angered the captain with her ignorance, which he had mistaken as resistance, or perhaps even as manipulation. But for once she hadn't been playing a game. She had honestly been confused at the thought he might expect her to completely undress. For reasons that now seemed foolish, she had expected him to enjoy ravaging her *in* this scintillatingly beautiful garment. Had she suspected otherwise, she could have worn more provocative undergarments, or at least could have explained to him, calmly and sweetly, that she hadn't brought much in the way of romantic attire, having expected the dress, and the moonlit beaches, to be enough to move Jack Ryerson to ecstasy.

She had wanted the captain to admire her during the meal, but it was Sean who continually praised her, with both his attitude and his words. McCullum simply scowled and made remarks that ranged from vaguely sarcastic to strangely self-mocking. And it didn't help that he was handsomer than ever this evening. He had dressed the part of the pirate, in his best black breeches and boots, with a jet-black shirt that intensified the bronze of his cheekbones and the dark richness of his thick, shaggy hair. How she wished she had simply allowed him to carry her to the bed and disrobe her before dinner. He would have sent the other diners away, and by this time she would have found some way to satisfy him. And she had no doubt that he would have found equally effective ways to make this night all she'd dreamed it would be. Instead, they were barely speaking to one another!

By the time the meal was nearing an end, he had regained most of his usual cheer, and seemed almost paternalistic in his attitude toward Erica. Solicitous, as though she were a child who needed counsel and protection. Given the manner in which she was attired, she would have found his attitude insulting had she not apparently insulted him first. Still, it was maddening, and she could scarcely wait to be alone with him and interrogate him as to this baffling change of heart.

"I should be on deck," Sean announced reluctantly, wiping his mouth with a starched white napkin. "It's been a pleasure, Erica. Captain. And Miss McCullum?" he added playfully to Polly. "Shall I escort you to your quarters so that your father and his guest can visit for a while?"

"Will you tell me a story?"

Sean started to agree, but Daniel held up his hand to

Introducing Ballad,
A NEW LINE OF HISTORICAL ROMANCES

*A*s a lover of historical romance, you'll adore Ballad Romances. Written by today's most popular romance authors, every book in the Ballad line is not only an individual story, but part of a two to six book series as well. You can look forward to 4 new titles each month – each taking place at a different time and place in history.

But don't take our word for how wonderful these stories are! Accept our introductory shipment of 4 Ballad Romance novels – a $22.00 value – ABSOLUTELY FREE – and see for yourself!

*O*nce you've experienced your first 4 Ballad Romances, we're sure you'll want to continue receiving these wonderful historical romance novels each month – without ever having to leave your home – using our convenient and inexpensive home subscription service. Here's what you get for joining:

- *4 BRAND NEW Ballad Romances delivered to your door each month*

- *25% off the cover price of $5.50 with your home subscription.*

- *A FREE monthly newsletter filled with author interviews, book previews, special offers, and more!*

- *No risk or obligation…you're free to cancel whenever you wish… no questions asked.*

Passion-
Adventure-
Excitement-
Romance-
Ballad!

*T*o start your membership, simply complete and return the card provided. You'll receive your Introductory Shipment of 4 FREE Ballad Romances. Then, each month, as long as your account is in good standing, you will receive the 4 newest Ballad Romances. Each shipment will be yours to examine for 10 days. If you decide to keep the books, you'll pay the preferred home subscriber's price of $16.50 – a savings of 25% off the cover price! (plus $1.50 shipping & handling) If you want us to stop sending books, just say the word…it's that simple.

4 FREE BOOKS are waiting for you! Just mail in the certificate below!

BOOK CERTIFICATE

Get 4 Ballad Historical Romance Novels FREE!

Yes! Please send me 4 Ballad Romances ABSOLUTELY FREE! After my introductory shipment, I will receive 4 new Ballad Romances each month to preview FREE for 10 days (as long as my account is in good standing). If I decide to keep the books, I will pay the money-saving preferred publisher's price of $16.50 plus $1.50 shipping and handling. That's 25% off the cover price. I may return the shipment within 10 days and owe nothing, and I may cancel my subscription at any time. The 4 FREE books will be mine to keep in any case.

Name _____

Address _____ Apt. _____

City _____ State _____ Zip _____

Telephone (___) _____

Signature _____

(If under 18, parent or guardian must sign)

All orders subject to approval by Zebra Home Subscription Service.
Terms and prices subject to change. Offer valid only in the U.S.

DN021A

Passion...

Adventure...

Excitement...

Romance...

PLACE
STAMP
HERE

BALLAD ROMANCES
Zebra Home Subscription Service, Inc.
P.O. Box 5214
Clifton NJ 07015-5214

interrupt. "Your uncle has work to do. You'll have to settle for Erica or myself for your entertainment."

Erica felt her heart sink, and could barely manage an encouraging smile as she turned to the little girl and awaited her answer.

"I like your stories, Papa, but I know them all," Polly said gently. "So . . . Erica, please."

The captain turned to Erica, and she saw something unfamiliar in his vibrant blue eyes. Apology? Dismissal? Whatever it was, it had a sense of finality to it that warned her not to argue. Even if it hadn't, her pride would not have allowed her to show her disappointment, and so she didn't even bother to ask if she'd be seeing him again that evening. She simply smiled coolly, thanked him for the dinner, and grabbed Polly firmly by the hand. "Let's go then, shall we?"

Daniel watched the females leave his stateroom, then turned to his first mate, suspecting he was about to lambaste him for having treated Erica so coldly. But to his surprise, Sean assured him, "You did the right thing, Danny. I'm guessing it wasn't easy, either, her looking the way she did tonight."

The captain grimaced in agreement. "Have you ever seen a more beautiful girl?"

"Never. She's wasted on that bastard in Boston. But still," he added hastily, "she wants him, and we respect that."

"Respect." Daniel nodded. "I'm trying to remember how much of that she deserves. Her feelings are hurt, but she still claims to love Ryerson, so that's that."

"And even if she didn't love the other fellow, you did the right thing," Sean persisted. "You don't need a girl like that in your life, Danny. You've said yourself you'll never marry again—''

"Marry?" Daniel grinned at his friend. "Is that what's been worrying you? You give me too much credit, Sean. My intentions toward that girl have been many things, but never honorable."

"I know you better than you know yourself," the first mate observed dryly. "I saw it happen once before—''

"Erica's nothing like Lilli, in case you haven't noticed." Daniel shook his head, annoyed by the comparison. "Lilli needed me, for reasons we both know. With Erica, it's not that way at all. She's just fine without me, and me without her."

"All I'm saying is, you did the right thing, sending her away tonight. For both your sakes."

Daniel glared at the friend who was so quickly becoming a pest. "Are you still here?"

Sean chuckled. "Get some sleep, Danny. You've a few more nights of this ahead of you, and it's best you're rested up for it. You're ornery enough when you *aren't* resisting temptation."

Snuggled under her covers, Polly beamed up at Erica and declared, "I want to look just like you when I grow up. And I want a dress just like that one."

"I'll have one made for you myself," Erica said with a smile. "Although it's been something of a disappointment to me, I must admit."

"Why?"

"Hmm? Oh, dear, I don't know. I suppose I expected too much from it. There's a lesson in that, Polly. Just as they always say, it doesn't matter so much how you look, or how you dress. It's how you behave, and what's in your heart, that counts in the end."

"What's in *your* heart?"

"I don't know. I suppose that's what I should spend the next few days discovering. I should take advantage of the solitude. . . . Well, never mind that." She smiled apologetically. "What sort of story would you like to hear?"

"You're dressed like a princess, so that's what you should tell about."

Erica laughed lightly at the simplicity of the child's world. Much like Erica's own world would be if she had her way. Games, illusions, wishes . . .

The silence seemed to frustrate Polly, who demanded finally, "Don't you know any princess stories?"

"Hundreds. I'm trying to choose one."

"What about the one Papa was telling? About the pirate who kidnapped the princess. Do you know *that* one?"

Erica nodded. "I know it by heart, and it's just like I said before. There's a lesson in it, if we're wise enough to learn it. So close your eyes—" She kissed the little girl's cheek, and then began, "Once upon a time, when treasure ships and smugglers still sailed the waters of the Caribbean, a handsome pirate captain assembled a bloodthirsty crew and they began to plunder and loot every ship that dared come within one hundred miles of their base on La Creciente."

"The buccaneers!" Polly exclaimed.

"Exactly. They built their huts just where your house is now. It was a secret hiding place—the only place they could relax and feel safe."

"What about the princess?"

Erica sighed. "With the princess, things were quite different. From the time she was a little girl, younger than yourself, she was a bit *too* safe. Always protected. Never allowed to wander or explore. She had no idea what the world was like outside the walls of her father's castle, except when minstrels would come to dinner and tell tales of love affairs, and battles, and exotic lands far, far away.

"That's what the princess wanted—to see those far-away lands. And so, when her father told her he was sending her to a new world, across the ocean, to marry a prince, she was wildly happy. She pictured herself and the prince falling in love and having adventures together. But her royal sisters laughed at her—"

"Why?"

"Because they said she would just leave one castle for another. New walls, on the other side of the ocean, that would still keep her imprisoned. And so, when the time came for her to board the huge ship that would take her to the prince, she wasn't sure what to expect. But at least, she'd have this one adventure, on the high seas, and for that she was grateful."

"She liked to sail, just like me."

"Yes, Polly. She had that in common with you. Unfortunately, the guards on the ship made her stay below, in her stateroom, all day long. She had books to read, and delicious food to eat, and servants to wait on her, but nothing had really changed. Sometimes she would try to sneak up onto deck to see the stars, but her chaperon would scold her, and soon they even put a lock on the outside of her door."

"Oh, no!"

"She was lying on her bed one stormy afternoon, reading poetry, when she heard a thundering roar. Cannon fire, again and again! She jumped to her feet and tried the door, but it was still locked. Then, without warning, she heard a pistol fire, and the lock clanged to the floor, and the door burst open."

"Oh!" Polly's eyes were round and incredulous. "Was it the pirate captain?"

Erica nodded. "He had a pistol in one hand and a cutlass in the other, and the princess was sure he was going to kill her on the spot. She thought of all the times she'd complained about the guards and the walls, but now, she understood them, and she cursed herself for having ever wanted adventure. Then the pirate looked at her—" Erica took a deep breath, embarrassed by the husky edge that had crept into her voice.

"Did he hurt her?"

"No, Polly. He just looked at her—not like she was a princess, but like she was just a girl. One of a thousand girls he'd seen in his lifetime. He could see she was frightened, and if he had been a gentleman, he would have told her not to fear him, but he didn't."

"Why not?"

"I suppose he liked it a bit. It made him feel powerful to see her feeling so weak. But she wasn't as weak as he thought. She didn't cry, or even cringe away. She reminded herself that she was a princess, and he was a criminal, and so she stood proudly and refused to plead for her life."

"I like her."

"So do I." Erica smiled wistfully. "Then the pirate threw open the chests that stored her jewels and clothing, and stuffed the jewels into a bag. Then he threw the princess over his shoulder and carried her up onto the deck, where a horrid battle was taking place. Swords were clashing, and the guards and soldiers that were protecting the princess were being defeated before her very eyes. The pirate handed her over to one of his men, and that man carried her along a plank that led to the buccaneers' ship. The pirate captain stayed behind, and as the princess watched helplessly from the pirate ship, the captain single-handedly vanquished her guards."

Polly squirmed with excitement. "What if he kills her?"

"That's exactly what she was thinking." Erica nodded. "And so she prayed for a miracle. She prayed that the prince would come and rescue her."

"The prince!" Polly exulted. "I forgot about him. Did he come and save her?"

"Not exactly. But when the fighting was over, and the king's ship had been set on fire, the pirate captain allowed the surviving guards to set sail in a small boat, with a message for the prince. To send a ransom of a thousand pounds of gold for the princess, and she would be released, untouched and unharmed. Then the pirates took the princess and her jewels to La Creciente to wait for the ransom."

"And so the prince saved her, by sending the gold? It would be a better story if he came and fought the captain."

Erica nodded. "It's what she wanted, you can be sure of that. But kings and princes are practical men. They leave the adventure and recklessness to men like the pirate captain."

"So, she got saved and married the prince and lived in a castle again forever?"

"Yes, Polly."

"That's good." The little girl snuggled further against her pillow and began to drift to sleep, even as she asked, "Was she happy?"

"That's the strange part of the story," Erica murmured, more to herself than to the child. "I think she was happy, in her own way. But I think, as her life went on, her most treasured memory was the moment when the pirate broke down the door to her cabin and carried her away to his island. It was as though her life hadn't really begun until that moment. If she had missed that one, perfect adventure, none of the rest—her marriage, her children, her riches, her lavish parties—would have mattered. Because something would have been missing. . . ."

"Well, we can't have that, can we?" a voice growled from the doorway.

"Oh!" Erica's hand flew to her mouth too late to stifle the gasp. A quick glance at Polly confirmed that the child was sleeping soundly despite the interruption, and so Erica slipped off the edge of the bed onto her feet and smiled sheepishly toward Daniel. "How much of that silly story did you hear?"

"Come over here."

She studied him warily. "Why would I want to do that?"

"I suppose you expect me to carry you?"

"Captain—oh!" She tried to wriggle free as his huge hands imprisoned her, hoisting her over his shoulder with maddening ease. "Daniel McCullum!" she wailed, her voice soft for the child's sake, but strident nonetheless. "Put me down this instant!"

But she knew he wouldn't comply. For reasons that were both confusing and thrilling, he had become the pirate captain again, and so, as he strode from the child's stateroom, down the passageway toward his own, she struggled only because it was part of her role.

Still, when he threw her onto the bed and towered over her, his blue eyes blazing with undisguised lust, she informed him haughtily, "Don't forget yourself, Daniel McCullum. There are limits to what I'll allow—"

"I have limits too," he countered cheerfully. "Limits to my patience, and you've reached them."

Erica flushed with anticipation. "I know that, Captain. I want to cooperate, only first, there's something I want to explain."

"Erica—"

"Hush." She knelt and sandwiched his face between her hands. "I want to apologize for the way I'm dressed."

"Huh?"

"If I'd known you wanted to undress me, I would have worn beautiful undergarments. I wasn't resisting you earlier, Captain. I just didn't want to disappoint you."

He eyed her in amused frustration. "You thought I'd be disappointed because your undergarments aren't beautiful?"

"It's worse than that," Erica sighed. "I'm not wearing any at all. This gown has its own—"

"You're wearing nothing under it?" He burst into laughter. "*That's* the grand disappointment? Are you listening to yourself, girl?" He shoved her gently back onto the bed and stretched out over her, grinning broadly. "Have I mentioned that you fascinate me?"

"I don't appreciate being laughed at," she complained, but her voice was too husky to communicate anything other than arousal, and so she added lamely, "Couldn't you at least try to be romantic about this?"

"You'll have your romance with the prince," he teased. "With me, you'll have to settle for passion." Then he lowered his mouth to hers and kissed her, gently at first, and then with a hunger that made her shiver from head to toe.

One arm encircled her, embracing and imprisoning, while his free hand traveled, exploring her bodice and then moving lower, gathering handfuls of fabric until her skirts were high on her legs. Erica's own hands were laced in his shaggy hair, pulling his mouth hard against her own so that she could kiss him greedily, propelled by the desire his mouth and hand were awakening. Then his rough fingers found the smooth skin of her thighs, and she gasped as he stroked her, his touch inching upward to a hitherto untouched place that was already throbbing in welcome.

"Daniel," she moaned. "Be careful."

"This is what you want," he reassured her, his voice thick with desire. "This is what you've wanted for a long time." Then he dared to touch her with a gentleness that made her instantly arch for more.

"There," he chuckled fondly. "Now you understand."

"No," she whispered in throaty disbelief. "I don't. I don't understand what you're doing to me. Daniel, this can't be enough. You said there were ways— Oh!" She arched again as his finger plunged into the wet, warm folds that had ached to be entered. "Oh, no . . ."

She wanted to think of Jack, for at least one last, loyal second, but all she could think was that she needed more, and she needed it quickly. Her loins were on fire, and Daniel's touch, deliciously thorough and crude, was only making it worse! And the bodice of the dress was suffocating her! The world was going mad, and with no thought to the consequences other than survival, Erica grasped at the huge bulge had been pumping insistently against her hip.

"Erica," Daniel groaned, and in that moment, she knew that despite his experience and self-control, his state was as mindless and glorious as her own. He had been seeing to her needs, and unselfishly neglecting his own, when the answer to both their predicaments was so painfully, sinfully obvious.

Too fevered to feel shame, she quickly worked the buttons that imprisoned him, and his throbbing member sprang hard into her hand, thrilling her for reasons beyond her ability to understand. She only knew she needed to please him this way, and every other way possible, and so she stroked him adoringly, enjoying his shocked expression for a moment before returning her mouth to his for a bold, exuberant kiss.

With each stroke, she imagined him inside her, until she felt almost furious at him for denying her. She could barely remember why she had wanted to preserve her virginity, but those ''limits'' were ravaging them both, and if they hoped to survive with their sanity intact, she had to convince him to transcend them. Moving her lips to his ear, she whispered, ''Do it now, Daniel,'' then grasped his member firmly and urged it between her thighs.

''Erica—''

''Don't argue with me,'' she pleaded. ''I never argue, remember? Just do this for me. With me. In me. Before I scream and lose my mind.''

''There are ways—''

''I don't want ways! I want this!''

He pulsed against her for a moment, as though weighing his options while sheepishly enjoying himself, then both his hands were between her thighs, spreading her legs wide apart, while his gaze locked with hers, seeking final, irrevocable confirmation. And he must have seen what he needed to see, because his hard, pulsating shaft was suddenly there, where his fingers had been, and he was thrusting, cautiously, but with no sign of doubt. Then his mouth crushed down onto hers and he thrust again, hard and hungry, plunging through her maidenhood with a sure, obliterating confidence so awe-inspiring that she could only guess there might have been pain.

''Erica?''

''I like it,'' she assured him shyly, surprised by the simple fact that they were joined together so intimately, and confused that the mindless throbbing of her loins seemed to have diminished. It was a beautiful, calm moment, a world apart from the deliverance she had expected, and so she asked hesitantly, "Is there more?"

He chuckled and nodded. "What's done is done, so we'll just enjoy ourselves now. If you want anything, just ask."

Erica moistened her lips, then wriggled a bit, to see how he felt, and the throbbing began anew. Delighted, she smiled up at Daniel, then flushed with embarrassment at the grin on his face. It was as though he knew how thoroughly she needed him now, and while she suspected it was mutual, she also knew he was in control, and so she decided to abandon herself to him completely. Wrapping her legs around him, she began to pulse, and to her amazed delight, it clearly startled and seduced him into a frenzy of long, greedy thrusts.

Need came rushing back, engulfing her loins, and she gyrated against him, learning quickly that for every motion either of them made, each was greeted with a decadent reward. She was sure that if she could only gain control of her erratic breathing, Daniel could help her find a steady pace, so that they could do this forever— wringing every ounce of pleasure from every movement until they expired in absolute ecstasy in one another's arms. Then, without warning, she was gripped by spasms of arousal so pure and strong they made her clutch frantically at his neck and wail his name again and again in hedonistic appreciation. When she arched against Daniel in one final, grateful paroxysm, it seemed as though he'd been waiting for just this signal, and his thrusts grew infinitely more rapid and demanding. Then, to her dismay, he withdrew from her, pumping for a final string of seconds against her abdomen, then groaning aloud as his own release came in warm, sharp spurts.

He gathered her against his chest then, and she could plainly hear the thundering of his heart. If she had needed any further evidence of his power and authority, this was it. Beside it, she felt insignificant, yet she knew in her own way, she had conquered him, for this one perfect night, and so she cuddled happily against him, needing nothing else.

"So?" he asked finally. "Are you angry with me?"

"No. Not at all."

"Good." He buried his face in her hair. "You'll have regrets later, I know. But if it means anything, that was something not to be missed."

Erica smiled. "I appreciate what you did, at the end. I hope it didn't ruin it for you."

Daniel chuckled. "It was fine. I couldn't very well send you back to Ryerson with a little McCullum in your belly, could I?"

"I suppose not. I wish I could have felt it though."

He pushed her back enough to stare into her eyes. "You're a difficult woman to satisfy, Miss Lane."

She laughed sheepishly. "I wasn't complaining. Just curious, as always. Do you always do it that way?"

"If I'd always done it, Lilli would still be alive. I mastered it after Polly was born, swearing I'd never plant a baby in her poor body again. But she wanted one, so she found ways to subvert my efforts."

Erica felt a surge of affection at the naive assumption. "Are you sure it was a baby she wanted?"

"Pardon?"

"I'll bet she just wanted to feel it, too."

He seemed shocked, then a shaky smile spread over his features. "That's an interesting theory. I'm not sure Lilli ever had your appetite for it, though."

"Or she didn't show it?" Erica sighed. "Like Abby, I suppose."

"What?"

She grinned mischievously. "Her 'litany of complaints'

about the island? No doctors, no parties, no playmates for the children. Don't you suppose she misses all *this* just a bit too?'' She laughed when he again seemed shocked. ''The only difference between Abby and my grandmother is an accident of birth. Grandmother was born and raised in France, where they understand these things.''

He stroked her cheek with the back of his hand. ''No regrets then? Other than my not coming inside you?''

She blushed. ''I wasn't complaining about that. But I do have one regret. I should have listened to you about undressing. I thought I was going to asphyxiate in this gown! It was so tight I couldn't breathe, and we grew so warm so quickly. You should have insisted.''

''I insist now,'' he replied quietly, turning her so that he could work the row of polished black buttons that had been so difficult for her to fasten alone in her stateroom. In contrast, Daniel made short work of them, then helped her slide the gown off her shoulders, baring her small, firm breasts. ''You're so beautiful,'' he murmured, nipping gently at first one peak, then the other.

''Mmm, you definitely should have insisted earlier.'' She sighed, relaxing back into the bed. ''That feels heavenly.''

He pulled at the gown until it was past her hips, then he gathered it into a ball and threw it across the room. ''So much for that.'' Taking off his shirt, he used it to wipe away the traces of himself that had been smeared across her belly. ''I've never seen a more beautiful woman, Erica. I almost despise myself for ruining you.''

''Almost?'' She pretended to glare. ''Except instead, you're insufferably proud?''

He grinned and nodded. ''When you've had a chance to rest, we could do it again, if you're willing.''

She wanted nothing more than to do just that—to fall

asleep in his arms, and wake up to more lovemaking—but she knew it would be a dangerous step in a direction she could not bear to go. For all that she adored being in this man's life and in his bed, she wanted to be a wife, not a mistress. And Daniel McCullum, to his credit, had made it clear he wasn't offering marriage, to Erica or to anyone else.

"I'm sorry, Captain, but it just wouldn't be proper for me to spend the whole night here." She eyed him sternly, warning against any teasing. "I have my reputation, remember. Undeserved though it may be."

"You're worried Ryerson will hear about this from one of us?" Daniel frowned. "It's more likely he'll notice on your wedding night that someone else has had the best of you."

"I've told you how inattentive he is," Erica drawled. "I doubt he'd notice at all."

"Well then, I'm doubly glad you chose me for the honor. I can't remember ever noticing anything quite so fully in my life." Then he eyed her sternly. "Remember my advice, though. Never tell him about this. Tell him what he wants to hear."

"That I was miserable and lonely the entire time? That I've learned my lesson and will never play games or seek romance again? *That's* what he wants to hear, isn't it?" She bristled at the thought, then gathered the blanket up tightly around herself and sighed. "I have so much to think about, Captain. I really must go back to my room now, and get a good night's rest."

"Whatever you want." He crossed the room to a foot-locker and pulled out a fresh white shirt. "Come here."

She slid out of the bed and stood before him, allowing him to stare for a long moment at her body—naked, except for the gold chain—before she slipped her arms into the wide sleeves of the garment. "This is much more comfortable than that silly dress."

"They both suit you."

She watched as he retrieved his breeches and pulled them back onto his lean, muscled legs. "You're going back on deck?"

"For a while."

Stepping into him, she raised up onto her tiptoes and kissed his cheek. "Don't you dare forget me, Daniel McCullum."

"That's not likely." He rested his hands on her hips. "You're saying we won't be doing this again? It'll take a week at least to reach Salem in this weather—"

"I have so much thinking to do. I can't imagine having time for anything else."

He nodded briskly and dropped his hands to his sides. "That's how it'll be then. Let us know what you need. We'll do our best to make the voyage a good one."

"Thank you, Captain." She stooped to pick up her gown, then smiled sheepishly and hurried out of the stateroom and down the passageway to her own quarters.

My dear Mr. Braddock,

It's so odd that I find myself writing to you of all people tonight, but there's no one else I can turn to for advice, and you have proven to me, through your reputation and our correspondence, that you have wonderful instincts in matters of the heart.

Of course, you don't even know we've corresponded, and so first I must introduce myself. I am the woman who wrote the letter from Boston governess Sarah Gibson. You matched her with a sea captain named Daniel McCullum, but in my heart I have no doubt that you intended him for me. You must have seen so much in my letter, and you must have guessed

*that the captain and I could please one another, and
you were so right. I have just spent the most blissful
night in his arms, and I have you to thank for it.*

*Unfortunately, the captain has no need of a wife.
His mother-in-law was well-meaning but mistaken
in that belief. In many ways, that makes my dilemma
simpler, my dilemma being whether I should break
off my engagement with my fiancé, whom I left
behind in Boston in order to travel to the Caribbean
and meet the captain, to see if he was well-suited
to Sarah. He was not, as I've indicated above.*

*My question is a simple one. Is it possible that I
really do love Jack, even though I don't miss him
one whit and I've given myself to another man
despite our engagement? I suppose you'd say I just
answered my own question, but there was a time I
thought I loved Jack madly. And Captain McCullum
is so dashing and charismatic and tender and com-
manding that I imagine any girl might momentarily
stray were he to pay attention to her. And it didn't
help matters that Jack has been neglecting me lately.
I was a rather easy conquest, especially given my
unladylike craving for an adventure or two before
I settle down.*

*Does it sound as though I regret the liaison with
the captain? Nothing could be further from the truth.*

Erica sighed and put aside the letter, then snuggled into
her bunk and smiled at the truth of this last assertion. If
she had regrets, they were over what she *hadn't* done,
not what she had. She hadn't taken the time to memorize
the sea captain's lean, powerful, naked form. She hadn't
satisfied her fantasy of burying her breasts in the rough
hair of his chest. She hadn't touched him or kissed him
in any of a dozen or so places he might have enjoyed. She

hadn't even kissed his manhood, and given the amount of pleasure it had given her that seemed a complete lapse of etiquette on her part!

She had begun the letter to Russell Braddock as a way of sorting out her thoughts, and she intended to finish it, too. If she hadn't resolved her uncertainty over Jack by the time they arrived in Salem, she might even consider sending it! If her mother hadn't been thousands of miles away, she could have sought counsel from her, but as it stood, there was no one among her friends who might understand this particular quandary.

Ironically, the only other person who might have offered good advice was Daniel McCullum, and she didn't dare tell him she was having doubts about Jack. He might feel responsible, and that certainly wouldn't be fair. If her love affair with Jack had been a strong one, it could never have been breached, no matter how dashing a candidate tried. It was either a weak love—but one perhaps worth strengthening and saving—or it wasn't love at all. In the end, only Erica herself could decide which it was. She only hoped she could make that decision before the *Moon Rigger* sailed into the harbor at Salem.

CHAPTER EIGHT

"Erica? Are you going to sleep all day?" Polly whispered impatiently as she nudged Erica's shoulder through the thick covers. "Aren't you hungry at least? Uncle Sean says you should eat before the sea gets any rougher, or you won't be able to hold it down at all."

Refusing to open her eyes, Erica nestled herself more fully into the narrow bunk of the guest quarters. "What time is it? It's still dark outside, Polly."

"It's almost noon. It's only dark because of the storm."

"Gracious." Erica gathered Daniel's white shirt about herself before pushing back the covers enough to sit up and rub her eyes. The rolling motion of the schooner had been rocking her so soothingly, it might have kept her asleep for the whole day, she realized sheepishly. Of course, the prior evening's romantic escapade had undoubtedly contributed to her deep, satisfied slumber, and as the memory of those hours came back to her, she sighed with confused longing. If only Captain McCullum had come to wake her. . . .

But hadn't she instructed him clearly not to come? And so he was being a gentleman, as always. And perhaps he was a bit relieved also. After all, her allure was based in part on her unavailability, was it not? Engaged women—his new favorites. She giggled inwardly at the silly reference, then remembered Polly and smiled. "It can't be much of a storm. I didn't even hear any thunder."

"You didn't?" The girl eyed her in disbelief. "It thundered all night! Didn't you hear Papa shouting to the men?"

"Your father was up all night? Oh, dear."

"All hands were up. Even me, except Papa kept sending me back to bed."

"You all must be exhausted. Perhaps, when the storm is done, you can just roll up all the sails for a while, and the whole crew can get some sleep."

Polly laughed at the suggestion. "When the storm is past, we'll be unfurling the sails, not furling them. Did you think we were sailing in all that weather? We'd be at the bottom of the sea by now!"

"I bow to your experience, Miss Captain." Erica smiled. "What will happen now?"

"Papa and Uncle Sean are arguing over what to do. Uncle Sean says we should try to head for shore while there's a break. But Papa says we'll just ride it out, same as always."

"I see." She moistened her lips, then asked as casually as possible, "What is your father's mood today? Does he seem grouchy? I mean, from lack of sleep?"

The little girl shook her head. "It's Uncle Sean who's in a mood. Usually, it's the other way round, but Papa's happy today."

Erica blushed with delight. "Isn't that nice? Will you

do me a favor, darling? Will you go and tell your uncle I'm famished? I'll just slip into something a bit warmer, and wash my face, then I'll join you in the chart room for tea, just as we did yesterday.''

"They won't want you on deck," Polly warned. "But if you go anyway, you should wear one of Papa's coats. And don't worry about your face. The rain will wash it clean.''

Erica laughed. "I hope the galley boy doesn't have that attitude. I was going to ask him to draw a bath for me when there's a lull in the storm.''

Polly grimaced at the notion, but admitted, "He'll do whatever you want. The crew has been teasing him about that, but he doesn't care. I guess he liked the way you looked in your princess dress," she added mischievously.

"That should be a lesson to you, for when you're the captain of your own ship.'' Erica smiled, rumpling the child's hair fondly. "I see you've been putting that new brush to good use. Your hair feels so soft and satiny.''

"Papa said so too.'' The child bit her lip before admitting, "If I can be a lady and still be a captain, that's what I want to be.''

"Does that mean no more swimming out to the schooner?''

Polly nodded. "Papa asked me not to do it too. So I'll stop. But I can still swim sometimes, can't I?''

"Gracious, yes! I'll have my dressmaker design something for you to wear—something practical but modest— and you can swim to your heart's content.''

"And will she make something for you, too? So you can swim with me and the boys when you come for visits?''

"Visits?'' She touched the child's cheek in apology. "I imagine most of the visiting will be done in Salem. My father used to take me to a beautiful beach in Newport when I was a little girl. You and I will go there one day soon. How does that sound? I'll have my friend Jack take us—'' She broke off, distressed at hearing herself describe Jack Ryerson as a mere "friend." Was she so certain he was no longer her fiancé? Had her heart made that decision while she slept? If so, it was both presumptuous and premature. And Jack Ryerson, for all his faults, deserved better than that.

She reminded herself of the vow she'd made right before she drifted off to sleep—to wait until she had put a little time and distance between herself and her charismatic seafaring lover before she made any decisions about Jack. Her fiancé couldn't compete with the passion and danger Daniel McCullum wielded so easily. Nor should he need to do so. Jack Ryerson never claimed to be anything other than what he was—a dependable, kindhearted, sometimes noble, young entrepreneur, devoted to his sisters and to Erica. When it came to choosing a husband, a girl could do much worse than he.

And there had been a time when she'd found delight and promise in his kisses, hadn't there? She no longer believed those kisses would erupt into mindless passion, as Captain McCullum's did so easily, but she also didn't doubt that lovemaking with Jack could be nice in its own way. The only question that remained was whether all of this admiration and appreciation was love, or something else. If it wasn't love, she would find a way to gently break it off, even though she admired the man. And if it *was* love, she would find a way to make up to him for her infidelity.

So, she didn't need Russell Braddock's advice after all. At least, not on the issue of Jack Ryerson. And on the issue of Daniel McCullum? She needed no advice in that regard either. She would be pleasant, and she would be grateful, and she would keep her distance as much as possible. She suspected the captain himself would be more than happy to do the same.

By the time Erica ventured out onto the deck, the crew was busy taking advantage of the much-heralded "lull" to mop, tighten, and inspect the *Rigger* from stem to stern. Standing at the foot of the main mast was the tall, lean figure of Captain McCullum, staring up at the rigging as though certain some dire yet invisible flaw lurked therein. Two crewmen had climbed the ratlines and were poised, waiting for their captain's instructions. When he sent one up to the platform, Erica gasped at the acrobatic feat required to keep one hand gripped to the line while hanging for an instant high in the air, almost perpendicular to the water, before scrambling onto the narrow foothold.

Once Daniel was satisfied with the state of the rigging, he gave the command to break out the topsails and, as Erica's eyes widened, the huge, billowing sheets of pure white sprang free in a breathtaking spread of canvas. In an instant, the *Rigger* was racing along, slicing through whitecaps that swelled at times to eight feet or more.

Mesmerized, Erica edged forward toward the bow, her gaze shifting across the horizon, noting the patches of pale, warm blue where the sun had succeeded in piercing the dense gray columns of cloud. Then a huge hand gripped her shoulder, spinning her around toward a familiar, gravelly voice that demanded, "Where do you think *you're* going?"

"Captain . . ." She raised her gaze to his, unsure of what she wanted to see. The proud grin—wide with the knowledge that he'd had "the best of her," as he called it? Sadness at the thought he wouldn't be having her again? Annoyance or anxiety, based on some perception that she had come looking for him, with a need to cling to him and make demands?

Instead, his expression was a mirror of her own confusion. Elation over seeing one another again, coupled with dread over having to acknowledge anew that whatever had happened had also ended.

"So?" he asked warily.

"So?" she replied, her cheeks flushing slightly.

It brought the grin finally to the surface, and Erica relaxed and smiled a bit herself. "I hear I slept through quite a storm."

"You had your reasons." He stroked her face with the tip of one finger. "Are you angry with me yet?"

"No, Captain. Not yet."

A sudden swell pitched the schooner high into the air, sending Erica hard against the captain, who steadied her with strong hands that remained on her waist even after she'd regained her footing. Startled and confused, Erica looked up at him intending to reprimand, or at least remind him, but instead she found herself silenced by the raw handsomeness of his rugged features.

He wanted to kiss her. She could see it in his eyes. Right here, in front of his crew, he wanted to sweep her off her feet and carry her back to his quarters for another round of pleasure. The only thing stopping him was a detail that might not even exist—her engagement to, and love for, Jack Ryerson. All she had to do was tell this sailor she had decided to break that off, and she would be in his arms in an instant.

Instead, she told him gently, "You should try to get some rest yourself, before the storm comes back."

"I'll go in a while." He hesitated, then asked casually, "Care to join me?"

She stammered only slightly as she reminded him, "As lovely as that sounds, Captain, I'm afraid it's impossible."

The muscles of his jaw tensed visibly, and she knew he was stopping himself from pursuing the subject, even though he undoubtedly suspected, as did she, that he might be able to change Erica's mind. To lure her into his stateroom on some pretense, then seduce her with tales of pirates and princesses. The thought that he could read all of that in her eyes—the longing, the weakness, the regret—embarrassed her, but she didn't look away. They both needed to go through this, one time. To seal their bargain, and their mutual resolve.

"Polly didn't sleep much last night, either," Daniel said finally as he released his grip on her waist. "Could you watch out for her today? She can be reckless, and the deck's slippery."

"I'll watch her," Erica said with a nod. "And I'll convince her to take a nap, too."

"Can't be done."

She smiled wistfully. "Now that she wants to be an attractive female as well as a sea captain, it can be done quite easily. I'll simply explain to her that sleep makes one more beautiful."

He stroked her face again. "All she needs to do is look at you to know that's the truth."

Then he motioned toward the galley boy, who was headed into the companionway with a large tray. "Go on now and eat, while the sea is quiet and the wind is steady."

"Quiet and steady?" Erica laughed lightly. "That must have been quite a storm I missed, if you consider this to be steady."

"Last night was only a warning. I expect we'll be hit by a beauty of a squall by late afternoon. That's why you should eat now. And try to stay in the cabin as much as possible today. There's a lot to be done, and the crew doesn't need a female underfoot—even a pretty one."

"Aye, Captain, I'll try to stay out of your way."

"I was only referring to my men," he corrected with a playful grin. "You can get in *my* way any time you please."

She smiled at the harmless flirtation—a means of balancing the yearning with the reality. It was almost as it had been before they'd made love—an engaged woman and a rogue. Or at least, two persons playing those roles.

"You won't even know I'm here, Captain," she assured him with a haughty, equally playful sniff. "I have less than a week to teach your daughter to be a lady, and I haven't written to my mother in ages. I imagine I'll be spending every waking hour in my room."

"Well, then ..." He turned his gaze skyward, inspecting the mast, and she knew he was concerned again, despite the fact that all appeared trim and proper.

"Captain? What do you see?"

"It's not so much seeing, as hearing. She just doesn't sound right. Probably jealous," he added with a wink. "Not used to having competition."

"Well, then, I'll just leave the two of you alone." Erica smiled. "And Captain?"

"Yeah?"

"Be careful. And get some rest." She turned away quickly, not wanting to see if her tender words had affected him. Perhaps he hadn't even noticed the soft, husky quality behind them. If so, she was grateful to the schooner for the distraction. It wouldn't do for Daniel to suspect how large a piece of her heart he now commanded.

As she entered the companionway, she glanced over her shoulder and saw that he was fully engrossed in his endless scrutiny of the rigging. For the moment, he seemed focused on the square topsail, which was furled loosely so that it caught only a fraction of the wind she'd seen it master when it was unfurled in all its glory.

''He'll be over you in weeks,'' she told herself wistfully. ''With any luck, it'll be that way for you, too, once you're home, with Sarah's loneliness and Jack's neglect to occupy your attention.''

She wouldn't have minded one last, lingering, love-starved gaze from Daniel, but knew it was for the best. ''And at least you still have the galley boy,'' she reminded herself philosophically, stripping off the captain's heavy wool coat as she entered the sitting area of the captain's quarters, so that her young admirer could see her pretty yellow dress and fuss over her accordingly.

When the afternoon squall hit, as predicted, it was with such violent force that Erica literally feared for their lives. Ordering Polly to stay with her despite the child's pleas to be allowed on deck for just a few minutes, she rapidly took stock of the decisions she'd been making as of late. All of them, she decided with a frustrated groan, had been poor ones. And somehow, all of those mistakes had led to this awful moment, which therefore appeared to be entirely her fault.

Then the stateroom door burst open, and she was instantly ready to throw herself into Daniel's arms and make yet another colossal error. But it was Sean, not Daniel, and so she grimaced and moved to stand before him as well as she could, given the wild pitching of the vessel. Lowering her voice so that Polly couldn't hear, she asked, ''Can the ship survive this pounding? Are the men being careful? Did you and Daniel get any rest before this hit?''

The first mate hesitated, then turned to Polly and instructed, ''Go to your own quarters and fetch your belongings. The captain wants you to bunk in here with Erica until morning.''

"But I want to—"

"Go!" he ordered gruffly. "And don't step one foot on deck if you know what's good for you. The captain swears he'll never bring you along again if he catches sight of you out there."

The girl nodded and scampered out into the sitting area.

"Sean? Are we all going to die?"

"No, we've been through worse. Just keep the little one below, so we've one less worry."

"I will. I promise." He was studying her quietly, and she could see that he had more to say. "Sean? Are you upset about something? Besides the weather, I mean."

"I thought you should know, the captain considered putting in to shore until it passed. On my suggestion," he added meaningfully.

"Oh?"

"I thought it would be prudent. We knew this squall would be a bad one. And while we were there, you could have found a ship headed directly for Boston, instead of sailing out of your way to Salem. It would have been more convenient for everyone. Especially Ryerson."

"That's true." Erica smiled as she looped one arm around the mate's neck, partially from a need to steady herself, but mostly out of pure affection. "Do you know what I like best about you, Mr. Lynch?"

"What's that?"

"When I step off this schooner and out of Captain McCullum's life, I won't need to worry about him. Because I'll know there's someone looking out for his best interests."

Sean studied her intently. "What will you do after you leave us? Are you still going to marry Ryerson?"

"I thought about that for hours last night."

"And?"

"It occurred to me that if I don't love him enough to

remain faithful to him, and he doesn't love me enough to come after me when I need him, perhaps we should reconsider our engagement."

The mate's green eyes flashed in frustration. "I thought so!"

"Don't be tiresome," she teased. "I can't believe I considered letting you marry Sarah. Or even Betsy for that matter! Does she have any idea how unfair you are? You assume I would knowingly ruin the captain's life? Stand in the way of his adventures? Destroy the very thing that draws me to him?"

"Are you in love with Danny?"

"I suppose I could be, if I weren't careful. But thanks to your warning, I've been careful." She flushed when he eyed her sternly. "Fine, I haven't been as careful as I should have been, but I wanted a little adventure for myself. Is that so wrong?"

"It's dangerous, Erica."

"Dangerous for myself, perhaps, but not for the captain," she assured him firmly. "He says it himself—he is free to flirt with me, knowing I'm engaged and therefore no danger to his freedom. And I *am* engaged, and will be still when I leave the *Moon Rigger*. And most importantly, the affair between myself and the captain is ended. I played a dangerous game, but that's done with. I intend to spend the rest of this voyage contemplating what I should do with the rest of my life."

For the first time, the mate's tone softened. "I'm sorry about Ryerson, but you can do better. You're a lovely girl, and a tender-hearted one. I'm glad you're not marrying a man who would let you run off without rescuing you from yourself."

"I suppose I'll always wonder what would have happened if Jack *had* come after me. It's confusing," she admitted. "I keep asking myself—well, never mind."

She patted his cheek. "Don't worry. I don't have plans to domesticate your friend."

He laughed in wry relief, and seemed about to offer some much needed advice on the subject when a loud commotion on deck made him turn away sharply. "Stay here. Keep Polly out of our way."

"I will," Erica promised, following him into the sitting area, where the little girl was already poised to run out to her father. "Polly McCullum! I need you to stay with me. I'll be scared to death if you leave me alone."

"And your father will keelhaul you," Sean warned cheerfully. "So take care of Erica, and when the squall's passed, we'll let you handle the wheel again."

He was gone before the child could argue, leaving both females to stare down the companionway with trepidation. It truly sounded as though a mutiny were at hand, and one glance at Polly's face told Erica she'd never be able to distract her, or herself, from the drama.

"I'll go see," she announced finally. "He can't punish *me*, can he?"

"Be careful," Polly pleaded. "Don't get washed overboard."

"I wouldn't dream of it," she said firmly, grabbing for Daniel's dark wool coat and wrapping it tightly about her shoulders. "I'll just be a minute."

The coat shielded her body, but nothing could have prepared her for the assault on her face as icy droplets of rain and fierce gusts of wind ravaged her in seconds. Through the blinding haze she could see crewmen running everywhere, and the few who were not, were strangely rooted to their spots, their expressions wooden as they stared up to the top of the main mast, as Daniel had done earlier.

Not sure what she might see, Erica struggled to follow their example, and immediately noticed how the half-

furled topsail seemed tangled in the complex lines and
ropes that held the whole mess aloft. She also saw that
Daniel was sending the same man up the ratlines as he'd
sent at noon. The sailor was a compact, wiry fellow who
couldn't have yet been eighteen years of age. A boy,
really, yet he seemed experienced, and was nimble to an
almost miraculous degree.

"He's the right man for the job," Erica told herself
nervously. "Probably does it a hundred times a day."
Still, as the wind drove icy pellets of rain against her
cheeks, she imagined how it must be battering the sailor.
How could he grip the ropes, with such slick, freezing
interference? And how in heaven's name would he keep
his footing, especially when trying to negotiate the platform!

To her horror, she had correctly predicted a near disaster, for as the boy used both his hands and one foot to
grip the underside of the platform, his remaining foot—
the only thing securing him to the ratlines—slipped out
from under him. For a long and perilous instant he seemed
to be falling free, toward the deck and certain death, and
Erica shrieked, softly and without hope of being heard
over the roar of the wind. Then she saw the sailor's hand
shoot out to grab a line, and he was steady again, beginning
the maneuver anew, his confidence apparently unshaken.

As Erica methodically quelled the pounding of her
heart, she watched the plucky young man skillfully and
successfully vault himself onto the platform. Every man
on the schooner cheered as he waved down to them, a
reassuring grin on his ruddy face.

Then he was climbing again, so high above the deck
now that Erica knew a fall would kill him. But there
was no other platform between the sailor and the tangled
yardarm, and so she trusted in his training, and tried not
to imagine the worst. Her own fingers were growing stiff,

just hanging at her sides in the driving rain, and she wondered how the others managed to wield tools and tie knots under such conditions. It explained why Daniel's hands were so rough. And so strong. So demanding of everything they touched.

She tore her gaze from the climber and stole a quick look at the captain. From the way his eyes never wavered, she knew he was mentally assisting the sailor, willing him to safely reach and disentangle the yardarm before something ripped, or worse, came crashing down to where they were standing. From the frenzied way the schooner lurched every time the wind whipped the topsail, Erica suspected that that was the true danger—the vulnerability of the vessel to gusts and crosswinds despite the fact that the other square sail had been fully furled and secured.

When the boy reached the tangle, Erica sighed with relief and again looked to Daniel, but his expression was still filled with concern, and so she shifted her gaze aloft, just in time to see the yardarm swing wildly, crush against the boy, then swing free again. Clearly disoriented, the boy panicked before their horrified eyes, clutching at the canvas and then lurching backward. He would have fallen then for certain, but his foot caught in a stay and so he dangled helplessly instead, screaming into the gale for help.

Three crewmen lunged for the ratlines, but Daniel thundered for them to stand down, peeling off his coat as he roared. Then to Erica's horror he pulled a knife from his belt and gripped the blade firmly between his teeth. Terrified, she sprang forward and caught his arm just as he began his climb. "Y-you're the captain, Daniel! Send someone else. Please—"

He caught her chin in one hand while he held the knife clear of her with the other, explaining rapidly, "There's no one else. Sean! *Take* her—"

"No!" She threw her arms around his neck and blurted into his ear, "I can't bear this! Promise you'll come back to me. Promise you'll make love to me again tonight."

"Take her!" he roared to his first mate, then to Erica, he added, "I'll hold you to that, wench," and thrust her away from himself.

Sean pulled her firmly into his own arms and murmured softly, "He'll be fine, sweetheart. I watched him do this dozens of times in the old days."

"But he's not a skinny boy anymore! How will he ever manage those horrible contortions?" She wrenched free and stood helplessly, watching as Daniel sped up the ratlines as though they were child's play. Then he reached the platform and before Erica could pray for his safety, he'd swung his body out and over, rolling to a stand with the ease of an acrobat. She wanted to cheer, as they'd done for the sailor, but there was no jaunty wave from Daniel, because there was simply no time. Instead, he was climbing again, seemingly more quickly than ever. Finally he reached the boy and grabbed him by his shirt until he could get a firm grip on his waist.

For the first time, Erica realized that the crewman was no longer screaming, or even moving. He was deathly still and silent, unable to assist his rescuer. Daniel seemed to struggle for a moment with the weight of the limp body. Then, in a series of quick, sure movements, he hoisted the boy over his shoulder while untangling the foot that had both imprisoned and saved him.

The crew went wild with appreciation and relief, shouting up to their captain and clapping their frozen hands lustily. Sean released his grip on Erica and began shouting orders, sending two men up to meet Daniel at the platform so that he could hand the unconscious boy to them.

Erica's eyes brimmed with tears of relief and she

hugged Sean happily, murmuring, "He'll be fine, won't he?"

"Sure," Sean soothed. Turning to a nearby hand he instructed, "Put him in my stateroom. Keep him warm until I can tend to him. And as for *you!*" He stared, seeming to look right through Erica. "I thought I told you to stay put! Come over here."

From behind her, Polly came running to Sean, wrapping her slender arms around his neck and clinging anxiously. "Did you see Papa? I thought he might fall, but he didn't."

"You'll be a long time waiting for Daniel McCullum to fall," Sean assured her heartily.

"Gracious, Polly," Erica sighed, dropping to her knees in spite of the flooded deck. "Did you see all of that? You must have been scared to death." To Sean, she added quietly, "My father was a doctor. I don't know much, but I'd like to help with the injured man if I can."

"Go along, then," he agreed. "As soon as Danny's done, we'll join you."

"Done?" She gasped, then she craned her neck and groaned, "Oh, no," at the sight of Daniel, knife in teeth, climbing perilously toward the tangle that had almost killed the sailor.

"Go on now," Sean urged. "Look, they have O'Rourke down. He needs you. Make yourself useful, and don't worry about Danny. He was born for all this."

Erica hurried to where two crewman were bundling their dazed friend into blankets. "Sailor?" she demanded softly of the injured man. "Can you hear me?"

The sailor stared up at her through bleary eyes and nodded.

"What's your name?"

"My name?" He hesitated, then almost seemed to guess, "O'Rourke? Aye, that's it. Michael O'Rourke."

"Can you move your legs, Michael O'Rourke?"

"Aye."

"And your neck?"

"Aye." He turned his head from side to side, wincing as he did so.

"Good. And I can see with my own eyes there's no damage to your handsome face, so we can all relax," she said with a smile. To the others, she instructed briskly, "Take him to the cabin. Try not to move his back or neck more than necessary, until I've had a better look at him."

"Aye, miss," they chorused, gingerly shifting O'Rourke onto a sling.

Although the squall was as fierce as ever, she noticed that the schooner was weathering it more solidly, and knew, before she turned her attention back to the captain in the riggings, that he had freed the topsail, which was now furled tightly out of harm's way.

Moving to rejoin Sean and Polly, she raised her voice enough to be heard over the wind and marveled, "He did it, Sean. It's just like you said: he was born to do this."

"Aye. Remember that," Sean scolded. Then to her surprise, he pulled her into a hearty bear hug. "What are you doing, Erica? You said it was ended, but clearly it's not."

"I couldn't just let him go—" She caught herself and admitted sheepishly, "I suppose I'll have to do it sooner or later, but not today, Sean. Please?"

"I was worried for him, but now it's for you that I'm troubled," he murmured into her hair.

"What's this?" Daniel's gravelly voice interrupted. "Mutiny?"

Erica pulled free and smiled shyly. "You were wonderful, Captain. You saved that boy's life."

Daniel shrugged. "Seems only fair, since I'm the one who sent him up there." Lifting Polly into his arms, he added mischievously, "Did you watch all that, so I can send you up next time?"

She giggled and nestled against his chest. "You're the bravest of all, Papa."

"It was all my fault," Sean grumbled, half to himself. "I'm the one who told you to furl that damned sail loose, to make some time before the squall hit."

"But I'm the fool who listened to you, so it's settled." Daniel laughed. "How's O'Rourke?"

"Erica's offered to nurse him back to good health."

"Is that so?"

"My father was a doctor. And—" She blushed under his appreciative gaze. "I should go right away. Excuse me, Captain." Despite the roll of the vessel and the force of the wind, she managed to curtsey as she backed away. "I'll see you at dinner?"

"I'm looking forward to it." He grinned.

"So am I," she dared to admit before she turned and sloshed quickly away.

Once she was certain O'Rourke was resting comfortably, Erica hurried to her stateroom and changed into dry clothes before returning to her patient's side. After that, she relaxed and enjoyed watching him sleep, awed by the fact that he had come so close to death so recently. It was a wonder he could sleep at all, much less confide to her, as he had before he'd drifted into dreams, that his only worry was losing the captain's confidence.

"You sound almost anxious to be up there again, battling the elements and all those horrid ropes," she had chided.

O'Rourke had smiled through his discomfort. "What's the point of being alive if you can't be aloft?"

"You sound like Captain McCullum."

''That's a real compliment, Miss Erica. I only hope the captain doesn't see me as useless now.''

''He almost got you killed, sending you up there. I suppose *that* was a compliment too?'' she had teased.

''Aye, the finest any man has ever paid me.''

And she knew exactly how he felt, because the finest compliment any man had ever paid Erica had also come from Captain McCullum, and that, too, had been through an indirect yet glorious route. With a rueful smile, she acknowledged that she was learning more on this vessel—about life *and* about men—than she'd learned in all the other experiences of her life combined.

Despite all of Sean's advice and information, she hadn't really understood how completely the sea could own a man until her bedside talk with Michael O'Rourke. She imagined that most of the men were like Sean—drawn to the sea, appreciative of it, but not consumed by the need to experience it. The O'Rourkes and the McCullums were probably few. But they had a sort of mystical, charismatic edge to them that other men—even other heroes—could never fully attain.

On the other hand, she wasn't attracted to Michael O'Rourke, and she took this as the final sign that she hadn't been in love with poor Jack at all. During the voyage on the *Valiant,* she had seen every handsome sailor, and several of the male passengers, as intriguing prospects about whom to fantasize, without any intention of acting on those daydreams. It had always been that way with Erica, in fact. It was the reason she saw herself as heiress to her grandmother's legacy. She seemed able to fall in love, for a moment at least, with any able-bodied man who tipped his hat to her!

Now, it was only Daniel McCullum. She couldn't imagine another touch, another voice, another bed. Every time she saw a sailor flex a muscle, it made her long for Daniel.

Every time the galley boy blushed, or Sean teased, or
O'Rourke murmured in his sleep, she wanted to rush to
Daniel and throw herself into his arms. All the other
males, and the thoughts she'd had about them, had been
preparation for the feelings that would erupt in her when
Daniel McCullum strode into her life.

Even Jack Ryerson, she realized sheepishly, had been
some sort of romantic rehearsal, allowing her to imagine
herself married and living in a grand house with darling
sisters-in-law and endless parties. Allowing her to determine, slowly and imperceptibly, whether such a life could
be enough to satisfy her. But she had chosen instead to
run away from that life, because in the end, it simply
wasn't what she needed to be happy.

It's a paradox, she decided wistfully. *I want to be
married to a man who can only be happy if he isn't
married! It's just as Jack always claimed: I'm impossible
to please!*

"How's our patient doing?"

"Oh!" She whirled to blush into Daniel's smiling eyes.
"I didn't hear you come in."

"You were daydreaming. If it was about anyone but
me, I'll have to kill him."

"It was about you," she assured him softly. "You
were so brave today, Captain. You took my breath away."

"That's what I want to hear." He pulled her up to her
feet and into his arms, then lowered his mouth to hers
and kissed her gently, tasting and savoring her lips before
parting them with his tongue and exploring the rest.

Erica heard herself sigh aloud as she wrapped her arms
around his neck and luxuriated in his lovemaking. She
loved the feel of his hands, caressing her hips and buttocks
through layers of soft, supple fabric. Then one hand slid
up to fondle her breast and she whispered huskily, "Not
here, Captain. O'Rourke could awaken. . . ."

"I'll have the galley boy sit with him for a while," Daniel offered, his voice tinged with need. "You'll come to my quarters? Right away?"

"Aye-aye," she teased with impish delight. "I live only to follow your orders, depraved though they may be."

He chuckled as he released her. "Be quick about it then," he insisted, then he swatted gently at her behind and left in search of the galley boy.

Erica waited until her cheeks had cooled a bit, then leaned over O'Rourke to confirm that he'd slept through the amorous interlude. Relieved to hear steady, oblivious breathing, she tucked the covers gently around his shoulders, then turned her thoughts to the lovemaking that awaited her. It would be everything the previous night had been. And it would be even more wonderful, because she knew what to expect, and she knew how she felt about the captain. And while it might have been thrilling for a time, giving herself to a rogue, the idea of giving herself to the man she loved was infinitely more exciting.

She stopped by her own stateroom, to brush her hair and to anoint herself with the last of a small vial of perfume she'd brought with her for the purpose of seducing Jack. Then she retrieved the shirt Daniel had lent her, noting with a blush that the galley boy had folded it neatly and placed it at the foot of her bunk.

Had he guessed the rest? she wondered. But of course he had. The whole crew had to know by now that she was enamored of their captain; the way she'd run into his arms when he started to climb the mast in the storm would have told them all they needed to know. And she doubted it was the first time Daniel had brought a woman along on a voyage to warm his bed. Nor would it be the last.

"I don't care," she insisted, raising herself on tiptoes

to study her reflection one last time in the small mirror on the back of the door. "In its own way, this love affair is perfect. No one can convince me otherwise. The captain will remember it fondly, and so will I."

She peeked her head out to make certain the tiny sitting area was empty, then dashed across and rapped gently on his door. When no one answered, she pushed it open and stepped inside to find herself alone with a rush of scintillating memories—of Daniel carrying her here in his strong arms, and throwing her onto his bed, and making love to her so boldly yet so gently.

Tingling with anticipation, she placed his folded shirt on his footlocker. Then, with a glance at the closed door, she quickly stripped off her yellow dress and underclothes, pulling the soft, white muslin garment on in their place. It was an outrageous thing to do, she knew, but it would ignite him. And it would ensure that nothing interfered with her need to feel his naked body against hers.

Her long, uncovered legs were chilled, however, and so she carefully turned back the coverlet, thinking it might be just as provocative, and much warmer, to be ensconced in the bed when he arrived. She had barely settled herself in the soft, downy layers when the door burst open and her pirate captain strode into view.

His practiced eye quickly noted her clothing, piled in a heap near the footlocker, and he grinned with anticipation. "Let's have a look at you."

"Let's have a look at *you*," she countered mischievously.

"Who's giving the orders here?"

She smiled sweetly. "I'm tired of playing pirate and princess. Wouldn't it be more fun if I were your queen, and you were my devoted subject—a knight, sworn to protect my honor and my life? Which you did today, you know. By your heroism, you saved us all. And I'm inclined to reward you, *if* you behave respectfully.''

"If I behave respectfully, it won't be nearly as rewarding," he warned.

"Are you so certain of that?'' She knelt in the bed, gathering the coverlet around herself and motioning for him to stand before her. "Come here and follow my orders. I assure you, you'll enjoy yourself.''

He shrugged and crossed to her, standing close, so that his mouth was even with, and just inches away from, hers. "What would you like, milady?''

Erica moistened her lips and smiled. "I want you to kiss me. Gently.'' When his hands moved toward her waist, she rebuffed them quickly. "Just a kiss, sir. For now.''

Daniel grimaced but nodded, and brushed his lips across hers, then moved closer and tasted her more thoroughly, but still with complete tenderness.

Sighing with delight, Erica pulled back and smiled. "That was lovely, sir. I believe you will be able to please me greatly. Now—'' She gestured disdainfully toward his shirt and breeches. "Take off those offensive rags.''

CHAPTER NINE

She wasn't sure whether Daniel simply didn't want to argue with her, or whether he was beginning to like the new game, but he didn't protest. Instead, his eyes locked with hers, then he quickly unbuttoned his shirt and stripped it off, dropping it to the floor. Next, he pulled off his boots, one by one, then unhooked his breeches, still without dropping his gaze from her own. She heard, without seeing, the last article of clothing slide to his feet.

He's daring me to look at him, she told herself with a shiver of delight, and so she motioned for him to step backward, then she slipped out of the bed and instructed coolly, "Don't move a muscle. I want to have a look at you."

She saw a flash of something in his dark-blue eyes— impatience? resistance? annoyance?—and so she arched an eyebrow sharply. "Are you questioning my command?"

"Just make it quick," he advised dryly.

She stifled a laugh and began to circle him, fixing her eyes on his lean torso and nodding approvingly. She hadn't taken the time the previous night to notice his bronzed back or trim, muscled buttocks, but now she studied them greedily before moving to stand in front of him again, lowering her gaze with exaggerated interest until it was fixed on his nearly erect manhood.

"Don't move," she reminded him, then she dropped to her knees and stroked the shaft reverently with her fingertips. To her awe-struck delight, it hardened to pure granite under her touch. Remembering her fantasy, she licked her lips, and with a tremble of excitement, leaned into him, trailing light, appreciative kisses from base to tip.

"That's enough!" he roared, catching her under her arms and hoisting her into the air, half throwing her onto his bed. As she laughed helplessly, he tore open her shirt, heedless of the buttons, and spread the plackets to reveal her full, needy breasts. Kneeling over her, he lowered his mouth and devoured her, from throat to nipples and then downward, until his mouth was buried in damp auburn ringlets and his hands were forcing her thighs to part and allow him ultimate access to her body.

"Wait," she gasped, but it was too late. His tongue was assaulting her, and she softly shrieked his name, stunned by the pleasure he was drawing from her. It was almost as though he intended to bring her to the same dizzying edge of ecstasy she experienced the night before, with just his mouth and imagination!

And he would have succeeded too—her fevered loins left her no doubt as to that—but suddenly, his tongue abandoned her and he climbed back up to whisper into her ear. "You were right. This game's a fine one."

She reached down to grasp his manhood in her hand. "I need all of you now."

"All of me, eh? How's this, for a start?" He plunged a finger into her and chuckled when she sighed with relief. "See now? It's me who should be making the decisions."

"Do whatever you want," she said, arching greedily against his hand. "Just don't stop." Stroking him firmly with one hand, she put the other behind his neck and pulled his mouth toward her own.

His lips and tongue savored her, then he pulled free and turned his attention to her thighs again, pushing them apart and moving his shaft into position. Towering above her, he asked, "You're ready? It could hurt again."

She answered by arching in impish insistence, and he shook his head as though amazed, then began to pump gently into the drenched, swollen darkness.

"Daniel," she crooned. "It feels so good."

"Does it?" He thrust harder, watching her expression intently.

"Do more," she suggested, wrapping her legs around him with a mischievous smile.

His eyes narrowed, as though suspicious of the invitation, then a roguish grin spread over his features and he began to enjoy her with long, powerful thrusts that made her arch with decadent appreciation. Every movement stoked the fire he'd ignited within her, while his kisses told her he adored her for the glorious pleasure her body was allowing him to share.

Clinging to his neck, she urged him, with throaty moans, to thoroughly enjoy her, until she heard his breathing grow ragged. All she could think was that he was going to climax with her this time, and the thought drove her past the edge, until her loins began to convulse in greedy, grasping spasms. She heard herself shriek his name again, and she was sure his low, gravelly voice answered, although his mouth was buried in her wild auburn tresses. Then her spasms began to subside, and she wallowed happily in the tremors that continued to rack her exhausted body as Daniel pumped gently, yet still with insistence. Finally, through her haze, she realized he was still in need, and so she whispered, "You're still so hard. Let me help you."

"Erica," he groaned, pulling himself from her and thrusting rhythmically against her hip. This time she used her hand to help him, and almost instantly she was rewarded by the feel of the steady spurts that signaled he had finally been delivered from the madness that had enveloped them both.

"Mmm . . ." She pushed him onto his back and knelt above him, then leaned down so that her nipples could graze against his wiry chest hairs.

"I adore you, Daniel McCullum. I hope you don't mind."

"I like you too," he admitted.

She laughed and stroked his chest. "I love so many parts of you, it's hard to choose a favorite."

"You didn't seem to have any problem earlier."

"I'm serious. Take these, for example." She caught his hands up in her own and brushed her lips across their rough, warm skin. "I never really appreciated them until now." When Daniel chuckled wickedly, she scolded, "I mean, because of the way you used them today, when you were climbing the mast. That's how they got this way—calloused and strong. From the biting cold and the rough ropes. They serve you well." Unstraddling him, she pulled up the covers over them, then snuggled against his chest. "Your life is so dangerous. So exciting. So perfectly suited to you."

"I can't imagine living any other way," he admitted, pulling her closer. "But feeling you here, like this, makes me understand why other men make other choices."

"That's such a lovely thing to say." She brushed a

dark curl from his forehead. "You should sleep for a while, Captain. You must be exhausted."

"You'll stay with me?"

"Yes."

His arms tightened around her. "Try to sleep, too. I'll be wanting you rested when I wake up." He paused. "That's how it's going to be from now until Salem, so don't pretend otherwise."

"I wouldn't dream of it," she said solemnly. "Go to sleep now, Captain. I'll be right here when you wake up."

To her surprise, he slept deeply, despite the roll of the vessel, the creaking of the rigging, the whistle of the winds. *It must sound right to him,* she guessed as she studied his handsome, relaxed features. *The same way it sounded wrong this morning. That's why he kept staring up at the yardarm. And that's why he can sleep now, because he knows instinctively that everything's fine.*

She knew when he woke he'd scold her for not resting, but her mind was too alive to be still. With every ounce of imagination at her disposal, she struggled to find a way to make this last forever; but it seemed it couldn't be done. It was just as she'd said to Sean that afternoon: the very qualities they loved in one another were the ones that would keep them apart.

From now until Salem . . . Hadn't Daniel summed it up perfectly in those loving, ominous words? Once they reached their destination, he would consign her back into Jack Ryerson's arms without a moment of regret. And she would watch him sail away, and that, too, would feel right, despite the ache he'd leave behind. She would always imagine him at sea—a rogue and a loner, "living aloft." And he would imagine her in Jack's arms—that would be his punishment, for being so irresistibly untame-able.

After two hours of deep sleep he stirred, and immediately his arms encircled her, pulling her flush against him. "I wasn't sure you'd stay," he murmured huskily.

"This is how it's going to be from now 'til Salem," she reminded him softly. "I don't want to miss a minute of it."

He murmured something unintelligible and nuzzled her neck. "Talk to me."

She ran her fingers through his thick, wavy mane of blue-black hair, grazing his scalp gently with her fingernails. "You want to hear another story?"

"No." His hands settled on her buttocks, which he stroked softly as he explained, "Tell me about Ryerson."

"Pardon?"

She tried to pull away in haughty reproach, but Daniel chuckled and restrained her. "I won't let him have you unless I'm convinced he's worthy."

"Oh." She sighed. "I suppose that's noble of you. Odd, but noble."

"So? Talk."

She hesitated, then relaxed and snuggled against his chest. "You needn't worry, Captain. Jack will take wonderful care of me."

"He let you run off with a sailor, without taking a minute from his precious business to come after you. That doesn't say much for him."

"He was being strong, for both of us. You're the one who explained that to me," she reminded him. "And I honestly think it's true. Jack is very strong, Captain. Very dependable. You needn't worry."

"I asked you a question," he complained, raising himself up onto his elbow and staring into her eyes. "Why do you love him?"

"Is that what you asked?" She smiled shyly. "Are you sure you want to hear this? I mean . . ." She blushed but held his gaze. "I've never felt even a twinge of jealousy over your love for Lilli, but still, I've no desire to hear the details."

Daniel chuckled. "Not even a twinge?"

She laughed in return. "To be perfectly honest, I find it utterly maddening." Moistening her lips, she admitted quietly, "It's a romantic story—me and Jack, I mean. Are you sure you want to hear it?"

"I'm sure."

Erica closed her eyes. "I'd heard about an enterprising young man named Jack Ryerson, from friends. And I'd seen him from a distance. He's quite handsome, Daniel. He has what they call 'boyish charm.' Armloads of it. But behind the innocent green eyes and disarming smile, he's shrewd, in a mathematical sort of way. The man can concentrate so intently, a train could run through the parlor and he wouldn't notice it. He can spend hours poring over books and accounts, sometimes missing dinner because of it.

"My father was enormously impressed with Jack, even before we met him," she continued softly. "A close family friend had been in danger of losing his livelihood— he was a textile manufacturer—before Jack stepped in and saved his factory. We were *all* so impressed and grateful, even Mother. But to me, the most amazing fact was that so industrious a man could have so adorable a face. Is this bothering you, Daniel?"

"No." He eyed her with wry disdain. "Your parents appreciated him, before any of you ever met him, because of his mathematical ability and because he saved a friend's livelihood? And you were smitten, before you ever met him, because of his *face?*"

"Not just his face," she defended herself quickly.

"He's tall, too. Perhaps even taller than you, although he doesn't have your . . . well, he's built differently. Lanky— that's the word Mother uses."

"Lackey?"

"Lanky!"

Daniel grinned. "So, go on. How did you finally meet him?"

"It was at an Independence Day fireworks display. I knew he was going to be there, and I believe our mutual friends had told him I'd be there—"

"And he came anyway? That's a brave man. You should have mentioned his courage sooner."

She glared, then shrugged her shoulders. "We were introduced, and then the fireworks began, and I wanted to see if he was a romantic, so I pretended to be frightened by the noise. And he put his arms around me, and at that moment, we both knew we were right for one another."

"He kissed you?"

"Jack? Kiss me in public? Never. Didn't I mention how reserved he is?"

"No."

"Well, he is. It was weeks before he kissed me, on the porch at my house on Sunday afternoon after dinner. Three months later, he asked Father for my hand. It wasn't long after that that Father died," she added wistfully. "But as Mother says, at least he rests in peace, knowing I have someone like Jack to keep me out of mischief."

"That's Ryerson's assignment for life?"

"Pardon?"

"Why aren't you married by now? I'm no mathematician," Daniel assured her wryly, "but it sounds as though you've been engaged for well over a year."

"A year and a half," she confirmed. "Jack isn't impulsive, Captain. He wanted to marry and start a family of his own at a certain age. Especially because of his responsibilities to his little sisters. He'll be twenty-eight years old in December, and so, December fits well with his plan. Of course, now it will be September, assuming—''

"Assuming what?"

She flushed, annoyed with herself for having hinted at any doubt aloud. "I was only thinking it might be a nice way to make things up to him if I agreed to keep the original date."

"To make things up to him?" Daniel teased. "Like having affairs with randy sailors?"

"Hush!" She buried her face in his chest and sighed. "You're impossible, Daniel McCullum. Doesn't it make you at all jealous to imagine me in Jack's arms?"

"Except you're not *in* his arms. You're in mine," he corrected her cheerfully.

"Yes, I know, but—well, never mind. I suppose you're right." She touched his cheek in apology, wondering what had possessed her to press the subject so.

You're never satisfied, Erica, she scolded herself silently. *Do you honestly want him to erupt with jealousy, and demand that you break your engagement to Jack and marry him instead?*

Of course, that was *exactly* what she wanted, despite the folly of it. It would be so perfect. So romantic. So overwhelming. But then she would have to say no, and that would ruin everything. His heart would be broken, and for what? Salvaging Erica's pride? What was the point of that?

Because if he asked her to marry him, it would mean he was in love with her, and so, his heart would be broken when she turned him down. He'd never understand she was doing it to set him free. He'd argue with her—

And what if he won that argument? she challenged herself cautiously. *What if he convinced you to marry him? To take you to La Creciente and make love to you forever. To raise his children, and give him more little darlings to love him. Even if it meant your love would hold him back, and keep him from the reckless, exhilarating life that makes him who he is. . . .*

"What are you thinking, Erica?"

"Hmm?" She laced her fingers into his thick black hair and explained lovingly, "I'm thinking about what you did today. Climbing those treacherous ropes, in that petrifying storm. You saved O'Rourke, and probably the rest of us too, and—" She brushed her lips across his. "You loved every minute of it, didn't you?"

He grinned and nodded. "Certain experiences make my blood boil, and that was surely one of them. You're another."

Then, as if to prove it, he pushed her back into the bunk and descended on her with a passion that made her heart soar from her chest.

From now until Salem . . .

Daniel made good on that promise, showering Erica with erotic attention that made her weak with happiness, so that the days blurred into the nights, and all else—chats with Polly, meals with Sean, hastily scribbled letters to her mother and Sarah—seemed unimportant pastimes as she waited for her lover to assault her anew. And as much as she relished the lovemaking, she grew to love the discussions she had with him too. The lessons and the lectures, about the schooner, the sea, and the sky. And of course, the games, wherein she was a dozen different women, but he was always the same proud, tall, conquering hero she had come to adore.

Every time she found herself wanting it to last, she reminded herself of the price. Daniel would give up the life he loved. And she would know she'd done that to him, for her own selfish purposes. And so she remembered the truth—that he wanted her to marry Jack. It was a truth that was also a lie, because she could never consider such a course now. But she continued to play the role of unfaithful fiancée well, for Daniel's sake.

It all bothered Sean immensely, and finally, she took him aside to reassure him one last time. "If he loved me, he'd try to convince me not to marry Jack. But instead, do you know what he did?"

"What?"

"He made me tell him all about Jack, down to the last romantic detail. He said he wanted to be sure I'd be in good hands. So I told him everything, without a hint that it might not come to pass. Now Daniel can sail away without looking back. That's what you wanted, isn't it?"

"It doesn't matter what I want. It's what Danny needs."

"That's what I meant."

Sean pursed his lips thoughtfully. "He asked about Ryerson?"

Erica nodded. "I could tell he was impressed."

"And jealous?"

"No." She flushed and admitted, "That hurt me, just a little. But we both know he has his reasons for wanting me to be in love with Jack, so I'm trying not to be *too* hurt by it."

"Are you in love with Danny?"

Erica hesitated, then took his hand in her own. "If I tell you, it's in confidence. But yes, I'm afraid I am. I'll get over it, though. My grandmother fell in love five times, and Daniel's only my first, so I have high hopes for the future." She dropped the bantering tone and added sincerely, "He needs the sea. And freedom. I'm grateful to you for explaining it all to me, Sean. And I've seen proof of it myself during this voyage. I love him too much to ever try to lure him away from all that."

"Are you sure he's not in love with you?"

"Absolutely." She cleared her throat hastily, alarmed by the hint of hurt in her voice. "He's fond of me, but he's not in love. If he was, he'd be jealous of Jack, just a little. Don't you suppose?"

Sean shrugged. "Could be he's jealous, but didn't let you see it."

"No. He laughed and joked, as though it were all just a game—" She cleared her throat again. "He once told me that my most attractive quality was my unavailability. In the end, it always comes back to that. I appeal to him because I belong to Jack, and he appeals to me because he belongs to the sea. The whole magnificent affair was doomed from the start."

"So, you'll be able to walk away?"

"I don't believe I have any true choice."

"Come here." Sean gave her a warm, loving hug. "We'll make Salem tomorrow morning. Did Danny tell you that?"

"I knew it was soon, but . . . tomorrow?" She sighed and pulled herself free. "I suppose I should gather my belongings and . . ." She sighed again. "You'll watch out for him? He's so reckless—"

"I'll do my best."

"And Polly's making such lovely progress."

"Aye, you've made a little lady of her. We'll see to it she minds her manners from now on."

"And Abby and the twins? Will you give them my love?" Erica wiped hastily at a tear trailing down her cheek. "I promised myself I wouldn't cry."

Sean embraced her again, this time patting her back in gentle consolation. "Go ahead and cry. It's a heart-breaking thing you're having to do."

"I'll have plenty of time to cry after I've left. For now, I don't want Daniel McCullum to remember me with puffy red eyes.'' She touched the sailor's face with tentative need. "He'll remember me, won't he, Sean? I mean, I know he meets dozens of women—''

"He'll remember you," Sean promised, his voice choked with emotion. "And he'll always wonder why he let you get away. And I'll wonder too, if I did the right thing, advising you this way.''

"I would have seen it on my own, so don't blame yourself. Not ever. Just take care of the McCullums, and yourself, so I don't need to worry.'' She pulled free and wiped her eyes again. "I'd best go fix my face before he sees me like this. Keep him occupied, won't you, Sean? I want to look especially pretty tonight, if it's to be our last night together.'' Her voice caught on that last phrase, and she had to turn away quickly for fear she'd end up in the first mate's arms again, this time truly sobbing.

Your last night together with him, and you knew full well it was coming, she chastised herself tearfully. *All you can hope to do now is make it a night Captain Daniel McCullum will never, ever forget.*

The galley boy drew a bath for her, and she luxuriated in the steamy water, forcing herself to concentrate on this last, romantic escapade. Then she enlisted the young servant's aid again, this time to heat the iron she hadn't used since she'd left Boston, and soon, her hair was pulled high on the crown of her head, cascading down in sumptuous ringlets, just as Erica's grandmother had once worn hers.

Her grandmother was in fact supplying the inspiration for this entire seduction, and as Erica slipped a brilliant sapphire ring onto her finger, she reminded herself that, along with her mother, Grandmother had been the most beautiful and confident woman she'd ever had occasion to meet. And she had been serenely, almost sinfully, content in her later years.

Because she took so many lovers in her youth, Erica teased herself gently. *Five that you know of, and doubtless many more. She would have approved of what you're doing here, on this schooner, for this brief time. And she would have understood that some loves, however passionate, simply cannot be expected to last forever.*

For the past few days and nights, the captain's quarters had become Erica's as well, and so as she readied herself, she had the benefit of a large mirror that hung to the left of the doorway. Dressed in a white silk camisole and lacy white petticoats, she frowned in indecision, wanting to choose just the right dress with which to charm her lover. He'd seen them all, of course. In fact, the only outfit he hadn't seen her wearing was the one in which she now admired herself.

And so, when the door burst open, she didn't bother to dash for cover, but stood, proud and hopeful, awaiting his always unpredictable reaction.

His blue eyes flashed with admiration as he took in the sight of her bare shoulders and soft, elegant curls. Then he cocked his head to the side and asked quietly, "What game is this?"

"I beg your pardon?"

"Princess? Queen? Duchess?"

Erica curtseyed shyly. "You flatter me, *Capitaine*, but I fear I'm only a simple peasant girl from the French countryside."

He studied her with wistful appreciation. "So? Are you your mother? Or your grandmother?"

She smiled with delight. "Grandmother, of course. Mother was born in Paris, and there's nothing simple about her."

"I want to hear about both of them," Daniel assured

her, stepping close and sweeping her into his arms. His lips brushed hers, once and then again, then he carried her to the bed and settled down, so that she was on his lap. "The grandmother first. She's the one I have to thank for all your pretty ways, after all."

"She would have adored you," Erica murmured, her arms loosely draped around his neck. "She would have understood what we feel for one another, and she would have approved."

Daniel caressed her waist fondly. "What will your mother say?"

"If I tell her, she'll pretend to be aghast," Erica admitted. "But she's Grandmother's daughter, after all, and so I'm sure she'll secretly understand. The problem with Mother is that she fell in love with Father so utterly and completely at so young an age, she doesn't realize how complicated love can be. Although I believe she may be learning it now," she added impishly. "It's the reason she went to Paris, I suspect. In any case, Grandmother's experience was quite the opposite. She fell in love five times—"

"Five?"

Erica blushed. "She married five times, at least, so I assume she fell in love—"

"She *married* five times?" Daniel pretended to glare. "She doesn't sound like a simple French peasant, Erica." He played with a ringlet of auburn hair, then admitted, "If she was half as beautiful as her granddaughter, I imagine men must have come from miles around just to catch a glimpse of her."

"Captain McCullum," Erica scolded. "Are you trying to seduce me? If you're not careful," she added playfully, "I'll decide to take five husbands myself, and I'll insist that you be one of them. We'll wait until the twins are grown, then we'll marry and sail the seas together forever.''

"I'd like that," Daniel said in a husky voice, then he lifted her gently off his lap and stretched out over her on the bed. "I could show you places that would amaze you, mademoiselle. There are foods, and birds, and stars, and sunsets that can't be seen unless you travel to the ends of the earth. With me."

Erica felt a traitorous sting of tears behind her eyes, and struggled to smile up into his shining eyes. She had meant the proposal as a mischievous game, and though he'd answered her in kind, she knew now that he didn't want this to end, at least not without preserving some hope that they might meet, and make love, again.

"If I'm going to be one of your five husbands, I assume you won't mind if I kiss you?"

Lacing her fingers in his thick, shaggy hair, she answered him by pulling his mouth down to hers and kissing him passionately, if only to hide the sight of the tears she knew were glistening in her eyes. It didn't help that he was more tender, and more loving, this time than ever before. Because it was their last night together, and he wanted it to be a night she'd never forget.

But Erica wanted more, and as her lover took her, her heart pounded, not only because of his provocative movements, but because of the words he'd spoken half in jest. He wanted her to sail to the ends of the earth with him. He wanted to be her husband. He had said those things as part of their romantic play, but he had meant them, whether he realized it or not. And suddenly, everything had changed.

Because it can be that way! she told herself dizzily as she arched in appreciation of his masterful lovemaking. *I can sail with him, and never tie him down. I can inspire him, and urge him to be reckless, and bold, and daring to his heart's content. And he can fill my life with such heart-stopping excitement and adventure that I'll wonder how other women exist on land without going mad from boredom.*

"Daniel!" she gasped again and again as his thrusts delivered her from chaos. Then he finished against her, groaned her name just as fervently, and gathered her roughly into his arms and growled, "I think I'm going to like being one of your five husbands."

"I'm going to like it too." She sighed, cuddling gratefully against him. It didn't matter that it was a game to him. All that mattered was, Erica intended to win.

She didn't bother to pack her belongings the next day, confident that she could make the trip to Boston, break off the engagement in person—she owed poor Jack that much, at least—and be back in Salem before the *Moon Rigger* sailed away. Sean needed time to court Betsy, after all, and surely the crew would demand at least a few days to enjoy themselves in the many taverns and ale houses that they could find in a seafaring town.

And then Erica would simply browbeat Daniel McCullum into submission. He wanted to be one of her five husbands? Fine. He could be the first. He wanted to take her to the ends of earth after the twins were grown? Fine. Except she wasn't about to wait that long, so he really only had two choices: he could leave the children in Salem with Abby, or bring them along.

And if Sean Lynch dared send even one disapproving glance her way, she'd give him a piece of her mind he wouldn't soon forget! She wasn't Lilli. She was a healthy adventuress. And if Daniel needed variety in his women as well as in his destinations and experiences, Erica could be any woman he chose. She'd proven that, hadn't she? And Daniel had loved every moment of it.

At times, during the last hours of their voyage, she almost suspected he had reached the same conclusion as she. He seemed light-hearted and at his ease. Wasn't that a good sign? After all, if he thought they were about to say good-bye forever, he might have been in a bit of a mood at least, wouldn't he? And certainly he would have been trying to have a few last trysts in his stateroom! Wasn't it a wonderful sign that he was cheerfully going about his duties, studying the rigging, watching through his spyglass, encouraging the less-experienced lads to climb high while the weather was clear?

The sun, which had been trying so valiantly for days to break through the cloud cover, had finally succeeded, bathing the schooner and its grateful occupants with clear golden warmth. Erica and Polly had commandeered a sunny section of deck and played card games as the sailors bustled around them, their steps jaunty as they contemplated the warm meals and soft beds that were now only hours away.

Then, without nearly enough warning, O'Rourke shouted "Salem, ho!" from his perch high above the deck, and the bustle of activity turned into a veritable frenzy.

"Hurry, Polly!" Erica gathered up the playing cards and tucked them into their tin. "We should get out from underfoot. And I want to watch us dock."

The little girl's smile was ever so slightly patronizing. "It'll be a while before that happens. And if Papa lets Uncle Sean pilot her, it will be even longer, because he's so fussy."

Erica grinned. "You're such an old hand at all this. But I intend to learn quickly." She took the child by the hand. "Tell me about your grandmother's house in Salem. Do you stay there often?"

Polly nodded. "Michael O'Rourke's grandma and grandpa live there. To watch over it while Grandma is with us."

"Oh! Isn't that lovely?"

"They're fun," Polly agreed. "But they're old. Sometimes, there are children visiting, though, and that's better."

"I see." She thought about her plans to bring Polly to visit Jack's little sisters, and shivered with delight. This was so much better! It was almost as though everything that happened was a sign she and Daniel would be together forever.

Glancing toward the quarterdeck, she saw that he was looking at her, a pensive smile on his face, and she waved shyly. Another sign. He was contemplating marriage, and so, like any healthy man, he was feeling just a bit overwhelmed. But he didn't look sad, as he would if they were about to part. And he wasn't grinning, as he might if he were actually pleased to be rid of the complications she'd brought to his life.

Because he loves those complications, and he loves you, she assured herself happily.

Up on the quarterdeck, Daniel took a last, admiring look at his pretty passenger, then turned back to the wheel, only to find that his first mate was studying him with pure disapproval in his green eyes.

"Problems?"

Sean shook his head. "Not with the *Rigger,* at least. I just find myself wondering if you know what you're doing."

"Huh?"

"With Erica," the mate explained warily. "Are you going to be able to take your leave of her when the time comes?"

Daniel shrugged. "That may not be necessary."

"What does *that* mean?"

"It means I've decided to keep her." He grinned sympathetically. "I know we made a pact, Sean, but I'm breaking it. Turns out, I'm more the marrying sort than I knew."

"Danny . . ." The first mate pursed his lips. "What about Ryerson?"

"No need to worry on that account." He chuckled. "She told me all about him. I wish you could have heard it. Her father chose him for her, as a means of keeping her out of mischief—that's exactly how she phrased it too," he marveled, half to himself. "Keeping her out of mischief."

"Not an easy job where Erica's concerned," Sean drawled.

"An impossible one," Daniel agreed cheerfully. "So I've decided not even to try. Fortunately, I like her sort of mischief just fine, so there's no need to do anything but sit back and enjoy it."

"On La Creciente?"

"She loves it there."

"And you'll have babies with her?"

"She'll insist on it," Daniel told him with wry satisfaction. "For reasons I'm too much of a gentleman to disclose."

"Have you told her how you feel?"

"There's no need to say it outright, but I will, as soon as she breaks it off with Ryerson. In her heart, she's done that already. She just needs to admit it to herself, and then to him." His tone grew more serious as he insisted, "She doesn't love him, Sean. I could hear that when she talked about him. She wanted to be in love—she was born for that, you know—and her father approved of the fellow, and so she gave it a try. Fortunately for me, he never made the most of the opportunity."

Sean grinned reluctantly. "That's why you weren't jealous when she told you about him?"

"Jealous of what? A mathematician who sits indoors and studies books while his beautiful fiancée runs off to the islands? I'm just grateful he kept her occupied for two years, until I could find her and marry her myself."

"What if she doesn't want to marry you?"

"Why wouldn't she?" Daniel began, then he chuckled ruefully. "She could do a lot better, I'm certain. But she agreed last night to allow me to be one of her five husbands. I've decided to be the first. With any luck, she won't have need of the others after all."

"Five husbands?"

Daniel nodded. "There's hope for *you* yet, if you're interested."

The first mate grimaced. "I've never seen you in so fine a mood. I suppose that's the proof of it. She's what you want, after all. Even though . . ." He hesitated for a moment, then asked, "You've decided against the clipper ship, after all?"

"What?"

"You said you'd be selling the *Rigger* and buying a clipper. In less than ten years, when the twins are old enough to either serve with you or learn a trade in Salem. If you and Erica start another family—"

"Between Erica and the *Rigger,* I'll have enough adventure to last a lifetime." He clapped his friend on the back heartily. "Be happy for me, Sean. She's everything a man could want, and she's all mine."

Sean studied him quietly. "You should go and talk to her then. No more games. It could get confusing, her seeing Ryerson again—"

"I told you, he's no threat." Daniel shook his head, wondering why the first mate couldn't see what was so clear. "She'll do what needs to be done, and then be back

before the week's out. She hasn't even pretended to pack
up her belongings," he added with a confident wink.
"One of her little games, and don't ask me to give *those*
up. I'm looking forward to fifty years or more, at least.
And so is she. I can guarantee you that."

Daniel had sent word ahead to Boston, and Erica was
confident that Jack would send a carriage for her. Perhaps
Sarah would choose to make the trip, which would be a
wonderful opportunity to share all the delicious details
of her affair without fearing Jack might overhear and be
offended. In hopes of catching a glimpse of the governess,
she positioned herself right alongside the rail as Sean
skillfully piloted the schooner up to the wharf while an
admiring throng of sailors, children, and passersby watched.

She hadn't really taken the time to plan what she'd say
to Jack, but in her heart, she knew he'd take the turn of
events in stride. That was his problem, wasn't it? He took
everything in stride. It had insulted Erica more than once,
and if he wasn't careful, it was going to keep him from
ever making a woman feel alive and indispensable and
adored.

Perhaps that's what you should say to him, she counseled herself as she scanned the crowd for a glimpse of
Sarah, or at least, Jack's driver. *Don't shield him from
the details of your love for Daniel. Bombard him with
them, so he can see how he needs to treat his true love.
Tell him about the kisses. The moonlight. The pirate and
the princess—well, perhaps not that, but everything else.
Make him see it and feel it and taste it, so that he's ready
when the real time comes.*

Then she saw a familiar face, but it wasn't Sarah or
the driver. It was Jack himself! Honestly amazed and
touched, Erica felt a twinge of regret for having doubted

that he'd come. In his mind, they were still engaged, and while the notion of traveling to the Bahamas had struck him as pure folly, traveling to meet his beloved at a nearby wharf was simply the gentlemanly thing to do.

She started to wave to the handsome figure, then was seized by an inspiration that seemed nothing less than brilliant, and so she spun instead and sprinted toward the quarterdeck, almost colliding with Daniel in the process.

"What's this?" he demanded. "Did you see a ghost?"

"Come quickly!" she insisted, tugging at his hand and pulling him into full view of the wharf. "Jack's out there, in the crowd! He came, in person!"

"What did you expect?" he chuckled. "We sent word ahead."

"Hurry!"

"I'm not interested in boyish charm and lanky bodies, so spare me—"

"Daniel! Pay attention," she pleaded, draping her arms around his neck as she spoke. "You have to kiss me like you've never kissed me before. This is my chance to show Jack what I've been begging him to do to me all these many months, so *please,* make it breathtaking."

Daniel stared down at her in confusion, his hands gripping her shoulders with a disconcerting need to remind himself whose woman she was. Except for the first time in almost a week, he wasn't sure he knew!

She wanted to show Ryerson how she longed to be kissed? Why did she care about all that now? Her cheeks were flushed, her golden eyes shining—over *Ryerson?* Because he'd deigned to come "in person" to Salem? Was that all it took for him to win her back? Or had he never lost her at all?

"Don't be stubborn, Daniel. Help me show him how perfect it can be if he just—"

"Gladly." With a burst of anger laced with injured

pride, he grabbed Erica against himself and kissed her roughly, then released her with a careful but irreverent shove. "Go on now. Run along to him so I can see to the cargo."

"Daniel—"

"Go! The man's been waiting long enough," he growled. "And now that he knows what you want from him, you can have that romantic reunion you've been dreaming of."

Her eyes had widened with alarm, further infuriating him. Had she expected him to bid her a gracious farewell as he sent her off to another man's bed? Her *first* husband's bed, no less! "Give him my best." He laughed harshly. "And thank him for taking you off my hands. I wasn't sure how I was going to get rid of you if he didn't show up."

"Daniel McCullum!"

"I'll have your bags sent along to Boston. Go on now. Ryerson looks to be in a randy way—"

"Daniel!" She was visibly struggling to keep from crying. "I haven't said good-bye to Polly or Sean or—"

"They knew you'd be leaving. We all knew it, so get on with it, and let us get back to our business."

She seemed about to protest again, then instead, she drew herself up proudly. "I'll never forgive you for this, Daniel McCullum. After all we've been, and done, and said. To send me away with harsh words ringing in my ears—" Her voice broke and she spun away, racing for the gangplank that the crew had just secured into place.

"Captain?" Sean stepped into view, his forehead creased with concern. "What was all that?"

Steeling himself against the rush of bitter humiliation that was assaulting him, Daniel explained in a quiet voice, "Turns out I was wrong. Turns out it was Ryerson she loved all along."

"No, Danny. I know for a fact—"

"Don't you have eyes, man? Look!" he snarled, pointing toward the wharf in time for them both to clearly see Erica, running and stumbling against strangers in her haste to reach a tall, well-dressed gentleman. When she threw herself into his arms, he hugged her passionately, then scooped her up and carried her to a nearby carriage and bundled her inside.

"She got what she wanted at last, Sean. To be carried away—by Ryerson."

"I can't believe my eyes," Sean murmured. "Did you two argue?"

"Erica never argues."

"You must have said something."

"Leave it be, Sean."

"No!" The first mate blanched, as though he hadn't known he was capable of such blatant defiance, but he continued doggedly, "She told me straight out that she loves you, Captain. I give you my word on that."

"Such an honor," Daniel seethed. "To be one of the five or so men she'll love in her lifetime. I might have been able to swallow even *that* particular insult, if Ryerson hadn't been one of the anointed."

Forcing himself to take a deep breath, he added more evenly, "You're a good friend, Sean, and you were right all along. There's only one female I can count on."

When Sean still appeared doubtful, Daniel warned, "Let it go, Sean. She was pretty, but she was a bother. I'm well rid of her. Let Ryerson satisfy her, if he can." He grimaced and added, more to himself than his friend, "I'll bet the bastard's having her right now. She'd like that—in a carriage, no less."

"Danny—"

"Didn't I order you to let it go?" he growled.

"Aye, Captain."

"Then get to work. And, Sean?"

"Aye, Captain?"

"Go and have a word or two with Polly. Tell her whatever you think's best. She'll be brokenhearted, poor little girl." His fist clenched and unclenched at his side. "I should have let them say good-bye."

"You did your best," Sean reassured him carefully. "You don't need this kind of grief in your life, Captain. You've said that more than once, so maybe it's for the best that she left, and left quickly."

Daniel nodded, knowing in his heart that Sean was right. For whatever reason, life had chosen to plague him with more than his fair share of loss. Why seek out new means of being hurt or tormented? He'd made up his mind, after Lilli died, that the only pain he would welcome from that day forward was the ache of a body that had put in a hard day's work, preferably aloft. It was time to rededicate himself to that simple principle, and put Erica Lane out of his thoughts, and dreams, forever.

CHAPTER TEN

"I hate you both! I truly do! Why didn't you come after me, Jack Ryerson?"

"If you'd settle down for five minutes, we could discuss it."

"Discuss it?" Erica picked up a sofa cushion and sent it flying against her hapless escort's chest. "You're the worst fiancé a girl ever had!"

"You're not exactly the ideal bride," he drawled. "Even without the details, I can assume the escapade you had with Sarah's intended was something less than acceptable—"

"It doesn't even bother you!" Erica glared through her tears. "Daniel wasn't jealous that I was in love with you, and now *you* aren't jealous that I fell in love with *him!* I hate you both!"

"You've made that clear, Erica. Shall I have my driver take you home?"

"Home?" She wiped her eyes and sniffed unhappily.

"There's no one there, Jack. I need a shoulder to cry on."

"So far, I've been more of a target than a shoulder."

"I'm sorry." She flopped onto the sofa and buried her face in her hands. "My heart is broken. You can't imagine how that feels."

"I can't? Did it ever occur to you that *my* heart is broken too? I've just found out that the woman I love has been carrying on with some sailor—"

"We weren't carrying on! We were falling in love. Or at least, I thought we were."

"That makes me feel so much better." Jack shook his head in amused disgust and settled down at his desk. "Are you listening to yourself, darling? You've known this man for less than two weeks, yet you're convinced that he's the great love of your life. And you expect *me* to listen to the details? The man who has loved you faithfully for two years without so much as glancing at another woman?"

Humbled, Erica stood and crossed to him, draping her arms around his neck. "That's such a sweet thing to say. But the truth is, dear Jack, you have no idea what it's like to fall in love. I didn't myself, until I met Daniel. I only hope it goes more smoothly for you than it has for me."

"I may not love you the way you want to be loved," Jack muttered, "but it's love just the same. Why else would I be willing to go through with the marriage, despite your obvious lapse of judgment?"

"You still want to marry me?"

"I'm afraid so."

She eyed him dourly. "In other words, you haven't heard a word I've said! Love is something completely devastating! It changes everything—your hopes, your dreams, your sensations. It isn't just a practical arrangement between two attractive friends.'' She patted his cheek and sighed. ''You'll see one day. And the truth is, you'll be even more devastated by it than I've been, because it will turn your orderly little world upside down. You won't be able to see straight, much less read your silly ledgers.'' The thought made her smile for the first time since she left the schooner. Then she remembered how much love could hurt and wrapped her arms around her ex-fiancé protectively. ''Poor Jack. I only hope she doesn't break your heart.''

''At the risk of repeating myself, my heart already *is* broken.''

Erica settled onto his lap. ''I know you think that's true, but the day will come when you'll fall truly in love, and you'll say to yourself, 'Erica was right. This is much, much more wonderful. And much, much more painful.' '' Patting his cheek, she added lovingly, ''I want that for you.''

''Pain?''

She laughed ruefully. ''Did you see the way the captain kissed me while you were waiting for me on the pier?''

''I missed that, fortunately.''

''Oh, Jack!'' She shook her head in frustration. ''How could you miss it? We did it for your benefit, so you could see how it should be done in the future.''

''Oh?'' He eyed her hopefully. ''You want me to kiss you in the future? That's encouraging, at least.''

''No, silly. I want you to kiss your future fiancée that way. Well, almost that way. It wasn't Captain McCullum's best,'' she mused. ''But I suppose I should consider myself fortunate since he clearly had no intention of wishing me farewell at all.''

''Bastard.''

''Yes,'' she agreed softly. ''That's precisely the word

for him. Somehow, I didn't see it. I wonder why that was.''

''Because you were angry with me for not coming after you, and you wanted to teach me a lesson. So you allowed yourself to be intrigued by him. It's really not that hard to understand, darling. And clearly, it was my fault, at least in part. So I apologize.'' He nuzzled her neck hopefully. ''Shouldn't we kiss and make up?''

Erica sighed and shifted away from him and onto her feet. Of all the distressing emotions this day had occasioned, this was surely the most foreboding. Jack's nuzzling—it had always sent shivers down her spine. Now nothing? Was it not enough Daniel had broken her heart? Had he ruined her for other men as well?

''It's no use, Jack. I think I'll just go to bed early tonight.''

''Here?''

She glared in disgust. ''You just admitted the whole thing was your fault. And even though that's not exactly true, I really don't want to be alone in that big awful house of ours. With Father gone, and Mother in Paris, it's so empty. Can't I stay here?''

''Absolutely. Stay as long as you like.'' He hesitated, then asked gently, ''How long do you suppose that will be?''

''Jack!''

''Fine! I'll just spend my days at the office, and my nights listening to you cry, indefinitely. Make yourself at home.''

''Good night, sweet Jack.'' She pecked his cheek softly. ''I'm so glad you were there today, to rescue me when Captain McCullum turned his back on me. If only you had come after me sooner—'' She shrank from his annoyed expression and added quickly, ''I'll just go visit Sarah again for a while. I've barely spent ten minutes with her, she's been so busy with the girls, but I'm sure the girls are asleep by now.''

Jack nodded, clearly relieved, and Erica smiled fondly. He'd been so sweet in the carriage, once she'd made it clear to him that amorous advances weren't welcome. And for ten straight hours since then, he had listened to her cry, and rail, and complain, and reminisce. It was enough to make her wish she'd never gone to the Caribbean. Perhaps if she hadn't, she and Jack could have been happy with one another, in a predictable sort of way.

But she had gone, and in many ways, it was ultimately for the best. But she couldn't expect Jack to understand that, so she sprinted up the stairs and knocked briskly on Sarah's door, opening it only when the governess had called out her permission.

"Sarah? May I come in?"

"Oh, Erica!" The nanny sprang from her desk and ran to embrace her friend. "Poor dear friend. We've had so little chance to talk, but Mary and Jane have had a thousand questions about—well, about you and your dismal spirits."

"I can't imagine what you told them, but thank you. I just wasn't in any mood to pretend."

"They've missed you dreadfully, and so have I. And Mr. Ryerson has been uncharacteristically grouchy. You would have been flattered," Sarah added impishly. "I believe it was just the jealous reaction you always wanted to see him have."

"I doubt that." Erica sighed, then she added warily, "You're the person who's behaving differently, not Jack. I don't think I've ever seen you so lighthearted. Has something happened?"

Sarah hesitated, then admitted, "Yes, I believe something wonderful has happened. But I don't want to talk about it. At least, not yet. I want to console you, poor

dear. I could tell from the letters how confusing it must
have been for you. But it must have been wonderful,
too.''

"The letters?" Erica winced. She had given Sarah the
letters she'd written on the *Valiant* and on the island, but
had pulled out the ones from the last days on the *Moon
Rigger,* for fear they may have revealed too much. Now
she realized that even the early letters must have contained
indiscreet details of her feelings for Daniel McCullum.

"I felt honored and grateful that you included me in
your adventure." Sarah smiled. "Come sit on the bed,
Erica. I want to hear all about it."

"I've been complaining to Jack for hours," Erica said
with a wry smile. "If something has happened in *your*
life—''

"If something has happened in my life, it's because of
you," Sarah told her solemnly. "If you hadn't convinced
me to write to Mr. Braddock in Chicago, I would have
gone along through my life, thinking every day was the
same. But you gave me hope. If I seem 'lighthearted'
now, it's because of that gift. Do you have any idea how
grateful I am?''

"Sarah . . ." Erica smiled uneasily, realizing that perhaps she shouldn't have omitted the letters detailing her
affair with Daniel. "If you think Captain McCullum
would be a good husband for *you*—''

Sarah's burst of laughter interrupted the confession.
"Really, Erica, I'm not a romantic. I leave all that to you.
I'm talking about hope, not romance.''

"Hope?''

"Yes." The nanny's voice lowered to an excited whisper. "I had almost given it up. To tell you the truth, I
have considered taking my own life more than once—''

"Sarah!"

"Don't worry, dear Erica. Because of you, I no longer

have such thoughts. I know I don't have to resort to such, well, such drastic measures to find peace. All because you were perceptive enough to recognize Russell Braddock's genius.''

Erica winced again, remembering Jack's advice: trying to arrange a love life for Sarah was hopeless. Because she was ''a bit off.'' Was it true after all? Talking nonsense, and admitting to suicidal impulses—

''You're frightening me, Sarah,'' she blurted. ''What does Russell Braddock have to do with finding peace?''

Sarah's brown eyes widened in dismay. ''I thought you more than anyone would understand. You're the only other person I know, beside Mr. Braddock, who truly believes in miracles.''

Erica sighed and crossed to her friend, embracing her warmly. ''I still believe in miracles. And I believe in hope. Especially for someone as wonderful as yourself. But what is it that you hope for, Sarah? Is there some way I can help?''

''You already have.'' Sarah smiled. ''I love the letters, Erica. May I keep them? They'll be my most truly treasured possessions.''

''Of course.'' It humbled Erica to realize that those lighthearted musings could mean so much to Sarah. But why not? The governess had never been anywhere. She had been tortured by tragedy, and relegated to a subservient role in life. Through the letters, she had a glimpse of Erica's world—a world of fantasy, and possibilities, and above all, confidence. Even that silly letter about Daniel's chest hairs—it might bring a tear to Erica's eye, but to Sarah, it was perhaps daring and provocative insight. ''I insist that you keep them. I wrote them to you, didn't I?''

''I'll never forget that,'' Sarah said with a sigh. ''And I posted the ones to your mother and Mr. Braddock.''

"Pardon?"

"I didn't read them," the governess assured her hastily. "But I can imagine what they said."

"You can?"

"You want advice on what you should do, now that you and the captain have quarreled. You don't need to go any further than your own heart, Erica. All the answers are there, if you're willing to listen."

Erica winced, suspecting that Sarah would now extol Jack's virtues shamelessly. The governess had always believed in that particular match, and after seeing Erica in tears this very afternoon, she undoubtedly despised Captain Daniel McCullum with all her heart. "You think I should give Jack a second chance?"

"Mr. Ryerson?" Sarah blanched. "I was talking about the sea captain. I was hoping—" She flushed unhappily. "It's all so confusing, isn't it?"

Erica cocked her head to one side, still disturbed by Sarah's morbid confession. It certainly brought her own woes into perspective.

"Do you know what I think, Sarah? I think you and I need to spend more time together—talking about *you* for a change. We've certainly beaten the subject of *me* to death, haven't we?"

"You've already done more for me than I can ever express." Sarah sighed. "I hate seeing you with those red, puffy eyes. You should try to get some sleep, Erica. Tomorrow will be a better day, I promise you."

Erica nodded and gave the governess a quick hug. "Tomorrow, you and I will talk about your future. I have dozens of ideas for you."

"That sounds lovely. Good night, Erica."

Erica moved to the door, then turned, intending to reassure her friend again. But Sarah was already back at the desk, pouring over the letters that Erica had written, as though transfixed by them.

Why? Because a stranger had found a true love for Erica, and Sarah now had "hope" that miracles were possible? If only that were true! Sighing, Erica closed the door behind herself, then headed to the guest bedroom to nurse her broken heart alone.

Daniel was beginning to despise the Black Tower ale house, if only because it was in Salem, less than a day's ride from the Ryerson household. But for reasons unfathomable to the ornery captain, Sean Lynch could not seem to get his fill of the place, or more particularly, of a red-cheeked barmaid named Betsy.

It seemed all the more incongruous, given Daniel's recent escape from matrimony. Of course, that was probably what had set Sean off, because no matter what else the affair between Daniel and Erica had been, it had set the *Moon Rigger* aglow with their passionate lovemaking.

"Captain McCullum?"

Daniel glanced up, and immediately scowled in recognition of his rival.

"I'm Jack Ryerson," the newcomer informed him hesitantly. "From Boston. Are you McCullum?"

Daniel wanted to wave the pest away, but remembered Erica's annoying comment—that her Jack was taller than her sea captain—and so he stood up and faced the man squarely. Even at best, he noted with grim satisfaction. He could only hope Ryerson had heard about Daniel's incursion into Erica's virginity, and had come to avenge it. Nothing would please him more than to take his fists to this "lanky" fellow's ribs.

"You want something from me, Ryerson?" he growled.

"Desperately," Jack admitted. "May I join you?"

When the annoyingly congenial gentleman had settled into the chair opposite him, Daniel demanded impatiently, "Did you come here to drink?"

"I'll have what you're having."

"Fitting," Daniel grumbled, then immediately he reprimanded himself. Erica deserved better. "What can I do for you?"

"I wanted to thank you. For bringing Erica home safely."

"It didn't take me out of my way." He shrugged, studying his adversary to see if he had guessed at the intimacies Daniel had shared with his fiancée.

"Good." Jack smiled. "I'd like to charter your schooner for another, somewhat longer voyage."

"Let me guess," Daniel drawled. "For your honeymoon? And I'm guessing Miss Lane doesn't know about this romantic surprise? Take my word for it, Ryerson. She wouldn't be comfortable aboard the *Rigger*. I can recommend—"

"Wait!" Jack slapped a serious handful of bills onto the table. "Take her to Paris. There are times when a girl needs to talk to her mother, and this is one of them."

Daniel stared at the small fortune, speechless and annoyed. He didn't want Ryerson's money, he wanted his woman! Not that he'd take her back, under any set of circumstances. But still, he wouldn't take the man's money.

"I'm not judging you, McCullum," Jack was confiding earnestly. "I can tell from the way Erica talks that she essentially threw herself at you. But you might have had the decency to end it nicely. Would it have killed you to kiss her good-bye and tell her you'd never forget her, or some such nonsense? It would have made *my* life simpler, I can guarantee you that. Instead, I've been living in a tear-filled hell of *your* making for five straight days."

"You should have watched more closely when you met us at the dock," Daniel complained.

"Ah, yes. The infamous kiss," Jack drawled. "The one that was supposed to teach me how to please my next fiancée. I'm glad to say I missed it, but thanks for trying. In any case, that wasn't a good-bye kiss, it was Erica's version of a gift to me." Rubbing his eyes, he sighed. "She really is insane, isn't she?"

"What are you saying?" Daniel demanded. "That we were teaching you to kiss your *next* fiancée?"

Jack looked up from his hands and shrugged. "She has it all planned, McCullum. Even after that fiasco with you, she's convinced life should completely revolve around romance, to the exclusion of everything else." Lowering his voice he added, "The truth is, as beautiful as she is, and as much time as I've invested in her, that aspect of her has always terrified me a little, and now, she's completely uncontrollable. Maybe there's a man in Paris who will be up to the challenge, but I intend to escape with my sanity still intact. I don't know you from Adam, but still, I advise you to do the same. Some females are just impossible from the day they're born. I believe our pretty Erica may be one of them."

"I think you're right," Daniel announced quietly. "The girl is insane. *And* impossible."

Jack Ryerson was visibly relieved by Daniel's reaction. "We understand each other then?" he asked carefully.

"We do indeed," was Daniel's careful reply.

Erica wanted nothing more than to wallow in misery over her star-crossed love affair, but her conscience wouldn't allow it. Not when she thought about Sarah Gibson and the cruel disappointments that tenderhearted woman had been forced to endure. There was something ominous in Sarah's mood these days. She had long periods of melancholia during which she refused to talk to Erica, interspersed with unfounded bursts of optimism during which she made enigmatic references to ''second chances,'' and Russell Braddock's ''genius,'' and miracles. It was as though the poor woman's mind was unraveling before Erica's eyes! Not only did Sarah consider the silly letters Erica had written to her to be her ''most precious possessions,'' she had actually considered taking her own life!

You think your heart was broken, Erica Lane, but imagine losing your entire family when you weren't yet fifteen years of age! Jack was right about all that. It did something to the poor woman's mind as well as to her heart!

It made her grieve for Daniel too, remembering how Sean had recounted the tragedies his friend had suffered in his youth. Having barely survived the loss of her father at age seventeen, Erica could only imagine how Sarah, and Daniel, had managed to cope with the wholesale loss of their entire families at so young an age.

Sean was right, she told herself coldly. *Daniel McCullum doesn't need someone else to love. He can love the sea, because it's always there—invincible and eternal. He can't love a woman again, or more children. Most of all, he can't love you! It's selfish of you to have wished otherwise, and it was practical of Daniel—coldhearted but practical—to put so final an end to it.*

If only he hadn't felt the need to behave so cruelly. Even knowing that he had acted to protect himself from emotions that might have consumed him, it didn't excuse the way he'd spoken to her on deck that last morning. Ordering her off the schooner, complaining that she was a pest, keeping her from saying farewell to Polly—those transgressions went beyond any excuse or justification.

And so, when Jack's butler announced that Captain and Polly McCullum had come to call on Miss Erica, she was supremely torn. He had protected his heart from her, and shouldn't she now do the same and have Jack send him away? But she had to see Polly—the child was innocent, even if Erica and Daniel were not—and so she hastily dressed in a modest but flattering green dress.

Just as Erica was pulling her wild tresses into a severe, matronly bun at the nape of her neck, Sarah flew into the room, gushing, "He couldn't stay away from you! And the child is with him, too! Hurry, Erica. I can't wait to meet them."

Erica stared in surprise. "You're not nervous at the prospect of meeting Captain McCullum?"

"I doubt he'll even notice me." Sarah grinned. "It's you he's come to see. He probably wants to sweep you into his arms and carry you back to the island—"

"I doubt it," Erica said sadly. "It's more likely that Polly missed me so much, he decided to bring her so that I can explain why I ran off so quickly. He may be an awful lover, but in the end, he's a good father."

"It's fate," Sarah corrected. "It's all happening, just as Mr. Braddock knew it would. Happily ever after—"

"Gracious, Sarah, it's not at all like that. Since when did *you* become a matchmaker?" She shook her head, amused and relieved to see the governess in such good spirits. Checking her reflection one last time, she then moved to the door, warning over her shoulder, "Come and meet them if you wish. But don't forget how he broke my heart. I wouldn't even consider laying eyes on him again if it weren't for Polly."

She hurried down the stairs and into the parlor, where Polly was accepting a piece of candy from Jack, while Daniel paced impatiently in front of the fireplace. Refusing to notice how handsome the captain looked in his proper coat and trousers, Erica dropped to her knees just as Polly ran to her and threw herself into her arms.

"Erica! I missed you!"

"I missed you too, darling. How beautiful you look. If I'd known you had this gorgeous lace dress, I would have insisted you wear it every day!"

"Papa bought it for me yesterday. He wanted everything to be just perfect when we saw you."

"You are always perfect, darling." She hugged the child tightly to her chest. "I'm just so very glad you're here. I'm sorry I left the schooner without any explanation or good-bye."

"Papa explained it."

"Oh?"

"He said there was a misunderstanding."

"Well . . ." For the first time, she looked directly up at Daniel. "What a perfect description of that entire voyage." Rising until she was standing tall and proud, she extended her hand to him. "Captain McCullum."

Striding over to her, he bowed slightly and kissed her fingertips. "Miss Lane."

"I don't mean to interrupt," Sarah murmured softly from behind them. "But I thought perhaps, if you'd like to be alone, Polly might enjoy visiting with us upstairs."

"That's a good idea, Sarah," Jack boomed. "The girls would love a new playmate. And, Polly? You should see the fancy dollhouse Erica made me buy last year. It cost more than the mansion you're standing in."

"Jack!" Erica scolded. Then she smiled down at Polly. "Would you like to see it? Since I've no need to visit with your father, I could take you myself—"

"That's not necessary," Sarah interceded smoothly. "Polly and I will have great fun alone. And I'm sure you and the captain will enjoy the opportunity to reminisce." With a shy smile, she held her hand out to Daniel. "I've read so much about you, Captain. It's an honor to finally meet you."

Daniel flushed, but gallantly kissed her fingertips as he'd done for Erica. "You read about me? Do you mean in Braddock's letters?"

"And in Erica's." Sarah giggled. "You needn't worry, Captain. I've no more interest in you as a mate than you have in me. But I admire you greatly, for a thousand different reasons."

Daniel grinned. "I'd like to see those letters one day."

"Well, you shan't," Erica snapped. "Polly, darling, perhaps it *is* best that you run along with Sarah for just a minute or two."

To her surprise, the child grabbed at her hand, clinging to it as though she'd never let loose. "I want to be with you. I've missed you so much. Uncle Sean said we might never see you again—"

"Gracious!" Erica knelt to embrace the child once again. "Remind me to scold him royally the next time I see him. Which will be often, believe me." She felt a sting of tears behind her eyes as she insisted softly, "Don't ever worry, darling. One of my fondest wishes is to see you as a grown woman, with suitors swarming about you, and sailors obeying your every command. You won't get rid of me for years, I promise you."

"You always say the right thing." Polly sighed, relaxing in relief against Erica's bosom. "I wish I could be like you."

"Oh, dear, don't wish *that*," Erica scolded lightly. "If you were like me, your father would be anxious to rid himself of you."

"What?" Polly asked innocently.

"Nothing, darling." Kissing the child's cheek, she asked, "Wouldn't you like to see the dollhouse, for just five minutes? Sarah will promise not to keep you long."

Polly nodded. "I've never seen a dollhouse." With a quick glance at Daniel for a nod of permission, she shyly accepted Sarah's outstretched hand, and the two moved into the foyer and climbed the stairs, chatting amicably as they went.

As soon as Polly was out of sight, Erica's face settled into a scowl. "How dare you come here."

"I've come to apologize—"

"Don't bother!" she snapped. "Jack, send him away."

"That wouldn't make much sense, since I'm the one who invited him." Jack chuckled.

"What?" she gasped. "What were you thinking?"

"I wanted to rid myself of what sailors refer to as an albatross. Isn't that so, Captain?"

Daniel grinned and reached again for Erica. "We've had a misunderstanding, you and I—"

"Are you referring to the fact that you are a heartless bastard?" She sniffed, jerking her arm away firmly. "Jack and I came to that conclusion ages ago. Is there another reason you're here?"

"He's going to take you to Paris," Jack explained. "To see your—"

"He is not!"

Daniel chuckled sympathetically. "You'd better let me handle this, Ryerson. You've taken enough of the risk."

Jack nodded gratefully and receded into the shadows.

"So?" Erica demanded. "Why are you here?"

"My daughter was inconsolable."

"Oh." She grimaced in apology. "You did the right thing, of course, bringing her here. But you did the *wrong* thing, sending me away without allowing me to explain it all to her in the first place. I know now why you did it, but still, it was unforgivable."

"I agree. I humbly apologize."

"Oh." Erica bit her lip, desperate not to be disarmed, or worse, seduced, by his charming manner. "I'll write to Polly every month, and visit her at least once a year. Now, go away.''

"I'm here to invite you to a party."

"What?" Erica stared in disbelief. "You think I'd go somewhere—*anywhere!*—with the likes of you?"

Daniel shrugged. "Sean felt you should be there. Since it was your doing—"

"Sean and Betsy?" She tried unsuccessfully not to grin. "Oh, Daniel! How wonderful! Of course we'll be there. Jack, I hope you don't have any plans—"

"I'm never setting foot in Salem again," Jack protested cheerfully. "It's bad luck. If you want to go, go with McCullum. Or don't. Just leave me out of it."

Daniel stepped close to her and repeated stubbornly, "We had a misunderstanding. I'll be damned if I'm going to spend the rest of my life miserable because of it."

"Don't blame me for the fact that you're miserable," Erica warned. "And don't blame those darling children either."

"What?"

"You should be sailing a clipper ship in the dark reaches of the unexplored Pacific, but instead you hug the coast, and blame everyone but yourself," she accused sharply. "Just don't you dare have the nerve to blame *me* for it. All I ever asked was to be treated with respect for the short time we had together. I never had any intention of asking, or wanting, anything more. You flattered yourself if you believed I did."

She thought Daniel was finally going to lose his temper, but at that moment, Jack stepped forward and murmured something to the sea captain, who then nodded and announced, "Are you coming with me to celebrate Sean's wedding or not?"

Erica spun to glare at Jack. "What did you say?"

"I asked him if I should go fetch his daughter," Jack

informed her smoothly. "So if you'll excuse me, I'll do just that."

Erica huffed in disbelief, but it was too late. Jack was taking the stairs two at a time, and she was alone with Captain McCullum. And to her distress, he was studying her in a way that evoked memories of every sinful encounter they'd enjoyed together.

"Keep you eyes and your wayward thoughts to yourself, Daniel McCullum," she warned shakily. "Jack may seem harmless, but if you dare touch me, he'll kill you. Don't doubt that for an instant."

"He's very fond of you," Daniel agreed. "Lanky, too."

She took a deep breath, then smiled coolly. "Would you do me a favor, Captain?"

"Anything."

"Tell me what Jack said to you, just then before he left."

"He reminded me that you're insane," Daniel revealed solemnly. "It gives us both perspective when you seem to be spouting nonsense."

"I see." She fought to maintain the chilly smile, and turned toward the stairs in time to see Polly skip into view. "There you are! Did you see the dollhouse?"

"It's beautiful," Polly gushed. "Sarah wants me to stay and play with the girls while you and Papa go to Uncle Sean's party."

"No!" Erica and Daniel protested in unison, then Erica added more gently, "We appreciate the offer, but I've missed Polly dreadfully."

Sarah's brow furrowed. "I know you don't want to leave her with anyone but family, Captain. But she'd be safe with me. We were having the most lovely visit. Weren't we, Polly?"

"It was nice," the child hedged. "But I want to ride with Erica in the carriage."

"Then it's settled." Erica sighed in relief. "I'll need a few minutes, though, to pack up a few belongings. So you can play with Mary and Janie until then."

"Bring enough for a week," Daniel suggested. "The party's tomorrow night, and the wedding will be Sunday afternoon."

She sent Jack an annoyed look, but knew better than to ask again that he serve as her escort. From the expression on his face, he was already counting the minutes before he'd have his study, and his life, back again. "I'll stay until Monday morning, but not a minute longer. Jack, will you at least have the decency to have your driver come for me then? And, Captain, it should only take a few minutes for me to pack."

"You're always worth waiting for, Miss Lane," he assured her. "Whom shall I expect? The princess or the peasant?"

Erica glared, but Polly clapped her hands in delight. "The princess! Our favorite! Right, Papa?"

"One of our favorites," he agreed with a roguish smile.

"And whom shall I expect?" Erica demanded quietly. "The pirate or the beast?"

"The devoted servant, despite his temperamental outbursts to the contrary," Daniel assured her.

Jack applauded briskly. "Excellent. Erica, go and get dressed. I have work to do."

She grimaced as she brushed past him on the stairs. "I despise you again, Jack Ryerson."

"I'm growing accustomed to it," he replied. "On the other hand, I'll always love you madly, so don't bother arguing with *that*."

"Love," she said with a sniff. "As though either of you know anything about it." Then she swept up the stairs without a backward glance, trying not to think about the fact that she and Daniel—and Polly of course—would soon be sharing an intimate carriage ride all the way back to Salem.

"And she said she's going to give me something special next week, for my birthday. She said I remind her of her brother," Polly chattered, as she'd done since the moment they'd left Boston. "She's so nice."

"Sarah and her brother were very close." Erica smiled. "It's lovely of her to compare you to him."

"He was just a little baby when he died," the child continued. "But she thinks he would have been a sailor, because they lived so close to the sea. Just like we do."

"That's what she chose to talk about all that time?" Daniel complained. "A dead boy? I thought you were supposed to be playing with Ryerson's sisters."

Erica glared at him pointedly. "All that matters is that Polly had a lovely visit, and saw the dollhouse. Would you like me to give you your own dollhouse for your birthday, darling? A wonderful one, with beautiful furnishings?"

"I can't wait! Will we still be in Salem on my birthday, Papa? I don't want to miss my gifts."

Daniel pretended to ponder the question. "I'd say that depends on Erica."

Erica had tried not to look at or speak to Daniel more than absolutely necessary, but had to ask, "Will Betsy be going with you when you sail?"

"I doubt it. She's welcome though. Sean knows that. Either way, we need to be headed back to the Crescent by the end of next week, if we want to be there before the hurricane season starts."

"Will you be coming back with us, Erica?" Polly asked hopefully.

"Gracious, no. I'll be off for Paris, I suppose. On a grand steamer ship."

She noted how Daniel's jaw had tightened, and wondered if it was because of the blasphemous mention of steam, or something a bit more flattering. Not that it mattered, of course. She had decided, during the first few hours of this carriage ride, to accept his apology eventually, but that didn't mean she had any intention of resuming any sort of affair with him. She simply wanted to salvage a friendship with him, and to acknowledge that a marriage between them would have been a travesty.

"Why don't you two females have your visit without me," he suggested suddenly, banging on the roof of the carriage as he spoke. As soon as the vehicle had come to a standstill, he was out the door, assuring Polly over his shoulder, "I'll meet up with you at your grandma's house in a few hours. See to it that the O'Rourkes make our guest comfortable until then."

Disappearing from view for a moment, he reappeared astride the tall chestnut steed he'd had tied to the rear of the carriage. "Au revoir, mademoiselles," he called out cheerfully, then he was gone in a cloud of dust, leaving Erica to wonder if she'd pushed him too far.

"Did he seem annoyed to you, Polly?" she asked sheepishly.

"Papa hates carriages," the child explained. "But he says ladies need them, because of our fancy clothes." Her voice grew wistful as she added, "I like horses, though. Don't you?"

"I adore them. We should have insisted we all ride to Salem on horseback," Erica said. "But this gives you and me a chance to visit, so there's no harm. And your dress really is so utterly darling, it would be a shame to ruin it. Have you any riding clothes?"

"Not girl ones."

"Well, we'll see about getting you something stylish but comfortable. There's no way around it, you need a whole new wardrobe. But at least you have something pretty to wear to your uncle's wedding. Have you met Betsy?"

Polly nodded. "She's been Uncle Sean's friend for a long time. She comes and eats at grandma's when we're in Salem."

"Is she pretty?"

The child nodded again. "Nice, too. I thought you knew her. Uncle Sean said it was you that brought them together."

"Did he? How sweet." Erica had noticed that the little girl's eyes were starting to droop, and so she draped her arm around her shoulders and squeezed lovingly. "Do you want to sleep for a while, darling?"

"Just for a minute," Polly agreed, yawning slightly before snuggling against Erica. "I missed you so much. I was afraid you wouldn't come back with us, but Papa said he'd find a way to convince you. And he did. So that's good."

Erica sighed. "For now, at least. And after this week, we'll find some way to visit each other often."

"Papa says he's going to marry you, and you're going to live with us on the island forever," Polly murmured, her voice growing softer with each word as she began to nod off to sleep.

"He said *that?*" Erica gasped, but the child was already asleep, and so she bit her lip and tried to imagine what Daniel could be thinking. Snapping at her one minute, wanting to marry her the next. Torn, just as she'd been. And wrong, just as she'd been, to imagine there was any way he could keep his children secluded on an island, safe and protected, yet still hope to lead the reckless, danger-laced life he craved.

So you'll just have to be strong for him, she chided herself wistfully. *Try to remember his angry words on the deck of the schooner that last morning—you're a pest, disturbing his world, just when it was growing manageable again after all the sadness and interruptions. Accept his apology, because you know in your heart he's not the beast he pretended to be. So let it go, and be grateful he allowed you to have this time with Polly before the* Rigger *sails away.*

Cuddling the child to her side, she closed her eyes and tried not to dream of the love she knew could never be simple; could never be right; and therefore, could never really be love.

CHAPTER ELEVEN

Michael O'Rourke's grandparents proved to be warm and welcoming hosts, settling Erica briskly into her new room, then plying her with food and sharing stories of their family. Most of all, they extolled the generosity of Daniel McCullum to such an extent that Erica almost weakened in her resolve to put the captain forever out of her life. According to Patrick O'Rourke, Abigail Lindstrom was nothing less than a pauper since her husband had absconded with all their modest, accumulated wealth when he'd run off to California after Lilli's death. It was only because of Daniel that the house hadn't been sold off. The captain had paid off all the debt Martin Lindstrom had left behind, then he'd hired the O'Rourkes to keep the place up, supposedly so that Daniel could use it on his visits to Salem.

"And us needing a place to stay, and honest work, after my unfortunate accident," Patrick finished, indicating the leg that had been bitten off at the knee by a hungry shark five years earlier. "Danny could easily have boarded up this place, for as little time as he spends in Salem, but he knew we were needing it, and he's got that soft heart, so here we are."

"You're underestimating your contribution," Erica assured him gently. "I've never seen such lovely gardens, or such a clean, cozy house. It's a perfect place for Daniel to rest after voyages such as the one we just made, where all the crew work so hard with almost no sleep at all. You'd be so proud of Michael if you could see what a wonderful sailor he is."

The grandfather's eyes shone with pride. "So Danny tells us. Of course, how Michael tells it, it sounds like we almost lost the poor boy, and would have, if not for Danny."

"You'll never convince 'himself' there, or me for that matter, that Danny McCullum isn't a saint," Mary O'Rourke added cheerfully as she set a huge piece of apple pie in front of Erica. "That's a fine husband you're getting yourself, Miss Erica."

She winced but didn't argue, since it didn't seem to do any good at all. Daniel had apparently convinced everyone that he and Erica were as engaged as Sean and Betsy, and she had decided hours earlier to let him be the one to convince them otherwise, once they'd had a chance to talk in private. In the meantime, she enjoyed being pampered, and visiting with Polly. And waiting for "Saint" Daniel to appear.

And when he finally did arrive, she knew it instantly, not from the sound of his voice, but from the silence, as Mary and Patrick O'Rourke beamed in the direction of the doorway, and Polly squirmed, a conspiratorial gleam in her eyes. Resisting an urge to turn around and stare into his royal-blue eyes, Erica dabbed at her mouth with a napkin and waited for him to announce himself.

He did so by grabbing her, gently but firmly, and spinning her right out of her chair and into his arms. "I thought you might have turned the carriage around and gone back to Ryerson again," he told her, his voice husky with relief.

She moistened her lips and tried for a casual smile, hoping her eyes weren't shining as brightly as his. "Jack made it clear he wanted me to go away for a while, and the O'Rourkes have made me welcome, so I'll stay until the wedding, if that's agreeable."

"There, Danny! Do you see?" Patrick boomed. "She isn't angry with you at all."

"She wouldn't show it in front of the three of you, even if she were," Daniel explained. "It's one of her most endearing qualities. So?" he added wryly to Erica. "Shall we speak in private?"

"It isn't necessary," she assured him, wriggling loose from his hands as she spoke. "I've completely forgotten the little misunderstanding we had aboard the schooner." To prove it, she raised herself onto her tiptoes and brushed her lips across his. "There, do you see? All is forgiven."

"She's angrier than I thought." Daniel grinned toward the O'Rourkes. "But since the stew smells so good, we'll just play her little game for a while." Sitting down in the chair Erica had just vacated, he pulled her smoothly into his lap. "So? What were you talking about when I walked in? The squall?"

Mary O'Rourke set a steaming bowl in front of him, along with a huge slice of fresh, warm bread. "About how you saved our grandson's life. And not for the first time."

"And about how you're such a saint," Erica added dryly. "Of course, they didn't need to tell *me* that."

"Do you see?" Daniel chuckled. "She's furious."

Erica grimaced and tried to wriggle away, but he steadied her easily with one hand. "I'm not going to let you get away, so don't bother trying. Just settle down now and have something to eat."

"I've had enough food to last a week." She hesitated, then relaxed a bit against his chest, guiltily enjoying the feel of him after the lonely nights at the Ryerson house. "But when you're ready for some pie, I'll share mine with you."

He seemed surprised, and grateful, at the conciliatory gesture. "We'll have our pie, and then our talk. Sean and Betsy will be coming around later. She wanted a chance to meet you before the party, since you're the one who convinced Sean to make her his bride."

Erica smiled shyly. "He just needed a tiny push. And she's better than a match with Abby's niece, don't you agree?"

Daniel nodded. "He loves her. If a man loves a girl, he should marry her. Isn't that so?"

Erica shrugged. "Someone should be sure to remind the captain of that when a boy comes asking for Polly's hand."

Patrick and Mary laughed heartily, as though fully appreciating the response Daniel would undoubtedly have when that first marriage proposal arrived.

"Remind me of it yourself." Daniel grinned. "You'll be sitting right there beside me, wondering if he's good enough for our little girl."

And so it went for the rest of the meal, with Erica attempting to politely dispel the rampant rumor of their impending nuptials, and Daniel effectively subverting her at every turn, until even she began to believe he might be able to change her mind with his charming, gravelly entreaties. But Sean and his intended—a ruddy-cheeked barmaid with an infectious giggle—arrived during dessert, preventing any opportunity for a serious talk that evening.

The first mate managed to pull Erica aside for just a moment, asking quietly, "Is it all settled, then? You and Danny, I mean? Or are you just behaving for the O'Rourkes' benefit?"

"I always behave." She patted his cheek. "Don't worry, Sean. I won't marry him."

"I've changed my mind about all that," Sean protested quickly. "He's been miserable without you."

"He'll be miserable for a while, and so will I. And then I'll find someone else, and he'll rediscover the sea, and it will all be for the best."

"You're so sure you'll find someone who makes you feel the way Danny does?"

"I have no illusions about that," she murmured sadly. "But we both know it was a love that couldn't last. Not without stealing his future from him."

"That's not how he sees it."

"Then we'll just have to convince him it's true. You'll help me do that for him, won't you, Sean?"

"You're a stubborn girl," the sailor complained. "When I wanted you to leave him be, you couldn't stay away from him. Now—"

"I know. I'm impossible to please." She patted his cheek again. "I'm going to go and see if Polly's asleep. I'll probably stay in there for the rest of the night, for Daniel's sake. Will you explain to Betsy why I had to sneak off, and tell her I can't wait to celebrate with you both at the ale house tomorrow evening?"

"Go on, then," he grumbled. "But don't be surprised if Danny comes in and drags you out of there, and into his bed. He's missed you something fierce these last days and nights."

She flushed and nodded. "I'm hoping he won't want to act so boldly with the O'Rourkes in the next room."

With a glance toward Daniel, who was trading yet another seafaring yarn with Patrick O'Rourke, she scurried down the hall to the guest room where she grabbed a nightgown Mary O'Rourke had unpacked into a dresser drawer. Then she hurried to Polly's bedroom and was soon climbing into bed, taking care not to wake the sleeping child. Her heart was pounding as she remembered Sean's prediction, but Daniel McCullum didn't appear. After a full hour of waiting, she finally relaxed and allowed herself to remember how wonderful it had felt, sitting on his lap, cuddling against him, looking up with shy confusion into his vivid blue eyes. Then his image faded into a dream of a handsome, gravelly voiced pirate, and the princess who kept trying valiantly not to love him.

When Erica wandered into the kitchen the next morning, Polly smiled with delight from her perch atop the table, where she was shelling peas for Mary O'Rourke. "You slept in my bed!"

"I hope you didn't mind."

"I didn't even know it. And then Papa said not to wake you, so I didn't."

"Danny told us how it is with you," Patrick O'Rourke added mischievously. "He said the longer we let you sleep, the prettier you'd be when you woke up. He was right."

"You're so sweet." She eyed the cozy group fondly. "Is Captain McCullum here? He and I can't keep avoiding our little chat, I'm afraid."

"He said you'd say that," Polly informed her cheerfully. "But he says it'll keep until tonight."

"Oh, really?"

"There are repairs needed on the *Moon Rigger*," Patrick explained hastily. "Danny wanted to oversee them. But if you need to talk to him now, I can walk you over there, if you don't mind going slowly."

"But you need to hurry back, because Uncle Sean will be coming to build the dollhouse." Polly's eyes sparkled with anticipation. "He said there's no need for me to wait until next week. He says it can have as many rooms as I want, and as many gables and doors and windows, too. I need your help choosing, Erica."

"I wouldn't want to miss any of it," Erica admitted, charmed by the thought of actually working with the designer of a future McCullum family heirloom. "And I wouldn't want to bother the captain if he's busy with the schooner."

"Come and have a cup of tea then," Mary urged. "I'll make you anything you'd like to eat. And Danny will be back in no time, I'm sure."

Erica settled at the table and smiled impishly. "As many rooms as you'd like? What do you think, Polly? Will it be a grand mansion, like Mr. Ryerson's? Or a pretty town house, like this one?"

"I want it to have a porch on the roof, like the cottages on the bay. What do you call it, Mrs. O'Rourke?"

"A widow's walk," the housekeeper explained gently. "For a sailor's wife, so she can watch and wait when a ship's late arriving and she's fearing for the worst."

"Gracious," Erica murmured. "Are you sure that's what you want, Polly?"

Mary gave her guest an apologetic hug. "What was I thinking, saying such a thing? It won't be that way with Danny, I promise you. He's too fine a captain to ever leave you widowed, dear."

"I know that." She glanced toward Polly and was

relieved to see that the morbid nuances hadn't affected
the child. And they shouldn't have affected Erica, but
they had, and she was pleased when Sean stomped onto
the back porch, toolbox in hand and a cheerful whistle
on his lips, ready to distract her from her overworked
imagination.

"There now. We've made a good start of it, at least,
wouldn't you say?" Sean stood back and admired his handi-
work proudly. "Is this what you had in mind, Polly?"

"I love it," the girl informed him simply.

"It's the grandest home I've ever seen." Erica smiled,
loving the way the child had insisted on having every
possible feature of every possible style of house combined
into one glorious, contradictory structure. Gables and tur-
rets, bay windows and portholes, secret passageways and
circular staircases—the framework was there for all.
Including the widow's walk, although they had judi-
ciously decided to refer to it as "the roof porch."

"As time allows, we'll put up the walls and floors and
finishing touches, and then we'll start with the furnishings.
I'll leave it to Erica to find the wee dolls for you," the
uncle added with a wink.

"And dogs and cats. And a horse?" Polly asked hopefully.

"Don't tell me you're wanting a stable now." Sean
pretended to groan. "Can it wait until tomorrow, at least?
If I'm not washed up and presentable before the guests
start arriving, Betsy may come to her senses and send
me packing." He studied Polly intently. "I know your
father said the party was just for adults, but you're welcome just the same, you know."

"I'll have fun playing with my dollhouse," the child
assured him. "And I'll have other toys to play with too.

I don't want to come to the party, but I want to come to the wedding, because of my new dress.''

"You'll be there, or there'll be no wedding at all," Sean assured her. "Betsy has plans for you to carry a bouquet of roses, just like hers.''

"Assuming she'll still marry you if you're late for your own party," Erica warned, then she laughed when he jumped to his feet in exaggerated distress. "Send Captain McCullum home if you see him, so he has time to bathe without making us late."

Sean pulled her aside. "Shall I tell Danny you offered to join him in the tub? That's how Betsy gets her way with me."

"That's enough, Sean Lynch. You know how I disapprove of matchmaking." She gave him a quick hug. "I'll see you soon."

"There'll be plenty of food, so don't bother having supper before you come," he instructed as he hefted his toolbox and headed for the door.

"Wait!" Polly ran to him and he dropped to one knee just in time for a loving embrace. "Thank you for the beautiful dollhouse, Uncle Sean. I've never had anything so wonderful to play with."

"Well, now that you're such a young lady, it's only fitting, don't you suppose?" He grinned toward Erica. "And you should be thanking Erica, too. It's she that's managed to change us all so much, all for the better, don't you know?"

"Amen to that," a gruff voice confirmed from behind them, and Daniel stepped into view, his eyes shifting from Erica to the dollhouse with clear appreciation.

"Captain McCullum." Erica blushed. "Thank goodness you're home in time to bathe for the party. And Sean? Betsy will be wondering where you are if you don't hurry."

The first mate nodded and, after another quick hug for Polly, he disappeared through the front door.

"Did you see the dollhouse, Papa?"

"It's a beauty," Daniel agreed.

"It has six gables and ten doors, and twenty-five windows. And a widow's walk, only Erica won't let us call it that, cause it makes her scared."

"I didn't think anything frightened our Erica," Daniel murmured, crossing to her and looking into her eyes. "You saw how it was on the *Rigger,* didn't you? I'm safest when I'm at sea."

"I know that." Erica forced herself to smile brightly. "I just didn't think it was an appropriate feature for a child's dollhouse. Come and see the rest of the place, Captain. Your daughter has quite an imagination, and your first mate is amazingly talented."

Daniel studied her for a moment longer, then moved to inspect the dollhouse, pronouncing it "a fine place."

Polly beamed, then informed him briskly, "Erica wants you to take a bath."

"Well, then, I will."

Ignoring his care-to-join-me expression, Erica backed away toward the guest bedroom, a formal smile on her lips. "I understand from Sean that we can walk to the wharf from here tonight, rather than taking a carriage. I'd like that, Captain. It will give us a chance at last to have our discussion." Without giving him a chance to reply, she turned and bustled away.

Daniel watched until she was out of sight, then asked his daughter, "How was Erica's mood today? Does she seem angry with me?"

"No, Papa. She seemed happy, except when we talked about the widow's walk."

"Did your uncle explain to her that we're safe on the *Rigger?*"

Polly nodded.

"It doesn't worry *you*, does it? The sailing? The dangers at sea?"

The little girl grinned. "It's safer than land, isn't it?"

He smiled proudly. "That's absolutely right." Seating himself in Mary O'Rourke's rocking chair, he gestured for the child to climb onto his lap. "How did I get so lucky, having two such brave females in my life?"

"I don't know, Papa."

"Does it bother you that we won't be bringing you with us to the ale house tonight? It's no place for a child, not even a brave one."

"I *want* to stay here."

It surprised Daniel—she had protested so vehemently about it earlier that week!—then he remembered the new dollhouse and smiled. "I forgot. You've a house to furnish now, don't you? That's quite a responsibility."

Polly smiled. "Do you know what Uncle Sean said, Papa? Betsy wants me to carry flowers at the wedding."

"You're turning into a proper young lady," he complained. "Do you have any idea how much that worries me? Or how proud it makes me? Give me a hug, and promise me you won't grow up too quickly."

She wrapped her arms around his neck and squeezed with all her might. "I promise, Papa." Then she wrinkled her little nose and added diplomatically, "Erica wants you to bathe, and so you should do it right away."

Daniel roared with laughter, hugged her again, and plopped her onto her feet. "Excuse me then, fussy miss. I'll try to make myself presentable."

When she giggled, he chuckled with contentment before striding out of the parlor and into the kitchen, to be sure Mary O'Rourke had followed his instructions and fixed a bath on the back porch, where he could soak for a while, enjoy a cigar, and plan how best to approach Erica. Not that planning would do him much good, he suspected. She was too unpredictable. But since that was one of her most attractive qualities, he wasn't about to complain about it.

Still, he wanted to make the most of this evening, and while he knew she would refuse to outright argue with him, he had to find a way to change her mind. Because whether she was angry with him or not, there was definitely something bothering her, and he knew instinctively it went well beyond his poor behavior at their last farewell. Something in her pretty golden eyes told him she'd decided they couldn't make one another happy, and he had come to believe fervently and completely that they could. That they were, in fact, each other's best chance at finding true happiness in the years and decades to come.

At least he had more information about her than he'd had on the schooner. Seeing Jack Ryerson's house had given him a clue as to the style of living to which she was accustomed. And if she'd had any input into the design of the ostentatious dollhouse, that impression had been confirmed. More troubling was the fact that she'd found the "widow's walk" disheartening. Was that what was holding her back from him? A fear that the next squall or yardarm could make a widow of her? If so, he had to find a way to reassure her.

Above all, he had to find a way to convince her of how much he loved her, because with Erica, that was really all that counted in the end. How had Ryerson put it? That she was convinced life revolved exclusively around romance, or some such indictment?

As Daniel stripped off his soiled work clothes and slipped into the steaming bath, he chuckled in sheepish acknowledgment of the fact that, for reasons he'd never regret, he had belatedly become convinced of it himself.

* * *

For the engagement party, Erica had selected one of her favorite dresses, a dark maroon silk with a tight, white bodice, the neckline of which was cut to reveal a hint of her high, firm breasts. She had always wanted to wear her hair loose around her shoulders with this particular outfit, but her mother hadn't allowed it. Of course, her mother had never met Captain Daniel McCullum, and so couldn't have known how important it could be to draw blue fire from his eyes with so simple and unassuming a maneuver.

She could no longer deceive herself as to what the evening would bring. After all, Daniel's misbehavior on the deck of the schooner had clearly been born of a heartfelt struggle between wanting her and wanting his freedom. He'd chosen a beastly way to deal with that struggle, but there was no doubt he regretted it and wished to make it up to her.

With yet another mistake, she told herself wistfully as she brushed her auburn hair to a burnished sheen. *A marriage proposal. It will break your heart—and his— to turn him down, but at least you can enjoy a few final nights in his bed, once you've made him understand, as he once understood clearly, that it can never be more than that.*

Confused, yet also heady with anticipation, she stepped into the parlor, weakening almost instantly as his eyes roved over her in lusty appreciation. It was all she could do to not echo his behavior and greedily memorize every inch of his lean form, dressed casually yet with striking effect in black trousers, black shirt and a dark-gray silk vest.

"So?" He stepped close and twirled a lock of her hair

around his finger. "Is this a sign you aren't too angry with me, after all?"

"I don't know how to answer that question, Captain," she murmured.

"I never expect an answer from you," he reminded her just as softly. "But I may ask you to make an exception, for one particular question I have on my mind tonight."

Flushing, she turned to Polly, who was engrossed with the dollhouse. "Your father and I will be going now, darling. Enjoy your new toy, and tomorrow you can tell us all the plans you've made for furnishing it."

The child barely looked up. "Have a good time. Are you going to sleep in my bed again when you come back, Erica?"

Erica expected Daniel to chuckle at that, and was awed by his wary silence. Did he not know how she shivered at his every look and word? How his simple gesture of touching her hair had reawakened warm, wonderful needs in her? Hadn't he guessed that she would be in his arms the moment they were alone together?

"We'll see," she told the child simply, leaning down to peck her on the cheek. Then she placed her gloved hand on Daniel's arm, as casually as she could manage, and suggested, "Shall we go?"

He had planned on insisting they talk the moment they were out of sight of the house, but instead they walked in silence for blocks. It was such a joy, simply to be alone with her. To have her arm linked with his, her pace matched to his, her thoughts almost certainly on him and him alone. But they were almost within sight of the wharf, and while the smell of salt and fish in the air usually made him long to hurry until the sea herself was in sight, this evening he knew he needed to be sure there were no distractions other than Erica's beauty, and so he stopped her in the shadows and turned her toward himself.

"I smell a beach," she smiled shyly. "Couldn't we talk there?"

He chuckled. "It's not much of a beach. Nothing like the one we're used to on the island."

"Remember how it was there?" Her golden eyes twinkled at the memory. "How we'd be so desperate to kiss, but I would insist that we talk first?" She slipped her hands behind his neck and whispered, "There's so much to say, Captain. But it's been so long since we kissed—"

"I want to apologize for that kiss," he interrupted with clumsy insistence. "I misunderstood—"

"It's fine. I understand completely why you had to send me away so harshly. It was too harsh, though, and you're right to apologize. And I accept."

"Well, then. . . ." He leaned his head down and brushed his lips across hers. "I never intended to send you away, Erica."

"I know that. You thought I'd go back to Jack without the need to do anything on your part. And when it seemed as though I might stay, you didn't know quite how to— how did you put it?—rid yourself of me."

"So much for accepting my apology," he said with a scowl. "Are you going to quote it all back to me for the rest of our lives? I was jealous. I'm not proud of it, but I was."

"Jealous?"

He eyed her with amused frustration. "You asked me to kiss you, to demonstrate for Ryerson how you liked it done. How you'd been asking him to do it—to *you*— for years."

Erica nodded, a tiny frown creasing her forehead.

"He'll make all the same mistakes with the next girl if someone doesn't teach him how to act. And since when are you jealous of Jack? As I recall, you found the story of his courtship amusing, not enraging."

Daniel cupped her chin in his hand and instructed gruffly, "Pay attention. I'm telling you why I was jealous. I thought you wanted Ryerson to learn from me, so he could please you when you'd gone back to him."

"Oh." She seemed to be weighing the statement in her mind, as though it didn't quite make sense. Then, to his relief, a soft, appreciate laugh bubbled up through her. "Oh, dear!"

"You looked so beautiful," he explained sheepishly. "So aroused. And for the first time, I wondered if it was for me, or for him."

"And you were jealous?" She sighed and leaned against his chest. "I should have known you couldn't be cruel, Daniel McCullum."

"And I should have known you were mine and mine alone. I'd been so sure of it," he confessed softly. "And then suddenly, I wasn't sure of anything."

"That's how I felt, too." She looked up at him with tentative anticipation. "If you'd like to kiss me—"

His mouth stopped hers, kissing her as she'd wanted him to kiss her that morning on the deck, with all the love and longing their short affair had instilled in them forever. Then she pulled free, just enough to look up at him and murmur huskily, "We'll be late for the party. But after that, I want us to be together again. I want to make the most of these last precious days—"

"No more of that talk," he protested firmly. "We'll be together forever, but that doesn't mean tonight isn't important. I've never ached for a woman the way I've done for you these past few nights—"

"I've been miserable too."

Her eyes were shining brightly—*too* brightly—and he knew she was on the verge of tears. Gathering her against his chest, he vowed, "I'll do my best to make you happy, sweetheart. If that means spending less time at sea—"

"*Less* time?" she gasped, wrenching away from him as though horrified at the thought. "No wonder you're afraid to love me, if you think *that's* the price I would exact."

"Fine." He eyed her warily. "Then I promise I'll be more careful—"

"There!" She stomped her foot in disbelief. "Just when I was beginning to believe we might—well, never mind." She stepped back from him and raked her fingers through her hair, as though tending to that detail would put them back on course. "We have a party to attend, and I don't want to walk into that ale house with red eyes, on the arm of a sullen escort—"

"And, so, even now you won't argue with me? Even with our future at stake? Forget about the blasted party!" he roared. "I love you and I want to marry you. Tell me your terms, woman!"

She stared for a moment, then the prettiest smile he'd ever seen tugged at the corners of her mouth. "You'll do whatever I ask?"

He nodded, annoyed with himself, but unable to resist.

"Well, then . . ." She moistened her lips, then took his arm. "Behave yourself. Escort me to the party. Make love to me tonight. And after that, I'll share my terms with you. Is that acceptable, Captain McCullum?"

He couldn't get enough of her that evening as he watched her sparkle and tease, chatting with the partygoers while always keeping one playful eye on him, occasionally snuggling into his lap and reminding him, in a whisper, of exactly what she expected from him in the hours between then and dawn. He had no idea what it was she would demand from him, but trusted now that her "terms" would be remarkably close to his own. She was so amazingly beautiful, and so clearly in love, and his own heart ached, along with his body, with the knowledge that they'd somehow managed to do the impossible and win one another's elusive hearts.

She was enjoying the role of captain, and he fully intended to allow her to play it for the entire night. Then, during a story he was telling to Michael O'Rourke about the days during the war with the South, in which the *Moon Rigger* had been hired by the Revenue Service to combat smugglers and deliver dispatches, he unexpectedly regained the upper hand.

"They had so many new recruits," Daniel explained to young Michael. "Not one of them knew the ropes, and so we agreed to rotate them, a few at a time, into our crew, for training."

"Do you mean to say your regular crew members didn't need to join the service?" Erica asked innocently.

"The service was grateful to have our help, enlisted or not."

"But the captain joined up," Sean interrupted helpfully. "Otherwise, the Service would have had the right to place another officer on board the *Rigger*. Danny wasn't about to allow that."

"You're saying you joined the service?" Erica demanded. "I didn't realize that. Did you wear a uniform?"

"Sure. The most uncomfortable contraption I've ever had the misfortune to own."

"Oh." The corners of her mouth drooped. "So I suppose you threw it out? Or returned it to them?"

Daniel cocked his head, intrigued by her reaction. "I have it still."

"On the island?"

He almost laughed out loud, so certain was he now that he could read her naughty thoughts. "It's hanging in my cabin on the *Rigger,* right out there in the harbor. Would you like to see it? I'm sure Michael here would be willing to bring us in the cutter."

She swallowed and nodded, her cheeks flushed with anticipation. "If it's not too much trouble. We should be leaving soon anyway," she explained quickly to Sean. "Polly will be wondering where we are."

"It's settled then." Daniel dumped her off his lap and shook hands briskly with his first mate, unwilling to allow Erica to cool down any more than necessary. He had a marriage proposal to make, after all, and it would be greatly aided by the mood that was enveloping her before his very eyes.

She hugged Betsy first, and then Sean, then turned to Daniel and admitted in a whisper, "I've missed being aboard your schooner, Captain."

"You won't be disappointed," he promised, adding softly into her ear, "You should have told me sooner that you wanted an officer instead of a pirate."

When she looked up at him with those dancing golden eyes and laughed with appreciative delight, it was all he could do to keep from scooping her up into his arms and taking her there on the spot. Instead, he urged her quickly along after Michael O'Rourke as they all made their way toward the cutter.

Erica sat on the edge of the captain's bunk and stared expectantly toward the doorway. Having insisted that he make a grand entrance, worthy of a military hero, she now questioned her own sanity without truly lamenting its loss.

All that mattered to her at that moment, besides the uniform, of course, was that he'd been jealous. Somehow, the lack of jealousy had been more hurtful to her than the momentary bite of his cruel words on the deck of the schooner that fateful morning. The words, after all, had masked his desire to keep his freedom. But sending her back into *Jack's* arms? That had been the truly crushing blow.

When the door swung open, and he swaggered into view, a gleaming cutlass hanging by the side of his severely tailored and decorated blue uniform, she almost drooled with anticipation, but instead, she fanned herself and asked with wide-eyed innocence, "Can I help you, Captain?"

He grinned wickedly. "I'm lonely."

Erica stifled an appreciative laugh and lamented, in the same naive, trusting voice, "If only there were something I could do to help you. But I'm just a helpless female, and you're so big and strong and powerful."

Daniel chuckled. "Help me out of this contraption, and I'll try to think of some way you can ease my misery."

Erica knelt and began to work the brass buttons of his jacket. "And will you ease my misery too, sir?"

Daniel's response was to attack her with lusty purpose, raising her skirt high on her thighs as she shrieked with unabashed delight. Then his mouth covered hers, and his hands began to explore her, and her breath grew ragged with true need, until she thought she might lose her mind if he didn't enter her soon.

But her military lover was suddenly in no hurry, caressing her between her thighs and nuzzling her neck as though he didn't realize how far her anguish had progressed. Finally, she pleaded, "I want you, Captain.

Won't you take me now? I can't bear the lack of you any longer.''

"Are you saying you want to marry me?"

She moaned in complete confusion at the unexpected ultimatum. "Daniel, don't. Not now."

"I want your terms, wench, and be quick about it. There's only so much a man can take."

"Or a woman," she agreed huskily, stroking him with reluctant appreciation of the erotically effective tactic. "Will you promise to be reckless? To sail around the Horn in a clipper ship, bound for ports unknown? To bring your children with you, or leave them with their grandmother—"

"With Abby?" He raised his head and stared down at her in confusion. "Where will *you* be?"

"With you, Captain. Always with you."

"Damnation," he whispered in defeat. "I accept your terms. I should have known you wouldn't settle for less."

It was dawn when Michael O'Rourke delivered the two exhausted lovers onto the gray, unremarkable beach that adjoined the wharf. Weary but supremely content, Erica had asked that they avoid curious eyes along the wharf by landing at so deserted a spot. This time, however, it wasn't necessary for the vessel to run aground. As soon as they reached shallow waters, Daniel jumped from the cutter and held out his arms to his fiancée, more than happy to endure the icy waters of Salem's bay if that was what was necessary to carry her to the safety of the beach and, if she wished, to continue to carry her for the five short blocks to the master bedroom of the Lindstrom house.

They waved heartily toward Michael, then Daniel set

Erica on her feet on the coarse brown sand. "Not exactly paradise, is it?"

"To me, anywhere you are is paradise, Captain," she countered, raising up onto tiptoes and kissing him with suggestive thoroughness.

"Take care, or I'll be having you here in full view of the ale house," he warned, pulling her against himself and nuzzling her ear.

Erica laughed and scurried away from him. "Remember yourself, Captain McCullum. We should behave at the house, for Polly's sake." She spotted a folded length of pink lace on the beach and observed wistfully, "Look at that. Doesn't it remind you of her pretty dress? It was so sweet of you to buy that for her, Daniel. After all these years of breeches, I believe it truly meant the world to her to know you saw her as a pretty young lady."

"What is that?" he asked, moving to prod the cloth with his toe. Then his handsome brow furrowed, and as Erica watched in cautious disbelief, he leaned to pick up a delicate dress, holding it before his eyes as though willing himself not to recognize it.

Erica's throat was dry with foreboding as she pleaded, "Daniel, no. Oh, please, no. . . ."

"She must have known we were out there." He stopped himself, his eyes glazed with horror as they stared out toward the *Moon Rigger,* sitting still and graceful, as she so often did in the harbor of the Crescent. Then without warning, he dropped the garment and cupped his mouth with his hands, calling out frantically over the empty waters, "Polly! Polly McCullum!"

Erica's mind reeled with shock and pain, remembering haphazardly the facts as she knew them. Polly, swimming out to the schooner whenever she wished. Defending her behavior with a cheerful grin, yet promising Erica she would never again engage in such unsophisticated conduct. Standing in Jack's parlor, suddenly a perfect lady in a perfect pink lace frock. Playing contently with her dollhouse, agreeing to wait patiently for the return of Erica and Daniel. But all the while loving the sea, and the schooner, and the freedom to plunge into the water whenever she pleased. . . .

Except this water was icy cold and unforgiving of youthful bravado, and so Erica began to call out also, in a voice laced with fear and uncertainty, "Polly! Polly, can you hear us? We're on the beach! Your father and I! Polly McCullum!"

Daniel grabbed her by the shoulders and said sharply, "She can't hear us. She's either on the schooner or too far out." He took a sharp, painful breath, then instructed, "Go and find Sean at the ale house. Tell him I need him and the rest of the men. Tell him to bring blankets for her. She'll be freezing—" He seemed to choke on the words, then shook himself and insisted, "Find Sean first. Then go and fetch a doctor. Are you listening to me, Erica?"

"Daniel," she murmured, dazed with foreboding. "This can't be happening."

"Pay attention," he growled. "I need you. My daughter needs you. Go and find Sean."

Before she could respond, he'd stripped off his shirt and boots and was running into the icy water, diving headlong into the shallow surf.

"Daniel!" she shrieked, but he was out of sight, and while she longed to stay until she caught sight of him again, she knew he was right. She had to find Sean. And the rest of the crew. The more men in the water, the better the chance of finding Polly before it was too late.

She sprinted along the length of the beach, then sped along the pier, ignoring the sailors who stared at her as she made her way to the ale house. Then she was pounding mindlessly on the door, calling out "Sean Lynch!" as though her life depended upon it. And it did, she knew. Her life and her soul. And Daniel's. Poor, darling, Daniel—

"Erica?" The sailor's bleary-eyed face had appeared in a second story window. "What in blazes . . . ?"

"Oh, Sean!" she wailed. "Thank God! Daniel needs you! Polly's lost—"

"What?" he roared, as awake as he'd been asleep only seconds earlier. "How? Where?"

"Come quickly! There's no time! There's no time," she repeated hoarsely, leaning against the wall to relieve her pounding chest. "Oh God, please. Please let there be time. . . ."

CHAPTER TWELVE

The beach was strewn with boots, coats and shirts, and Erica stumbled more than once as she alternately paced and prayed, springing toward the water every time one of the sailors emerged from the chilly blue-gray water. But it was always the same. The would-be rescuer's arms were always empty, and each time one dragged himself onto shore for a brief rest and a cup of Betsy's steaming coffee, the women would see the same bleak expression, and would know better than to ask for words of hope.

Each time a figure appeared in the distant waters, Erica strained her already swollen eyes in hopes of catching a glimpse of Daniel, but to no avail. The cook from the *Rigger* had positioned a rowboat halfway between the shore and the schooner, and from time to time, Erica could see the other men go there, hang onto the side for a moment or two to catch their breath, then plunge once again into the murky depths. But it was never Daniel who rested, or even seemed to surface.

"They're killing themselves," Betsy murmured finally, coming up behind Erica and draping a blanket around her tense, chilled shoulders. "It's been almost two hours—"

"I know. I see. I-I'll make them stop soon, I promise." She watched as an exhausted Michael O'Rourke took a final swig of warm coffee and trudged back to the water's edge. "They want to keep looking, Betsy. They *have* to keep looking until we're sure—" Her voice caught in her throat, and she shook her head defiantly. "If they're still looking, they must think there's still hope."

"O'Rourke says they're not looking for Polly anymore, they're looking for a body. For a proper burial."

"What?" Erica stared in dismay. "She'll be cold and sick—"

"She'll be dead, Erica. Everyone knows that now. It's been too long." The kindhearted barmaid's voice cracked, as Erica's had done, but she continued stubbornly, "The little darling can't be alive."

Erica spun and pointed toward the doctor, who had come running at the news and was still sitting, patiently, on a nearby rock. "*He* hasn't given up hope."

"He's waiting to make the pronouncement. And—" Betsy hesitated, then admitted, "In case the captain needs attention."

"Attention?" Her gaze shifted warily from the doctor to the icy waters, stunned by the implication. He was there for Daniel? Because Daniel would be mad with grief, and half dead with exhaustion . . .

"Oh, no . . ." She covered her face with her hands and fell to her knees as sobs began to wrench through her. "No, no, no. Polly . . . Polly! Please, no—"

Strong arms, still drenched from the sea, pulled her into a hasty embrace, and when she opened her eyes, Sean's grief-stricken face confronted her. "There, there," he crooned, his voice crusted with pity and disbelief. "Let it all out. It's a cruel world, to take our lovely Polly from us. Cry all you like. All you need. Get it all out now, so you can help Danny.''

"Poor Daniel," Erica wailed. "My poor, darling Daniel. To lose that precious child. It can't be true, Sean."

"But it is," he assured her mournfully. "She can't have survived, not in those waters for this long."

Erica choked back a second wave of sobs and steadied her voice with tentative resolve. "Does Daniel know?"

"Hard to say," Sean murmured. "He's past exhaustion, I'd guess. Diving without even thinking any more. Without letting himself think."

Betsy knelt beside them and slipped her arm around Sean's shoulders. "Michael says he and the others intend to keep searching until they find the poor babe's body."

"Aye," Sean agreed. "If we don't find it soon, we'll be burying them both by day's end."

"Both?" Erica winced, remembering all she'd heard about Daniel and grief. How he'd almost lost his mind when he'd lost Lilli. How he'd buried his whole family in Ireland before he was eight years old. How he'd struggled to protect himself from more, knowing in his heart he might not survive it himself. Grabbing Sean by the arm she instructed tersely, "Bring me out there. In the rowboat or the cutter. It's time someone made him rest."

"I've tried, Erica," the first mate assured her gently. "He almost throttled me when I dared suggest even a short rest. I've done what I can do—asked the men to keep watch on him, so we can grab him when—well, there now. It's happened, hasn't it?"

Sean's eyes were fixed on something just beyond the water's edge, and through tear-filled eyes, Erica could see it too. Two men, dragging a third—

"Oh, no!" she shrieked, jumping to her feet and dashing madly to help the others pull Daniel's lifeless body onto shore. As Erica cradled his head, Sean and Betsy covered him with blankets that had been warmed by the fire, while the doctor knelt and placed two practiced fingers alongside Daniel's throat.

"He's alive," he announced quietly. Opening a flask, he grimaced apologetically at Erica, then poured a few drops of liquid through Daniel's lips. "Brandy," he explained. "Quicker than almost anything, for the moment."

"It's fine," Erica whispered. "Just help him any way you can." Clasping her lover against her chest she whispered desperately, "Daniel? Can you hear me? Captain McCullum, darling, please wake up."

He stirred slightly and groaned, "Erica?"

"Oh, Daniel." Hot tears streamed down her face. "Daniel, thank God. There's a doctor here. He wants you to sip—"

Daniel's huge hand knocked the flask away in wary disbelief. "Where's Polly?"

"Daniel—"

"Sean!" he roared, sitting up and twisting to stare into his friend's face. "Where's Polly?"

"Take it easy, Danny," Sean soothed. "We're still looking, but—"

"Why aren't *you* looking? Why'd you stop me—?"

Sean's fist crashed into Daniel's jaw at that moment, and the captain fell back into Erica's arms, unconscious once again. "Forgive me, Erica," the first mate muttered. "But someone had to do it."

She stroked Daniel's face lovingly. "You did the right thing."

Shrugging to his feet, Sean addressed the throng of sailors who had gathered to watch in silence. "Get some rest. Have a meal. Once you have your strength back, meet me here for another go at it. Our captain needs to see his daughter's body, or there'll be no stopping him. Not ever.''

Murmuring their agreement and commitment, the men retrieved their boots and clothing and shuffled away, mostly in the direction of the ale houses near the wharf. Then Sean and Michael O'Rourke hefted Daniel into the doctor's carriage, where Erica once again cradled his head in her lap for the short, mournful ride to the Lindstrom home.

Erica had expected the poor father to be tortured by nightmares, but instead his slumber was eerily still, and so she snuggled at his side, forcing herself not to sob or sniffle, unable to sleep at all herself. She struggled not to remember Polly, so adorable and stubborn, diving into the waters of the Crescent and swimming defiantly out to the schooner despite all Erica's entreaties to the contrary. If only she had listened. . . .

Polly, Polly, Polly, she mourned silently. *You promised you wouldn't do it again. If only we had realized you might miss us, and might know where you could find us. If only you had known how cold—how very, very cold and cruel—these waters are. Daniel was right to keep you in the Caribbean, where you were safe. How could we have ever considered moving you here? And now you're gone. . . .*

She shuddered with loss and despair and, with a mournful glance at Daniel's face, quickly slipped out of the bed and stole quietly from the bedroom. If she stayed, she'd end up crying and he would wake, and then—

She shuddered again, remembering the look in his eyes just before Sean had blessedly saved him from himself. He would have gone back into that water and searched until it killed him. Of that, Erica had no doubt. She only prayed he'd stay asleep until Sean or Michael came with the chilling but needed news that the body had been recovered at long last.

Mary O'Rourke sprang from the table and ran to Erica when she appeared in the kitchen doorway. "Is Danny awake?"

"No, he's sound asleep." She gave the housekeeper a sympathetic peck on the cheek, then patted Patrick's shoulder before easing herself into a chair. "I dread the moment when he wakes up and asks. . . ."

"Aye." Mary poured a cup of tea and handed it Erica. "He'll need you then, more than ever. You should try to rest yourself."

"I can't." She tried to smile at the weary couple. "Has Sean come by? Or Michael?"

Patrick hesitated, then admitted quietly, "It's just the two of them now. Sean sent the others home. There was an incident—" He flushed and covered his face with his hands. "They found an arm—"

"What?"

"It wasn't Polly's," Mary explained hastily. "It was a grown man's arm. But it was clear to them all that it was a shark that done it. Bit it clear off, and recently too."

"It's not unusual in these parts," Patrick finished woodenly. "But they're thinking, if that's what happened to the wee girl, there may not be much to find."

Erica wrapped her arms around herself, but still could feel all the warmth drain from her body. "Sean thinks that's what happened? To Polly? Last night, while Daniel and I . . . ?"

"She was a strong swimmer." Patrick shrugged. "But used to warm water, not cold. We may never know."

Erica shook her head, dazed with renewed horror and guilt. "If only we had come straight home. We should

have known she'd want to see us—to see *me*. I should
have realized—''

"Don't blame yourself," Mary interrupted, standing to
fetch a bright green shawl, which she wrapped tightly
around Erica. "We've been doing that ourselves, this
miserable day. If we'd only thought to check on her,
one last time, before she went out that window. . . ."
Returning to her seat, she dabbed at her bloodshot eyes
and sighed. "Poor, darling Polly. So headstrong, and so
precious."

Erica bit her lip. "She climbed out the window of her
bedroom?"

Mary nodded. "We thought she was sound asleep."

"And she dressed in her beautiful party dress, to please
me." Erica pulled the shawl more closely about her shiv-
ering shoulders. "She promised me she'd never swim out
to the schooner again, but when she realized we left the
ale house, she must have guessed we'd gone to the *Rigger*
and couldn't resist the thought of surprising us."

"She was a mischief maker," Patrick confirmed unhappily. "Always wanting to please her father, and make
him proud. Wanting to be a sea captain one day. Did you
know that?"

"Yes. Yes, I knew about that." She tried to smile at
him but could see he was looking past her, and so she
spun in her chair, then sprang from it at the sight of Daniel
in the doorway. "Oh, Daniel!" She wrapped her arms
around him and hugged with all her might. "Daniel, how
are you? Mary made some soup—''

He allowed the embrace, then pushed her away gently,
instructing Mary, "I'll have a bowl of soup, and some
bread if you have it."

The housekeeper bustled into action.

"Erica?"

"Yes, Daniel?"

"I want you to do something for me."

"Anything," she said with a sigh, relieved at his rational tone.

"I want you to go back to Ryerson's house. I'll have Sean or Michael take you tonight. When I find Polly, I'll send word."

"Oh, Daniel . . ." She took one of his hands in hers and kissed it mournfully. "I think it's too late to find her, darling. I'm so, so sorry, but you mustn't keep torturing yourself."

"It's true, son," Patrick agreed, crossing awkwardly to extend his hand to Daniel. "Our hearts go out to you. She was a fine lass."

"Aye." Mary quickly joined them, throwing her arms around Daniel as Erica had done. "Will you ever forgive us, Danny?"

He looked surprised, then touched her cheek gently. "Don't talk like that. There's no blame here, not with anyone. Is that clear?"

The housekeeper wiped her eyes with her apron and nodded. "I'll just get that soup then. Erica, will you have a bite too?"

"Have something to eat before you go," Daniel agreed. Then he followed Mary to the stove, taking the bowl as soon as she'd filled it, and putting it to his lips for a long, appreciative gulp. Then he turned to Erica and repeated simply, "Have something to eat, then go back to Ryerson's."

"I want to be with you," she protested. "We'll have our soup, then we'll get some rest—"

"I've had enough rest. But Polly won't rest at the bottom of that damned harbor, will she? I intend to find her if it takes all night, and I don't want you here worrying while I'm gone."

"Fine, I'll come with you then."

"Patrick?" Daniel growled. "Will you find Michael and ask him to take Erica to Boston?"

"He and Sean are still looking for the little one."

Daniel's expression softened. "Are they? They should rest. I'll send them home."

"Daniel?" Erica felt her lower lip begin to quiver. "Please don't send me away."

He seemed about to argue; then he shrugged. "Stay with the O'Rourkes then. Don't come down to the beach. It'll be dark soon, and cold. And you may not want to see her, after all this time in the water. So stay here."

"When will you be back?"

"When I find her."

She watched as he took a heavy wool coat from a hook by the door. "Daniel?"

"Yeah?"

Taking a deep breath, she went to him and slipped her arms around his neck. "I love you."

"I appreciate that."

She winced, but couldn't afford to allow the frank words to hurt her, and so she persisted stubbornly, "At some point, if you don't find her—"

"I'll find her, or die trying," he replied, so coldly and with such finality that Erica knew it was what he wanted: to find the girl, or join her at the bottom of the harbor forever, so that she would never be lonely, and he would never need to mourn.

She wanted to reprimand him, or pull him into another, more insistent embrace, but all she could do was remind him, in a firm and loving tone, "You have two little sons who need you desperately. And I need you desperately too. Don't lose sight of that. Or of us."

* * *

For three days and nights, life in Salem was a nightmare of Daniel McCullum's making, as he spent every waking hour scouring the bottom of the harbor, returning to the house only when pure exhaustion drove him to it. He'd take a few gulps of soup then, and a swig or two of brandy for good measure, before dragging himself into the bedroom, dead asleep before his body hit the mattress. If he knew Erica was there, waiting to snuggle in loyal silence at his side, he gave no indication of it. Instead, he slept as he'd slept that first day—like a cold, lifeless rock of a man, impervious to the warmth and love she was so desperate to lavish upon him.

She wondered sometimes if he blamed her, somehow, for what had happened, but in her heart she knew he blamed himself, and that was far, far more unsettling to her. Her own grief over the loss of the child was great, and she could only imagine how monumental it would be for a parent. A father, bursting with pride at the girl's antics; defending her habit of swimming out to meet him; cherishing and teasing; and most of all, protecting. Wasn't that the duty he took most seriously? Wasn't that the reason he had insisted the children grow up on La Creciente?

On the fourth day, when Daniel staggered back to the house at the end of another grueling search, his body was ravaged by fever and his breathing was plagued by deep, resonant fits of coughing. Terrified, Erica bundled him into bed, and for forty-eight hours the fever raged unabated, plunging Daniel into a delirium that finally seemed to allow him to mourn the loss of his only daughter.

Through it all, Erica held him tightly, desperate to absorb every gut-wrenching sob and chest-shattering spasm that racked his beleaguered body. Her own state of mind and body mirrored his so irrationally that Mary O'Rourke began to fret openly, insisting without success that Erica needed to take at least one meal with the family and step outside once per day to fill her own lungs with fresh, sweet summer air.

Then, on a breezy Friday morning, just one week after the loss of Polly McCullum, Captain McCullum stirred and, when Erica's hand went instinctively to his forehead, she discovered his skin was both cool and dry, and she roused herself fully from sleep and whispered, "Daniel? Are you awake?"

"Erica?"

"I'm here, darling." She ran her fingers through his hair and smiled gently. "Can I get you something? Something to drink or eat?"

"Polly's dead."

"I know. It's so dreadfully unfair." She sat up enough to slip her arm around his neck and was relieved when he didn't pull away. "I'm so sorry, Daniel."

"You told me it was dangerous, but I didn't listen."

"No, Daniel. It wasn't dangerous in Crescent Bay. Only unladylike."

"She's *dead*. Don't tell me it wasn't dangerous."

Erica nodded sadly. "You need to rest a bit, then have something to eat. The O'Rourkes will be pleased to see that you're recovering at last. It's been days, Daniel. And you've been dreadfully ill." Sandwiching his face between her hands, she added carefully, "I know you don't care about yourself right now, but I do. I love you, and I need you. So do the twins."

Daniel tried to sit up, then fell back, exhausted by the effort. "You were right about that, too. I'm grateful to you for reminding me about them."

"The boys?"

He nodded. "Every time it felt like my lungs were going to burst for lack of air, and I found myself welcoming the thought, I remembered what you said. Those boys need a father, and I'm the only one they have."

"That's right," she soothed. "That's why you need to get some more sleep. The doctor says it could kill you if you try to get back on your feet too quickly."

"I'll sleep," he agreed. Then he eyed her sternly. "I don't want to see you here when I wake up."

"Pardon?"

"Once I've had some decent rest, I'll be leaving for the island. It's best to say good-bye now—"

"You can't sail in this condition. And even if you could . . ." She smiled apologetically. "Don't be angry over this, Daniel, but Sean already sent for Abby and the boys. I imagine they could even be on their way here by now."

"He sent for them?" Daniel frowned. "To sail here on someone else's ship?"

"He sent specific instructions, so that they'd be perfectly safe. He did it for you, Daniel. And I encouraged it. The boys need to be with you as soon as possible, don't you agree?" When he nodded, she snuggled against him and pleaded, "Won't you try to sleep again, for just an hour or so? We both need the rest. And then we'll have something to eat, and talk a bit more, and little by little we'll make it through this. Together."

Daniel drew a calloused finger along her cheek. "I'm so sorry I put you through this."

She caught his hand in her own and brought it to her lips for a gentle kiss. "Go to sleep, darling."

"Erica?"

"Yes, Daniel?"

His voice grew so soft that she almost didn't hear him when he told her, "I have nothing left to give."

While she recognized that a trace of his former delirium had returned, the despair in his voice still threatened to break her heart. "I'm not asking for anything, darling. Just hold on to me, and we'll survive somehow."

"Nothing to give . . . nothing . . ."

"Hush, now." She embraced him fiercely and willed him back to sleep, murmuring again and again, "Just let me hold you, Daniel McCullum. Just let me hold you until you heal."

She stirred and, when she didn't feel her lover's body molded to her own as it had been for so many days and nights, she panicked and almost bolted from the bed. There was no sign of Daniel, and she could suddenly imagine him diving mercilessly, choking back his grief as he filled his lungs with cold, gray water. Heedless of her unkempt mane of auburn hair and wrinkled nightgown, she dashed into the kitchen, then groaned in embarrassed relief to see him sitting at the table, being served by an adoring Mary O'Rourke.

"Daniel McCullum, you scared me half to death!" She hurried to him, wrapping her arms around his neck. "Look at you. So strong. And no fever at all. What a relief."

"You should have something to eat." Daniel frowned. "You look terrible."

She grimaced and slid into the chair next to his. "I'm famished, and I know I look a sight, but honestly, Captain McCullum, I'm just so pleased to see you up and about. Mary, he looks better, doesn't he?"

"Aye." The housekeeper nodded. "He's having soup again. Would you like the same, dear?"

"That sounds wonderful."

"Serve her," Daniel agreed briskly. "Then leave us for a few minutes. I need to speak to Erica in private."

Mary bit her lip but did as he asked, sending Erica a sympathetic glance before stepping out onto the back porch.

Resisting an urge to scold him for his rudeness, Erica pushed the bowl of soup away and waited patiently.

"I want you to go to Ryerson's for a few days. I want some time alone, to consider what's happened."

Erica sighed in frustration. "It's a big house, Captain. If you want me to give you some privacy—"

"I want you to go to Ryerson's. Or if you're not comfortable there, to your mother's house. I'm asking you to do it for me."

"I need to be with you," Erica countered stubbornly. "In bad times as well as good. That's what love means—"

"Don't tell me what love means!" he growled, then he reached for her hand and patted it firmly. "I hope you never have to learn about love the way I've had to do. Here." He put his other hand on top of hers too. "If I used the fingers of both these hands, I couldn't count the number of persons I've loved and lost before their time. I wouldn't wish that on another soul, least of all you. But don't tell me about love, because you only know a part of the story."

"Daniel—"

"I have nothing left to give to someone new. I have my sons, and that's all."

"Wait!" She stared in shocked dismay. "You aren't just sending me away for a while? You're saying you don't intend to marry me? Not ever?"

Daniel looked away. "We've known each other for less than two months. Don't make more of it than it is."

She shrank from the finality in his tone. "Don't push me away, Daniel. You need me, whether you know it or not. And I need you. We need to mourn together."

"I've done my mourning." He stood abruptly, his eyes dark and unreadable. "I'm going to the wharf. I've asked Michael to hire a carriage and take you to Boston. He's ready whenever you have your things together. All I ask is that you be gone when I return.''

''To the wharf?'' she whispered. ''Good Lord, Daniel, you can't be intending—''

''I'll search for an hour at a time. No more than that.'' He hesitated, then added softly, ''I fully intend to keep myself alive and healthy, for the sake of my sons. And I'm eternally grateful to you for reminding me of that responsibility. If you hadn't, I might have done something to myself—to them—that would have haunted them the rest of their lives.''

''Daniel . . .''

She tried to move into his arms, but he stopped her with an expression that was both harsh and vulnerable. Then he asked simply, ''Do you remember when you said you wanted me to be free? Prove it to me now. Walk away from me. It's the only thing I need from you now.''

Erica took a deep breath, then spoke from deep within her exhausted, battered heart. ''If you send me away, I won't come back. I'll want to come to you, and beg you to reconsider, but I will not. If you send me away, it'll fall to you to come after me. And as much as I love you, Daniel McCullum, I won't wait forever.''

''That's more than fair. Except you shouldn't wait at all. I'm not worth even that,'' he assured her quietly. ''And,'' his expression darkened once again, *''I won't be coming after you.''*

After the initial surge of hurt, Erica found that she was simply numb. Whether it was the horror of Polly's death, the alarm over Daniel's irrational conduct in the hours thereafter, the grueling hours nursing him back to health, or the abruptness of his dismissal, she was simply too exhausted to feel anger, betrayal, or even confusion.

Perhaps this was what Daniel had been trying to tell her. A person could become numb if pushed beyond his or her limits. It had happened to him, because of the sheer volume of grief life had inflicted upon him. And now, it had happened to Erica, because the great love of her life had been neither great nor lifelong.

After a wordless carriage ride with Michael O'Rourke, she had crawled into bed at Jack Ryerson's house without explanation. Her host had been his usual generous, bewildered self, peeking in on her from time to time, but seeming somewhat relieved when she protested that she wanted to sleep ''just a few more hours.'' She was grateful to him for seeing that his sisters didn't descend upon her, but was somewhat disconcerted that Sarah didn't find a moment or two to visit and commiserate.

''Except, what would she say?'' Erica challenged herself unhappily. ''Wouldn't she agree with Daniel? She'd say you never understood her grief over the loss of her entire family, and she'd be right, of course. They're both right. They both endured more than they could bear. Daniel went half-mad with grief over Lilli, and almost fully mad over Polly. And Sarah clings stubbornly to the idea her brother was never fully lost to her. No wonder they mock you for your romantic optimism. They know it's based in raw luck and ignorance, and they're correct to resent you for it.''

Vowing that she would tell Sarah just that the next time she saw her, Erica finally decided to break her silence in the face of a dinner invitation, delivered by Jack's butler on a silver tray, requesting the honor of her appearance. So like Jack, she told herself sheepishly. For all his faults, he truly could not stand to see another person in pain or grief. If only she could have fallen in love with him the way she'd fallen for Daniel McCullum.

And apparently Jack was thinking the same thing,

because when she made her way to the dining room, the mood was undeniably romantic, from the soft glow of candlelight to the profusion of fragrant bouquets to the strains of a violin being played in the adjoining courtyard. Delighted and confused, Erica demanded, "What's all this?"

"Do you like it?"

"Yes. I don't understand it, but it's lovely."

He bowed gallantly. "It's my way of saying I'd still be honored to marry you."

"You would?" She stared in disbelief. "After your narrow escape?"

"You're still the most beautiful girl I've ever met. And the most disarming."

"And I'm in love with someone else."

Jack took a deep breath. "He doesn't intend to marry you. Not ever. He tells me he's made that clear to you."

"You spoke with Daniel?" She sank into a chair and asked sadly, "Are you saying he suggested this?"

"Not entirely. He worries, though, that you'll wait forever for something that will never happen." Jack sat beside her and gathered her hands into his own. "He's serious, darling. At first, I thought it was just the grief talking, but the man's heart has closed up tight. The fact that he can resist *you*—your beauty, your warmth—shows how unreachable he's become. Don't you see that?"

Erica nodded, then reached for the chilled bottle of champagne in the middle of the table and poured herself and her suitor a glass of bubbling spirits. There was nothing to say. Jack was correct in his assessment of the situation, although foolish to believe he could be happy marrying a woman who didn't love him. Still, it was flattering, and if she hadn't been so miserable, she knew she would have found it momentarily enjoyable.

"Don't be stubborn, Erica. I'm not asking for an answer

tonight. Even if you decide to turn me down, you need to be realistic and allow other men to court you eventually. You can't just live here for the rest of your life, unless you can make the situation a bit more favorable to me," he added teasingly.

"I suppose that's true." She scanned his face hopefully. "What else did Daniel say?"

Jack grimaced. "The man has lost his mind, Erica. I'd rather not repeat what he had to say."

"Grief can make a person say and do things they otherwise wouldn't. Look at Sarah," she added, then she scowled. "I suppose you'd say I just made my point for you. She never really recovered from her grief. And perhaps Daniel won't either."

Jack eyed Erica warily. "Except, of course, Sarah recovered. But only because of happenstance, not because of a true recovery. Is that what you're saying?"

Erica took a long sip of champagne and almost smiled for the first time in days. "What in heaven's name are you talking about, Jack? I've never heard you babble before! It's frighteningly amusing."

"I'm talking about Sarah."

"What about her?"

"She told me she wrote you a letter before she left." He still seemed to be proceeding cautiously. "You know what's happened to her, don't you? I mean, the irony hasn't been lost on anyone, least of all me. Still, we should be happy for her, shouldn't we? After all these years of doubting her sanity—"

"Wait!" Erica slammed her glass down on the table. "Sarah left? Why? Wait!" she ordered again before he could answer. "Does this have something to do with all the hope and miracles she was talking about during my last visit?"

Jack grinned and nodded. "Hope and miracles—that

about sums it up, doesn't it? I know you'll be pleased, Erica, because it will suit the optimist in you, and so—'' He took a deep breath and announced, ''After all these years of claiming her brother couldn't be dead, she's found him. Alive and well, and living in Somerset.''

''What?''

''Isn't it amazing? And disquieting, but only in the best sense. Although I suppose I resist the irrationality of it—''

''Jack!''

He laughed sheepishly. ''Fine. An old family friend saw a boy—just the right age, and bearing an uncanny resemblance to Sarah's late father. Someone remarked on it to Sarah, and of course, she reacted with alarming optimism.''

''That was the hope?'' Erica whispered. ''She said she wasn't yet certain when I visited last. She must have heard the rumor, but hadn't verified it. And you're saying she has now found proof?''

''The couple that took the boy have confessed to her, on the condition that she not inform the authorities. They took the baby from the burning house, darling. They lived in Boston then, and were supposedly walking past the place when they saw smoke and flames. The husband went inside and saw that the parents were dead, but the little boy was still breathing. The couple hadn't been able to have children of their own, and somehow they managed to justify taking him for all these years. They claim they never knew there was a surviving sister.'' Jack took a deep breath. ''I'm not certain I have the story as straight as Owen does, since he's the one who last spoke with Sarah.''

''Owen? Oh, of course. Sarah's mother was his house-keeper before the fire, was she not?''

''Exactly. And after the fire, Sarah took her place in

that position for almost two years, but his wife didn't approve of so young and pretty a servant. They were only too delighted to recommend her to me as a governess after my parents died. She'll be impossible to replace,'' he added wistfully. ''But I suppose it's best that she and her brother spend time together—''

''After eight years apart? I should imagine so!'' Erica felt her spirits soar. ''It's a miracle, just as Sarah claimed. I can't believe she didn't say anything to me—'' She paused and grimaced in silent apology to her friend. ''I suppose by then she had heard about Polly?''

Jack nodded. ''Odd, isn't it?''

''I'm rather glad I didn't receive her letter in Salem,'' Erica mused. ''We never found Polly's body, you know. News like this might have raised Daniel's hopes. Even without such encouragement, we had difficulty convincing him to stop his fruitless search.''

''I can imagine,'' Jack said with a sympathetic sigh. ''If anything happened to Jane or Mary, I'd cling to any hope, however remote, that they could be saved.''

''And you might even shut out those who wanted to comfort you,'' Erica agreed. ''But only for a time, isn't that so?''

Jack took her face between his hands. ''I wish I could tell you what you want to hear, darling. But if I had a woman like you who wanted to comfort me in a time of loss, I'd cling to you, not push you away. The man isn't just grieving, he's tormented. You have to protect yourself from that, or at least allow me to protect you.''

Erica wiped a tear from her eye and nodded. ''You're doing a lovely job of it, Jack. I'll always be grateful to you for tonight. But if you don't mind, I'm so very tired.''

He stood and offered his arm to her. ''May I escort you to your room?''

''Of course. Except, please escort me to Sarah's room.''

"Pardon?"

Erica smiled. "She told you she wrote me a letter. Perhaps in all the confusion, she forgot to send it. She was so distracted, even during my last visit. I imagine once she had confirmation that the little boy was alive, she must have become almost delirious."

"She was distracted. It was especially evident in the letter of resignation she left for me," Jack agreed as he escorted her up the staircase. "If Owen hadn't explained it all to me again yesterday, I wouldn't have fully understood even now."

"Why do you suppose she went to him instead of you?"

"For money." Jack chuckled fondly. "At the risk of sounding like a gossip, I can assure you Sarah's relationship with Owen was something more than the one she had with me."

Erica winced. "So? His wife's suspicions were well-founded? How odd. I had imagined Sarah to be— well . . . "

"A virgin? I'm afraid Owen took care of that particular detail after the fire, all in the name of comforting the poor girl. Or at least, I've surmised as much. We haven't ever actually discussed it, and I'm depending on you to be discreet." He blanched as he added, "Just this one time?"

Erica laughed lightly. "Out of respect for Sarah, not Owen, I will be glad to keep it to myself. Come help me look for my letter."

They entered Sarah's room and Jack quickly scooped up a handful of papers from a desk drawer. "I've located a treasure trove of them here."

"Oh . . ." Erica flushed as she accepted the letters she'd written to Sarah from the Caribbean. The last thing she wanted was for Jack to read about her exploits with Captain McCullum! Then she saw that Sarah had circled certain passages, and she studied them, at first with wistful curiosity, then with genuine confusion. Polly's birth date, Polly's habits, Polly's bravado and ambitions—

"It's all about Polly, Jack."

"I beg your pardon? Why would Sarah— Oh, look here, Erica. This must be the letter she spoke of, and you're absolutely correct. She must have forgotten to post it."

"Let me see!" Erica snatched it eagerly and began to read aloud:

> *Erica,*
> *Forgive me for not saying farewell. For all your faults, you have been a true friend. I will never be able to thank you and Owen enough for discovering the Happily Ever After Company. It has been the answer to all our prayers, has it not? And Russell Braddock is a miracle worker, just as you always hoped. Now you will live happily ever after with your sea captain, and I will be content with my precious Robby and the husband and father Mr. Braddock will find for us. Take care.*
>
> > *Yours always,*
> > *Sarah Gibson*

"Russell Braddock?" Erica murmured.

"That's where she's gone," Jack explained. "Didn't I mention that? She wants to marry right away, so that she and her new husband can begin to provide a proper household for her little brother. And you've made such a point of this Braddock fellow, it must seem as logical to her as anything else that's happened."

Erica sank onto the bed, weakened by the direction her imagination had taken. Robby Gibson would be nine years old—the same age as Polly. Polly—who dressed like a boy and reminded Sarah so much of her dead brother . . .

"I want to hear every detail, Jack. Everything Sarah said, and everything Owen said, too. And after that—" She paused for a deep breath, alarmed by the racing of her pulse. It wouldn't do to become overly excited, after all. She had to think clearly now, more so than at anytime during her life. Then she smiled up at Jack, who was studying her anxiously. "I want you to send a telegram for me. Tonight."

"Tonight? Why—" He coughed and added dutifully, "I'd be happy to. It's a nice idea, actually. We can send our congratulations and best wishes to Sarah in Chicago, at Mr. Braddock's home, before she embarks for parts unknown. Is that it?"

Before she embarks for parts unknown . . . Erica nodded briskly. "Tell me every detail, and don't leave anything out. It's time to discover, once and for all, if Mr. Braddock is really the miracle worker we all believe him to be."

Erica dressed in modest black silk and pulled her hair back into a severe knot at the nape of her neck before stepping into Jack Ryerson's carriage the next morning. She hadn't been able to eat or sleep, but knew it was important to appear rested and solemn when she arrived at the Lindstrom home. Still, she couldn't resist spending her time in the carriage reading and rereading the letters they'd found in Sarah's room, and in what seemed like minutes rather than hours, she was tucking the pages into her valise, summoning her haughtiest smile, and allowing Jack's driver to escort her onto the porch.

The O'Rourkes descended upon her, as expected, and she greeted them warmly once she'd made certain that Daniel wasn't around. Mary quickly confided that the sea captain was at the wharf.

"But he's been keeping his promise," she assured

Erica. "The poor man searches for the body for an hour or two, then comes home to rest."

"And his health?"

"He looks a fright, but it could be far worse, so we must be grateful. The cough's still there at night, but I'd say he's on the mend. Physically, I mean. The other . . . " She shrugged as if to say her employer was still crazed with grief, and then she added loyally, "He loved that girl. We all did. I don't judge him."

"Neither do I," Erica said with a smile.

"It's lovely to see you again, especially with you leaving as quickly as you did, but I have to ask," Mary murmured. "Why have you come back? He isn't ready, and may never be. Why put yourself and him through this again?"

"Excellent question," a familiar voice drawled from the shadows, and Erica turned slowly toward Daniel, haggard and frowning, but still the only sight she wanted to see, other than Polly McCullum.

She eyed him dourly. "I assure you I have a legitimate reason for coming, Captain. Assuming I'm welcome in Abigail's home, of course."

He winced and abandoned his sarcastic tone. "You're welcome anytime, of course. We just didn't expect to see you so soon."

"Well, I have a life to lead," she said with a sniff. "And a favor to ask. In private," she added, with a brief, apologetic glance toward Mary and Patrick. "I believe you owe me a courtesy or two, Captain, and I'm here to collect on that debt."

"I'm in no mood for games, Erica."

"I've lost my taste for them as well," she admitted quietly. "Mary? Patrick? Would you excuse us for just a moment?"

The couple exchanged worried glances, but could

apparently sense the futility of trying to intervene, and so, after Mary extracted a promise that Erica wouldn't leave without sharing a meal with them, they disappeared into the kitchen.

"What's this about, Erica?"

"That's all you have to say to me, Daniel McCullum?" When he simply nodded, she forced herself to take a deep breath despite the rawness of the wound he continued to inflict. "Is there any word from Abby?"

"Sean's gone down to intercept them. It'll be a week or more, I'm guessing."

"That should give you enough time to do me the small favor I mentioned."

Daniel gestured toward the parlor. "Sounds like I should be sitting down for this, so . . ."

Erica smiled her haughty smile and settled into Mary's rocking chair while Daniel took the sofa. "Jack told me about the conversation he had with you."

"I don't know what he said—"

"He suggested that since you would never marry me, I should reconsider his proposal."

Daniel's expression grew wistful. "He's a good man who can provide well for you. And he's clearly fond of you."

"True," Erica agreed. "But I want something more. I want what I had with you, only this time, I want it to last."

"Erica," he growled.

Silencing him with a glare, she insisted, "Please don't be tiresome, Captain. I wasn't suggesting a match between you and myself. I simply want a similar match, and to achieve that, I believe I must consult Mr. Russell Braddock of Chicago."

"Braddock?"

Erica shrugged. "He's the one who found you for me,

is he not? It's only logical to assume he can find someone else for me—someone with your qualities, but who is capable of loving me forever. Do you see?''

Daniel stared for a long moment, then chuckled wearily. "I never know what to expect from you, Erica."

"Did you expect me to fight for our love? To demand that you give it another chance? To throw myself into your arms and beg you to take me back?" She paused to collect herself, not wanting him to hear the true anger behind the taunting words. "If I thought there was a chance that might be effective, I suppose I'd try it. My pride, after all, has been demolished where you are concerned."

"Erica—"

"No!" She glared again, this time without any attempt to hide her feelings. "You wanted me to marry Jack. Why not some other man? A man who can make me happy?"

Daniel seemed to consider it carefully before nodding. "I'd never stand in the way of that."

"Will you facilitate it?"

"Pardon?"

She moistened her lips, then delivered the plea she'd been practicing all the way from Boston. "Will you take me to Chicago, Daniel?"

"Me? Why not ask Ryerson?"

"I'm asking *you!*" She fought unsuccessfully against a rush of tears, then realized they might be for the best and sank back into her chair, sobbing mournfully. "I'm asking you, Captain, for one last favor. After that, you need never see me again. Considering all we meant to one another—all I gave to you, freely and because of true love—I should think you could do this one last favor for me. You're the only person I trust and love enough in the whole world to ask this of."

He sank to his knees before her, and for an instant she thought he was going to take her into his arms and make this whole nightmare disappear, at least for one short, reassuring moment. Then, he tilted her chin so that she was looking straight into his deep-blue eyes, and announced softly, "I'll take you to Braddock to find someone to love you. And after that, I'll ask you to let me go forever. Will you be able to do that, Erica?"

Forcing herself to meet his gaze directly she admitted, with honest and sincere finality, "I've already done it, Captain."

CHAPTER THIRTEEN

They traveled together, and there were moments when Daniel actually allowed Erica to see what he was thinking and feeling, but for the most part, he stared out the train window with eyes that clearly were not looking at the landscape. Although she might have wished he would confide in her, or at least allow her to comfort him, she knew that if he did, he might also see what *she* was thinking and feeling, and what would she do then? Tell him her suspicions? Never! She would never raise this man's hopes only to dash them cruelly in Chicago.

No one believed me that my brother was still alive, but I never lost hope. . . . Those had been Sarah's words in her letter to Jack resigning her post as governess. Now it was Erica whose heart was filled with hope, perhaps just as insane and delusional as Sarah's had been. But if they didn't go to Chicago and see for themselves, wouldn't that be even more insane?

She had considered making the trip with Jack rather

than Daniel, but if her suspicions proved true, she wanted the reunion to take place without any further heartrending delay. And poor Jack had been through enough that last night. She had peppered him with so many questions that he had playfully threatened to withdraw his marriage proposal once and for all. But he had dutifully answered every question to the extent he was able.

Did anyone actually see the little boy? "Yes, Owen saw him, or rather, caught a glimpse of him through the window. The child was too shy to actually come up to the offices, and so he waited for Sarah on the street below."

Did Owen describe him? "Only to say he was healthy-looking, despite his ordeal. But he also seemed confused, which is understandable, don't you suppose?"

What day was that? "The same day you left with McCullum, actually. Or rather—" He had hesitated, then remembered, "Sarah left my house for the last time that same afternoon—it was her regular afternoon away, so I didn't think much of it until late that evening when I found her letter of explanation on my dresser. But the visit to Owen must have been that next morning. Yes, yes, I'm sure of it now."

While inconclusive, Jack's words had been music to Erica's ears, especially when she'd sent him to Owen Sawyer's house to learn the exact date of the infamous fire, and the half-asleep financier had confirmed that it had happened on the very same day Polly McCullum had been born, hundreds of miles away.

"Erica?"

She forced her thoughts back to the present and smiled sheepishly at Daniel. "Did you want something?"

"You seemed so faraway." He cocked his head to the side. "Were you thinking about the past or the future? The island?" he added quietly. "Or the husband you'll ask Braddock to find for you?"

"Does it make you jealous, just a bit?"

He nodded. "I've been firm with you because I want you to understand that there's no hope for us. But I'd be lying if I said I won't miss you."

His eyes began to fill with tears, and she knew his thoughts had drifted to Polly. Wrapping her arms around his neck she soothed, "I miss her too, Daniel. We can help each other through this, don't you see? If you would just let me comfort you—"

"You've done enough," he assured her, pulling free abruptly. "Mary claims I would have died of exhaustion or worse if you hadn't been there those first few days after—after it happened. I believe that too. I remember the warmth of you next to me, like a beacon in a storm. That's how I'll *always* remember you, Erica."

"Are you saying you don't need warmth anymore?" she murmured, her voice almost choked with tears. "There will be other storms, Daniel. For you and for me. We'll need each other then—"

"I don't *want* to need you. You or anyone else, ever again. Haven't I made that clear? I want you to find someone else. I'll be content to sail, while the boys grow up with Abby in Salem."

"I'll sail with you! And when the boys are older, they'll come along too."

"Erica!" His blue eyes flashed with sudden fury. "You told me you'd given up on all that. Do it *now*—right here, this minute—or I'll be off this train at the next stop, I swear it."

"Fine!" She turned away, fighting the sobs that she knew would only anger him further. She'd been so careful not to provoke him and cursed herself now for allowing his moment of tenderness to subvert that plan. If only he hadn't called her a beacon. If only she hadn't shown him just how needy and clinging she could be.

Is that why you've brought him along with you? she chastised herself in silent misery. *To rekindle romance? This man and his love are lost to you—he's made that clear enough. But his child may need you still, so try to remember what lies ahead. That poor sweet girl has either fallen into the clutches of a truly insane gentlewoman, or she lies at the bottom of the harbor, half-devoured by sharks. So don't you dare cry, Erica Lane. Think of Polly, and be strong for just a little while longer. . . .*

"As soon as I know you're in good hands, I'll be leaving," Daniel informed Erica as he took her arm and led her up to Russell Braddock's front door. "I assume from your silence that you prefer that arrangement," he added in an awkward attempt at teasing.

Erica forced herself to look straight ahead, fearing that he might read the expression on her face and know that she was suddenly filled with dread and foreboding. What if she was wrong? What if Sarah's little Robby really was alive? It would be no less a miracle than finding Polly alive and well, would it? What had she been thinking, dragging Daniel along with her on this impossible journey?

"Erica." He turned her toward himself and tilted her chin up so that their gazes locked. "I know you're angry with me, and I don't blame you. I shouldn't have allowed your feelings for me—"

"This isn't the time or place to discuss my feelings for you," she protested weakly. "Perhaps you should wait in the carriage."

"I know you trust this fellow, Erica, but I'm not going to let you go in there alone. That's final. You should have chosen Ryerson as your escort, but you chose me, and we've come this far. So unless you're reconsidering the

lunacy of marrying a total stranger, I suggest we proceed.''
He chuckled softly as he inclined his head toward the
house. ''It looks like we've attracted some attention. I
believe I just caught a glimpse of the sainted Mr. Braddock
in that bay window. So?''

''Oh, Daniel.'' She threw herself against his chest,
clinging to him unhappily. ''Will you forgive me if I've
made a mistake? It was only out of love and hope that
I've done this.''

''There, now.'' He embraced her warmly. ''Shall I take
you back to Boston? Or even to Paris, if that would be
best. Ryerson says a girl needs her mother at a time like
this.''

Erica's head snapped back as she finished the thought:
a girl needs her mother, *or her father*. And if Polly McCullum was somewhere in Chicago—

''Can I help you?'' a kind voice interrupted from the
front stoop. ''I'm Russell Braddock. I've been expecting
visitors. Are you by any chance Miss Erica Lane of
Boston?''

Erica's heart almost stopped at the sound of his voice,
knowing that she was about to hear the truth, and she
would then be either jubilant or destroyed. Overwhelmed
by anticipation and dread, she felt her knees begin to
buckle. If it hadn't been for Daniel's arms, she knew she
would have crumpled to the ground.

''Erica?'' Daniel growled as he caught her. ''It's not
too late to change your mind. This is nonsense—''

''Mr. Braddock?'' Erica extricated herself from her
escort, steadied herself, and cautiously approached the
matchmaker. ''You received my telegram?''

''Yes, dear.'' He smiled reassuringly. ''I've grown very
fond of your correspondence, as a matter of fact. Can I
assume this gentleman is Captain McCullum?''

''That's right.'' Daniel strode forward, positioning himself between Braddock and Erica before extending his hand in greeting. "I didn't realize Miss Lane sent a telegram. You're aware, then, that she's here for another match? You should know that I personally disapprove, but I also have no right to stand in her way, so I'm here to make certain it's all handled respectfully."

"Another match?" Braddock arched an eyebrow in Erica's direction. "You forgot to mention that."

"I know." She hesitated, then asked carefully, "Are they here?"

"Yes. They showed up on my doorstep two days ago. I believe they're in the atrium at this very moment."

"Oh, dear." Erica stared into his warm eyes, wanting to ask the next question but unable to find the words. "Tell me . . ."

"They're both well," Braddock assured her. "I did as you requested, and didn't mention that you were coming."

"Erica!" Daniel yanked her away from Braddock and cupped her face in his hand. "You're as white as a sheet. What's this about?"

"Oh, Daniel. I need you, just one more time—"

He didn't hesitate, pulling her into a protective embrace before demanding over her head, "What's this about, Braddock?"

"I'm not exactly certain," the matchmaker confessed. "Erica sent a telegram saying that her friend Sarah would arrive with her brother, and asking if I would keep them here until she could join them."

"Sarah and her brother? I thought he was dead."

"Daniel?" Erica murmured. "Promise me you'll forgive me if I was wrong to bring you here?"

He seemed completely confused, but still nodded. "I promise."

"Then, Mr. Braddock?" Erica took a deep breath and insisted, "Will you take me to the atrium?"

The matchmaker led them up the steps, across a lovely tiled entry hall, and into his richly paneled study, off of which one could glimpse a lush, glass-walled garden. Erica couldn't see Sarah or the child, but could hear the governess' voice, pleading and scolding. If only she could hear the child, but she could not, and so she took another deep breath and gave Daniel a shaky smile. "Wait here, Captain. I'll just be a moment."

"I've come this far," he complained. "On a pretense, which shouldn't surprise me—"

"Hush!" Erica spun away from him and strode into the atrium, unwilling to spend one more moment in suspense. She saw Sarah first, and then the child, dressed in knickers and boots and a starched white shirt. With a ruddy, suntanned face, and jet-black hair that was closely cropped but still managing a bit of a wave. Like her father's.

"My God," Erica whispered. "Polly, darling?"

The child turned, her eyes looking first at Erica, and then beyond her, and then she was shrieking, "Papa! Papa!" and catapulting past Erica and into Daniel's arms.

The sea captain sank to his knees and hugged the child frantically. "How is this—? Sweetheart, Polly, sweetheart. Saints be praised, *look* at yourself! You're alive!"

"Robby!" Sarah wailed. "No, Robby—"

"Be quiet!" Erica pointed an angry finger toward the governess. "Don't say another word to her. *Not ever again!*" When Sarah cowered, Erica's voice softened, but only slightly. "How could you have done this? Didn't you know it would kill him? Didn't you know how they love each other—"

"You don't understand!" Sarah wailed, sinking onto a bench and covering her face with trembling hands. "It was a miracle—"

"How could you have done this?" Erica repeated, but

she, too, was sobbing, as much for her former friend as for Daniel and Polly. Moving to kneel before Sarah, she whispered, "What were you thinking? Couldn't you see how much she missed her father?"

"You don't understand. . . ." Sarah began to rock back and forth, as though she'd fallen into a trance. "You never understood. You never believed me. Please, please don't do this to me again."

"Erica?" Russell Braddock tapped her on the shoulder. "I'll take care of Sarah. The others need you now."

She patted Sarah's arm, then after giving the matchmaker a grateful smile, turned and watched, through a haze of tears, as Daniel, still stunned, but also radiant, cradled Polly's sobbing figure in his arms as the little girl recounted the details of her kidnapping.

"At first, it was fun, but I missed you so much, Papa. Sarah kept telling me you and Erica were on your honeymoon. She said you went to Paris, but you'd come for me one day soon. I-I'm so glad you finally came!"

"Your father's been searching for you every moment since you disappeared," Erica told the child softly as she knelt beside father and daughter. "I've missed you too, darling. Do you have a little hug for me?"

Polly nodded and wrapped her arms around Erica's neck. "I never want to dress like a boy again! Never, never, never. She kept calling me Robby—"

"I know, darling. Sarah is a very confused person, and I'm so dreadfully sorry I ever introduced you to her. Can you forgive me?"

"She was nice to me," Polly admitted with a confused sigh. "She gave me gifts, and told me she loved me. But I don't love her, Erica. I love you and Papa. And my brothers, and grandma. Are they here too?"

"They'll be in Salem soon, waiting to see you. Everyone misses you, darling. There are *so* many people who care about you. But your father—he loves you more than words can describe. Do you know that?''

Polly nodded. ''I kept wishing he'd find me, and he did.''

''We have Erica to thank for that,'' Daniel murmured. ''I'm so grateful, Erica. How long have you known?''

''I only guessed a few days ago. Forgive me for not sharing my suspicions, but I wasn't certain, and I couldn't bear to raise your hopes.''

Polly looked from one to the other, an impish smile beginning to light her swollen eyes. ''Are you married? That makes you my mother—''

''We've been too busy looking for you to even think about marriage,'' Erica hedged. ''It's so wonderful to see you smile again.''

A movement from the doorway caught her eye and she beckoned for Russell Braddock to join them. ''How is Sarah?''

''She's resting comfortably. I've sent for a doctor, but in the meantime, my housekeeper will sit with her. I don't want to intrude,'' he added gallantly. ''I just wanted to see if there was anything you needed.''

''Please stay.'' Erica took his hand and squeezed it. ''We're indebted to you for your assistance.''

''We can never repay you,'' Daniel agreed. ''Erica has been singing your praises for weeks, and now I know why.''

''I beg your pardon,'' a melodious voice interrupted, and a pretty, dark-haired female stepped into view. ''Have I missed something? Again? Why didn't you tell me more guests had arrived, Father?''

''This is my daughter, Noelle,'' Braddock said with a smile. ''Sweetheart, this is Erica Lane, from Boston. And Captain Daniel McCullum, from—''

''From the Caribbean!'' Noelle clapped her hands in hearty appreciation. ''And here they are, together. You've

done it again, Father. All from reading between the lines."
Beaming, she added to the newcomers, "It's wonderful
to meet you both."

"Captain McCullum is Polly's father," Braddock
informed his daughter mischievously.

"And who is Polly? Oh, wait! It's *you*, isn't it?" She
crossed to Daniel and took the child from his arms and
into her own. "I *knew* you were a girl! Father, didn't I
tell you?"

"You were absolutely correct."

"I kept telling him," she informed Polly briskly. "One
look at those eyelashes and I just knew. But do you
suppose he'd listen? Men are so stubborn sometimes, but
of course you know that, with a stubborn father like the
captain here." She rumpled the child's short hair and
demanded, "Why on earth did that strange woman call
you 'Robby' and dress you like an elf?"

"It's a long story, Noelle," Braddock scolded.

"I don't want to hear it, and neither does Polly," she
retorted, setting the child onto the floor and covering her
ears with her hands. Then her gray eyes began to sparkle.
"Would you like to see my dolls, Polly? Some of them
are almost as pretty as you are."

Polly's own eyes were twinkling from the barrage of
compliments and energy. "May I, Papa?"

When Daniel winced, Braddock assured him, "Our
daughters will be safe together, Captain. And we do have
a matter to discuss, before the doctor arrives."

"Five minutes," Daniel agreed reluctantly. "But
before you go—" He gave the child a long, hearty hug.
"I love you, sweetheart."

"I love you too, Papa."

The captain watched until the two daughters were out
of sight, and even then he seemed to struggle to return
his attention to the matter of the kidnapping. "What do

you suggest, Braddock? Polly tells me she was treated with care, and this Sarah is obviously deranged. I wouldn't want to see her punished if she can be helped instead.''

Braddock exhaled with relief. ''I was hoping you'd say that. You have a perfect right to turn her over to the authorities, of course, but there is another way I can handle it. If Sarah's willing to cooperate.''

''Wait.'' Erica eyed the matchmaker impatiently. ''You're not going to marry her off to some unsuspecting customer, are you? I'm not sure you understand how insane she is. She kidnapped Polly, and made us believe she'd drowned. The captain has suffered dreadfully, Mr. Braddock. We can't allow anyone else to be hurt.''

''I agree.'' He smiled reassuringly. ''This happens in my business occasionally, Erica. A girl comes to me who is simply not ready to be a bride, or perhaps life has been so cruel to her that she will never heal enough to prepare her for that role. Fortunately, some of the profit I've earned from my matchmaking has enabled me to find shelters for girls like Sarah. She won't be allowed to hurt anyone, including herself. But with any luck, she'll be happy and productive. How does that sound?''

''We'd be forever grateful to you.'' Erica gave Daniel a sympathetic grin. ''I think Captain McCullum is missing his daughter.''

''Come this way, then, but I warn you. My daughter's doll collection is enough to frighten any sane man. You'll suspect I overindulge her, and I suppose I do. But I also suspect you're one man who can understand why I can't deny her anything.''

''You're lucky to have her,'' Daniel agreed vehemently.

Braddock's eyes warmed with understanding and he clapped the sea captain on the shoulder before turning to usher his guests toward the staircase.

* * *

They found Polly seated in the middle of Noelle's lace-bedecked four-poster bed, surrounded by dolls of every size and description. When she spied Daniel, she exclaimed, "Look, Papa! Noelle says I can choose any one of them I want. As a gift. Which one should I choose?"

Erica could see that Daniel's eyes were misting at the mere sight of his precious daughter, alive and well, and so she intervened hastily. "Which one do you like best, darling?"

Polly smiled. "There's one that looks just like you. See?" She held a redheaded bride into view. "Shall I choose this one?"

Erica smiled cautiously and reached for a pretty doll in a dark blue dress. "What about this one? A lady sea captain, and a beautiful one. Except ..." She fingered the doll's loose braid and lamented, "This knot in the ribbon has come loose. What do you think of that?"

Polly bit her lip, and it was Daniel who boomed, "Looks like she needs a reef knot to hold that pretty hair in place."

The little girl hesitated, then took the doll and carefully knotted the ribbon around her hair. "Like this?"

"Perfect," Daniel pronounced. "Just like Sean and I taught you."

"A lady sea captain? Is that what she is?" Noelle demanded. "I always wondered! She's one of my prettiest dolls, but I never realized she knew about oceans and weather and all such things. It suits her perfectly."

Polly flushed. "She *is* pretty, isn't she?"

"Not as pretty as you," Noelle conceded. "But lovely nonetheless. Still, I think you should take the bride with the red hair. I've always thought she was special. Unique, in her own way. And a little lonely too. She needs a husband, and soon. Just like me, although Father doesn't see it at all.''

''Noelle,'' Russell Braddock chastised. ''Remember your manners.''

Erica winced at the flash of pride in Noelle Braddock's eyes. Was it so different from the way she herself had felt, only months earlier, when her mother had dared to gently question the wisdom of her engagement to Jack Ryerson? Erica had refused that day to listen to her mother's suggestion that, while Jack was beyond question a wonderful man, he might not be quite impetuous and playful enough to suit Erica's nature.

It seemed so long ago. Yet she couldn't help wondering what Simone Lane would say about the hopeless affair with Daniel McCullum—an impetuous, playful yet moody man whose resistance to marriage, while understandable, was also profoundly hurtful.

Subdued, Erica advised Polly quietly, ''Take the pretty sea captain, Polly. She'll be less trouble in the long run.''

Russell Braddock winced. ''Why do I have the feeling we aren't talking about dolls any longer?''

Polly McCullum seemed to understand also, and eyed her father cautiously. ''Are you going to marry Erica soon, Papa?''

''We've decided against it,'' Erica interjected, trying for a cheerful tone. ''That's one of the reasons we're here. Mr. Braddock is going to find me another husband.''

''Erica!'' Daniel protested. ''Don't tell her that.''

''Why not?'' Erica felt a surge of pride every bit as strong as the one Noelle had manifested moments earlier. ''Polly wants me to be happy. And for that, I need a man who can't imagine life without me. Don't you agree, Mr. Braddock?''

The marriage broker smiled nervously. ''I didn't realize you were unhappy with your match with the captain.''

"He brought me here so that you could find me someone else. Does that sound like love?"

"No," Braddock admitted. "It doesn't."

"Be reasonable," Daniel protested. "I was out of my head with grief—drowning in it! I didn't want to drag you under with me. But in time—"

"Don't you dare say *that,* Daniel McCullum!" Turning to Braddock, she explained unhappily, "He didn't send me away because we'd lost Polly, but because he feared the next loss. And now he's grateful she's alive, and so he can see a future with me again, but nothing has really changed."

"*Everything* has changed," Daniel corrected firmly.

Russell Braddock pursed his lips, then tentatively intervened. "I've learned a thing or two about men and women over the years, and I am almost certain that eventually—in six months or so, perhaps, when the captain's grief had grown more manageable—he would have come after you, Erica."

"There." Daniel smiled in grateful relief. "Listen to Mr. Braddock, sweetheart."

"And?" Erica turned to stare directly into the marriage broker's eyes. "After six long months, would I have taken him back?"

"No," Braddock replied sadly. "I don't believe you would have." To Daniel, he explained quietly, "She would have loved you still, of course, but you would have proven to her that you weren't willing to share your life with her—the good *and* the bad. That's what marriage is about, Captain."

"He told me he didn't have anything more to give," Erica whispered, choking slightly on the painful memory.

"I believe that was true." Braddock sighed. "And I believe he's learned a lesson—"

"But you can't be certain, and neither can I. How can

I give my heart to him, completely and forever, knowing that one day he could send me away again?''

"Fine," Daniel growled. "Don't promise yourself to me forever, then. Follow in your grandmother's footsteps instead."

"Pardon?"

His eyes began to twinkle. "You can be my second wife, and I'll be your first husband. The first of five. You can trust me that much at least, can't you?"

Erica flushed under his playful gaze. "This isn't a game, Captain."

"I know that." He stepped close and insisted huskily, "Question my character and my sanity, but never question whether I love you, sweetheart. If only I didn't! For all the torture of the last weeks, loving you made it one hundred times worse. I ached for you, but couldn't ask you, or the twins, to share in my cursed existence any longer. Do you doubt whether I love my own sons?"

"I suppose not."

"Yet I was going to turn their care over to Abigail completely, and turn you over to Ryerson, although God knows," he groaned, "the thought of him touching you made me mad with jealousy."

Erica suppressed a smile, wondering if he realized how much she had longed to hear such words. "Perhaps I should reconsider your offer, Captain. You would make a wonderful first husband—"

"Wait!" Noelle wailed. "Father, speak to them!"

Erica smiled toward her distraught hostess. "I'm afraid the captain and I have a penchant for variety. I myself am in love with a sea captain, a pirate, a prince, a soldier, and a knight. With any luck, I can have them all if I agree to Captain McCullum's proposal."

Noelle opened her mouth to protest again, then her gray eyes began to sparkle with belated understanding, and she turned to Polly and suggested, "Come and look in this trunk with me. We'll find you one of my favorite old dresses to wear to dinner. A blue one, to match your eyes. How does that sound?"

"It sounds nice," Polly said eagerly. "May I borrow a dress from Noelle, Papa?"

Daniel nodded wistfully, and Erica knew he was simply grateful to have his little girl safe, whether in breeches or a fancy dress. And suddenly she realized how exhausted he must be, from the deadening mix of grief, illness and emotion that had plagued him these last torturous weeks.

"We should give these two some privacy while they change for dinner," she suggested softly. "Mr. Braddock, is there somewhere the Captain can rest while you and I visit? I'm anxious to tell you all about my ex-fiancé. If ever a man needed your services, it's Jack Ryerson. I fear that without our help he'll never manage to find a loving partner. And there's the matter of Abigail Lindstrom also—"

"You want to find a husband for Grandma?" Polly giggled.

"I believe I may already have found one." Erica smiled. "Really, Mr. Braddock, she's perfect for you. Vivacious and attractive and intelligent—"

"You're daring to match *Father?*" Noelle dissolved into a heap of laughter. "We knew you were bold, Erica, but this? It's so wonderfully hilarious!"

Russell Braddock flushed to a dark crimson. "I appreciate the thought, dear, but I have no intention of remarrying."

"Neither did Captain McCullum, and look at *him,*" Noelle warned gleefully.

"That's enough," he scolded, then he turned to Daniel and grinned sheepishly. "Your assistance would be greatly appreciated, Captain."

"There's no stopping Erica when she decides to make

a match,'' Daniel sympathized. ''But I can keep her occupied until dinner if you'd like. Polly?'' he added quickly. ''Will you be content with Noelle for a while?''

The little girl's eyes roamed the doll-filled room as she nodded vigorously. ''I love it here.''

''Well, then . . .''

Seeing how difficult it was for him to tear himself away, Erica took his arm and guided him gently into the hallway. ''You really should rest, Daniel. Alone, I mean. I can visit with Mr. Braddock—''

''I need to make the final arrangements for Sarah,'' the matchmaker interrupted. ''There'll be time enough over dinner for you to rave about your Abigail.'' With a circumspect smile, he gestured down the hall. ''The last two rooms on the left are empty guest rooms. Please make yourselves comfortable. I'll send someone to announce dinner in an hour or so.''

As soon as the matchmaker had hurried out of sight, Erica turned to Daniel and smiled shyly. ''How are you, Captain?''

''Happy,'' he admitted, resting his hands contentedly on her hips. ''And hopelessly in love.''

Inspired by the commitment that shone in his cobalt eyes, she raised herself onto tiptoes and gently kissed his lips. ''I trust you remember my terms, Captain McCullum?''

''Vividly,'' he assured her with a chuckle. Then, to her profound and eternal delight, he proved it, by scooping her up into his loving arms and carrying her away with him forever.

MEANT TO BE

... Coming from Zebra Ballad, June 2001 ...

Despite her pride in her father's matchmaking skills, Noelle Braddock wasn't about to let him ply his trade in *her* love life, especially when she'd already found herself the perfect suitor in Adam Prestley, a suave and successful banker. And so, when her father had the nerve to invite a brash young war hero—a buckskin-clad sharpshooter, no less!—to stay with them during the month before her wedding, she dutifully resisted the inexplicable thrill she felt whenever he was near.

Lieutenant Zachary Dane hadn't much cared about marriage until he wandered into Russell Braddock's dining room and spied a vision of lacy loveliness being fitted for a pure white wedding dress. Zack wasn't sure whether Noelle was a girl or an angel. He only knew he had to have her, and from the mischievous sparkle in her eyes whenever they were together, he suspected she felt the same. So he mounted a campaign, so bold, so romantic and so unorthodox, it would either completely infuriate the feisty bride, or make her see, once and for all, that their love was truly MEANT TO BE.

ABOUT THE AUTHOR

Kate Donovan was born in Ohio and grew up there and in Rhode Island, then moved to Northern California to attend college at Berkeley and law school at King Hall on the UC Davis campus. Today she divides her time equally among her many loves—a great husband, charming son, and delightful daughter; her love stories; and a career as an attorney in Sacramento, California. This is her seventh book. You can e-mail her at katedonovan@hotmail.com.

COMING IN MARCH 2001 FROM
ZEBRA BALLAD ROMANCES

__COWBOY FOR HIRE: The Dream Maker #1
   by Alice Duncan   0-8217-6878-6 $5.50US/$7.50CAN
While working at a health spa Amy Wilkes is "discovered" by a producer.
Whisked off to a movie set in California, Amy is transformed into a
stunning starlet and meets her new leading man Charlie Fox. Sparks fly,
on and off the screen, between Amy and Charlie, and a real-life passion ensues.

__THE STAR-CROSSED BRIDE: Once Upon a Wedding #2
   by Kelly McClymer   0-8217-6781-X $5.50US/$7.50CAN
Three years ago, Valentine Fenster tried to elope with Emily Weatherley,
his true love. Unfortunately, their plans were thwarted and Valentine
was forced to promise never to pursue her again. But when he learns that
she is betrothed to an abusive marquis he can no longer stand aside.
Some promises *are* made to be broken.

__HIS REBEL BRIDE: Brothers in Arms #3
   by Shelley Bradley   0-8217-6790-9 $5.50US/$7.50CAN
A fearless warrior, Kieran Broderick was bound to fight for the English
crown. So when King Henry decreed that he take an Irish wife to quell
rebellion there, he reluctantly agreed. Yet when he picks Maeve O'Shea
he finds himself facing his most daunting battle of all. Kieran is determined to conquer the rebellious beauty.

__A MATTER OF HONOR: The Destiny Coin #3
   by Gabriella Anderson   0-8217-6789-5 $5.50US/$7.50CAN
Eager to flee London, Lorane St. John stowed away on a ship bound for
America. Her plan goes awry when she is discovered by the ship's
dashing captain. Infuriated, Nicholas Grant is determined to send her home
when they reach shore. Instead, Lorane finds herself stirring up trouble
in Boston society—and winning the love of the man who is her very
destiny.
